W9-BHJ-341

THORPE

THORPE

by MARY DUTTON

The World Publishing Company

Cleveland and New York

Published by The World Publishing Company
2231 West 110th Street, Cleveland, Ohio 44102

Published simultaneously in Canada by
Nelson, Foster & Scott Ltd.

Printed in the United States of America

FOR BECKY

AUTHOR'S NOTE

On this page I say thank you to some of the people who made the writing of this book a joy:

> *to* my parents, who waited
> *to* Meda Sellers, who cared
> *to* Molly Epps, who listened
> *to* Phoebe Larmore, who believed
> *to* Manon Tingue, who advised
>   and
> *to* Laurene Chinn, who Is.

This is not a chapter from history. It is a novel, written in love and in gratitude, and was not intended to portray actual persons, places, or events.

The Angel that presided at my birth
Said: "Little creature, formed of joy and mirth,
Go, love without the help of any thing on earth."

William Blake
Couplets and Fragments

THORPE

prologue

The yard is covered with weeds and most of the fruit trees out back are dead. The front porch has pulled loose from the old breezeway house. It sags crookedly, and all of the window glass is gone.

We stand in the weeds, my brother and I, on the spot where Daddy dug a hole for Mama's cape jasmine bush. James takes off his glasses and wipes his face with his handkerchief. He steps onto the sagging porch and peers down through the hall of the old house. "Coming in?"

The heat of the July sun is more comforting than the cobwebs and cool shadows of the old house, and James sees my hesitation. He turns from the hall door and comes back into the sunshine with me.

"Let's go down and see if Donie's house is still standing." The hot stillness is oppressive, and he wipes his forehead again. "And if you're game, we'll walk on down to the old Pig White place and see if it's still ghosted."

"Ghosted." I echo James' last word. "You know damn well there's no such thing as ghosts." We laugh as the gate swings shut and open again behind us. The latch is gone.

We go along the fence and into the tall trees to walk along the path that is no longer there. In the distance we can hear the oil wells pumping on Uncle Elmer's farm, and the sun is not so hot under the dampness of the trees. The trees get bigger and thicker and the undergrowth harder to penetrate, and the years are now closing in on us with the shadows that dance among the leaves. The ghosts have not waited at the Pig White place. They are advancing to meet us, and the sound of the oil wells does not invade the world into which we are entering.

We are standing in front of Donie's house.

Blackberry vines have covered the little house with its lean-to kitchen and bedroom. The shutters are gone, and as we stand in front an owl flies out the window and sits sleepily in one of the pinoak trees. Butterflies hover over the vines, and the heady scent of the overripe fruit that has fallen to the ground is like the scent of the pink wine tonic that Sister Mearl used to take. Bees also are hovering, and from the house comes a faint continuous buzzing as though from a hive. And faint and sweet and clear, calling through the years, I hear Thee's voice.

Honey in th' bee-ball, bee-ball, bee-ball,
I cain't see y'all, see y'all, see y'all.
All ain't hid, holler haa-ay—yo-oooooo. . . .

"We will leave Donie's house as it is," Mama said once to Aunt Neevy. "Donie may find that Chicago is not the Promised Land. She may decide to come back. And if she does, her house will be here, waiting."

It is still waiting. Donie, Donie, where are you?

We do not go past Donie's house and into the woods to find the old Pig White place. We have seen enough ghosts.

We go back through the trees to James' sleek air-conditioned car. Back over the railroad track and the little dirt road to the highway.

"Want to turn and go on to Strawne?" James asks as he stops at the highway.

My fingers go under the strap of my cool yellow cotton dress, find and rub absently at the thin line of the scar that is still there. And I hear again the hoot of an owl and the ugly laugh and see the ghost horses gathering around the flickering torch, "No," I answer slowly. "No, let's go home."

14

We ride in silence. Neither of us can summon the laughter needed to dispel the ghosts that have entered the car. They are there with us, and I am six years old again and James is eleven and all of the joy and the pain and the love and the terror is also in the car.

I

> *"Arkansas, Arkansas, 'tis a reindeer*
> *In a place I call home, sweet home—"*

I sat on the doorsteps in the sunshine and hugged my knees and
sang. I was waiting for Daddy and James to come out of the pink-
brick schoolhouse across the street. I pulled my bloomer legs down
over my knees to keep warm and watched Mama raking the dead
leaves away from the flowers she had covered last winter. She was
being careful not to break any of the little green shoots that were
pushing up through the leaves, and she wouldn't let me help her.

"Arkansas, Arkansas, 'tis a reindeer—" I sang it again.

I only knew the first two lines.

Mama looked up from her flower bed.

"'Tis a name dear,'" she said. "For goodness sake, Thorpe, if
you're going to sing it over and over, sing it right!"

Mama stood up, and there was mud on her dress. She came over
and sat down on the step beside me. "Listen. Because I can't
stand too much more of that reindeer." She pulled my head over
against her shoulder and rubbed her face against my hair to show
she wasn't cross, then she sang it for me.

> *"Arkansas, Arkansas, 'tis a name dear,*
> *'Tis a place I call home, sweet home.*

17

Arkansas, Arkansas, I salute thee!
From thy shelter no more I'll roam."

"You got mud on my arm," I said when she'd finished.

Mama stood up. "Well, quit pulling your bloomer legs down over your knees like that," she said. "Go in the house and get a sweater if you're cold. And remember, ' 'tis a *name* dear.' " She went back to her flower bed.

Well, of course I knew it was a name. James had told me that when he taught it to me the night before. It was the name of the state we lived in and you had to sing the song every morning at school, first thing. I went into the house after a sweater.

When I came back out, Mama was raking the leaves into piles for Daddy to move. She stood the rake beside the fence and started up the steps. As she went by me, she stooped and straightened my collar over the sweater and pushed my hair behind my ear.

"Let's go in and make a pie," she said.

I thought about it. It was fun to peel apples and roll crust. But it was more fun to be lifted to Daddy's shoulder when he came in the gate and carried into the house.

"Do I have to?" I looked up at Mama. "May I stay out here and wait for Daddy?"

Mama waited for a minute and then went on into the house.

I heard her in the kitchen. She was singing the rest of the song about Arkansas.

" 'Tis a place full of joy and of sunshine,
Rich in pearls and in diamonds rare—"

When she got to the part about "I salute thee," I saluted like James had shown me the night before. But I wasn't sure which hand you were supposed to use, so then I saluted with the other hand. Afterward I felt silly saluting with both hands out on the porch all by myself. I looked around to make sure nobody saw me.

James was coming out of the door of the schoolhouse. He ran across the street and through the front gate.

"Hi," he said, and dropped down onto the bottom step. "Do you have a headache? What were you doin' with your hands up over your eyes like that? Look what I've got."

He had a box Mama had helped him cover in red crêpe paper,

18

and when he opened it, there were about a thousand valentines inside. He dumped them out onto the steps.

"Look!" he said again. "Let's read them."

I had one valentine. *One*. It was propped up on the radio in the living room, and it was from my Sunday School teacher. Miss Mildred had given everybody in the class one. And here was James with a whole boxful, because he was ten and in the fifth grade and everybody he knew had given him one. We looked through them.

"Gaw." James held out a big red-and-white flowered valentine with lace on it. "Look at this one from old Soggum Thompson!"

I was looking at another one. "Didn't you give Soggum one?"

"Well, sure, but—" James looked disgusted. "I didn't give him one that said TO MY FAVORITE UNCLE!"

"Look at this one!" I held it toward James. "It says TO MY TEACHER!"

"Gaw," James said again. "Some of them don't even read what it says before they write your name on it!"

"Maybe they were running out of valentines," I said. "And your name was last on the list. Maybe—"

James looked at me and curled his lip. "You always make people feel better," he said. "The way you figure things out. Stupid, gaw! How Daddy ever taught you to read, *why* he ever did, is something I'll never know! You—"

"Ha-ay, James!" A gang of boys was at the gate, yelling. "Ha-ay, James! Les go play shinny!"

James dumped the rest of the valentines into my lap and stood up. "You can have them," he said. "All of them. I guess you can't help being stupid." He started toward the gate.

"The box, too?" I wanted to go play shinny with them, but I couldn't. Because the last time they had let me play shinny one of the boys had whacked me across the shinbone too hard. James had whacked him back and after Mama had doctored James' black eye she had said no more shinny for me.

"You can have the box, too." James turned and came back and helped me pick the valentines up from the doorsteps around me. "Next year when you start to school maybe you'll have your own valentine box. Maybe. Pull up your bloomer legs and go into the house to look at the rest of them. It's gettin' cold out here."

"Remember your *Ings!*" I called to his back as he went out the gate, but he didn't answer. Daddy had signs up in the dining room and in the bathroom, but with James they didn't help much. RE-MEMBER YOUR INGS the signs said. Daddy said the reason they didn't help was because Mama didn't make us realize it was important to speak correctly, and Mama said she didn't see what was so important about sounding different from other people.

I went into the house with the box of valentines. Daddy still hadn't come out of the schoolhouse, but it was getting too cold to wait outside.

In the kitchen Mama was polishing the legs of the shiny green stove she'd gotten for Christmas, and I could smell spice and apples baking together. I spread the valentines on the table and sat down to count them. It was hard to do, because I didn't know as many numbers as I did words. Every time I got to twelve I had to quit and start over. I went over to the trash can and rescued my favorite calendar. Mama had taken it from the wall of my room because 1934 was all gone and the pages were all torn off. I started to my room with the calendar.

"Put that thing back in the trash, Thorpe." Mama looked up from the stove leg. "You don't want that thing. It's turning brown around the edges, and it makes your whole room look junky."

She stood up and looked down at me and laid her polishing cloth on the table beside the valentine box. "Move over here." She pulled out a chair. "I'll help you count the valentines."

I put the calendar back on top of the trash can. Maybe James could rescue it for me when he came home. I sat down at the table with Mama.

"There are thirty-six of them," she said a few minutes later. "Go put them up now, and let's set the table. It's time for Daddy. Do you want a glass of milk while you're waiting?"

I didn't. I didn't want to set the table, either. I went back to the front door and stood there, looking out. Toward the schoolhouse.

The door of the schoolhouse opened and old Will Jackson came out. He stood there on the steps looking around.

"Is old Will Jackson Daddy's boss?" I had asked James once, after I'd noticed that old Will went in and out of the schoolhouse a lot. "Is that why he goes in and out so much?"

"Daddy doesn't have a boss, stupid. He works with people, not for them," James had said. "I guess old—I guess Mister Jackson

20

bosses everything in the county, in a way, though. He comes to the schoolhouse so much because he's president of the school board. See?"

I didn't, exactly, but it was all right. I was glad, because I'd have hated for Daddy to have a boss who looked like the picture of the North Wind in James' reader.

The schoolhouse door opened again and Daddy came out. He stood just outside the door, and they looked at each other, Daddy and old Will Jackson. Then old Will walked over to his pickup truck and got in and slammed the door and drove off.

Daddy came across the street, and I ran to meet him at the gate.

"Thorpe," Daddy said. "Thorpe."

He wasn't whistling or singing or walking proud, and he didn't lift me to his shoulder. His brown-dotted bow tie hung tired and crooked, and his eyes were dark gray with wrinkles around them. He let me take his hand and we walked to the porch. On the porch Daddy sat down in a rocking chair and stared into the cape jasmine bush.

"James got a whole box of valentines today," I said. "Would you like to read them?"

Daddy didn't answer. I sat down on the floor beside his feet and we both looked into the cape jasmine bush. We sat there on the porch for a long time. The sun got lower in the sky and went away behind a cloud that was the exact color of Daddy's eyes.

James came back through the gate.

"Hi." He stopped on the porch and looked at Daddy.

Daddy raised the fingers of one hand from the arm of his chair and let them fall back down, *plunk*. "James," he said. That was all.

"Oh, there you are! I thought you'd all disappeared!"

Mama had come to the door. She had on a fresh blue dress with a ruffle down the front and her cheeks were pink from cooking. Her gold-brown hair was all loosened and wavy. Mama always looked prettier all loose and pink than she did with her face powdered and her hair pressed down into tight little waves to go somewhere. She walked over and leaned her face against the top of Daddy's head.

"Tired?" she asked.

"A little." Daddy put his hand on her cheek and held her face against his head. Then he moved his hand and stood up.

"Is supper ready?" he asked. "I have to go to a school-board meeting tonight." We all started into the house.

"You better not make a mess!" I called through the bathroom door to James. "I don't want to get fussed at for being messy when I come out of the bathroom after *you've* made a mess!" Mama polished the things in the bathroom as much as she did the green stove and the rest of the things in the house.

Daddy went into the bathroom when James came out. He just stood there and looked into the mirror over the lavatory.

"Jim!" Mama called from the kitchen. "It's not time for a school-board meeting! Is this a called meeting?"

"Yes!" Daddy shouted back from the bathroom. "It's a called meeting. And I am invited. Requested. Commanded."

"Whatever for?" Mama asked as we came to the table. "Why do they want you there? Is it about new textbooks or something?"

"Probably." Daddy stirred his coffee, but he didn't eat.

"Well, it's nice they want you." Mama put a pork chop on his plate. "These things were twenty-five cents a pound, and I shouldn't have paid it. What we need is another grocery store in Strawne so Walter Byrd would realize there's a depression on and people can't pay twenty-five cents a pound for meat. What do people do that don't have it?"

"What's a depression?" I asked, but nobody answered.

"Oh well, I remember Mama used to fuss about the prices Walter's father charged for groceries when I was a girl," Mama said. "You know, Jim, Will Jackson is beginning to realize you've got more common sense, and education too, than anybody on the board. That's why they're—"

"Excuse me." Daddy looked at Mama and set his coffee cup down. "I may as well start getting ready."

"This early?" Mama looked at his pork chop. "But you didn't eat! There's plenty of time to finish your supper."

"Excuse me," Daddy said again. He pushed back his chair and went into the bathroom again and we heard him getting his shaving things out.

"Order some new books for the fifth grade," James called after Daddy. "I've read everything in the room."

"I do hope he isn't coming down with something," Mama said.

"He didn't eat a bite. You kids go ahead and eat. James, I want you to help me move that pile of leaves before it gets too dark."

It was an afternoon and evening pretty much like all of the ones I could remember, and none of us knew that it would be the last one like it for a long time.

2

"Oh, God in Heaven, Jim!" Mama's voice was clear.

It came through the walls and through the dark into my room. I sat up in bed to listen.

"You didn't do it! You couldn't!" Mama was still talking. "You didn't let nigras have books from the schoolhouse, books our children handle and use, and then go up there tonight and *admit* it to the whole school board!"

"Admit what?" Daddy shouted. "Admit that I've been making some unused reference books available to Nathaniel Darsey and a few more boys like him? And encouraging them to learn how to do something besides cut logs and do yard work? Yes, Venie, I—"

"But you knew better!" Mama was shouting too. "Jim, you *knew* better!"

"I know a lot of things, Venie." Daddy's voice was tired and quiet. "And sometimes I have to do what I can about them. Those boys needed help, and I was trying to give it to them."

"Boys!" Mama screamed. "Those boys? You mean those nigras! You have a boy of your own, you know. Did you stop to think about him, or his future, with his father laughed out of the country for being a—a bleeding heart, a *nigra-lover,* a—"

Mama started crying. She cried for a while, and after that she talked some more. "Oh, God," she said. "All this fancy vocabulary you have, and you don't even know what *family* means! *Did* you think about us at all?"

Daddy said, "Oh, for God's sake!"

They were quiet for a few minutes except for Mama's crying. Then she started talking again.

"Jim," she said. "It's not final yet, is it? I mean, you just flew off the handle and, and— Anybody's liable to do that, once in a while. But you could still go back to the school board and explain. You could, Jim. You could go to Will Jackson right now, tonight, and talk to him about it. Explain to him that you'd made a mistake and lost your temper about it. Tell him that you're sorry and that you don't mind being under observation for the rest of the term. You can explain to him and to the school board that you aren't going to do anything else foolish."

"Mistake?" Daddy shouted again. "Foolish?" Then his voice got quieter again. "Oh, Venie, Venie, books are written in black and white. Aren't they?"

I heard Daddy walk across the room. To Mama, I think. He might have put his hand on her shoulder.

"Lavinia," he said. "It's not the end of the world. There are other places, other school boards. If you weren't so set on living here where you grew up, we could go—"

"Don't touch me!" Mama cried. "Other places, other school boards! And most of them paying off in written promises that the grocery stores hate to honor! This is nineteen thirty-five, Jim! Bread lines and soup kitchens all over the country, and you have to toss away one hundred dollars a month cash and a teacherage to live in rent-free! Our place in the community, everything. You have to lose it all!"

"You're right, Venie. I have to. But I promise you won't stand in a bread line. We may have to move on, but—"

"We will not move on. I thought we settled that, six years ago, when we came back here from dragging around to all those schools in Missouri. I spent enough years living among strangers, Jim! And I am not going to start dragging around all over the country again like boll weevils looking for a home just because you can't get along with people! I am not going to raise my family among no telling what kind of strangers and no kin at all and—and——" Mama cried harder.

"All right, Lavinia," Daddy said. "All right. But I am not going

25

to teach under the supervision of an illiterate fanatic. You know damned well that the only times I've left teaching positions in the past was to go to better ones, and there's no comparing this situation with those instances. My resignation still stands, Venie. But we won't leave Strawne, I promise you. I'll try to get a job as bookkeeper for the railroad. Maybe I can go to work in one of *Mister* Will Jackson's sawmills. Would you like that?"

Mama kept crying. "You know there aren't that many jobs here or anywhere else. What makes you think you can find one anywhere?"

"Then I'll get on the PWA!" Daddy shouted. "I can lean on a shovel in the sunshine! But we won't leave your little nest. We'll hole up here and stay, but I'll be damned if Will Jackson's going to pad the hole for us! Does that settle it?"

Mama said one more thing to Daddy before they both were quiet.

"God in heaven," she said. "You—you Don Quixote!"

It started raining then, soft, spattering sounds on the roof and against the window. In the next room Mama was still crying. Rain blew in through my open window and was cool and soft on my face, but after a while I put my pillow over my head and I could not feel the rain.

I heard the light click on in James' room. A few minutes later I heard him over at the wall getting a book from his shelf, and I knew that he had been listening too. I got up and tiptoed through the living room to James' door, and he opened it before I tapped.

"Go back to bed," he whispered crossly.

"I can't," I whispered back. "I'm not sleepy."

James opened his door wider and I went in. He lay back across his bed with his book, and I perched on the edge of the bed and pulled my gown down over my legs to keep warm.

"It's cold in here," I whispered. "I bet you Mama raked the leaves off her flowers too early. I bet they freeze."

He looked up from his book. "I don't think that'll matter now."

I sat there on the edge of his bed, shivering. James kept trying to read, but he wasn't turning any pages.

"James," I said. "What's a donkey hody?"

"A what?" James closed his book and held his finger between the pages.

26

"What part of a donkey is the hody? You know, what Mama called Daddy. What is—"

"Oh." James put his book down on the bed. He grinned, and his grin made me feel better already.

"Oh gaw," he said. "You mean a Don Quixote."

"That's what I said. A donkey hody."

"Well, it's not any part of a donkey, stupid. It's a man's name. Or rather, it *was*. It's in one of Daddy's books. He was just a good, stupid man, who went around fighting at windmills and—well, anyway, his name was Mister Quixote. *Don* means Mister. See?"

I didn't see, exactly, but it was all right. What James meant was that Mama hadn't been calling Daddy anything except good and stupid. That wasn't so bad. I never had been called good very much, but I'd been called stupid lots of times. Anyhow, it didn't mean anything like I had feared . . . sometimes James called people the south end of a northbound horse, and I couldn't bear to think Mama had called Daddy anything like that. . . .

"You better get back to bed."

James went over and opened his door again, and as I went out he pinched my nose, real easy. "G'night, stupid," he said. James looked awfully skinny in his nightshirt, and his cowlick stood straight up.

"Good night," I said, and eased out into the living room. The light from James' door shone across the living room. He stood there and held it open so I wouldn't stumble over anything. Just as I crawled back into bed, his door closed again and his light clicked off. Then I heard him talking to himself in the dark.

"Aw, gaw. What part of a donkey is the hody!"

For a while after that, everything looked the same. But it wasn't at all. Daddy and James went to school the next morning, and the iceman came in with this black rubber thing on his shoulder under the ice and took the money Mama had left on the box and put the ice in.

"Nice day, Miz Torrance," he said. He stood there holding his tongs and watched Mama put Daddy's toast and eggs in the garbage. "Go' be a early spring."

"Is it?" Mama didn't smile or anything like she usually did. The iceman waited a minute and then went on out to chase some kids away from his truck.

When Daddy came home that evening, he sat out on the front porch and looked into the cape jasmine bush again, and James stayed home and played with me because nobody came by and yelled at the gate for him.

That was the way the days went; looking the same, but not the same at all. Once James came home with a black eye and nobody said anything at all and at supper that evening Mama told me to hush asking about it.

On Thursday Donie came, with her extra shoes under her arm, and went out in the back yard and washed for us like she always did. Donie brought extra shoes when she came to wash because her feet were always muddy from walking through the woods to town. She always wore a flowered apron over her dress, and her face was dark-brown and strong. Donie walked like a queen and looked like a Hershey bar.

After she'd finished rubbing and boiling the clothes and had them hanging on the lines to dry, Donie scrubbed the back porch with a bucket of suds from the boiling pot. Then she stood the rubboard on the bench and turned the tubs upside down, and came into the kitchen to eat. Mama poured a cup of coffee and sat down at the table with Donie and they talked.

"Go' be a early spring." Donie said the same thing the iceman had said. She buttered a piece of cornbread. "Fish awready bitin down in th' Little Luter, an Callie say Miss Una done try to run away twice."

Miss Una was old Will Jackson's wife, and she was always trying to run away, and Callie or somebody was always bringing her back. Callie was a big tan woman who lived with Miss Una and went everywhere Miss Una went.

Mama smiled, for the first time that day.

"It's a sign of spring," she said, "when Una tries to run away. But I thought she was better. She was at church Sunday, and she acted like she felt a lot better."

Donie lifted one shoulder. "Callie probly lyin. She like to brag, an she ain got much to talk about, livin out there day in, day out, like she do. She sho ain got much else to talk about, except Naye-thaniel, an I think she worrit about him."

"Nathaniel is Callie's grandson, isn't he?" Mama looked up from her cup. "Isn't he the one that's supposed to be so smart?"

"He smart as a whip," Donie said. "I don know where he git

28

it, raised up out there in that little room behin Mister Will's barn. Naye-thaniel th' only chick 'n chile Callie's got, since her Willielou died a-bornin 'im. Callie aw-ways think they a cut above mos of us, her being a Darsey from Louisiana an all, an now she ack sometimes like they bout halfway Jacksons theyselves."

"Maybe they are," Mama said, and then she looked at me like she'd just remembered I was at the table with them. "Thorpe, it's time for your nap."

I went into my room, and they were still at the table talking when I went to sleep.

One day soon afterward, there was a new principal at the schoolhouse, and Daddy didn't have to go to school any more. The new principal's name was Mr. Whitehall, and we had to move out of the yellow house so he could move into it.

Where we moved to was about three miles out into the country, out into the big gray house with trees all around it and the long hall down through the center. It was the house Mama had lived in when she was a little girl, and nobody had lived in it for a long time.

We went out to the house one day, Mama and Daddy and James and me, and Donie was there waiting to help us. All day we scrubbed and cleaned and swept down cobwebs, and the next day Uncle Elmer came over in his truck and they loaded everything except Mama's shiny new stove.

Mama had swapped the beautiful green stove to Aunt Neevy and Uncle Elmer for a cow.

Mama said it was called a breezeway house, because the long hall was to let the breezes blow through and into every room.

There was a lot of breeze that day we moved into the old house. Soft warm breeze that brought the smell of Easter into every room. The smell of violets pushing up through the rotted pinestraw under the trees and of the redhaw and the cypress swamps down around the Little Luter Creek where Daddy had taken us fishing once. A smell that told you that maybe spring was already out there in the trees around us. Spring, in her flowing green dress and wearing flowers in her hair, like in one of James' readers.

"The first day of March—" Mama said. "Where will the first day of April find us?" She sniffed.

Mama had hay fever all the time Daddy and Uncle Elmer were loading our stuff out of the yellow house, and her nose and eyes were still pink as she stood in front of the tall window in the living room of the old gray house and tried to open the faded red drapes Grandma Thorpe had left there.

Daddy and Uncle Elmer kept walking in and out with chairs and beds and things, and nobody answered Mama. Nobody was saying much of anything. Daddy hadn't talked much since the night of the school-board meeting, and Uncle Elmer wasn't allowed to talk much when Aunt Neevy was around, so I guess he'd kind of lost the habit.

Aunt Neevy was Mama's sister. She was older than Mama, and bigger and not as pretty. But the old gray house belonged half to her, and so Aunt Neevy had come over with Uncle Elmer to show us how to move in and where to put things, and she was in the kitchen talking ninety miles a minute to Donie about what went where.

"I'll—I'll git that cow over here tomorrow, Venie." Uncle Elmer came through and stopped beside Mama at the window. "And we'll take good care of your stove, don't you worry. And in case you want to swap back again when Jim—well, he'll start teachin' again, don't worry. He will."

Mama held a fold of the dusty old drapes and looked up at them. "I don't want the stove back. Ever. It's Neevy's. Mama's old wood range is good enough—good enough—"

Mama found her handkerchief in her pocket and blew her nose. Uncle Elmer went to the back of the house. I went out the gate to the truck and watched Daddy unload his big red chair. He lifted it ahead of him and looked down at me.

"Don't get in front of any of us, Thorpe," he said. "Or you might get stepped upon." He looked around the yard. "Where's Dawn Starr?"

Dawn Starr was my cousin, and usually she would have been with Aunt Neevy and Uncle Elmer, but we were lucky that day.

"She's in school. I didn't ask, but I guess that's where she is." I opened the gate for Daddy. "This is a schoolday you know, and some people still have to go. Aren't we lucky? No Dawn Starr, and no school either!" I followed Daddy onto the porch.

He lowered the chair to take it through the door.

30

"We sure are," he said. "Just born lucky, that's us." He went into the living room with his chair.

"Thorpe!"

Mama was calling from the end of the hall.

"Thorpe, find the broom and come sweep out all the mud we've tracked in. It looks enough like a barn around here, with the floors all rotted and the porch falling down! I guess we shouldn't have moved that broom. It's bad luck to move a broom from one house to another. But God in Heaven knows we can't afford to be superstitious right now."

I got the broom and swept the mud right through the hole in the corner of the dining room. Mama came and watched me for a minute, and then she looked up at the wasp nest in the ceiling over us.

"Jim will have to get rid of those wasp nests," she said. "They'll all start hatching out when the house gets warm. Remind me to show him this one— Oh!"

Mama jumped and put her hand against her face, and I thought a wasp had already stung her.

"Why," she said, holding out her hand and looking down at what the breeze had blown against her face. "Why, it's a dogwood petal. Still green, but a petal. I guess it will be an early spring."

She leaned against the wall, and her shoulders shook.

"Oh, now, Venie, it won't be so bad." Aunt Neevy had walked up behind us. "Your dishes are all put up, nice and orderly, and I told Donie to mop the kitchen. Let's go in the livin' room and start."

They went into the living room and I followed them.

Aunt Neevy looked around the room. "Venie, this table would look better over under the window. And I don't really like your couch against the wall like that. What do you aim to put in this corner?"

Mama looked around at her chairs and tables and didn't answer. I stood in the door and watched them.

"You know, Venie," Aunt Neevy stood in the center of the room holding the little end table she was moving across to the window. "You know, Jim got out light. He could've been held to that contract, and made to finish out the term on whatever conditions— They *didn't* fire him, did they?"

"Certainly not." Mama looked over toward Daddy's big chair.

"I've always had that table beside Jim's chair. You didn't hear that they did, did you? Fire Jim, I mean."

"Well, no." Aunt Neevy put the little table under the window. "You need it here, in the window. Course I've heard it two or three ways, but—"

"I'll bet you have." Mama dragged a box of Daddy's books over to the bookcases along one wall.

"But what I heard mostly was that the school board reprimanded Jim and told him that, well, they might be watchin' him a little closer from now on, and he said that he wasn't finishin' out a contract under *probation* for anybody and they could—" Aunt Neevy looked over at me standing in the door. "Did Jim really tell them they could take their contract and—and do what he told them to with it?"

"I'm sure I don't know what he told them." Mama took some books out of the box and shoved them into the bookcase, hard. "I'd rather not talk about it, Neevy."

"Well, he's just lucky." Aunt Neevy looked around for something else to move. "I don't know another man in the county the night riders wouldn't go after, for what Jim did. To chastise, maybe, or *warn,* anyhow."

"Don't be silly."

Mama stood up and went over and took the little table from under the window and put it back beside Daddy's chair. "That trashy bunch? Who among them has the energy to *ride,* I'd like to know! Sit around the pool hall and stand around street corners and talk big about what heroes they were twenty years ago when they whipped old Pig White's husband and he died next day. Probably none of them even been on a horse since, thank God. They—"

"They're not all trash, Missy. Papa was a night rider, and you knew it well as I did, even if we weren't supposed to. And there's still law and order to be kept, with the sheriff thirty miles away in Wellco. Somebody has to watch after smart nigras and white trash."

"Well, Jim's not either one, so let's talk about something else." Mama squatted in front of the bookcase and started putting up books again. "You've always had the idea, Neevy, that there's something outlandish and—and different about Jim. Why, for goodness' sake, Neevy, Jim's father taught history at the College of the Ozarks. And his mother played all kinds of musical instruments!

32

If they hadn't both been drowned when that riverboat sank—" Mama moved over a little bit, to another shelf for the books she was holding. "But you know all that. Jim comes from just as good a family as we do, and you know it!"

Aunt Neevy sniffed. "In other words, they left him saddled with a bunch of crazy notions and not much else. I still say he's lucky the night riders didn't—"

"The only way the night riders would come after Jim, and you know it," Mama said, "would be to get him to join them. And they know he won't do that. He's already settled all that with them."

"Join them! Humph!" Aunt Neevy picked up the little table again. "He's too namby-pamby for them! They want *men*. It's always been funny to me, you had to go all the way to Arkadelphia and enroll in college with money scarce as it was and Papa on his deathbed, just to find and marry a namby-pamby, no-good—"

Mama stood up again, and her face was red.

"You never did understand Jim, Neevy. You never did try to, and let's leave it at that. Jim's not namby-pamby at all. He's strong and good and you tell me another man in the country who'd give up a whole way of life for what he believes in! Jim quit his job, yes, and—" Mama's voice rose higher and shook. "Now you just put his table back over there beside his chair and don't you move it again!"

"Daddy's not a namby-pamby."

I spoke up from the door to let Mama know I was on her side. "He's a donkey hody."

Mama whirled toward the door.

"He is not! You get in your room, Miss Smart, and start putting those toys and books up onto the closet shelves! And don't you ever let me hear you say a thing like that about your father again! And quit hanging around doors getting into conversations that don't concern you!"

I slinked off down the hall to my room and got busy. But I could still hear them talking.

"We should have had somebody living in this old house all these years." Mama had come out into the hall and her voice was quieter. "It wouldn't be so run-down if there'd been somebody in it. Neevy, let's don't fuss about—"

"I'd like to know who'd have rented it," Aunt Neevy said. "Nobody moves into these old houses now except nigras and white trash. Who'd want their children to walk a half a mile down a dirt road to catch the school bus? That's why Eloise was so happy to take cash for her part and spend it like a fool. And we're bigger fools than Eloise for givin' it to her. We'll never get that much back—"

"She needed it," Mama said. "Let's don't get off on Eloise."

Eloise was Mama's baby sister. She lived in New Orleans, and she was real nice. Eloise was not married, and she was pretty.

"Needed it for wild parties and fine clothes," Aunt Neevy kept on. "Needed it for junk to send home and make a big show, and everybody knowin'—"

Aunt Neevy was talking to the wind that blew through the breezeway. Mama had gone into the kitchen and was making a lot of noise moving the dishes that Aunt Neevy and Donie had put up in the pantry.

There wasn't much more talk after that. Pretty soon Donie and Aunt Neevy and Uncle Elmer went home and we settled down to living in the old gray breezeway house.

It rained that night, and the roof leaked through right onto my bed. When I got up to move my bed, I heard James in his room moving his. And the only thing that blew into the breezeway was rain. Before Daddy got the doors closed the rain had blown in through the front and out through the back.

Mama stood there in her gown watching Daddy push the doors closed against the rain and wind. "At least we have running water," she said.

Daddy said he was glad by God that somebody thought it was funny. That was after the wasp stung Daddy. When he'd crawled into bed, a big red wasp had been between the sheets waiting for him.

All night long Daddy ran around scratching his hip and putting buckets under things, and the next day he got rid of the wasps.

But the day we moved in the old house was full of the promise of spring, and in spite of all the things that happened while we lived in the breezeway house, I started loving it that day and I never stopped loving it.

Easter must have been in April that year, but it might have been in a warm March. I wouldn't be six years old until November, and I didn't notice that the seasons and the months changed. Only that all kinds of days came and went, hot ones, cold ones, rainy ones, and sunny ones. A new hill to run down and a new flower to find at the bottom, a new game with James under the pink cloud of the peach trees out back, a new word in an old book and Daddy always around to explain it. . . . They were good days.

One day Mama got out a box of stuff Eloise had sent to us and started sewing on our Easter clothes.

You could tell which one of Eloise's big sisters she liked best, because she was always sending us stuff. Even when it wasn't anybody's birthday or anything, here would come a big box from Eloise, and it was like Christmas every time. The last box had been full of material for our Easter clothes.

Mama had spread the blue velvet for me and the bottle-green wool for James. After she cut it all out, she dragged her sewing machine over in front of her bedroom window and started sewing.

I sat on the floor picking up the scraps of cloth and watching her foot work the pedal up and down, and I wished that, just for once, Eloise had sent pink silk step-ins like the ones she wore. Instead of all that yards of stuff for bloomers.

Eloise had a lot of pink silk things with lace and little pockets on them, and on the pockets it said things like OH YOU KID. She had one pair that said I LIKE MEN. Eloise had pretty clothes and a lot of friends. Most of the friends who came with her to see us were pretty girls like herself, but once a man had brought her to Strawne in his big black car, and they had taken James and me to Wellco to a carnival. But the man never did come back with her any more. Because of what Mama had said, I guess. Mama had come into my room after we were home from the carnival that night, and had said that she didn't know whether Eloise should let her men friends come to Strawne or not because with an older, well-to-do man like that, somebody might misunderstand, and Eloise had laughed without sounding a bit happy and said she hoped to God they *did* misunderstand. "Not that it matters one hoot in hell to me," Eloise had said, and then they both cried. . . .

"You're a lucky little girl."

Daddy was standing in the door watching Mama at her sewing machine. "To have a mother," he said, "who can take a piece of material and a needle and make something straight out of a fashion magazine—"

"And to have somebody send your mother the material to sew." Mama didn't look up from her sewing machine. "That makes the difference."

Daddy stood there a minute or two longer. Then he went out and got into the car and left.

He went to work the next day. He went to work like he'd told Mama on that awful night, at old Will Jackson's sawmill up on the highway. He wasn't around the house all day, but I guess Mama liked it better that way. She was happier.

A week later she was still sewing on our Easter clothes. It was on the Saturday afternoon before Easter that I heard her singing as she sewed:

> *"What a fellowship, what a joy divine,*
> *Leaning on the everlasting arms—"*

She looked up from her sewing, out into the lilac and snowball bushes, and she sounded happy.

I stood in the door for a minute, watching her and listening. Then I wandered out onto the back porch. James was lying on the porch in the sun, reading. He looked up at me and put his finger to his lips and nodded toward Mama's window, and I knew he'd been listening and enjoying it too.

"Mama sounds better, doesn't she? Not so cross. Do you want to play baseball?"

"Not right now." James turned a page of his book. "Maybe after a while."

James went back to reading. I wandered on down to the barn to talk to Dammit for a while. At least Dammit would look at me and listen.

Dammit was the cow Uncle Elmer had brought over and swapped for Mama's shiny green stove. Her real name was Brownie, but nobody except Mama ever called her that. Daddy did most of the milking and feeding and stuff, and every evening you could hear him down at the barn. "Back that leg, dammit," he'd yell. "Stand still, dammit!" So we called her that too.

Dammit was standing at the gate, looking out toward the mailbox and chewing. Once in a while she'd switch her tail around and hit herself on the back with it, but nothing much else about her moved.

"Are you lonesome too, Dammit?" I reached through the fence

and rubbed her nose. It felt like the blue velvet Eloise had sent. "It would be a good day to walk in the woods with Daddy," I said. "But Daddy's not home. He went across the log over the Little Luter to spot timber for old Will Jackson."

I picked a handful of blue daisies and stuck them through the fence to Dammit. She didn't even look at them. I held them in front of her and started singing to make her look.

> *"Daddy's gone to spot tim-ber*
> *For o-old Wi-yull Jackson.*
> *We hope he'll be back soo-oon—"*

"Gaw!" James had walked up behind me. "Singin' to a *cow?*"

He reached over the fence and got the shovel that was leaning against it. "Let's go over under the pecan trees and dig another hole."

One Saturday James had dug a deep hole under the pecan trees and then he had leaned over it and listened to the Chinamen talking on the other side of the world.

"We'll dig deeper this time," James said. "We may have to dig all the way through to China, but we'll make it deep enough for you to hear them today."

"Maybe I'll never hear them." I followed James and watched him start digging. "Maybe I'll fall through and you'll never see me again."

He kept digging. "You have to hear them to be really educated. Rake the dirt back out of the way."

I raked the dirt back with my hands and patted it down smooth around the edge of the hole. James dug for a long time, and the hole looked awfully deep. Then he lay down on his stomach and put his head over the hole and lay there listening to the Chinamen talking.

I sat down on the ground and watched him. Then James got up and I lay down and listened.

The ground was cool and damp and the sand was gritty against my face. Once I thought I heard the mumble of voices, but I couldn't tell for sure. I lifted my face from the hole and looked at James and shook my head.

"Didn't you hear them?" James asked. "Gaw, are you deaf or what?"

I was ashamed. "What do they say?" I asked.

37

"Well, heck, wait." James started toward the house. "Wait here," he said, "and we'll trick them, and then you'll hear them!" He ran around the house and into the back yard.

I lay there looking into the hole. James had dug through a lot of sand. The dirt underneath was darker and softer and smelled wet. I heard Dammit moo over at the fence. She had moved down and was watching me. I wondered if the cows in China had to walk upside down.

"Move over."

James had come back with an old lard can full of water, and he poured it into the hole. The water went right into the dirt, not even making a puddle. By the time he'd finished pouring, it was all gone from the bottom of the hole.

"Now listen," James said.

Still nothing, for me.

"Aw, gaw." He lay down on his stomach again. "Get up and let me listen while the water's still running through."

I stood up and watched James listening again. "What do they say?" I asked.

James rolled over onto his back and put his arms under his head and looked up into the pecan trees.

"Well, at first," he said, "right after I dug it, one of them said Hark. Hark, he said, do you hear the sound of digging? And the other one said Methinks. Methinks I do, he said. There were only two of them."

"And what did they say the last time? After you poured in the water?"

"Well, the first one said Shiver my timbers, it's raining. Out of a clear blue sky, he said, it's raining. Cats and dogs. He said I cannot go to Canton in the rain."

"And the other one? What did he say then?"

James reached for a blade of grass and stuck it in his mouth and chewed it and watched me as he talked.

"Oh, the other one, he said, Drink your tea, it's quit already. Methinks. That's what he said. Methinks it has quit." James chewed his blade of grass. "The rest of their talk was just talk. You know, about rice, and chopsticks, and stuff like that." He stood up. "Let's do something else for a while. Maybe you'll hear them next time."

"Let's go home," I said, "and see if Mama will let us make

some more hot chocolate to sell down at the tie yard. Like we did last Saturday. Maybe Billy Bob Jackson will pay us today for what he drank last week."

Down beside the railroad tracks that you crossed to get to our house, the trees had all been cleared away, and there were big stacks of crossties waiting to be hauled away on the train and used on railroad tracks all over the world. Every Saturday Billy Bob Jackson came out in his big shiny car and checked and counted the ties before they were hauled away to be used. James said it was so he would know how much money to pay the men who had made the ties from the big trees in the woods around us.

Sometimes there were men at the tie yard with Billy Bob, singing and laughing and sweating as they lifted the big crossties up onto their shoulders and loaded them into boxcars on the railroad track. The men said our hot chocolate was sho good, and they paid us two cents a cup for it. . . .

"I cannot go to Canton in the rain," I sang as I stood in a chair over the big wood stove and stirred and waited for James to open a can of milk. "I cannot go to Can-ton in the rain, rain, rain—"

"Don't you make a mess and leave it, today." Mama stood in the kitchen door watching us. "And don't stay down at that tie yard long. I'm about through sewing, and after I press these things I want you around to try them on. Don't spill that stuff on the irons on the back of the stove, either." She went back to her room to sew some more.

At first Mama had been cross about having Grandma Thorpe's old irons always sitting on the back of the stove, but she used them. James wiped up the milk he'd spilled, and we left for the tie yard with the pitcher of cocoa and four cups.

The tie yard was quiet that day. There was nobody there except Billy Bob and Nathaniel Darsey. Billy Bob was going around marking things on the ends of ties with a little brush and a can of black paint, and Naye was following Billy Bob around and writing in a little blue notebook he had in one hand.

Naye looked up from his notebook. He smiled and waved his pencil at us, and his brown eyes and his white teeth sparkled in his brown face. I'd never heard of Nathaniel Darsey before that night of the called school-board meeting. But since we'd moved, we'd been seeing Naye every Saturday at the tie yard, because he worked for Billy Bob. We liked to talk to Naye, because he talked to you like you were real people, and not just kids hanging around in somebody's way.

Billy Bob looked around at us. Then he went back to marking the ties like he hadn't even seen us.

We stood beside a pile of ties until they'd finished a stack. James set the pitcher on a crosstie and I put the cups with it. Billy Bob wiped the paint off his fingers onto his khaki pants and lit a cigarette. Naye added up the figures he'd written down, and Billy Bob blew out a big puff of smoke and watched him.

"You add them figures right, boy," Billy Bob said to Naye. He looked at us. "Ain't nothin' gits by old Billy Bob, is they?"

"Yassuh. Nawsuh." Naye finished and handed the blue notebook to Billy Bob. "You mought bettah check 'em, be sho they right." Naye's voice sounded like cream would, if cream could have a sound. It was rich and deep and smooth, and somehow it made you think of music. Sorrowful music when his eyes weren't laughing, dancing music, clapping music, when they were.

Naye had told James that he was seventeen, but sometimes Naye's eyes made him look older than Daddy or Uncle Elmer.

Old Will Jackson was Billy Bob's father, and that was why Billy Bob worked at the tie yard. James said old Will had to put Billy Bob somewhere he could keep an eye on him. Billy Bob must have been about twenty-five that summer we lived in the breezeway house, and he was about a foot shorter than Naye, but he was a lot wider. James said Billy Bob had a beer belly, but of course he didn't say that where Billy Bob could hear him.

"—and forty-eight, and sixty-six, and seventy-two—" Billy Bob looked down at the notebook and frowned and bit his lips, but you could tell he wasn't really doing the figures. Naye looked across at us and wiggled his eyebrows and his ears. James wiggled his ears back like Naye had taught him, but we all kept our faces straight. After we stood there for a while, Billy Bob put the pencil and notebook on a tie and came over and looked into the pitcher.

"Mighty hot for cocoa today," he said. "But I guess I'll take a cupful. Hope it don't make me sick."

He knew it wouldn't. James poured a cupful and handed it to him, and he swilled it all down without taking the cup from his mouth.

40

Then he swiped his hand across his mouth and pushed his straw hat onto the back of his big round head. He looked down at James with that ugly grin that made his front teeth stick out even worse.

"Is it garnteed?"

"Well, sure." James held out his hand and waited for Billy Bob to reach into his pocket for two cents.

The constable's badge pinned on Billy Bob's shirt pocket began to shake before his laugh came out, and we all knew exactly what was coming. Billy Bob never laughed at anything except his own jokes on other people.

"Well," he was still grinning. "To be honest, I b'leve it was a little too sweet. But I'll be fair with you. I tell you what. I'd hafta think on it twice before I paid for anythin' that might make me sick, but you pour me another cup. An' if I ain't sick by next week, I might pay you."

He drank the second cupful and swiped his mouth again and picked up his paint can and brush.

"You hurry, boy," he said to Naye. "I ain't paying you t' stand around in the sunshine drinkin' stuff."

"Yassuh."

Naye stood still until Billy Bob went back to marking ties. Then he picked up a cup and held it for James to pour cocoa. After he poured Naye's, James poured a cupful for us, and we all three leaned against a stack of ties and drank it.

Naye took off the white handkerchief that was tied around his head and mopped his face with it. Then he shook the handkerchief and tied it back around his head.

"Kind of warmish out here in the sun," he said. "Too warm for this time of year."

James watched him.

"How come you talked that way to ol' Billy Bob while ago?" he asked. "That yassuh, an' nawsuh an' sho, an' all that stuff?"

Naye smiled down at James and reached into his pocket and handed James a nickel. Then he opened his eyes real big and rolled them around.

"That Mistuh Billy Bob, he sho want a black boy to know he black," he said. "No, you keep the change to pay for part of what he drank. He'll never pay you for it, you know."

"I know." James thumbed his nose toward Billy Bob's back.

"But he won't pay you back either, and so you'll just be the loser instead of us. You—"

Naye rolled his eyes again. "Ah has mah ways."

James thumbed his nose again. "Ol' Bullet-head! That's all he is. Ol' Bullet-head. Ol' Beer-belly."

"Somebody ought to have the law on him," I joined in. "For cheating people."

James and Naye laughed.

"Be kinda hard to do," James said. "He is the only law between here and Wellco. The law's not comin' twenty-five miles, clear from Wellco, to arrest another law for splashin' mud on people, or twistin' their arms, or cheatin' somebody out of four cents." He looked up at Naye. "Does ol' Billy Bob ever arrest anybody?"

"Mmm, no." Naye picked up his notebook and pencil. "Most of the time he just kinda roughs them up. Not white folks, of course."

We stood there leaning against the ties and looking at Billy Bob's back, thinking how mean he was. It wasn't any wonder that Miss Una was always trying to run away. If I had to live with Billy Bob and old Will both, I thought as I looked at Billy Bob's mean back, I'd run away and not even Callie could catch me and bring me back.

"Gaw," James said after a while. "All that money and stuff old Will Jackson has, and he still can't buy Billy Bob a set of brains. What were his brothers like, Naye? Didn't he have two brothers that ran away and joined the Navy or something?"

Naye nodded. "Pretty rough boys. But I guess they had to be. Main thing I remember about them is how they used to beat me up. Then they'd laugh about not being able to see the bruises. They used to burn up the books Gramma got for me. And she just got me more books, instead of—" He shook his head. "Miss Una's a good little woman. But her menfolks, they're somethin else. And I'm hushin right now."

"I know something," I said. "I heard Daddy tell Mama once that old Will had bought Billy Bob a constable's badge now and we'd see what came of that. And Mama said well it would keep the law off of him when he pulled his shennagins, if *he* was the law. What's a shennagin?"

"Hey, boy!" Billy Bob had stopped to light a cigarette and he was looking back toward us. "This ain't no holiday! Git over here!"

"Yassuh!" Naye left us to go and write down some more numbers to add. "See ya," he said, and flipped his hand.

When we started gathering up the cups to go home, James frowned at me.

"You talk too much," he said.

"About what?"

"About stuff you hear at home. Don't you ever do that again. You hear?"

"Well, gollee, all I said was that I heard Daddy—"

"Well, just don't say it!" James started home, talking over his shoulder at me. "Just don't say anything about what you hear anywhere any more."

"You said that you'd heard that he roughed folks up," I said. "Why do you have to act like there's some kind of secret about what *I* say?"

"I was just poppin' off." James frowned again.

"Well, why don't you remember your *Ings* when you're doing it?" Some people got to be smart alecks the minute they were eleven years old. "Just wait 'til Daddy hears *you!*"

"Oh, you!" James stopped and waited for me. "Come on. Let's give Dammit the rest of the cocoa. Maybe she'll give chocolate milk tonight."

We stopped at the barn and poured the rest of the cocoa into an old pan for Dammit, but I guess she thought it was too sweet, too. She wouldn't touch it.

"Let's go home and try on our Easter clothes." I loved to try on new clothes. They never looked quite like I had thought they would, because something always came loose or hung down or slid around, but still I loved it.

James didn't exactly love it, but he knew we had to, and so he followed me back to the house, walking slower and slower.

"I can-not go to Can-ton in the rain, rain, rain," I sang. "I cannot go, I cannot go, I can-not go to Can-ton in the rain!"

Mama was in the kitchen pressing our Easter clothes.

"Here." She caught James by the arm and pulled him toward the ironing board.

"Take these in and try them on, so I can be sure they fit. You, too, Thorpe." She handed us our new clothes.

I didn't mind at all, anything except the bloomers, but James pulled away and glared at the bottle-green suit Mama was trying to hand to him. James sure hated to try on clothes. I think it was because Mama stuck pins in him when he didn't stand still.

"Gaw," he said. "Again? Do we have to? Can't I wear mine just like they are now? They fit good enough for me."

"Oh, hush!" Mama pushed him toward his room. "I didn't say go cast yourself in irons. And I want you to quit saying *gaw* so much!"

Mama looked tired. "After Eloise sent us all this nice material and I sewed night and day, the least you can do is try it on."

We went into our rooms.

I had thought at first that the nicest part about the blue velvet was who ever heard of blue velvet bloomers, but the bloomers were tan pongee, and too big, like always. Still, looking in the mirror, I thought I looked pretty good. I reached for the blue velvet tam o'shanter Mama had made and pulled it down over all my hair, tucking up the wisps that hung down in the back.

When I went back out into the hall, James was already there with his bottle-green suit on, and Mama was straightening his stiff white collar. She set his straw hat closer to the front and stepped back.

"Move closer," Mama said. "So I can see how you look together." She straightened my tam. "Let your bangs show." Then she bent over my head.

"What in the world? Thorpe, there's sand all in your hair!"

"I know," I said. "I guess I got it when I was listening to the Chinamen. I mean, when I was trying to."

"When you were *what?*" Mama took the tam off and brushed at my hair.

"James dug this hole, Mama, and we listened to the Chinamen talking underneath the world, but I couldn't hear them. I'm too stupid."

Mama looked at James and raised her eyebrows.

"James!"

James pushed his new hat to the back of his head. "Well, gaw, Mama. It's just a joke. She's so stupid. She b'leves everything anybody tells her."

I wasn't really listening to them. I was watching myself in the big yellowed mirror Grandma Thorpe had left on the wall. "May we keep our new clothes on to show Daddy?" I asked. "May we go meet him at the creek and surprise him?"

Mama knelt down on the floor beside me and straightened my collar, and her hand on my neck was gentle. "I guess so," she said. She brushed some sand from my forehead and kissed the spot she had brushed. "You may walk as far as the creek if you promise not to run or fall down. It's time for him now, so go ahead. And don't get in a hurry."

She followed us to the porch and we started to the gate, walking stiff and straight.

"Remember," Mama called, "stay on the path. Don't cross the creek and don't get hung on the brush and tear something!"

We didn't run at first. We walked nice and straight and we stayed on the trail. James looked nice in his new suit, but he looked kind of funny, too. Like he was ready to start singing or dancing or something, in his stiff hat and his stiff collar and his green-spotted tie.

"What's so funny about me?" James asked. "Why do you keep looking at me with that silly grin?"

"All you need is a banjo," I said.

"Well, pardon me, Missis Astor," James said. "But how do you think *you* look, with that—that cap thing pulled down over all your hair and your bloomers draggin'?"

"That cap thing"—I stopped and glared at James "—is a tam o'shanter. But you never remember the right name for anything, anyhow. And they always drag. My bloomers. My legs are too skinny, I guess. But Mama'll roll my hair tonight and make it curly for tomorrow. Will I look better then?"

"Aw, you look awright." James looked ashamed. "I guess, considerin' who it is, you look real good." He reached up and broke off a branch of redbud from a tree. "Let's take this home to Mama. Tag!"

He tapped me with the redbud branch. That was when we started running.

At the creek, we sat down on the end of the log to wait for Daddy. The log had been there across the creek for a long time, and the top of it was smooth and shiny. James got up and walked out on it but after a few steps, he turned back.

I stood up and put one foot out onto the log.

"I wish Mama'd let us walk across." I took my foot off. "I've been across it with Daddy. Lots of times."

"Mama won't even cross it herself." James sat back down and threw a stick into the Little Luter. We watched the stick float off downstream and sink in a whirlpool.

"Women are just that way," James said. "When you're a woman, you will be, too." He looked at me and then he shook his head like he didn't have too much hope I'd ever be a woman. "Anyhow, the reason we can't go across it right now is 'cause you're too little."

I drew myself up taller.

"Stand up and stretch your arm out. Come on."

James stood up, and I moved over beside him.

"See, I can't even stand under your arm any more!"

He laughed. "I guess not, stupid, on tiptoe. But you're still too little. And so, because *you* would fall off if you tried, I can't walk across it either!"

"You couldn't anyhow. Not barefoot and using a balancing pole, you couldn't."

James laughed again. "I could walk that thing with my eyes shut!" He stepped up onto the log. "You stand still and don't make a sound, and you'll learn something!"

He stretched out both arms. And then, using the redbud branch for a balancing pole, he shut both eyes and started walking.

I thought about yelling *Boo!* but it seemed like kind of a dirty trick when I wasn't even mad at him or anything, so I didn't.

James went on, toward the other bank of the creek, waving his hands up and down for balance. Of course, his back was to me, so I didn't know for sure that his eyes were shut, but they must have been.

He was just about halfway across when he fell.

I saw his foot slip. And then his hat fell off, because he was waving his arms harder. The hat sort of floated down. James didn't. He hit the water before his hat did, and a second later his new straw Easter hat settled lightly down onto the water and floated past him.

James went all the way under when he hit the water. After a

minute he stood up and his hair was plastered down over his eyes.

I ran out onto the log, and I had reached the place that made James slip before I remembered that the log was old and slick and I was too little. I stood there on the log and looked down at James standing there with his beautiful Easter suit all wet and muddy. Then I sat down on the log and slid off into the water with him.

I hit with a splash, but my head didn't go under. So I took off the blue velvet tam and dipped it into the water. Then I remembered Mama sitting up at night sewing on it and I put it back on.

"Well, stupid!" James shouted at me, and pushed his hair back out of his eyes. "What are you doin'!"

Downstream his hat whirled around about three times and got full of water and started sinking.

"Don't cry," I said to James. It was all I could think of to say. "Don't shout."

James shouted that he wasn't crying and he wasn't shouting. It was just that damned muddy creek water in his eyes and he was using a perfectly normal voice.

That was a long time ago. I only saw James cry one other time after that day. The second time was about a year later. There wasn't any muddy water in his eyes then, and I pretended not to notice. I don't guess he ever cried again.

3

The day we fell into the Little Luter we stood there in the water
and argued about who was crying and shouting and who wasn't.
While we were arguing and crying and shouting, we heard somebody, somewhere, singing. We stopped arguing and listened—

"Mermaids," I said. "Combing their long green hair with
golden combs!"

"Aw, gaw." The water was cold, and James shivered. "Mermaids in a *creek*? Anyhow, it sounds more like Neptune!"

"Oh, Mary, doncha weep, doncha moan. . . . Oh, Mary, doncha weep; doncha moan. . . . Pharaoh's army done drown-ded—"

"Well if it's Neptune," I said, "he's got a saw instead of a
pitchfork. Look!" I pointed to the other end of the log.

Stepping up onto the log and starting across it was the biggest,
tallest man (except Daddy) you ever saw. He had a cross-cut
saw over one shoulder, and in one hand he had a bottle of kerosene with pine straw sticking from the top of the bottle. I knew
it was kerosene in the bottle, because it was like the bottles that
Daddy fixed to take into the woods to sprinkle on the big saws.

We watched the man as he came toward us and as he squatted
on the log to look down at us.

"E'nen, chillun," he said, and you would have thought he saw
people in muddy blue velvet and bottle-green suits standing in the

48

Little Luter every day. He smiled. "Yall bout ready t' git out now?"

The man's face was the color of the caramel apples that Eloise had brought to us once. He was wearing faded blue overalls fastened at one shoulder with a bent nail, and his shirt looked like it was made out of patches left over from other clothes. He stuffed the bottle of kerosene into his back pocket and held his hand down to me. "I hep you git out," he said.

After he had us both back up onto the log, he raised me to one shoulder and shifted the saw on his other shoulder to balance us, and we followed James back to the creek bank. When we were all three on dry ground again, the man pulled an old rag from his pocket and started to wipe us off. Then he looked at the rag and at us and put it back into his pocket.

"That ol rag get yall dirtier," he said. He looked at James. "Yall mus be Mister Jim's an Miss Venie's chillun. Zat right?"

James shivered and nodded.

"Well," the man said. "I'm Lewis Johnson. I live right aroun that bend in the trail yondah. Now the way I see it, Miss Venie go' have a hahd time unnerstannin all this, so why donchall jes come along home wi me, an I wrop y' in a blanket so y' be dried out an warm befo y' try explainin it."

We were shivering too hard to argue.

We followed Lewis through the dogwood and pinoak trees, and when we got to his house we found the nicest surprise. Donie was standing in the door of Lewis' house. Donie, who still came up the trail through the trees and washed for us on Saturday mornings—and who started scolding like a bluejay before we were inside her front door.

"Now ain that somethin!" Donie backed into the house and Lewis led us inside. "Ain that— Where yall been? Ain that them good cloes Miss Venie been setten up nights makin? How come—"

"We fell in the creek." I quit shivering long enough to answer. "Donie, I didn't know you lived here! We saw smoke coming from this house the other day, but we didn't know it was *your* house, or we'd have been—"

Donie grinned. "It ain my house esackly, honey. It a Thorpe house, lak the one you live in. Yo grandaddy built this house fo my Mama, and Miss Venie she say it mine fo as long—" She frowned. "It ain houses we need t' talk about, now. How come you out splashin in no creek in nem good cloes?"

"We didn't mean to, Donie. James's foot slipped, and I—I fell in, too." I looked down at the puddle on Donie's floor around us. "The log was slick."

"Down nair on at log wif them good cloes on! Sometimes I wondah ef me an Miss Venie right, not bleven in whuppen kids! You blong t' some folks I know, they'd sho lay it on you now!"

She turned to the door that opened from the kitchen. "Don stan aroun grinnen at somebody else's bad luck! Git me a pan o' water an a rag!" She wasn't talking to James and me. She was talking to the boy and the girl who stood in the door watching us.

The girl had her hand over her mouth to hide her grinning, but the boy's grin showed all his teeth, and his eyes sparkled like brown glass. The girl's hair was in about eight little braids, pinned down close to her head. The boy's hair stood up in a little ruff on top, and his knees under the cutoff pants he wore were skinnier than mine or James'.

"You, Josie," Donie pointed her finger at the girl. "You git me a pan o' water an a rag in here, so's I kin clean this mess offa Miss Thorpe." She looked back at James. "You big enuf t' wash yoself, so you git in th' kitchen behin that stove an get busy!"

She sat down on the floor beside me with the pan of water. "That po thing! That po lil ol thing!"

"She means Mama," I whispered to James. He nodded and swallowed and went into the kitchen. I could hear him in there talking to Lewis and to the boy with the ruff of hair on top.

"Setten up at night fo two weeks, sewen an plannen!" Donie was scrubbing me and scolding. "An look at chall now! Well, you go' hafta take these drippy things off. I see kin I fin somethin fo you t' put on!"

"Donie," I whispered, "are those your children? What are their names? I didn't know you had children!"

"Well, cose I got a fambly!" Donie was still cross. "My girl, she name Josie May an we call 'er Josie. My boy, he name Theotus, but we call 'im Thee. You know, they bout th' same age as you an Mister James, cept fo Josie. I guess she a year or two older than Mister James."

She stood up and went over to the big shiny brass bed with

the peacock embroidered on the bedspread. She pulled the bed out from the wall.

"Now you git over behin this bed an strip. While I fin you somethin dry to put on."

I got behind the bed and stripped, and then I put on the gray flannel bloomers and the red silk dress that Donie had found for me. The bloomers wrapped around me twice, but Donie found a big safety pin and fixed that. She also found a pin to put at the top of the dress to keep my bosom from showing where the collar hung down. What she'd found me to wear felt a lot better than those cold drippy velvet clothes I'd pulled off.

"Yall kin come back in now, ef you ready," Donie called into the kitchen, and James came back through the door with Lewis and Thee behind him.

James was wearing an old purple bathrobe with a piece of green rope tied around his middle. He might have been wearing pants underneath, but you couldn't tell. The bathrobe came down past his ankles, and he kept pulling the green rope tighter and pulling the bathrobe back up to blouse over it.

Thee sidled over behind Donie and pulled on her skirt. When she leaned over, he whispered into her ear, but we could all hear what he said.

"Kin we give em a pig?" he whispered.

"A pig?" Donie frowned. She looked back at James and me. "They in enuf trouble wi Miss Venie *now*. They don want no pig!"

"He say they like to have one." Thee pointed at James. "He say they ain got no pets. An you done say we haf t' git rid o' that runt, so th' ol sow kin feed the rest. Why cain't we give it to them?"

"Miss Venie wouldn' nevah let em keep no *pig*. I know Miss Venie better'n to send a pig ovah to her house. She got enuf worries now, without no pigs!"

"Please, Donie!" I pulled on the other side of her skirt. "You mean a real *live* pig? Please, Donie, she'll let us keep it! I know she will!"

Donie looked at Lewis.

He grinned. "I don care, ef you want t' let em try it. We go' haf t' git rid o' that runt, that's right. An Miss Venie mought let em keep it."

Thee and Josie ran out the door. When they came back in,

51

Josie was carrying a little black-and-white pig. She handed it to James, and it kicked and squirmed. James handed it to me.

It was a beautiful pig, with its curly tail and pink nose, and I started loving it when James handed it to me. I held it in one arm and rubbed it, and its body felt like Daddy's face did every morning. I bent over it and kissed it.

"Gaw," James said. "You better not let Mama see you kissin' a pig, or she sure won't let you keep it!" He rubbed its side. "It *is* cute, isn't it?"

"Yall bettah go now," Donie said. "Mister Jim be home by now, an Miss Venie she be worrit sick cause you ain wif 'im." She turned to Lewis. "You go wif em, an you go in an tell Miss Venie not to worry bout th' cloes. You tell er I clean em up an steam em an git em back up to er firs thing in th' mornen, like new an in pleny o' time fo church."

"Kin we go, too?" Thee asked.

"Aw, I guess so," Donie said. "Ef you behave yoself. Git goin, now, all uv you, befo Miss Venie stahts thinken they done fell in an drownded."

We went out Donie's door and down the trail again, with Lewis walking in front and James behind him wearing the purple bathrobe. Behind James, I clutched the pig with one hand and held my long red skirt lifted with the other. I was in the middle of the line, with Thee and Josie behind me.

Ahead of me, James kept grabbing at his bathrobe. His green rope belt wasn't tight enough and his robe couldn't decide whether to come open or fall down around his feet or both. Nobody talked at first, and the only sound was the squishing sound of our shoes that were still full of water.

James looked like he'd looked one Christmas when he was a Wise Man in a church program. And he must have been thinking about the Christmas program too, because pretty soon he turned around and grinned at me and hitched up his purple robe and started singing.

"Oh, I'm a King of Orientar—" he sang.

"Bearing pigs we travel afar," I answered.

"But we wouldn't walk if we had a car!" James sang.

We were all singing and giggling except Lewis. Lewis looked like the Pied Piper without a pipe. We started another song but before we were halfway through it we were at our front gate and

52

I quit singing and got busy trying to wrap the pig in my red silk skirt before Mama came to the door and saw us. We walked around the house to the back door, and by that time I had him pretty well wrapped.

Mama came to the door when she heard us out back, and when she opened the door I darted past her into the house and poked the pig under my bed. Pretty soon after that Mama exploded and nobody thought about singing or giggling.

Mama didn't really explode until after Lewis told her about how and where he'd found us and that Donie would take care of our clothes. Thee and Josie stood in the back yard and grinned while Lewis was telling her, and after they went away—

After that, like Eloise said when she was telling things, after that was when the soup hit the fan. Mama whirled onto Daddy first, and he wasn't doing a thing but holding his book and listening.

"Don't you dare laugh!" Mama acted like it was Daddy who'd fallen in the creek with new clothes on. "Don't you crack a grin! If you do I'll take that everlasting book and—and make you eat it for supper."

"Why should I laugh?" Daddy was biting his lip and his face was red, but it was perfectly straight.

"Oh, go ahead." Mama's lips trembled. "Go ahead and laugh. They are hilarious, aren't they? Here Eloise goes out and buys the cloth and I sew and press night and day for two weeks! They left here looking just beautiful, and I was happy for the first time in weeks. Then they come home—" Mama's voice broke. "They come home wearing rags. Nigra rags!"

She reached for the big pin at the neck of my dress. She unpinned me, but when she reached for the dress to help me take it off, and her hands touched the red silk, she drew them back and wiped them on her skirt.

"Take those things off. Both of you." Her voice was lower. "Take them off and drop them on the porch. And go in the kitchen and get into the bath water your *father* is going to fix for you."

"But Mama, we've already had a bath. We had one at Donie's house."

Mama didn't hear me. She was listening to the sounds that came from my bedroom. Crash! went something falling to the floor, and click-click went the sound of pig feet running across the room. Something else fell, and it must have fallen on the pig. He squealed.

"What did you bring into the house, Thorpe? What was inside your skirt when you came in here with that Coxey's army parade?" Mama shook my shoulder.

I was busy pulling off the red silk dress. I held it over my head for a long time, hoping Mama would think I hadn't heard her. She yanked the dress off my head and handed James the towel she was holding.

"Wrap this around you," she said, "and go into Thorpe's room and bring out whatever you two brought home."

James went into the house. I heard Daddy in the kitchen filling the tubs for our baths.

"Bath water's ready," Daddy called. He came out onto the back porch and started gathering up the clothes we had pulled off and dropped.

"James!" Mama called.

James came to the screen door and looked out at us. "I didn't see anything in there," he said carefully. "Except the usual things."

"What usual things?" Mama gave me a hard look.

"Oh-hh," James said. "A ball. Some books. And some toys and stuff."

"What else?"

"And a bed, and things like that."

Daddy opened the screen door and put his hand under James' chin and lifted it. He made James look at him. "And what else?"

"And a dresser and a chair and some clothes and a pig and—"

"A *pig?*" Mama closed her eyes and she was quiet for so long that I wondered if she was counting or praying. "A pig?"

"They gave him to us and may we keep him he's so beautiful and I'm going to take the first bath." I brought it all out in one breath and slid past all of them and into the kitchen. I jumped into the tub behind the stove.

On the back porch Mama was still talking.

"So now we have a pig. A nigra pig."

Nobody said a word. Mama's voice rose again.

"No, you may not keep him, Missy. You hurry and get out of that tub so James can get in. As for you, Jim Torrance, you

get that pig out of my house. And in the morning, you, person-
ally, can go with them to take it back. But for right now, just get
it out of my house! And I don't want to hear it even mentioned
by any of the whole crazy lot of you. And if you kids want to dye
Easter eggs you'll have to get up early in the morning. We're not
going to do it tonight."

Nobody mentioned the pig on Easter morning. During breakfast we could hear him out in the back yard, in the old box that
Daddy had found for him. Mama watched us go out the door
with a plate of scraps for him, but nobody said a word about him.
While we were in the kitchen dyeing eggs, Lewis brought our
clothes to the back door, and when Mama saw that the clothes
looked like nothing had happened to them, she started feeling
better.

A few minutes later Mama straightened my tam o'shanter and
took a comb and tried to plaster James' rooster-tail down in back,
and we were off to church.

THORPE'S CHAPEL BAPTIST. The paint on the churchhouse was
flaking off in places and the big trees that grew right up to it
and met over it looked a little tired and droopy, but the sign over
the door was clean and fresh. Aunt Neevy made Uncle Elmer
keep it that way.

Even when we'd lived in the yellow house in Strawne, which
was for all of my life until we'd moved, we hadn't gone to the
big white church in town, with the stained glass windows. We'd
driven out to the country every Sunday, to Thorpe's Chapel. Because Grandpappy Thorpe (Mama's Grandpappy Thorpe) had
given the land for Thorpe's Chapel. While they were still holding
tent-meetings in Strawne, he'd built Thorpe's Chapel. Aunt Neevy
said so. Every time she had a chance.

People came to Thorpe's Chapel from up and down the highway on both sides, and from the woods around it. Some people
drove out from town, like we'd done, and some people still came
in wagons or rode horses. The horses and wagons were left out
back, between the churchhouse and the graveyard, but the cars
turned in from the highway and parked down the sides and in
front.

"Goodness!" Mama never said God-in-Heaven on Sundays. She always said goodness. "Look at the cars! We'll have a houseful today."

Daddy turned off the highway into the parking lot and Mama turned around to inspect us. We drove past Doctor John's Ford and eased in beside Uncle Elmer's Buick. Doctor John was one of the people who drove out from town, and he always parked at the edge of wherever he went. Beside Doctor John's muddy car, Uncle Elmer's car looked like new. It always looked that way. You wouldn't dare eat anything in it, and Aunt Neevy said there'd never been a cigarette smoked in it.

Mama looked in her purse mirror and pulled her hat a little lower over one eye. I stood up and twisted my bloomers straight. James felt for his rooster-tail and found it and tried to pat it down, Daddy sighed and we were ready to go into the churchhouse.

Brother Mearl stood in the door wiping sweat from around the collar of his white shirt. Brother Mearl must have gone to church earlier than anybody else every Sunday, because he was always there to shake hands with you when you got there. James said that Brother Mearl's coat was always unbuttoned because his stomach was so fat, but I thought it was so he could get it off quicker when he got wound up. He shouted a lot when he got in the pulpit, and as his face got redder and wetter he started stripping. First his coat and then his tie would sail through the air to a chair in the Deacon's pew. By the time he'd finished preaching his shirttail would be half out and his two top shirt buttons gone.

But just because Sister Mearl had died last year didn't mean that Brother Mearl went around without those buttons. You'd think it was some kind of honor to get to sew those buttons back on, the way the women at Missionary Society meetings argued about it. Mama didn't argue about wanting to sew on any buttons, but she had Brother Mearl over for Sunday dinner a lot.

I didn't hear much of his sermon that day, because I was praying. The churchhouse ought to be about the best place to ask for something that you wanted real bad, and so ever since we'd taken our seats after Sunday School I'd been praying that Mama would let us keep the pig. I prayed some, too, that Brother Mearl wouldn't go home with us for dinner. If we had to argue about it, I didn't want him around during the argument.

"—Will you come, sinner, will you come?" The sermon was about over. Brother Mearl's coat and tie hung from the chair, and he looked tired and happy. "Will you leave them cards and that likker and them painted women in the gutter where you found them and come?"

Nobody came. Brother Mearl's voice sank down to a whisper. "Come," he whispered, "before it's too late. Come, before the weeping and gnashing of teeth. Before the rocks fall from the mountain—"

We sang "Just As I Am" and then Miss Mildred played through it again, slow and soft, but nobody came. Old Will Jackson prayed a long time for all of the people who wouldn't leave the gutter and come to Brother Mearl, and church was over.

We didn't have to argue at all about keeping the pig. Out of a clear blue sky without anybody begging or having to promise anything, Mama changed her mind.

After church we had an egghunt. When it was over and James was giving me some of his eggs because I'd only found one, Aunt Neevy and Mama came out of the churchhouse and stood beside our car, talking.

"Hurry, Mama. Hurry!" Old Dawn Starr ran up to them, with her fat blonde Shirley Temple curls bouncing around her pudgy pink face, and started pulling on Aunt Neevy's arm. "Hurry. I want to go home and see about my pony."

I looked up from my Easter eggs. "Does Dawn Starr have a pony?" I asked James.

"Well, I don't know, stupid. I never saw it, if she does. Go ask her." James put our eggs in the car.

It could be true. Old Dawn Starr made up stories and told a lot of things that weren't true, but it *might* be. I thought about it for a moment, and then I went over to where Dawn Starr was still pulling on Aunt Neevy's purse.

"You don't have a pony," I said real loud. "Not a real one that eats hay!"

"I do too!" Dawn Starr hopped on one foot and twisted the

purse strap around Aunt Neevy's arm. "Don't I, Mama? Tell her, Mama. I got it yesterday, didn't I?"

"Quit pulling on my purse." Aunt Neevy frowned down at us and then she looked at Mama and kind of laughed. "Oh-h, Elmer finally traded for that little old pony that Will Jackson's had for sale all year—"

"And I have to let you and James ride him." Dawn Starr was still swinging on Aunt Neevy's purse. "Because Mama says you and James prob'ly never will have any ponies and things like that because Uncle Jim's such a—"

"Dawn Starr!" Aunt Neevy jerked her purse so hard it flew up and hit her on the chin.

"We do, too. We have lots of things. We have— We have—" I looked at Mama to be sure she was listening. "No, we don't. We don't have any kind of pet at all. We can't even keep things when people *give* them to us. We—"

"We have to go home and build a pigpen," Mama said and put her hand on my arm. "That's what we have to do. Thorpe, go find your father and tell him we're ready to go."

"—but remember," Mama said in the car on the way home, "you have to feed him, and keep his pen clean. You have to promise to do that."

"We promise!" James and I said.

"And if I ever catch you riding that—that pony, I'll beat you to death!"

"Well!" Daddy slowed the car to a stop in front of our gate. "I don't know what I missed in the sermon today, but whatever it was, I wish I'd listened!" He smiled at Mama and we all went into the house happy and nobody explained to Daddy that it wasn't the sermon.

We spent most of the rest of that day arguing about a name for our new pet. And that evening, when we were down at the barn watching Daddy finish building the pen, it was Daddy who came up with a name.

"Why don't you call him Peccavi?" he asked as he laid the last rail on the top and nailed it into place. "I think it would be most appropriate."

"Peccavi," I said. It had a lovely sound. "Peccavi."

James liked it too, and so we had a name for our pig.

It was a long time later that James learned, from one of Daddy's books, what *peccavi* meant, and we discovered that we were yelling "I have sinned" every time old Peck got out of his pen and we had to call him back. Mama had never called him; she'd always made us do it, and the day James found the name in the book, we finally knew why.

4

After that Easter Sunday, Donie brought Thee and Josie with her most Saturdays when she came to wash, and we played out back, Thee and Josie and James and I. They knew some beautiful games, Thee and Josie. Games with words that, if James knew, he hadn't taught to me.

> *"Bum bum bum, here I come. . . .*
> *Where you from? . . . New Or-leans!"*
> *"Honey in the bee-ball, bee-ball, bee-ball,*
> *I can't see y'all, see y'all, see y'all. . . .*

and

> *"Better run hide, the patterole'll gitcha!*
> *Better run hide, the patterole'll gitcha!"*

Saturdays. We played under the trees and sang the words to the games, while Donie kept time rubbing a shirt collar on the washboard. Inside the kitchen Mama baked an eggless, milkless cake and Daddy sat on the couch and read one of his books.

We must have had two or three—I don't remember exactly how many—good Saturdays before the Thompson kids started bothering us. They were our neighbors, too, living up on the highway like they did, but we'd never visited them. The Thompson kids started coming around after the trees out back had little green peaches and pears on them.

You wouldn't hear a sound out back on Saturday morning, but then you'd go out in the yard and all the trees would be full of Thompsons, with the little ones over squatting behind the fence waiting for the bigger ones to throw them some green peaches. There were ten of the Thompson kids. I'd seen the old house up beside the highway where they lived, but I hadn't known any of them. I'd heard James talk about some of them, of course, because old Soggum was in the same grade at school as James, and he was the one who gave James the valentine that said TO MY FAVORITE UNCLE. . . . Their old house was ragged-looking, with the fence all falling down and tin cans and old tires all over the yard, and a broken chair on the front porch where Mr. Thompson sat and watched the cars go by.

James would chase them out of the peach trees. After that the Thompson kids would all squat behind the fence and yell things at us about playing with Thee and Josie. So James would go out and chase them off again, but he'd always quit playing with us and go into the house. Or else he'd go down to the tie yard and talk to the men there.

But the Thompson kids quit coming around. Mama thought it was because she went out one Saturday and promised them some ripe fruit if they'd quit stealing the green, but I think it was because James caught old Soggum out behind the fence one day and made a believer out of him. James had said he was going to *murder* somebody if they kept stealing our peaches, and one day he made old Soggum believe it.

By the time we were rid of the Thompsons, school was out and James was home all day, and Saturdays stretched out into the whole week. Sometimes we had to work in the garden for an hour or two, and sometimes—not very often—we went to Strawne and bought groceries at Mr. Byrd's store. But most of the time, through the days and weeks that made up that summer, we were free to do as we pleased.

We walked through the woods. We ran, we hid, we dropped from the trees, and we waded in the creeks. We stopped by Donie's house on hot afternoons for a glass of buttermilk. We learned to cross the log over the Little Luter . . . with our eyes open. And James and Thee finally learned to cross it with their eyes shut. Lucky for them, we wore old clothes in the summer, and they dried out pretty quick.

"Draw a magic circle and dot it with a T-H-O-R-P-E!"

I stood with my hands over my eyes and my face against the smokehouse, and James—or Thee or Josie—stood behind me and drew a circle on my back with one finger, and jabbed me between the shoulders with each letter of my name. I knew it wasn't Josie jabbing, because she never did learn to spell any of our names right. We had taught Thee how to spell all four names, but that Josie just didn't learn . . . she probably would have said "—with a P-Q-R-H!" or something like that.

"James!" I guessed, and they all shouted No!

So I had guessed wrong, and I had to be *IT* while we played the rest of the game, which was really only hide-and-seek. It was the first part of the game I liked. The words, the delicious terror of guessing wrong, the tickle of the finger on my back—but mostly the words. The beautiful words. I shivered as I pressed my face against the rough gray boards of the smokehouse and waited for James and Thee and Josie to hide. . . .

Draw a magic circle! We were *in* a magic circle. The old gray house was home. Daddy had a job. We had friends, we played games, and over us the pink and white cloud of the fruit trees had turned into a green tangle of leaves.

"Ready!"

"Ready!"

"Ready!"

They had called, and away I went to find them. . . .

"Us got to quit fo a while," Josie said after I had found all of them. "Us gots t' take some shirts down t' Mister Martin. Come on, Thee."

"Okay." Thee ran after her, and they started out the gate. "See yall," Thee turned to call back to us.

"Wait, Josie!" I hung on the fence and grabbed at her sleeve. "Wait! Who's this Mister Martin? You took some stuff to him last week. Does he live around here? Can I go with you?"

"Ef you want to. Go ast." Josie grinned and waited for me. "He jes Mister Martin, thas all. He live down on th' trail pas our house, an he jes Mister Martin. Mama arn 'is shirts, an she say not stay out too late t' take em to im. He jes Mister Martin—"

"Come back, James!" I yelled. "Let's go ask Mama!"

But James had already started out the gate to the tie yard, and he didn't want to come back.

Inside the house, Mama was just settling down to listen to Stella Dallas on the radio. And the radio wouldn't work.

"Must be a battery gone," Mama was saying to herself when I ran into the living room. She frowned and fiddled with the knobs.

"Mama," I pulled on her skirt.

"Just a minute, Thorpe." Mama pulled the radio out from the wall and looked at it. "So now our only contact with the outside world is the newspaper. A newspaper a day old, brought out by the mailman. Who, Thorpe? Go to whose house?"

"To Mr. Martin's house. To take some shirts that Donie arn —ironed."

"Mr. Martin?" Mama frowned. "Who in the world is Mr. Martin?"

"He lives down on the trail past Donie's house! May I go, Mama? Please, they're waiting for me!"

Mama smiled.

"Oh, for Heaven's sake, you mean old Martin Ahrens! I'd forgotten he lived back down there!" She bent over the radio again and twisted a knob. "I guess so. If you promise to go straight to his house and no farther, and come straight—"

I flew out the door after Thee and Josie. We stopped by their house and got the shirts that Donie had ironed and wrapped in old newspapers, and trotted around the back of their house and down the trail.

We stopped once on the way to Mr. Martin's house to watch an old green bullfrog jump from the bank into Rocky Bottom Creek. While we were watching, a big fish jumped up after a bug and flopped back down into the water.

"Look at that ol goggle-eye perch jump!" Thee went down to the edge of the creek and held onto a big grapevine that hung from a tree and leaned out over the water. "Man, I like t' have me a pole an a can o' worms bout now! I bet I catch that big rascal!"

"Yeah, you catch at ol goggle-eye bout like I catch a star when 'e fall." Josie shifted the bundle of shirts to the other hip and grinned down at Thee.

Josie didn't talk much. Her voice was thick and low, and her words always came out slow, like she had to think about them first. Even when Josie was being funny there was something sad about the way she talked.

"You git back up on 'is bank fore you git muddy an git it on ese shirts," she called down to Thee. "Jes cause mud don' show on you don' mean it won' show on ese shirts."

We all laughed and Thee came back up on the bank. We went on around a bend and up a little hill, and there it was. Mr. Martin's house.

The little house was made of logs and the roof was wood shingles, maybe all from the trees somebody had cut down to make a place for it. The flowers that grew around it and climbed over it were every color you ever saw, and behind it you could see some apple trees and a garden. We stepped up onto the porch.

Josie tapped on the door, but it was Thee who called. "Mister Martin?" he called. "Mister Martin!"

The man who opened the door for us was tanned, like he'd been out in the sun a lot. His hair was so white it sparkled and his eyes were the color of the blue daisies we had picked down by the mailbox.

"Theotus. Josie. Come in, come in." The man opened the door with one hand and smiled down at us. In his other hand he held a giant-sized strawberry. He stepped to one side to let us in, and I saw that his shoulders were rounded and kind of stooped. He followed us into his house, and you would have thought we were real people come to visit him instead of children.

"Ah, clean shirts again. Thank you, Josie. Put them on the dresser. I was hoping for visitors today, so I could show this." He held the big strawberry out toward Thee. "Can you imagine a strawberry this big and perfect growing right out there in that patch behind my house?"

"Gol-lee!" Thee's eyes were big and brown. "I can magine it, Mister Martin. Them strawberries grow fo you. Anything grow fo you."

Over in the corner beside the dresser a possum was curled on the floor asleep. Curled except for one leg. That leg stuck out straight because it had a splint on it. You never saw so many books. The books were on shelves that went all around the room and up to the ceiling. I couldn't help looking toward the books

64

and trying to read the titles of some of them, even while Mister Martin was still talking to us.

"Well then," he was saying, "if you can imagine a whole bowlful of strawberries like this, then you may have that bowlful to take home with you. And a bowl for Josie, and a bowl for this young lady after we've been properly introduced."

Josie looked down at the floor and tried to dig her big toe into the boards. Thee looked at Mister Martin and at me and frowned, and then he grinned.

"Oh," he said. "Oh. She Thorpe."

"I'm Thorpe Torrance," I said. "I live in the big gray house where the dirt road ends. The house with the porch about to fall down. But Daddy's going to fix it. Some day."

"And I—" Mister Martin held out his hand and it was the first time I ever shook hands with anybody, except playing. "I am Martin Ahrens. How do you do, Thorpe."

That was how I met and loved Martin. Martin, who was to be one of my best friends for as long as we lived in the breezeway house. We shook hands and the magic circle grew bigger to make room for Martin. I wanted to tell him so, but I did not know how to say it.

On that night a year later when I saw his face in the light that flickered and burned in the old Pig White yard, I told him. And I did not have to use words.

"Strawberries?"

Daddy hitched his chair closer to the table and took a clean white handkerchief from his pocket. He wiped away the drops of water from his bath that were trying to run down his forehead. The rest of us were already at the table, hungry.

Daddy wouldn't come to the table until after he'd had his bath, and until last week, supper had been late every evening that summer. Last week James and I thought of a way for Daddy's bath to be finished sooner so we didn't have to wait so long for supper, and everybody liked the idea but Mama. Every day we drew a tub of water from the well and left it in the sunshine to warm, and when Daddy came home he dragged it over to a hidden place between the peach trees and the smokehouse and took his bath.

65

With no mess to mop up after him, you'd have thought Mama would be happy about the idea. She wasn't.

"Strawberries on Friday evening?" Daddy smiled across the table at Mama. "Who's been here since I been gone?"

Mama said "Jim!" but she didn't sound cross.

James and I laughed. What Daddy had said was from a song he had learned after he went to work at the mill. It went

> *Who's been here since I been gone?*
> *Who's been carrying my good work on?*

That was all of the song we ever heard, because after the first two lines Mama always said *Jim!*

I looked at the big red strawberries in the bowls beside our plates and felt proud. I had brought home something that was making us laugh and be happy.

"The strawberries are from my new friend." I felt important. "From my friend I met this afternoon. James, you should have gone with me. You never saw so many books, and my friend said he would be happy if I read every one of them. And you, too, because I said I have a brother who likes to read, and he said—"

"Whoa, whoa!" Daddy sounded just like Uncle Elmer. "Who is this new friend you've managed to magic up along with big red strawberries?" He looked at Mama again.

"His name is Mr. Martin," I said, still important. "Mister Martin Ahrens, and he says we can call him Martin but Thee and Josie can't. Donie told them never to call anybody anything without Mister in front of it. He said he used to give Mama and Eloise strawberries when they were girls."

"He did," Mama said, talking mostly to Daddy. "He did, and I'd forgotten. And actually, I wasn't such a little girl when old Martin built that little cabin and—" She looked around the table at all of us. "You know, it used to fascinate us, the way it happened. It was right after the end of the World War. Old Martin came wandering up one day, and sat out on the front porch and made some kind of deal with Papa for that little corner of Papa's low-ground field. I thought I was grown, and I didn't roam the woods too much, but Eloise did. It was Eloise who worshiped him. I remember Neevy used to fuss—"

"Oh, I know who you mean!" Daddy passed the potatoes to James. "I've seen him around, in town and walking through the woods. The tall, stooped gentleman, with the face of an arch-angel. An archangel who's suffered the tortures of the damned."

That was it. That was what was in Martin's face. Suffering.

"I used to see him in the park in town, on Saturdays," Daddy was still talking. "Holding some kind of services. I used to stop and listen, and what the old boy said made pretty good sense. But I guess he quit doing that, because he refused to take up any collection, and his listeners evidently decided that if it wasn't worth paying for, it wasn't worth hearing. I think he still preaches in places he's asked to, and—"

"He's not ordained," Mama said. "He shouldn't."

"Oh, well," Daddy reached for the butter. "I think he spends a lot of his time with the Negroes and the river-rats, so that automatically classifies him as some kind of nut. And I'm get-ting onto dangerous ground, so let's talk about something else."

"I've seen him," James said. "In town and down at the tie yard. Wasn't he gassed or something in the War?"

"I think he was gassed," Mama said. "He gets some kind of pension from the government. I know I heard him tell Papa one night out on the porch that he'd seen too much death and ugli-ness and evil, and that he just wanted to find his own corner somewhere and do what he could to stop some of it. I think he had a family when the War started, and when he came home they were all dead and buried. From the flu epidemic. I'm not sure that Thorpe should be wandering around—"

"Let Thorpe alone." Daddy reached across and patted my shoulder. "He's harmless. Let her find friends wherever they hap-pen to be."

But Mama had started worrying. "Neevy used to say he was a crazy old coot—"

Daddy said, "If that's what Geneva said, I don't think we need to worry. For me, that settles it. The woods should be full of such coots. Let her alone, Venie. Let her listen to the people who have time to talk to her. It's soon enough she'll become aware that she's too busy and too important and too hurried, herself, to listen. Either to sages or angels or crazy old coots." Daddy reached for his bowl of strawberries.

"Oh, you always have to start—to start philosophizing!" Mama sounded cross, and nobody said anything else.

I didn't feel so important after finding that everybody else in the family already knew my new friend, but that was the way things usually went. The friendly talk about the strawberries would have turned into a quarrel if anybody had said another word.

"That's right!" Mama turned on the radio, and it worked because Daddy had already fixed whatever was loose in the back and thanked God that he didn't have to go to Strawne in search of a tube or a battery.

Static crackled and spewed into the air around us.

"That's right." Mama sat down and looked at Daddy in his big red chair. "Sit there with your nose in a book and soak up some more philosophy to spout off at the supper table. And while you're soaking it up, be sure your children are running through the woods with nigras—"

Daddy looked up. "Well, now, slow down there. I didn't let her go. You did. And you did the right thing." He started reading again, and then he looked up once more. "For once."

"And when you're not doing that," Mama went over and turned the radio down, because the static was louder than she was. "You're out in the back yard rolling around naked under the peach trees singing at the top of your voice! What do you expect—"

Daddy put his book on the table and took off his glasses, but he didn't look up. He looked down at the floor. "You know you're remarkable, Venie," he said. "You really are. You take for your example an ordinary, everyday, *very private* bath in a damned washtub, and make it sound like an orgy! And the whole thing done to make it easy on both of us! I'm damned if I know how to please you!"

"May we go outside and play cat-a-bat?" I said. "The moon's bright as day."

We went outside, James and I. James was teaching me how to hit a ball, but we had both already discovered that the safest way was for me to hold the bat perfectly still and let James hit it with the ball. It worked out pretty good that way.

"Now stand still," James said. "And *don't* try to run to meet the ball and hit it." He had a knot on his head where I'd tried that, last week. James backed away and worked his arm and then his wrist around, to limber up.

"James, wait." I let the bat fall to the ground. "An orgy is a giant, isn't it, that eats people? Do orgies take baths? Under our peach trees?"

Either James didn't know or he wasn't in the mood to talk. He didn't say anything until he'd walked back across the yard and fixed my bat in the right position again. He started off, and then he turned.

"That's an *ogre*," he said. "That eats people. Now shut up and hold your bat."

That was the way the summer went.

Sometimes we went to Aunt Neevy's and had to spend the day playing with old Dawn Starr, and sometimes they came to our house and ruined whole days, but mostly I lived inside the magic circle that had widened to make room for Martin and his books.

I hated those days with Dawn Starr, because she usually managed to get us in trouble, one way or another. Like the time James called her Pudgy and she cried and told Mama. Mama made James say I'm sorry, and of course he wasn't.

That's the kind of person Dawn Starr was. She didn't like to read, and so she always wanted to talk about things you didn't care one hoot (like Eloise said sometimes) in hell about. Things like boys and babies and things like that. Dawn Starr knew perfectly well that babies came out of stomachs, but she always tried to make something nasty out of it.

James didn't like her any more than I did, and he wouldn't hide with her when we played together. There was a lot we could have told Mama and Aunt Neevy about Dawn Starr, but we didn't. James said those things were Dawn Starr's problems, and not ours. He said we had problems enough of our own.

The summer went too fast. The days kind of slipped by, all pretty much alike except for Sundays. On Sundays we went to church and watched Brother Mearl's shirt buttons pop off. Sometimes Brother Mearl came home with us for dinner. Most of the time, though, Brother Mearl went home for Sunday dinner with Aunt Neevy or Miss Mildred.

Miss Mildred was my Sunday School teacher. She lived in Strawne in a big sprawling white house, where all the railroad men

69

stayed, and the salesmen that came through town once in a while. On Sundays, Miss Mildred and her two boys drove out to Thorpe's Chapel for church. Miss Mildred had a husband, but he never came to church with her, and the only place I'd ever seen Mr. Walter Hagan was in the Post Office window, frowning while he read all the post cards.

"The way Neevy and Mildred Hagan struggle and vie to be— to be—"

We were in the car on the way home from church one Sunday, and Mama bit her lip, frowned, and looked out the car window.

"To be top-button-sewer-on-er?" Daddy finished Mama's sentence and slowed the car for the turn onto the dirt road.

Mama looked at Daddy and laughed. "Something like that. Anyhow, the way they act you'd think they were both eligible to be the second Sister Mearl." She leaned her head against Daddy's shoulder.

Daddy turned off the highway onto the dirt road that went to our old house. "Now if I'd said that you'd jump down my throat in a flash." He put his arm around Mama's shoulders and pulled her closer and drove along the dirt road with one hand on the steering wheel.

"I shouldn't have said it either." Mama sat up straight again. "But they're so silly! Here they are both running everybody crazy to get Brother Mearl ready for that revival in New Orleans and I bet you that Elmer and Walter Hagan both have holes in the heels of their socks."

I didn't know about Walter Hagan, but Uncle Elmer's socks had holes. I'd seen them more than once when Mama had made me go over and spend the night with Dawn Starr. Uncle Elmer always pulled off his shoes and leaned back in his chair and read his *Progressive Farmer* until he went to sleep and snored. After he'd slept a while and Aunt Neevy had read her chapter in the Bible, she woke him up and they both drank a glass of Crazy Water Crystals and went to bed.

Progressive Farmer was all there ever was to read in Aunt Neevy's house besides the Bible, which was another reason I hated to spend the night there. It was the same thing every time. Aunt Neevy read the Bible and Dawn Starr and I whispered in the corner about boys and Uncle Elmer Progressed himself to sleep in his socks with holes.

70

"Well—" Daddy turned with the road at our mailbox. "Maybe Elmer and Walter Hagan will get their socks mended while the preacher's gone. Maybe the preacher will find himself a nice meek little widow at the revival and bring back a wife!"

Mama would have liked Daddy to say Brother Mearl the way everybody else did, but Daddy never called him that. He always said He or The preacher or sometimes The minister. Mama never argued with him about it. James said it was because she knew when to let well enough alone.

Daddy guessed right in a way about Brother Mearl's week at New Orleans. Brother Mearl brought back a wife. But Daddy sure missed it in another way. She didn't look like she'd ever been or would be a nice meek little widow.

5

Either we were late to church the next Sunday morning, or everybody else was early. It could have been that everybody else was
early. There weren't many telephones around, but news sure
traveled fast. Brother Mearl was waiting for us at the door. He
shook Mama's hand, and Daddy's, and after the God bless you's
and Praise the Lord's were over he followed us up the aisle and
went on to the pulpit. He bowed his head for a minute while
everybody got quiet. He took out his handkerchief and mopped
his face and looked down at the big Bible open in front of him.

"We turn today, beloved, to the thirty-first chapter of Proverbs. Begin reading with the tenth verse."

It took the people a minute to get their Bibles open and a
sound like a sigh went up and floated out through the open windows. You could tell they hated to look down at the Bibles instead of craning their necks around toward the strange woman
with yellow hair. She sat on the front bench, and if she'd ever
been to Thorpe's Chapel before that Sunday I hadn't seen her.

The leaves of the Bibles rustled as everybody found Proverbs.
Aunt Neevy kept looking up from her Bible to the woman.

"Who can find a virtuous woman?" Brother Mearl read, and
their voices rumbled and chanted and whispered and blended

together. "For her price is far above rubies. . . ." The voices read on: "and her candle goeth not out by night—"

"You sent me to New Orleans last week, beloved." The reading was over and Brother Mearl looked up from his Bible again. "You sent me to save souls. And I want to tell you this morning, that's what we did last week! We saved Praise the Lord two hundred strong! Two hundred souls brought into the Light and the Grace. We sang hymns and we prayed and I tell you before the week was over we had a bigger attendance than that old carnival did just up the street from us! Praise the Lord!" He stopped for a minute, and looked down toward the strange woman.

"On a Tuesday night of that week, a little woman came down through the sawdust of that aisle, to the altar. She knelt there at the altar and I knelt beside her, beloved, and all night long we rassled with that old Devil there in the sawdust. By morning she saw the Light, beloved. Trembling, exhausted, she knelt there in the sawdust an' she was saved. Saved! And beloved"—his voice dropped to a whisper—"I got me a license an' I *married* that little woman I had rassled the Devil for!"

There wasn't a sound in the churchhouse except the pasteboard fans going back and forth—and most of them had stopped.

Brother Mearl looked out and around at all of us and spoke again. "And so, instead of a sermon today, beloved, I ask you to walk up here to the front row and extend the right hand of fellowship to the second Sister Mearl. Praise the Lord! Sister Mearl, will you stand?"

She stood up and turned to face us. Underneath the big pile of yellow hair her face was scrubbed and clean and shiny-looking. It was also white and frightened. Her dress was green-and-purple silk, and it curved in and out like Eloise's dresses did. You could see places at the neck that were kind of puckered like somebody had ripped off some flowers. Or maybe some bangles, like Eloise wore.

Everybody in the church heard Aunt Neevy gasp, and that was when Daddy started smiling. Mama kept her face straight, but it was red. James' mouth made a round *O* and his eyebrows went almost up to his rooster-tail. Mama kicked him on the leg. Aunt Neevy's face looked like it had frozen after she gasped, and her chin worked up and down like Miss Una Jackson's chin. Up at the piano Miss Mildred kept reading the songbook. She hadn't even turned around to look at the second Sister Mearl.

I guess Brother Mearl's marriage was the biggest thing that happened that summer. Everywhere you went there were people talking about it. Some of them didn't even go to church at Thorpe's Chapel.

"Well, he sure got took in. That's the kindest thing I can say about the whole deal." Aunt Neevy had come by the house one afternoon after Missionary Society, and she and Mama were in the living room talking. "But maybe there's a hidden blessing in it. For you, anyhow, Venie."

"For me? What do you mean?" Mama looked puzzled.

"Why, it gives people something to talk about besides Jim Torrance," Aunt Neevy said. "Maybe people will forget what a fool Jim acted for a while, now. Who can find a virtuous woman, my foot! Well, he couldn't have picked a verse that fit his choice better, at that. I'm just real upset with Brother Mearl. He went down there and converted carnival workers on money our church furnished him to save honest souls! She might wipe off all her paint an' make him think all she ever worked at was the sharpshooter's booth, but she don't fool me. She's a sharpshooter all right, but I bet you, the way she looks, she was one of them—them *girlies!*"

"Oh, Neevy." Mama took a deep breath and let it out slow. "How can we judge her when we don't even know her? She seems like a nice enough person, if she weren't scared to death of all of us. I—"

"Oh, yes." Aunt Neevy's mouth was a tight line. "I've heard that *you've* already been over to call on her! Well, Venie, I don't think this is the right time for *you* to start associating with carnival workers. You know—"

"What I know," Mama said, "is that you ought to try getting up on the right side of the world some morning. Thorpe, go move the coffee pot up to a front eye of the stove to heat."

Mama turned and watched me go out into the hall and down to the kitchen, and I heard her say: "Let's have a cup of coffee and forget about Sister Mearl——"

The clock in the kitchen said four-thirty, but out in the back

74

yard Daddy was dragging his tub of water around the corner of the smokehouse to the peach trees. He had a towel and some things under one arm. His gray pants were on a coat-hanger in the biggest peach tree. I moved the coffee pot up over the fire and went out the back door.

I sat down on the washbench and called around the corner to Daddy. "May I talk to you while you bathe?"

He stuck his head around the corner.

"Please do." He pulled his head back and in a minute he stuck it out again. "Here." He tossed his overalls and shirt out to me. "Take these and hang them on the back porch before we start our conversation."

I hung Daddy's work clothes on the porch and went back to my bench. "Daddy, did Sister Mearl work in a real carnival? I mean, like the one Eloise took us to?"

"Yes, I believe so." Daddy's voice floated from under the trees. "But I believe she's hung up her rifle now. Didn't you see it, over the fireplace, when we called on her the other night?"

I had seen it. And after Daddy had gone outside to smoke a cigarette, Brother Mearl had said that the rifle was hung there by the Grace of God, to serve as a reminder of the sins that she had left behind her.

"Is it a sin to shoot a rifle?" I called through the trees to Daddy.

The back door opened and Mama and Aunt Neevy came out onto the porch. "—no coffee," Aunt Neevy was saying. "But I do want a sack of them big Elberta peaches. Dawn Starr loves them, with sugar and cream. Our old tree finally died."

"Well, get all you want," Mama said. "They're half yours, anyway. Here, let me go inside and get a box." She went back inside.

Aunt Neevy came down the steps and over to the washbench. "Out here talkin' to yourself?" she asked me. She looked around the yard. "Thorpe, is that a pair of good pants hangin' in the trees?"

"It—it looks like it," I said. "It looks like a pair of Daddy's."

Aunt Neevy reached up into the trees and unhooked the coat-hanger. When Mama came back outside, she was still standing there holding them. "A pair of perfectly good pants," she said to Mama. "Hanging in the trees. Honestly, Venie, I don't see how you ever— In the trees! Here, Thorpe, take them in the house!"

75

"But—" Mama's eyes moved fast around the yard and to the back porch, and she saw Daddy's overalls hanging on their nail. "But I hung them out to air! In the sun. The wind blows the lint off."

"Well, there's no wind now, and not much sun time left." Aunt Neevy gave me a little push. "Take them on in, Thorpe, before they stay out hanging in the trees all night."

I took Daddy's pants into the house.

"Hurry," Mama said. "So you can climb up in that tree and get Neevy some of the good peaches at the top."

"Oh, I can reach them." Aunt Neevy started into the trees. "I'll just reach back in here and pull a few and—"

"*No!*" Mama pulled on Aunt Neevy's arm and dragged her over to the washbench. "You're tired. My, you look fagged! Now you just sit down here and rest and let Thorpe fill that box with peaches." Mama's eyes were sparkling, like she'd thought of something funny. She sat down on the bench beside Aunt Neevy.

"Remember," Mama was still talking, and her voice was loud. "Remember how we used to play out here until after dark? Well, let's stay out 'til dark one more time. Let's sit here and visit, and— Of course, the mosquitoes get bad around dark, but what's a few mosquitoes?" She was almost shouting.

Aunt Neevy stood up and Mama pulled her back down.

"What's wrong with you, Venie? Thorpe, that's enough peaches." Aunt Neevy stood up and frowned down at Mama. "Venie, you sound feverish. I'm goin' home, and you better go in the house and take an aspirin. Sit out here 'til dark, my foot!"

Aunt Neevy took her peaches and left, and before she was out of the gate Daddy bounded out from under the trees with a towel around his middle.

"In about two more minutes," he said to Mama, who was still sitting on the washbench, "I'd have come out just like this, Geneva or no Geneva! Tired and hungry and devoured by mosquitoes— By God, you don't think I'm that modest, do you?"

Mama was laughing so hard she had to wait a minute to answer. She wiped her eyes on her dress hem. "Well, it was a good try! Anyhow, if you're going to come home early and undress in the back yard, you might announce yourself!"

"I didn't come home early," Daddy said. He started toward the house, walking straight and tall and proud, the towel still around his middle. At the steps he turned. "Your clock is exactly thirty minutes off."

That was on Friday of the last week before school started. The next day we all went to Strawne and bought some shoes and things at Mr. Byrd's store, and Mama bought me a red dinner bucket with Orphan Annie and her dog on the lid.

I'd talked a lot about starting to school, especially to Thee, because he was starting, too. And I knew just exactly what I'd take in that Orphan Annie dinner bucket.

I'd take an egg sandwich and an apple and some cookies, and I'd give my friends at school some of the cookies and maybe the apple, too. Because I would have a lot of friends. Nobody would want the egg sandwich, and so I'd eat it. I didn't like egg sandwiches much myself, but Mama believed in them. Mama swapped buttermilk to Donie for the eggs, and fresh milk for the chickens that she fried on Sunday.

So I was all ready, with a drawer full of new bloomers and the dinner bucket scalded and waiting, open, on a shelf in the pantry.

And it was on that Saturday night after we got home from town with the dinner bucket that something ugly started creeping and oozing into our house and into our lives, changing everything.

6

Every Sunday for weeks old Will Jackson had been reminding God we needed rain. He still reminded God of the widows and orphans in these low grounds of sin and sorrow, but lately he'd been talking to Him more about rain than about widows and orphans.

The Saturday we went to Strawne and bought the Orphan Annie dinner bucket was hot and dry. There wasn't any breeze at all. The clothes that Donie had put on the line hung down straight and still and wet, and the four-o'clocks and moonglory vines around the smokehouse looked like they were about ready to give up.

It was hotter in town. The dust and heat rose up from the sidewalk and hit you in the face. The sidewalks were empty because most of the people who were out in the heat of that August afternoon were standing under the shade of the awnings in front of the drug store and the pool hall. Over in the park in front of the bank some kids were playing in the little ditch of muddy water that ran from the artesian well, but we knew better than to ask if we could join them. Mama had never let James play around the artesian well when we'd lived in Strawne and he'd played with those kids all the time. Mama hated mud.

James stepped off the sidewalk to watch them.

"Get back on the sidewalk," Mama said crossly to James. "Can't you even stay presentable until we get inside the store?"

We followed Mama and Daddy into Mr. Byrd's store. Inside the store was worse than outside. It smelled like cow feed and licorice and like the boxes where Mr. Byrd kept the baby chickens that he sold every spring. The big fan that hung down from the ceiling wasn't cooling anybody; it was just stirring up all the smells and mixing them together.

Behind the counter Mr. Byrd was fanning himself with a box top and looking down at the yellow glasses in the box he'd just opened. He gave Mama a big smile and came out from behind the counter to meet us.

"Hello, Venie, Jim," he said. "Got a big grocery list for me today?" He went back to the counter and took one of the yellow glasses from the box.

"No," Mama said, "not much. Just a few things today, Walter."

"Better stock up today, Venie." Mr. Byrd held the glass up to the light. "This might be your lucky day. You like this glass?"

Mama smiled and nodded.

"I'm gonna give you a whole set of these glasses today, Venie. For just five dollars worth of trade. Just got 'em in today, and the first set goes to you! How about that?"

Mama looked up from her grocery list to the shelves of coffee and rice and canned peaches.

"Is coffee really sixteen cents now?" she asked. "When did it go up from twelve?" She took one of the glasses from the box and looked through it toward the window. She tapped it with her fingernail and it went *pinnnggg*. "Can it accumulate, the five dollars?" she asked. "Do I have to buy it all today, or can I get the glasses when my purchases total five dollars? I guess you'd better give me a pound of that coffee."

Mr. Byrd went back behind the counter and took a pound sack of coffee and put it on the counter. "Well, gosh now, Venie," he said. "That ain't no problem. Anybody can use five dollars worth of groceries *and* dry goods this week, with school starting 'n everything. That dinner bucket over there for the little one here, it'ud make sixty-nine cents on that five. An' back here in th' meat market, I've got a good rolled roast f' just thirteen cents a

79

pound, f' tomorrow's dinner. An' over there's them bananas I got to sell by evenin', twelve cents a dozen—"

Mama picked up the dinner bucket and looked at it and put it on the counter beside the coffee. Then she went back to the meat case and we all followed her. She didn't get a roast. She had Mr. Byrd wrap her up a pound of steak for fifteen cents. Aunt Neevy and Dawn Starr came in while he was wrapping it, and Trudy came in through the back door with a grocery list for Miss Mildred. Trudy was Thee's and Josie's aunt. She cooked for Miss Mildred so Miss Mildred didn't have to go out in the heat for groceries on Saturday evening. She sent Trudy.

"My, that looks little for Sunday dinner meat," Aunt Neevy said when Mr. Byrd handed the steak over the counter to Mama. "You must not be planning on any company!"

"Hello, Geneva," Daddy said from where he was leaning against the corner of the meat case. Then he came up to Mama and spoke to her real low. "Venie, do you want those glasses? If you do, go ahead. I guess we can stay away next Saturday—"

"Oh, pish-posh," Mama said, and laughed up at him. "You know I don't want those old glasses. They're not worth over fifteen cents, at most! She looked down at her list. "Now you run on to the auto store and get that thing you need for the car, and I'll stay here and visit with Neevy for a while. We'll just come on to the car when we're through."

On his way out, Daddy signed the ticket for the groceries, and it came to two dollars and forty-six cents. He took the two sacks with him. Mama and Aunt Neevy stood over beside the rack of ladies' dresses and talked.

"Gaw," James said on the way home. "We'da had to buy twice as much to get those glasses! Gaw, wonder how many sacks it'd take for five dollars worth of stuff all at once?"

"Aunt Neevy could tell you," I said. "She got a set."

"Oh, hush." Mama turned to the back seat. "Reach in that sack and get us out a banana apiece, and quit worrying about something I didn't even want."

James handed two bananas up to the front seat. Mama peeled one of them halfway down and held it toward Daddy.

"Here," she said. "We'll have to glut ourselves on them, be-

80

cause by tomorrow they'll be too ripe, but at twelve cents a dozen, I couldn't resist."

The wind coming in the car windows was blowing away the smells left over from Mr. Byrd's store, and inside the car was just warm and happy.

I wish it could have lasted.

Mama was tired by the time we got through with supper and I should have known not to argue with her. So it was really all my fault, all those words they shouted out in the back yard later.

It started in the living room. I was sitting on the floor beside Mama's chair, letting her roll my hair. On Saturday night Mama always rolled my hair on these old socks, and while she was rolling it that night, I kept asking questions about the schoolhouse that James had shown me on the way to town. The schoolhouse that Thee and Josie would go to.

"You're being silly, Thorpe," Mama said and gave my hair a yank. "You haven't heard them fussing about it, have you?"

"But Mama!" I twisted my head to look up at her. "Did you look at their school? It's got these old pieces of tin nailed on top and the windows are gone and there's this old crosstie pulled up in front for a doorstep and—" I put my hand up to the back of my neck. "If you leave that hanging down, it'll get wet when I get in the tub. Mama, why can't they go to the same school we do?"

"Be still." Mama wanted my hair to be extra curly the next day, because I was going to sing with the six-to-eighters in church, and Miss Mildred hadn't taught us anything in Sunday School except the song for weeks. It could have been the song that made me start worrying about Thee's and Josie's school. It was a nice song, but James had said a while ago that if he had to hear it one more time he would throw up. Mama had made me quit practicing it and that was when I'd started talking about the school. Nobody can just *sit*.

"They wouldn't take care of a nice school building if they had one." Mama sounded cross. "They wouldn't know how." She yanked at a sock. A sock that was tied to my head.

"That pulls," I said. "Why can't they go to school with us in the big brick schoolhouse? There's plenty of room for everybody."

Mama twisted the last sock and tied it and stood up. "Come on in the kitchen and take your bath." She went into the kitchen and started dipping water from the reservoir on the stove into the washtub behind it. Her voice came back into the living room. "James shouldn't have shown you the school!"

James was lying on the floor cutting an old innertube into strips. He didn't look up for a minute. Then he said, "Well, gaw!" and frowned across at me. "I wouldn't have shown her if I'd thought about causing all this fuss. How'd I know she'd act so stupid about it after we got home?"

"Come on, Thorpe." Mama had come back to stand in the living-room door. "There are some things in the world that nobody can change, and this is one of them," she said crossly. "God didn't intend for them to—"

"Well, they're my friends." I started to the kitchen. "I'm not trying to change anything. I'm just talking about my friends."

"They are not your friends! They are nigras! And God didn't intend us to be friends with them or He'd have made us all one color and—"

Daddy looked up from his book. "Now she's going to tell you," he said, "how God intended them to be hewers of wood and drawers of water. And how God cursed—"

"And speaking of drawers of water," Mama glared at Daddy, "the reservoir's empty. Again. I don't see why you can't fill it just once without being reminded."

Daddy flung his book down onto the couch and went down the hall and out onto the back porch.

I went into the kitchen and got into the tub behind the stove. Mama had followed Daddy out onto the back porch and into the yard, and I could hear them out there shouting at each other.

"You wait," Daddy said, "until bedtime every night to tell me the damned thing's empty! Why can't you tell me before dark? Are you really that afraid you'll make it a little easier for me?"

"If you'd check it sometimes, without being told!" Mama yelled. "You know it's there! But no, if you had that much common sense we wouldn't be living out here where we have to draw water from a well and pour it into that old tank on the cookstove to warm it! It's your choice, you know! We had a good life, until you started handing out textbooks and playing—"

"I know, Venie." Daddy sounded tired. "We did have a good life, and we still could. We can still go—"

"Please, please don't start *that* again!" Mama's voice was

closer, like she had come back up onto the porch. "Don't try to make any of this appear to be my fault, please! I'm not the one who can't get along with people. And if you can't get along with them here, what makes you think it would be different anywhere else? I'm *not* going to drag my children around all over the country and raise them among no telling what kind of strangers! At least we have relatives and friends here!"

"Then there's nothing I can say, Venie," Daddy said. "Except that I'm sorry and that I'm doing all I can under the circumstances."

"You're sorry! Well, sorry doesn't cut wood nor draw water nor milk that mangy old cow. Old sorry can't even afford ice to cool us nor a decent set of water glasses to put on the table!"

Mama came into the house ahead of Daddy and banged the door behind her. Daddy kicked it open and I heard water slosh onto the floor.

"Well, I'll be damned," he said. "I'll be damned. I *told* you to go ahead and get those glasses! You do a lot of this to yourself, you know. Like milking the cow. If you'll just quit grabbing a bucket like some damned martyr and running down there to milk her before I even get home from the mill, I'll do it. You know you don't need to be doing things like that now."

Mama was so wound up she didn't even hear him. "—no, Mister Big Sorry," she was saying, "had to go and put in overtime as a bleeding-heart librarian or something. Something bigger and more know-it-all than anybody else in the country and look where it got him! Out here—"

Daddy slammed the water bucket against the stove, hard, and water sloshed onto the linoleum again. He poured the rest of it into the reservoir and started out after another bucketful. At the door he stopped, and his voice was quiet.

"You know, Venie, you and that—that *Brother* Mearl of yours are so fond of the Book of Proverbs. Well, I think you'd better read it again. Read the part that tells about a dry morsel being better than a houseful of sacrifices with strife. And in another place it says it is better to dwell in the corner of a housetop than with a brawling woman in a wide house. And about—"

"He's not my Brother Mearl!" Mama snapped back at Daddy. "He's *our* minister! And for somebody who goes to church as rarely as you do, I think you could quote something besides the Bible!"

"Oh, God, where's my housetop corner?" Daddy said. "To me, there's a vast area of difference between believing the Bible and believing the stuff he disgorges. You show me one thing, just one, that man has ever done or caused to be done, that really benefits his fellow man, and I'll go to church every Sunday and swallow back my— Oh, hell, how'd we get started on this?"

The screen door closed and Daddy went down the steps to the well again. When he came back in, his voice was still quiet.

"I saw Nathaniel today, Venie."

Mama didn't answer, and he came into the kitchen.

"Nathaniel's a *nigra* now, Venie. Not a Negro. He's making ties for Billy Bob Jackson. And doing the s.o.b.'s bookwork for free. I guess he's educated in one field, anyhow. What we do to smart-aleck niggers around here. Because he'll become just another *nigger,* and that should make all of you very happy."

He stood there for a moment waiting for Mama to say something. When she didn't, he went back out and banged the door again.

I jumped into my gown that Mama had made from flour sacks and yanked it down so hard I tore the lace she had made around the bottom and ran into my bedroom. But I could still hear them after I went to bed.

James said a long time later that the next day was the last really good Sunday we had.

I brushed my hair next morning and went into the kitchen, and Mama looked at me and sighed.

"I know it's a waste of time to try to curl that hair, and I don't know why I keep trying. But I did think it would curl a little!" She straightened my sash in back and told me to pull up my socks and we were off to church, with James' neck and ears still red from Mama scrubbing them so hard.

Most of the time Daddy didn't always stay for church, but that day he did. Because of the song. He pulled in beside Doctor John's Ford and got out of the car and went in with us just like it was Easter Sunday.

"Look at the ghosts," I whispered to James while Mama and Daddy were shaking hands with Brother Mearl.

Shadows were dancing over the tombstones under the big oaks, and they did look like ghosts. Brave ghosts, out skipping and dancing in the hot sunshine of a Sunday morning in August.

"You know dam— You know cotton-pickin' well there's no such thing as ghosts!" James whispered and pulled his arm from my hand. He'd barely remembered where he was in time to keep from saying it.

"The old Devil has got a-holt of the second Sister Mearl to-day." Brother Mearl stood at the pulpit and looked at his Brothers and Sisters. "And I ask your prayers for her. He got a-holt of her and he gave her a headache, brothers, that made her take to her bed! But praise the Lord I'm here to tell you that he's got to turn loose! We're gonna pray, sisters, and we're gonna wrench that old Devil a-loose and throw that headache out the window after him!" He knelt and we all bowed our heads while he prayed for the spirit to be stronger than the flesh so Sister Mearl could praise the Lord with us next Sunday.

When we stood up to sing the special song, I saw Daddy's arm along the bench behind Mama's back, and he was fanning her with a songbook. I knew then that the quarrel was over, and I sang louder. Louder than anybody, James said later.

Mama looked happy and pretty, with Grandma Thorpe's gold watch pinned to the front of the blue silk dress Aunt Neevy had given her and its gold chain against the white skin of her throat. At home we had this big piece of blue silk that Mama had taken out of the skirt of the dress, and she was going to make a blouse for me with it. But as I sang and looked at her that Sunday, I knew she should make a dress for the new baby when it came, instead of a blouse for me. Of course I couldn't tell Mama that yet, because I wasn't supposed to know about the new baby. Nobody knew that I knew about it.

We sang through the chorus again.

> *. . . though we be white, though we be red,*
> *Or yellow or black, He died in our stead.*
> *For we are all children of Jee-e-sus. . . .*

From the pulpit Brother Mearl kept smiling and saying Amen. When we'd finished he said "Amen. Suffer the little children to come unto me praise the Lord. Amen." Miss Mildred played through the chorus again and ended it with a little ripple that went clear to the end of the piano and turned around to smile at everybody, and it was over.

On the last bench, beside the door, Martin smiled too. Martin was at church that Sunday especially for me, because I had told him about the song and had practiced it to him. He looked nicer than anybody. Except Daddy. Martin had on a black suit, and the shirt that Donie had boiled and ironed for him was as white as his hair.

I felt sorry Sister Mearl wasn't there sitting on the front bench with her hat on crooked over her big bun of yellow hair and her scared smile. Once, when she'd caught me looking at her, Sister Mearl had winked at me and maybe that was why I missed her that first Sunday she wasn't there, but I think it was because I'd wanted her to hear the song. She'd have liked it.

When I slid onto the bench beside Daddy he smiled and made the OK sign. The OK sign was made with your hands clasped together, and it meant that everything was fine. It meant, that day, that I had sounded good and that nothing had come untied or hung down. I smiled back and we settled down for the sermon.

While Brother Mearl was preaching I kept thinking that I hoped he would go home for dinner. Or maybe to Aunt Neevy's. Because Aunt Neevy had been right, in Mr. Byrd's store, about the steak. It sure was a little pound.

After the sermon old Will Jackson stood up and prayed for a long time. While he was praying he kept unfolding and stretching and folding again the five-dollar bill he was going to put in the collection plate.

After Uncle Elmer said the last prayer, Aunt Neevy swooped down onto Brother Mearl and said why didn't he just go home with them for dinner and then Sister Mearl wouldn't have to cook his Sunday dinner because she knew the poor thing wasn't used to it. We left while she was still talking to him, so I don't know how it ended, but at least he didn't go home with us.

After dinner Mama went into her room and lay down to rest. James put on his old blue cap and said he thought he'd go down to the tie yard for a while. He stopped in the front door and looked at Daddy and me in the living room.

"Mama sure rests a lot," he said. "And she was sick yesterday morning. And this morning, too."

Daddy didn't say anything.

"It's because she's that way again," I said. "She's pretty sure she's that way again."

"What way?" James looked at Daddy again, and then he said, "Oh, gaw, no kiddin'?" and without waiting for an answer he ran to the edge of the porch and jumped off and leaped over the gate. As he went over the gate, I could see from the door that his face was all white and his freckles were showing like he was sick, too.

Daddy leaned back on the couch and picked up his book, but he didn't start reading.

"When have you been eavesdropping on your Aunt Geneva?" he asked. "Because I can't believe your mother used that expression, even if she told you about the baby."

I squatted down at the bookcase to look for *Tales from Shakespeare*. "Mama hasn't told me anything, but I heard her and Aunt Neevy talking in Mr. Byrd's store yesterday."

Daddy waited.

"They were whispering," I said. "But I knew what about, because Aunt Neevy put her hand up to her mouth like she always does when she's talking about somebody who's preg— about somebody who's that way. Well, anyway, when she's talking about babies and stuff like that. And I heard them."

Daddy winced and took off his glasses and put them on the table. "Spare me," he said. "But for God's sake, since you already know the word and what it means, say *pregnant*. You do know what it means, don't you?"

"Well, of course I know," I said. "But I'm not supposed to. And anyhow, it's one of those words I'm not supposed to use. And you mustn't mind Aunt Neevy knowing about it, Daddy. Mama always tells her everything and she's happy because Mama's—pregnant. She said something nice about it."

Daddy picked up his book again, and picked up his glasses and wiped them. "Well," he said, "Geneva's approval—or disapproval —doesn't matter too greatly in the case of our having another baby. That's one thing she can't very well supervise. But just for the record, what nice thing did she have to say about it?"

I found my book and stood up with it. "She said that's all we need right now. Another mouth to feed, she said, is *exactly* what we need right now. I think so, too, don't you?"

Daddy stared at me and didn't answer. He stared for a long time before he spoke again.

"I wonder what James finds so interesting down at the tie yard?"

I could have told him what James liked about the tie yard on Sundays, but I didn't. I stared down at my book. It was the dice games James liked. And the words he heard. Once James had even found a pair of green dice on the ground down at the tie yard, and he kept them in a little box in his pocket with my two front teeth.

Daddy put his book on the table again. He yawned. "I think I'll just do some cobbling." He got up and started down the hall.

I took *Tales from Shakespeare* and went outside and lay down under the peach trees behind the house, but it was too hot to read. I thought about how cross Mama had been last Christmas when Daddy had gotten me the *Tales* instead of the doll in a pink dress. She had said that Daddy was making a freak out of me and that it was not right.

Daddy came out onto the back porch with the heavy shoe iron last he had found in the barn and started looking up on the shelves where he kept his nails and things.

"Well, hell," he said after he'd looked for a few minutes.

I watched him, and I knew what he was looking for. But I knew, too, that he wasn't going to find it. He was looking for the little box of shoe nails that he'd bought after he'd found the old shoe last in the barn. James and I had used his shoe nails to put the leather straps on our Tom Walkers. We'd had a lot of fun on our Tom Walkers that summer. . . . Mine weren't very high, but James' put you up as tall as the porch. James had let me walk on his until I fell, but after that he made me use my own, and it wasn't as much fun. I tried to tell James that it really didn't matter about my two front teeth that he'd picked up after I fell because they were already loose, but after Mama turned white and cried James wouldn't let me back on his old Tom Walkers. . . .

Daddy said hell again. He stood there for a while, looking up at the shelves and down at his boots.

"I guess I'll just wear the ragged sons of— Hmmm, what's this?" He reached up onto a shelf.

"It's carpet tacks."

Mama was standing in the back screen. She looked cross and

sleepy. "It's carpet tacks that I bought last year. To fix that old red chair, and I do think you could watch your language a little better on Sunday afternoon."

"Well, where are my shoe nails and why the hell did you get red tacks?"

"Because the chair's red. And I don't know what happened to your shoe nails. I don't use them, but if you can use those, please do so. Only please do it quietly and less profanely, because I'd like to take a nap. Fix all the shoes you want, with any color nails you can find, but please do it quietly."

"Now how in the hell can I hammer *quietly?*"

Mama didn't answer. The screen door banged and she had gone back into the house.

Pretty soon Daddy was hammering away. And singing. "Greensleeves was my deli-ight—"

I wished they both sang more and argued less. I lay under the tree and thought about the songs Mama used to sing when we lived in the pretty yellow house. Songs about train wrecks and Floyd Collins and Little Marian Parker. They were sad songs, but it always gave you a good feeling to hear her singing them.

"And who but my La-ady Greensleeves—"

Daddy didn't hear James coming in the front gate. He hammered and sang and James walked around the corner of the house and stood behind him.

"Papa needs a new pair of shoes," James said. He rattled the box in his pocket. "Seb'n come eleb'n, Papa needs new shoes!"

"My mother used to sing that song," Daddy said to James, and hammered some more. Then he quit hammering and looked around at James. "Where did you hear that, what you just said? And what's that rattling in your pocket?"

"It's my front teeth!" I crawled from under the peach trees and ran to stand beside James. He was getting pretty good at rolling a seven and I didn't want him to have to hand over his dice box. "James keeps my front teeth in this box in his pocket, Daddy, because of what Josie said."

"Oh?" Daddy trimmed a little strip of leather from his boot sole. "And what did Josie say?"

"She said ifen a dawg step on nem toofs I go' have dawg tushes grow back in where they came out. We didn't really believe her, but we didn't want to take any chances. James said I'd sure lose them, and so he took them and put them in this box. Daddy, may we go down to Rocky Bottom and wade for a while?"

Daddy put his boot down and looked at us.

"Ohhh—I guess you may." He picked up his boot again and held it beside the other one. "But remember, you're only asking for permission to wade. Not to swim. Stay around the edges, remember. Stay out of the Mouth of Hell. And James, for God's sake, hold onto that box of teeth. We sure don't want her starting school tomorrow with a set of dawg tushes right in front."

We had found the Mouth of Hell earlier in the summer; it was a wide, deep place in the middle of Rocky Bottom Creek. James had said that the first thing President Roosevelt had done after he got to the White House had been to send divers down here to see how deep Rocky Bottom was. The divers had come back up from the water and said that the creek didn't have a bottom. They said it opened right into the mouth of Hell itself, and so President Roosevelt had passed a law against anybody under eleven jumping into it.

We went into the house and put on some old cut-off overalls and left before Mama woke up and said we couldn't go.

The trail to Rocky Bottom went past Donie's house, and Thee and Josie were out in the yard when we went by. Thee was crawling around on the ground running an old vinegar bottle around things like he was driving a car. Josie was lying on the washbench watching some chickens scratch in the dirt.

Donie and Trudy were outside, too, sitting in the shade of the house in some chairs they'd brought out from the kitchen. Donie was patching a shirt that Thee had torn in one of our pecan trees, and Trudy was fussing at her about it.

"You know the devil make you rip out ever one nem stitches wi' yo nose!" Trudy shook her head and her gold earrings rattled and swung. Trudy was Thee's aunt. She lived down the railroad track at Strawne and cooked at Miss Mildred's boardinghouse, but she came to see Thee and Josie every Sunday and she always brought them things. Just like Eloise did us.

"The devil min' his bi'ness, I min' mine."

Donie didn't look up from her sewing. "Anyway, that all he got agains me, I be drinkin ice tea while you shevil coal." She bit off the thread and stuck the needle in her collar. "An I ain be burnin cause my famly went aroun ragged, anyway. Maybe the Lord unnerstan, if the devil don't."

"Why don' you git em some new cloes, anyhow, an thow them things away?" Trudy took the shirt from Donie's lap and looked at it. "You done patchin patches!"

"New ones, my foot." Donie took the shirt back. "I do well t' git em shoes, by winter. You talk mighty big since movin into that new house. How come Miss Mildred built you that new house, anyhow?"

Trudy grinned and shook her earrings again. "Same reason Miss Venie let you live here all time. She lak my work. I a good cook."

"You still jes two dollars a week good? She still jes lak yo work that much?" Donie looked at Trudy and frowned. "What I think is, you better be careful what you do in that house. I know you, an I know too et Miss Mildred k'n see frum her back doe everything goes on down there. You jes watch it, that's what you do."

Trudy grinned again. "She done seen it. We foun out where we stan las week when I tol her I goin to Wellco an cook in a caf-fay. She say she done seen who been comin an goin all night, an if I leave she have me arrested fo—fo——"

"Hi, Miss Thorpe, Mister James!"

Lewis stuck his head out the door and saw us at the washplace with Thee and Josie. "Goin craw-dad fishin today?" He came out the door and went over to a big long saw that was on a rack in the yard, and started filing it. Lewis was a nice man. He always had something friendly to say to us, and it was Lewis who had taught us how to fish for craw-dads.

"No craw-dads today," James answered Lewis. "Mama says we can't fish on Sunday any more. We're going to Rocky Bottom and wade around the edges. Just to cool off."

"May Thee and Josie go with us?" I watched Lewis filing the saw he would use in the woods tomorrow.

"I don care," Lewis said. "Jes go on in nem ol clothes you got on. Ef you ain dried out time you git back, you k'n change then."

"An stay out o' the middle," Trudy said. "You jes stay out o' that deep part," and as we went down the trail, we could hear her fussing at Donie again. "You thow that shirt away, I git im a shirt in town tomorrow. An I git im shoes, too, when it gits cold enough to wear 'em."

Josie was getting so fat that she couldn't walk fast, and so James and Thee ran ahead of us. They were already in the creek, yelling and laughing and splashing water on each other, when we got to the edge. We sat down in the water, and Josie was puffing from the walking, but the water was clear and cold and pretty soon she quit puffing and said she felt better.

Then the Thompson kids came. All ten of them.

They ran down into the water splashing and pushing and yelling. When they saw us they all crawled out again. They stood on the bank and looked down at us and at each other.

"Come on in!" James threw a big splash of water up on old Soggum and laughed up at them. "Come on in and cool off!"

"Naw." Old Soggum glared at us and came down to the water and pulled the two littlest Thompsons up onto the bank and pushed them down onto the ground. "Naw," he said. "Lester, you hold John-bo. Don't let 'im git back in there." Lester was the next-oldest Thompson; he was about a year younger than Soggum, I guess.

"What's the matter?" James called up to them. "Didn't you come down here to go in the water?"

"Yeah, but not with coons." Soggum glared down at us. "We don't go in the creek with *coons*."

James stood up and glared back at Soggum. Then he went up and sat on the bank and his face was red. Lester and Junie Thompson started fighting, and Junie's nose started bleeding and Soggum caught them and bumped their heads together to make them quit.

"Go on home," Soggum told Junie. "You ain't goin' in the creek today, anyhow, so go on home. You ain't killed."

"You go with me!" Junie wiped her nose on her dress. "You go home too, or I'll tell Mama you went in the creek with coons."

James slid back down into the water with us.

"I'm a shark!" He fell into the water and grabbed Thee's feet and pulled him under and they both came up laughing. "Don't pay any attention to them," he said to us. "Don't any of them have good sense, anyhow."

Up on the bank, Soggum twisted Junie's arm behind her back and made her cry again, but when she left he went with her. He

yelled at the rest of the Thompsons to come on. They all whined
and quarreled, but they followed him. When he got to the edge
of the trees, Soggum turned and yelled back at James.

"You're too big a coward to come up out of that water and say
that to my face!"

So James got out of the creek again. And that was when the
Thompsons all turned and started running. Soggum, too.

James watched them until they were out of sight. Then he
grabbed a big old grapevine that hung down over the bank and
let out a whoop.

"I'm Tarzan!" he yelled, and jumped and swung out over the
water and dropped right down into the Mouth of Hell.

On the way home we stopped by Donie's house again. While
James was talking to Lewis in the yard, I went inside and Donie
gave me a hot biscuit.

Donie had put new papers on the walls of her front room, and
on my way out I stopped to read some of them. Trudy saved the
colored funnies from Miss Mildred's boarding-house and brought
them to Donie to paper her walls, and with the purple and green
and orange peacock on the bedspread it made a beautiful room.
And last week when I'd pasted some colored funnies on the walls
of our front room at home I'd had a terrible time getting them off.
Mama had been cross for days.

James was calling me. I backed out the door still reading but
without knowing what Mutt and Jeff had done about the sick dog.

"Want a bite?" I stuck the biscuit up at James' face, but he
said no thanks. The biscuit was warm and crusty and it smelled
like buttermilk and bacon grease. We turned off the trail to go
by Martin's house and get some books to read.

From the path through the woods to Martin's house, we could
hear Sister Mearl's rifle cracking away at her bottles. Brother
Mearl had made her a shooting gallery, from empty bottles with
bags of sand behind them, but James said that she didn't really
need the bags of sand. He said that Sister Mearl never missed
anything she was shooting at.

So she hadn't really hung up her rifle. Not for good. I had
seen her shooting gallery once, when James and I had wandered
over there one afternoon, and Sister Mearl had said that when I
was older she would teach me to shoot. She said that you could

work a lot of things out of your system that way. And then she had looked scared and said that maybe I shouldn't tell Brother Mearl she said that, because he was a man of God and couldn't understand. I hadn't told anybody. I liked Sister Mearl. I wasn't glad our first Sister Mearl had died, but since she had to, I was sure glad that Brother Mearl had picked such a nice second Sister when he was reviving people in New Orleans. . . .

Martin was out at the edge of the trees that came right up to his back yard, putting out food scraps for the squirrels. He had said once to us that he hated to tempt the wild animals with all that food growing just over the fence in his garden, and so he left food outside the fence for them.

"Don't you know you're wasting your time?" James asked Martin after we went over to the trees and spoke to him. "Don't you know that half of these animals you feed and make friends with will just get caught in Billy Bob Jackson's traps and he'll stand around half a day watching them die?"

Martin stood up with his empty bowl. "We have to keep trying. And how is the schoolgirl today?"

It was a nice thing to say. I wouldn't really be a schoolgirl until Monday, but that was one of the nice things about Martin. He always knew what to say, because he knew things without being told, things like people being sick inside because nobody slowed down long enough to listen. You came away from Martin's house feeling better because he showed you that the important thing was to listen and keep on trying to understand. Martin was kind, like Daddy, but with more time.

We went into Martin's house and he gave us an apple from a bowl he always kept on his table. We talked for a while. I wanted to ask Martin why the Thompsons wouldn't go in the creek with Thee and Josie, but I decided to wait until another time. Until I had it all sorted out a little better.

When we were ready to go, Martin helped us choose our books, and James took *Swiss Family Robinson,* which was his favorite. I wanted one of the big books with skeletons in it—James had said they were doctor books, because one time Martin had studied to be a doctor—but Martin still shook his head and smiled, and so I took *Oliver Twist.*

The sun was going down behind the trees when we left Martin's house, and the trees were still. Not a leaf moved anywhere. Nothing moved except the big clouds that were spreading and trying to cover the sky.

"Now you run straight home," Martin said as we left. "Before it gets any darker. Venie will be worried about you."

He was right. Mama worried if we were out for too long. Mama worried about a lot of things.

The sky clouded over after we started for home, and now and then a great drop of rain would hit in the leaves over us. The woods were still, and you could smell the ground underneath the leaves. We walked fast. I shivered in spite of the heat.

When we came out through the pines behind our house, we felt better. All that was left of the sun that had been so hot all day was a streak of red light at the top of the trees on the other side of our house. The old house looked all gray-silver. I felt another little shiver. This time, of happiness.

It had been a good day. The song, our friends, our house, the way we lived—everything. James went on ahead of me, and I wondered if Mama had ever seen the old house all gray-silver and felt happy about it when she was a little girl.

"James!"

He stopped at the gate and waited, and I wanted to hold him there to see with me. "James, aren't you glad we live here now, instead of that tacky old yellow house in Strawne?"

"Oh, I d'no." James opened the gate. "In Strawne, I think Mama was happier. We had more money then, and the iceman left ice every day, and—"

I was already beginning to forget what it felt like, living in the yellow house in Strawne. But I remembered the iceman. . . . Mama always put money on the icebox for him. And once Dawn Starr had taken the money from the top of the icebox and we had gone down to the fruitstand on the corner and bought bananas with it. The bananas had made Dawn Starr sick because she ate all of them, and thinking about it, I was glad. Glad she had been sick, not glad she took Mama's coat money.

Dawn Starr was my cousin, but she was not my friend, not even if she did give me her clothes when she'd outgrown them.

A drop of rain hit my face and the wet dust around me smelled good, but after thinking about Dawn Starr I didn't want to stand out there any more.

7

The next morning the trees along the dirt road that led to the highway looked like they'd all been scrubbed and put into new school clothes too. The leaves had all perked up to catch the rain in the night, and the red and yellow ones shone.

There were mudholes in the road, and little gulleys of water along its sides. And that was how old Billy Bob Jackson could splash us that morning without hardly swerving from his tracks. There we were, walking out to the highway in our new clothes to catch the schoolbus, and here he came, ninety miles a minute.

We saw him coming, but we couldn't get off the road in time, and anyway, if we had, we'd have been in a ditch of water—

"What's a sob?" I asked James, after Billy Bob had gone on around the curve toward the tie yard.

"A what?" James was wiping the mud off my dress with the clean handkerchief Mama had stuck in his pocket.

"A sob. What you called Billy Bob just now. I know what s o b spells, you know. I'm not stupid. So what is one?"

"A— Oh, it's just something I heard down at the tie yard. Don't always be asking fool questions!" James looked at his handkerchief and shook it and then folded it, mud and all, and jammed it back down into his pocket.

"You heard it at home, too." I wiped at his shoulder with the

96

end of my sash that tied in back. "Daddy has called him that before."

It must have been a sorry thing to be, a sob. Nobody liked Billy Bob Jackson, because all he did was drive around with his big ugly face hanging out of his car window grinning and killing things and scaring people. But James had said once that we couldn't go around saying what we really thought about Billy Bob, because he was *Mister* Will Jackson's son, and *Mister* Will Jackson had a finger in every pie in the county.

When we got to the tabernickle at the highway, the Thompson kids were already there, fighting and throwing rocks at each other. One time Mama said it looked like Mrs. Thompson would worry about them all killing each other, and Daddy said she probably figured it was easier and took less time to get another one than to try to stop the fratricide, but I thought it was because Mrs. Thompson never had time to teach them anything. In the summer she was plowing and pulling corn and in the winter she was milking and cleaning the barn and having babies. She wore old long handles of Mr. Thompson's stuffed down inside a pair of his old rubber boots. Mrs. Thompson didn't talk much, and you never saw her smile at all. Old Jelly smiled all the time. Mr. Thompson's real name was Tadwell, like it said on his mailbox, but everybody called him Jelly. I thought it was because he was fat, but James said it was short for Jellybean. Once I had asked Daddy what Mr. Thompson did when it got too cold to sit on his porch and watch the cars go by, and Daddy had said well he must do something else once in a while because there was Soggum and Lester and let's see now, Junie—and Mama had frowned and said hush.

Soggum was on top of the tabernickle, dropping rocks down onto Junie and Lester, who were underneath the eaves yelling up at him to quit or they'd tell the teacher.

"Go ahead," Soggum shouted down to them. "No old teacher ain't my boss! Nobody ain't my boss!"

James pulled Lester and Junie away from under the eaves. "Don't stand there where he can drop things on you," he said. "Move out."

Up on top of the tabernickle, Soggum looked down at a big rock he was holding and drew back and aimed it at James, but he didn't throw it. They glared at each other, and then Soggum dropped the rock real easy over the edge of the roof and climbed down.

"Hi, Thee!" I yelled. "Hi, Josie!"

Thee and Josie were coming over the hill. When they reached the tabernickle, they did the oddest thing. They went across the road and Josie sat down on an old stump. Thee stood beside her, and they looked across at us. And somehow, everything changed and was different.

It was like they were looking at us *through* something. Or from another place. A place that was not clean and shiny like the first day of school on the morning after a rain.

I went across the road to them and put my hand on Josie's shoulder. It was all right then. She was there and I could touch her. It was Josie, and she was sitting on an old sweetgum stump, right there across the road from the tabernickle.

"Hey, what's the matter?" I tried to pull her up from the stump. She had six little red bows in her braids and she had on the high-heeled white shoes that Trudy had given her and red socks. "You'll get sweetgum on your dress! Come on over here to the tabernickle with us."

Thee watched us while he tried to stuff his white shirttail down into his pants in back. Donie had starched it so stiff that it stuck out around his middle and I wondered if it scratched him. He raked his bare foot around in the mud in a circle and scratched at his ruff of hair that always stuck up in front.

"Naw," he said. "We stay over here an wait fo the bus. Mama say to."

Thee had on short blue pants that had belonged to James, and they were starched stiff, too. So stiff they hadn't pulled apart at the creases yet.

They both looked nice that morning, Thee and Josie did. Nice in a way that told you somebody cared and had worked hard to make them look that way. Not anything like the Thompsons, who could put on new shoes or silk dresses and still come to school with their hair matted and egg still on their faces. Josie had on a new blue flowered dress that Trudy had brought to her. It was brand new, but it was already too tight. It was so tight that it hiked up in front, and Josie kept pulling at it. Watching her pull at her dress, I forgot to ask them about Donie telling them to wait on that side of the road.

98

"You're sure getting fat, Josie," I said.

"I know. I fat 'n helfy, but I don' feel good." Josie lifted her foot to pull a sticker from her red sock, and she didn't put her foot back down. She just kept it there on the stump in front of her and stared down at it. "I like to stay home today, but I cain't."

"She thowed up this mornin," Thee said. "All over the porch." He grinned and ducked his head, because James had come up behind him and was scuffing his knuckles over Thee's ruff. Lightly. Not hard like old Soggum did sometimes that nearly took Thee's scalp off.

"Thorpe, you come on back over here." James took my arm. "Come on over here now, and stay on your side of the road. It's time for the bus." He scuffed Thee's ruff again and told Josie to put her foot down because Soggum and Lester were sniggering about it, and I followed him back across the road.

On my side of the road? *My* side? I stood there holding my Orphan Annie dinner bucket and the bus came around the curve and down the highway toward us.

Soggum was the first one on the bus, and the rest of the Thompsons followed him, pushing and hitting and yelling, like always. Leo turned from the steering wheel and looked toward the back of the bus and told them to be quiet or by God he'd make the whole bunch get off and walk.

Leo was my friend. Besides being the schoolbus driver, he was our mailman, and he always stopped to talk to me at the mailbox. Especially when we got letters from Eloise. Once when Eloise sent us pictures of herself, I had told Leo about them and he had asked if I couldn't get him one of them, but Mama wouldn't let me have one. Not when she found out that it was for Leo—

"Come on, Thorpe," James said, and nudged me toward the bus, but I was waiting for Thee and Josie.

"Come on, Thee," I yelled. "Don't just sit there. Hurry!"

"Oh, fool!" James shoved me inside the bus door. "Get in!"

James stepped up into the schoolbus behind me. As he passed me on his way to the back of the bus, he leaned over and said something to me, real low, like he was cross with me. "They don't ride the same bus we do!"

"Here's your seat, Thorpe. Right behind me." Leo lifted his foot from the brake and the old bus made a grinding sound, and we were off to the first day of school, leaving Thee and Josie there, sitting on their stump watching us.

Not happy or sad or anything. Just watching.

In the back of the bus, James was glaring at Soggum again about something old Soggum had said. James' fists were doubled, and the grin on Soggum's face faded and he kept quiet. For a while. Then he looked away from James and started mumbling to the kids around him.

"Aw, you think I pay any 'tention to Leo? He ain't my boss. He ain't nothin'! Settin' up there behind that steering wheel like he's a king, an' he ain't nothin'. Ast anybody. His ol' Daddy was a jailbird, died in the pen, f'r stealin hawgs. An' on that ol' mail truck, I bet he steals all the letters with money in them. He ain't nothin' at—"

James put his hand over Soggum's mouth and Soggum bit it. It bled.

James pushed Soggum's face back. He got his hand loose and wiped it on the one clean spot still left on his muddy handkerchief. "You wait for me this evening," he said to Soggum. "When we get off the bus, you just wait for me. Damn you."

Soggum was right about Leo not being a nothing. Leo was not a nothing. The something he was was my friend. Thinking about it, I was glad he was, because before we all piled off the bus in the schoolyard I already had a feeling that I was going to need friends.

"It's Miss Keeter," Mama said that night after supper, and she was laughing. "For Heaven's sake, Thorpe, didn't you even learn your teacher's *name?*"

The first day of school was over. I was finding out that I hadn't even learned the one thing that I'd been sure I had learned. But Mama didn't laugh much any more, and so right then I wasn't feeling ashamed of it. I was feeling glad that I was so stupid I hadn't understood the teacher's name and had made Mama laugh.

We went into the living room. Daddy wasn't there, but James was sitting on the couch, studying. Mama sat down in the rocking chair with a comb in her hand and I sat down on the floor at her feet.

"What was school like?" Mama reached for the glass of water

on the table beside her chair and combed water through my hair. She was rolling it on socks again.

"Well," I tried to think how to say it. "Mostly it was just watching and listening, and doing what you're told. It was like going to a meeting and watching people go in and out of a room and trying to learn the secret word so you could go in and out with them and—"

"Oh." Mama laughed again. "Well, anyhow, your teacher's name is *not* Mosquito! It's Miss *Keeter,* and good Heavens, she must be as old as the hills. She taught me when I was a little girl. Does that pull?" She tied the sock and waited to see if it was too tight.

"Well, yes, it does." I turned my head back and forth and nodded up and down. "It pulls when I move my head. But one must suffer for one's pride." The little mermaid in one of my books had said that when she lost her tail and grew feet, and it was a good thing to say sometimes.

Mama laughed again.

"You shouldn't laugh when she says those stupid things." James looked up from his book. "But I guess it's too late now. She's had too much stuff read to her, and Daddy shouldn't have ever taught her how to read."

"They read to you, too," I said, but I knew James was right. I said and did a lot of crazy stupid things, and I bet I was the only kid in the first grade dumb enough to think her name was Mosquito. And that was why James had to carry my two front teeth in a box in his pocket. I probably *would* have lost them and had dawg tushes.

"Well." James put his books together and pushed them back on the table. "Prob'ly you're not the only one. It does sound like Mosquito when you say it fast."

"And she looks like one," I said. "Like a mosquito." I looked at Mama. "She's not soft and pretty like you, Mama. She's just all arms and legs and a ball of hair on top." I sat there and thought about the cross look on Mosquito's face, and about how she had buzzed around the room, bothering people.

James sat down on the floor beside me and dealt the Old Maid cards Eloise had given us. "What are we?"

"What?" I looked at the cards I'd picked up, and then at James.

"If she's a mosquito, what are we?"

I sorted the cards around in my hand and Mama said Sit still and I sat still and looked down at the cards and thought.

"What's Mama?" James reached for a card.

"Oh, that's easy," I said. "Mama's a butterfly. In a glass jar. She's soft and pretty and good, and she doesn't leave her kids and her home and everything and fly out and swoop around over the whole world. She stays in her glass jar, like you put butterflies sometimes, and she doesn't mind, because it's glass and she can see through it and she doesn't even know it's there. The glass, I mean."

"In a jar? Mama?" James looked puzzled, but I didn't tell him anything more about Mama, because there wasn't anything more to tell.

"What about me?" James handed me the Old Maid and sat there, smirking when I saw what it was. "What am I?"

"Oh, you're a bulldog," I said. "Fierce and unafraid. You always fight for what you think is right, but you don't fight the little dogs. You take care of them."

"And I guess you're one of the little dogs?"

"Me?" I leaned back against Mama's legs. She was through rolling my hair, but she sat there, listening to us.

"I'm just old Peanut, I guess," I said. "Always running the wrong way with the stick."

Peanut was this old puppy that Aunt Neevy had given us when we lived in Strawne. You could *not* teach that dog to do tricks. He always got too excited because you were noticing him. If you threw a stick for him to fetch, he picked it up and ran the wrong way. Or else just around in circles. If you called him to come get a bone he stood there and grinned like he wasn't sure he was the dog you meant. Mama tried to teach him tricks, but she always got disgusted and went back into the house and left him standing there in the yard grinning. One day he started running in circles and wouldn't quit. He ran around and around, and then he fell over on the ground and jerked and twitched all over. Mama said it was running fits and she gave him some turpentine, but he still ran and fell and twitched. Pretty soon after that, Daddy took Peanut and his gun and went hunting, and when he came home Peanut wasn't with him. Peanut never did come home.

"What's Daddy?"

James tugged at one of the socks on my head, and I quit thinking about old Peanut to think about Daddy.

What was Daddy?

He was DADDY. There wasn't any way to say it. He was the biggest kindest wisest most wonderful man in the world, and he knew everything and could do everything. He stood up next to God and President Roosevelt. Nobody would ever get Daddy into a fruit jar, because Daddy would break the damned jar and get out and——

And he had come into the room while we were talking. He stood there smiling at us, ready to go to a meeting of Masons.

"Is this a home or a dog pound?" he asked. He bent and took my cards and reshuffled them so James couldn't tell where the Old Maid was, and handed them back to me. "You know, someday the Peanut will learn which way to run. Which way is the right way for her, I mean. And then she'll run a true course. So will the bulldog. He may tackle a tiger or two, but if he remembers how to hold on he'll do all right."

Daddy didn't look too happy about going to Masons. He never did. James said that Daddy used to go to lodge meetings like he enjoyed them, but I couldn't remember that. I thought that he went only to please Mama.

James tried to pick up his cards from the floor with the hand that Mama had cleaned and bandaged, and Daddy noticed his hand. Daddy looked down at James' hand and then at his lip. James' lip was swollen and purple.

"Want to tell me about the first day of school, James?" Daddy asked. "Was it that bad?"

We all looked at James, waiting for him to answer. We watched him, waiting, while he sorted his cards and pulled out a pair of aces and put them down on the floor with the rest of his discards. Then he looked up at Daddy.

"Yes sir," he said. "I'll tell you about it. It wasn't bad. I had something, all day, to look forward to. Something I enjoyed doing."

James' lip and hand looked bad and he'd had a hard time eating supper, but we'd hoped Daddy wouldn't notice.

I looked up from my cards. "If you think James looks bad, Daddy, you ought to see old Soggum's eye. He can't hardly see. And besides, old Soggum *cried.*"

"Well," Daddy said, "I won't ask any more questions. Just remember, son, try not to hit the first lick."

He looked a little happier than when he'd come into the room. He went out the door and down the walk whistling "Onward Christian Soldiers."

The rest of that first week went by without any more fights. Everything about school was different from the way I had thought it would be, but of course we kept going. I went, and I sat there at my desk and tried to make myself invisible to Mosquito, and I tried to do the things she told us to, but it was hard. I kept thinking about her instead of listening to her and she kept saying that she had very little use for a dreamer and that she was afraid that was what I was.

Back in the summer, Daddy had made a deal with Miss Mildred to build some extra cabinets in her kitchen if she would give me piano lessons, and Mama had said I was too young to be worried with it, but that maybe he'd better go ahead because it would be good training for when he got on the PWA and they had yelled again and I had been going for a piano lesson every Wednesday. Except that the first week of school I didn't go. Mama had said that the first week of school was enough strain. She was right. It was.

For one thing, there were Thee and Josie, still sitting on the sweetgum stump across the road every morning, and the rest of us over around the tabernickle. It worried me so much that Mama said if I so much as even mentioned it again she was afraid she'd do something drastic.

And then even that changed. The next morning, on Friday, Thee was sitting on the stump by himself. His ruff of hair stood up just as perky, and his shirt was starched and stiff, but he looked little and lonely and sad, sitting there on the big stump with his bare feet dangling so far from the ground.

I guess James thought so, too, because he stood there and kicked clods of dirt around on the ground and then he picked up a rock and threw it at the tabernickle. Hard.

"Damn," James said when he threw the rock. It hit the side of the tabernickle and fell to the ground. The Thompson kids quit fighting and pushing and we all looked at James to see what he

104

was mad about. James looked across at Thee, and then he went over to Thee's side of the road. I followed him.

"Hi." James stood by the stump and grinned at Thee. His grin was crooked.

"Hi, Mister James." Thee had one foot in his lap, looking down at it like he'd just discovered he had it. He didn't look up.

"Where d'ya get that Mister stuff?" James scuffed Thee's ruff of hair, but Thee still didn't look up.

I squatted on the ground in front of the stump and looked up at Thee. "Where's Josie?"

Thee kept his head down and only his eyes moved. He rolled his eyes to look up at us.

"Josie ain goin to school no mo."

"Not going to school any more? Not ever? Why?"

"She jes ain. She faint at school yestidday an the teacher say she cain come back. She ain goin no mo."

Josie? Not going to school any more? I turned to James.

"You told me yesterday that I had to go to school until I was sixteen whether I wanted to or not! Josie's not sixteen! Why does she get to quit?"

James dug a little ditch with the toe of his shoe and looked down at it. "Oh, gaw, Thorpe." He looked up the highway. "Come on, it's time for the bus."

I pulled at James' shirt and his shirttail came out and I held on to it. "I don't care, I'm going to quit too. You said we had to go to school. You said the law made us. You said—"

"I know what I said!" James jerked away from me and stuffed his shirttail back in. "Quit pulling on me. It's different with—with them. I mean, nobody cares if—Aw, come on! See ya." He flipped his hand to Thee and started back across the road.

Josie was thirteen. Did they have different laws, too, like they had different schools and different buses and different sides of the road?

"Bye, Thee." I went across the road.

Thee didn't answer. I stopped and looked back. He was looking down at his foot again and just before I ran for the bus a big tear rolled down his cheek and plopped into the dust under his other foot.

I thought about that tear all the way to Strawne. Mama had said that that was the way things were supposed to be and that they didn't mind, because they knew it. But Mama had been wrong. Thee minded. And the terrible part was that he could never, never do anything at all about it.

Mosquito (I only had her two weeks, and in that two weeks she was always Mosquito, to me) was cross with me at school that day because I had lost the list of things we needed for school. Things like scissors and paste and stuff. It really didn't matter about my losing it—except that she had to make me a new list—because I couldn't have gotten the stuff until Saturday anyway. But, of course, she didn't want to look at it that way. She didn't even want to hear about that we only had money on Saturdays when Daddy got paid at the mill.

At home that night I heard Mama and Daddy talking, and I learned that soon we might not even have that much money.

"Will's talking about closing the sawmill down, Venie," Daddy said that night. He was sitting in the kitchen with Mama, watching her wash dishes so he could dry them. I turned the radio down a little bit so I could hear them.

"Closing it *down?* Here, why don't you dry these pots and get them out of my way. For Heaven's sake, why? I really don't think we should worry about it, because I don't think he'll close it down, but what will we do if he does? You know—"

"Venie, listen to me."

Daddy's voice wasn't loud enough and I had to strain to hear it.

"Venie, Will came by the sawmill today and we had quite a talk. And by golly, the old boy's got quite a plan for me. He's a devious old devil, but he's tenacious, and the plan's a long-range one. A hell of a long range, I decided, reaching way back and probably way forward. . . . Venie, are you listening? Because I don't think I could stand to have to tell this more than once."

"Of course I'm listening. No, hang that pot over there." Mama came out into the hall and looked in the closet for the broom. "I hope *you* listened. What is his plan?"

"You're damned right I listened. It was on his time, and there wasn't anything else I could do, was there? I listened, and then I had to grit my teeth to keep from spitting right down on top of that damned arrogant red bald dome, or from shoving my fist into his filthy face. I wonder, if I'd knocked him down, if he would have had Billy Bob come and arrest me?"

It was quiet in the kitchen for a minute. Then Mama said, "Ohhh, go ahead. What's his plan?"

"Well, all I have to do to begin teaching again and be a respected citizen is to stay for one of the meetings and take the—"

A burst of drums came from the radio, and I could not hear what it was that Daddy had to take, but it sounded like he said "the awful White Supremacy."

"Then for God's sake, take it," Mama said. "Is that all?"

"All?" Daddy said. "*All?*"

Mama put the broom back into the hall closet, and when she went back into the kitchen her voice was softer.

"I know it's bitter medicine, Jim," she said, and I had to strain again to hear her. "But for God's sake, couldn't you just take it and forget it? You wouldn't have to ride with them. You could always have something else you had to do, and anyhow, they don't really do anything when they ride. They think they're keeping law and order. Can't you give them credit for what they think they're doing?"

There wasn't any sound from the kitchen at all. When Mama spoke again her voice was cross.

"What do you think you'll do, then, if he does close the sawmill down?"

"I'll tell you what I'm already doing," Daddy said. "I'm sending out letters to every school board in the state, and I'm giving them Geneva's telephone number, so if anybody, anywhere, needs a principal—or a teacher—I won't even have to wait for a letter back. And how am I going to buy stamps for all of these letters? I've quit smoking. Or hadn't you noticed? I'm not going to sit on my can any longer, Venie, waiting for one little hole in the woods to accept my way of thinking. Now does that answer your question?"

"Yes. But I have another one for you. Just how do you plan, when that seven dollars a week you've been earning isn't even coming in, how do you plan to move a family and a houseful of furniture into some strange town somewhere and live until you get your first check and pray God it's a real check instead of scrip and just how do you plan to do all that?"

"Well now," Daddy said. "Let me sort that one out. I'll ask for an advance. I'll borrow from the bank. The old car's paid for and the tires are still fairly good, so it ought to carry a little mortgage. Enough for that. Next question?"

"You have it all figured out, don't you?" Mama's voice sounded tired and cross. "Without even consulting anybody, you—"

I quit listening. I'd heard the rest of it all before, and the radio was better. The man on the radio talked about Crazy Water Crystals, like Aunt Neevy and Uncle Elmer drank at night, and I wondered if the awful White Supremacy that old Will wanted Daddy to take was anything like Crazy Water Crystals. It sounded worse.

Mosquito had made another list of school supplies for me and when we went to Strawne on Saturday to get them I saw the red coat.

Daddy and James had turned to go to the Post Office, and I had started across the street to go into Mr. Byrd's store with Mama when I saw the red coat. It was in Mr. Byrd's window, and around it were blue overalls and khaki shirts and bolts of gray flannel and some cans of motor oil.

"Oh, Mama!" I swung onto her arm and pulled her to a stop in front of the store. "Oh, Mama, isn't it beautiful!"

Mama didn't look at the gray flannel and the overalls. She knew what I meant. She had already taken her little grocery list from her purse, and she stood there holding it as we looked at the red coat.

"It's beautiful." Mama nodded and looked down at her grocery list, then back at the red coat. She looked at the coat and at me and started to say something, and then she bit her lip and we both stood there. Mama took my hand from her arm and went inside the store.

I stayed outside to look at the coat. I looked at it until Mama came back out with her groceries.

"For Christmas, Mama. Instead of a doll. Please!" The coat looked soft and happy, and, wrapped in it, you would be wrapped in love. People would turn again when they passed you on the street, to see how beautiful you were—

"Oh, I don't know, Thorpe." Mama bit her lip again and looked cross. "That plaid coat that Dawn Starr gave you last year is a pretty coat, and perfectly good. And you need other things worse. I don't know." Mama turned her back on the coat and started down the street. "Let's take these groceries to the car."

108

Down in my stomach and up under my ribs, I felt sick. The plaid coat that Dawn Starr had given me was pretty, but it had been Dawn Starr's coat first. Even that wouldn't have mattered, if Dawn Starr could have kept her mouth shut. But I knew just exactly what would happen the first time I wore it to school. At recess Dawn Starr would look out and see me wearing the coat and she would run from the third-grade room shouting to the world that she had given it to me.

"Come on, Thorpe," Mama said in a tired voice.

I ran to catch up.

"Pull up your bloomers," Mama said.

I looked down at my knees. At least I had on the right ones. They were supposed to match your dress, and sometimes I forgot and wore the wrong pair.

"When I get grown," I said as we crossed the street, "I'm going to wear pink silk every day. Like Eloise does all the time, and like you do on Sunday. Soft and silk and pink—"

Mama took my hand and jerked me up onto the curb. "Be quiet!" she said and looked up and down the street. "You don't talk about your—your underwear when you're out on a public street!"

We turned the corner to go to the car, and I forgot all about underwear. We were crossing the alley that ran behind the bank and behind the only doctor's office in Strawne. Just as we were half across, the back door to Doctor John's office opened and some people came out into the alley.

The sign over Doctor John's back door was faded and it hung crooked, but if you'd read the one in front, you knew that it said JOHN FREDERIC JOHNSON, M.D. And under the M.D. part, the sign in back said COLORED ENTRANCE. Lewis and Donie were standing under the sign, looking up and down the alley and at each other, like they were lost. Thee and Josie were hanging onto Donie's skirt like they always did in town or around strangers, and Josie was crying.

Then Lewis turned like he was walking in his sleep and walked down the alley, with his head bent. He walked like he'd never raise his head and look up again. Donie stood there and patted Josie's shoulder, and her head was straight but her eyes looked like she was asleep, too.

I ran down the alley to them.

"Hi, Thee. What's the matter with everybody? Is Josie sick?"

Donie had turned and was walking after Lewis, her arm still around Josie and her hand still patting up and down, up and down, on Josie's shoulder. They didn't even notice I was back there talking to Thee.

"Is Josie sick?" I asked him again.

Thee looked after them, and back at me, and his eyes were big and brown. "I do' know," he said. "I do' know why everybody cryin. It about Josie. She jes faint too much and she cain go back to school, and we bring er down to Doctor John an when he come out the back room with her an Mama, everybody go to cryin. She mus got somethin, but I do' know. She jes faint too much."

He turned and ran after Donie, and they all went into the back of the Cheerful Corner Café. I went back up the alley to where Mama waited.

"Mama, did you know Josie's sick? She faints too much and she's crying and Thee said—"

Mama wasn't listening. She was already scolding before she reached for my shoulder and shook it.

"—and don't you leave my side until we get in the car to go home! God in Heaven, don't I have enough to worry about, without you traipsing up and down alleys after nigras!"

"They're not nigras, Mama." I pulled my shoulder loose. "They're my friends."

"They are not your friends!" Mama walked faster. "You *have* to remember that, Thorpe!"

"Well." I trotted along behind her. "If you're going to walk that fast, I can't stay at your side. You keep going off and leaving me— Hi, Miss Una!" I slowed down to wave at Miss Una Jackson, who was standing in front of the Post Office with Callie. Mama slowed and waved and tried to smile but it didn't come out real good.

Miss Una nodded like a little bird pecking, and waved at us. Her hands looked like little bird feet, and her head bobbed up and down as she called out to us. "Venie, Thorpe," she called. "Wait and I'll—I'll walk with you."

Callie put her big tan hand on Miss Una's shoulder and turned her around, and they went inside the Post Office. We watched them go inside, and Mama shook her head and bit her lip.

110

"Miss Una goes around town with a nigra," I said. "Why can't I?"

Mama didn't answer. We walked on toward the car.

"Mama." I looked up at her face. "Will you slow down a little so I can keep up with you? Mama, why does Callie go everywhere Miss Una goes? Why wouldn't she let Miss Una walk down the street for a little way with us?"

"Oh, Thorpe." Mama looked sad. "Una's—well, she's sick. It's not the same at all for her to go around with Callie. Mr. Jackson pays Callie to watch after Una and to take care of her."

"Why doesn't Miss Una go to Doctor John?"

"Because he can't help her. She's not that kind of sick. Now quit asking silly questions and come on! Let's get these groceries to the car and rest a while."

We couldn't. We had to go back to Mr. Byrd's store again and get the things on my school list. Seeing the red coat had made me forget the list, and Mama was cross about that.

I sure hoped the next baby would be a boy, or at least a different kind of girl, so Mama would feel better. Most of the things I did made her cross.

On the way home Daddy stopped at Ben Joe Hudson's filling station at the edge of town to get gas. Ben Joe and High Pockets, who was Ben Joe's brother, were Mama's cousins, like nearly everybody else in Strawne and around it. Ben Joe ran the filling station and High Pockets worked their farm. Their farm covered most of the land between Brother Mearl's house and Strawne, and when High Pockets wasn't busy at the farm he sat around the filling station and talked to people. High was the tallest man in town, and I liked him.

While Ben Joe was filling the tank, James and I got out of the car and went over to talk to High. High gave James a beanshooter he'd just finished whittling, and then he picked me up and set me up on his shoulder. In the car, Mama frowned. Daddy paid for his gas and High took me to the car and threw me into the back seat.

After Daddy had pulled back onto the highway toward home Mama turned to the back seat and frowned again.

"I don't know," she said. "Maybe you're hopeless. You run down the street with nigras and you jump onto men's shoulders and— Thorpe, you're in school now. It's time for you to start growing up!"

"For God's sake!" Daddy looked from the highway to Mama and his frown was worse than any she could have made. "What's the matter with you, Lavinia? Are you so tired and worried that you have to take it out on a child? She won't be six years old until November! Do you have to see *me* in her every time you look at her?"

Mama looked down at her lap. "I don't know, Jim," she said in a tight little voice. "Maybe you're right. I don't know any more."

Daddy didn't answer. He looked straight ahead down the highway, and nobody said anything else all the way home.

On the second Monday of school Mosquito told us about Recitation Day.

"Next Friday," she said, "I expect each person in the room to take part. You may say a poem, tell a story, or sing a song. But you must do something. If you don't, you may stay after school and think of something for the next week."

That wasn't any problem at all. Everybody knew songs and poems and stories, and so I didn't worry about it.

What I did worry about was Thee. On Wednesday of that second week of school, Thee was still sitting on his stump every morning, drawing circles in the air with his toes and watching us all climb onto our bus. Of course, his bus came later, but it wasn't the same at all, having to sit there on his side of the road by himself and then having to climb onto his bus without anybody pushing him or yelling at him to hurry. It just wasn't the same.

On our bus the Thompson kids were still fighting and pushing and Leo was still having to shout at them to quiet down. At school, old Junie Thompson was still holding her reader upside down and pretending to read it. And not hearing a cross word from Mosquito about it. You'd have thought Mosquito didn't even *care* what Junie did.

What had made Mosquito get really cross with me and stay that way, was finding *Tales from Shakespeare* in my desk. It was her own fault that she found it, because my desk suited me fine, but one day at clean-up time she decided that it was still messy.

"I'll clean it for you, this time," Mosquito had said, and she had stuck her pencil into her knot of hair and squatted on the floor and started pulling things from my desk. Then she had pulled out *Tales from Shakespeare*. "No wonder you can't find room for your things! Where did you get this book, Thorpe, and what is it doing in your desk?"

"I read it," I said. "Not right now, of course, but sometimes when—"

Mosquito stood up and her glasses slipped down on her nose and she looked over them at me.

"You read *Shakespeare?*" She took the pencil from her knot and tapped it against her big teeth. "Thorpe, bad things happen to little girls who tell stories. Now if this book belongs in your home, I'm sure your mother doesn't know you've taken it from the shelf. You take it home, and you leave it there!"

I had an idea what kind of stories she meant. Not the kind you'd tell on Recitation Day. But the only girls I knew who told bad stories were Dawn Starr and Junie Thompson, and I didn't care what happened to them.

I couldn't bear to take *Tales* home and leave it. So after school that day I took it out and hid it in an old ditch at the edge of the schoolground, and after that I sat in the ditch at recess and read and listened to the other kids jumping rope and playing Red Rover.

What I really wanted to do was play Red Rover, but you had to be in the third grade for that. So I read, and I listened to the lines of kids calling for each other.

Red Rover, Red Rover, let Danny come over.

How good it must feel to be called for! To be *invited!*

Red Rover, Red Rover, let Dawn Starr come over.

Or Cynthia or Wilbur or James. . . .

Sometimes I thought of *our* magic circle. The one we'd had in the summer. I wanted to draw it big enough to go around everybody on the schoolground, but I was learning that you didn't do it that way. They drew the circle and you had to wait until they let you know they wanted you to be in it.

I waited.

It was a long wait. Every time I got to the end of *Tales* I started over and read it again. One night it rained, hard, all night long. It filled the ditches and the gutters and left mudholes in the road again, and the next day I thought I'd lost *Tales* for sure. I thought it had washed away. I found it, after a lot of looking, washed up in a brush pile at the side of a ditch. I dried it off on my skirt and found a little cave to keep it in, but after that it was real thick and it always had a funny smell.

"Thorpe! What in the world is that on your skirt?"

I had started into the building when the bell rang, and Mosquito stopped me at the door. She stood just inside with some of the other teachers, and they all looked at my skirt.

"It's— I fell down. In the ditch and it was muddy." There. I had told the kind of story she had meant, and bad things would probably happen to me.

"In the ditch? What— Never mind. Just go to the washroom and clean yourself up. I certainly can't look at that the rest of the day!" She turned her back on my muddy skirt and started talking to the other teachers.

Dawn Starr's teacher—the one with the pretty red hair—smiled down at me and took my hand. "I'm going to the bathroom. Come along, and I'll help you. That's a lot of mud you have there."

We went along the hall.

"Let me run in and get my purse," Miss Wooley said when we'd reached her classroom door. "I'll be right back out."

I waited outside Miss Wooley's door, and down the hall I could hear Mosquito and the other teachers still talking.

"Isn't that Jim Torrance's daughter? She's an odd little thing."

"She's Jim Torrance's daughter exactly," Mosquito said. "Not much chance for her, is there? I tell you, I've taught here for thirty years, and that man was the only principal we've ever had that I absolutely couldn't get along with. I don't hold it against the child, you know that, but—"

"Thirty years! You must have taught a lot of their mothers and fathers."

"I have. I taught that child's mother. Her mother was a Thorpe, you know. She was a sweet child from a good family. Lavinia Thorpe. But she sure drove her ducks to a bad market."

"They usually do," one of the other teachers said.

Miss Wooley came out of her classroom.

"Now let's go scrape off the top layer of your mud," she said. We went into the bathroom and she closed the door and reached for a paper towel.

James and I didn't ride the bus home after school that day. We walked over to Miss Mildred's boardinghouse for my piano lesson. Miss Mildred wanted to give me two lessons a week, but Mama argued with Daddy that I was a child and not a guinea pig, and so I only took one lesson a week. Before school started we had gone in the car on Wednesday evenings after supper, but going from school was better, because that way we could walk home afterward, along the railroad track.

"I have to run to the Post Office before it closes," Miss Mildred said when we'd finished the lesson. "But if you think Venie won't mind, you could stay and practice for a while. You need a piano at home to practice on."

She went out the door still talking, and I stayed and practiced and listened to James and Miss Mildred's boys playing shinny out in the back yard. Miss Mildred wasn't really a Miss, of course. She had a husband and two boys. Mr. Walter Hagan was her husband, and he did stuff like mowing the lawn and telling Winfred and Wilbur when it was time to quit playing and come in. Sometimes he worked at the Post Office, but most of the time Miss Mildred did that, and Mr. Hagan sat on the porch and talked to the railroad men until it was time for him to go and yell at the boys. "Call your dogs off!" he'd stick his head out the back door and yell, and Winfred and Wilbur would come inside and James would sit on the porch.

After Miss Mildred left, Trudy came into the room and stood behind me. "Jesus, lover of my soul," I played, because church songs were all Miss Mildred knew, and when I had learned the right hand she was going to teach me the left. Trudy stood there behind me, and I wondered again what Aunt Neevy had against smelling like a nigger. Trudy smelled like doughnuts and like the Irresistible perfume she'd given Josie and maybe a little like she'd been sweating, but you didn't mind that because you knew it was from standing over a stove cooking good things to eat. Donie always smelled like hot soapy water and starch, and I didn't know how Lewis smelled, because the only time I'd ever been that close to him I couldn't smell anything except creek water. But I'd have bet that Lewis had a kind, happy smell, because Lewis was a kind, happy man.

Trudy had on a stiff white uniform. Her hair had been straightened and curled again, and she had on lots of red lipstick. Trudy's feet weren't pretty. They were kind of spread, even with her shoes on, like maybe she'd stood on them too much. She had a paper bag in her hand, and there were grease spots on the paper.

"Here." Trudy put the paper bag on the green velvet piano runner, and kicked her shoe off and leaned over to rub her foot. When she leaned over, you could see that inside her white uniform she was soft and round like Mama and Eloise, only bigger and, of course, dark. "Here's a doughnut fo you, and one for Mister James. An the extra ones is to take to Theotus and Josie May. Now you hurry and scat with em, befo Miss Mildred come back. I jes finish em, and she ain count em yit."

I scatted. When we were outside the gate, I opened the sack and handed James a doughnut. We cut across the vacant lots to the railroad track, and started the walk home.

I loved that walk home because we had to go right by Trudy's little house, and there was always music coming out of its doors and windows. Victrola music, loud and happy.

It was the house Miss Mildred had built for Trudy, and the boards were still new and smelled like pine. I didn't blame Trudy for liking her little new house better than the houses down in the flats, where all the old rusty cars and wagon wheels and tin cans were. Trudy had blue morning glories around her doors and windows, and even when she was at work there was always Victrola music coming out of her house because of her friends who lived there with her.

"Hurry," James said. "Quit lagging. Come on!" He never, that whole year, let me listen for as long as I'd have liked to to the music from Trudy's house.

On that Wednesday, a big shiny blue car pulled up to Trudy's front door, and a man wearing a yellow hat and smoking a cigar was standing in the door looking off toward town.

"E'nen, chillun." The man in the yellow hat took the cigar from his mouth and blew out a big puff of smoke. It smelled good, and inside the house somebody was singing with the Victrola. Somebody else laughed, and squealed, and then somebody said "Aw naw, now!"

James was still hurrying me, so I ran to catch up with him.

"James," I watched him lick the sugar from around his mouth when Trudy's house was behind us. "James, how is this doughnut different from one we would go inside Trudy's house and eat?"

James glared at me.

"It just is!" He glared again. "Why do you have to ruin everything we do by asking stupid questions? You just don't go inside their houses and eat or visit or anything, that's all." He walked faster and when he was ahead of me he turned and looked down over his shoulder at me.

"They're *nigras!*"

8

Nobody was home at Donie's house. We stood in the yard and called, and then we stepped up onto the rickety little porch and knocked, but nobody came to the door. We didn't know what to do about the doughnuts, so we decided to go around to the back door and leave them in the kitchen. The kitchen was warm and quiet. The floor was scrubbed white with the homemade soap that Donie poured from a jar onto her floors to scrub them, and you could smell the biscuits rising in a round pan on the back of the stove. We left the sack of doughnuts on the table and tiptoed out again. I don't know why we tiptoed.

When we got home, they were at our house.

Mama was talking to Donie when I came down the hall and into the kitchen. Our floor wasn't as clean as Donie's. "Does Josie know what's the matter with her? Does she know whose it is? Do you?"

I put my books and Orphan Annie bucket on the table and got ready to answer Mama's questions about the day at school. Donie sat there at the kitchen table, bent over, with her elbows on the table and both hands holding her forehead. She didn't even notice that I'd come into the kitchen.

Mama didn't ask me about the day at school. She didn't ask about anything. She looked up from the fire she was stirring in the cookstove and waved one hand around at me like she was pushing me away.

"Run outside and play, Thorpe. *Now*."

"I'm hungry."

"After a while. Run on out and play now."

I went out the back door. Thee and Josie were in the back yard, picking up pears that had fallen from the trees. I wanted to pick up pears with them and take them down to Peccavi in his pen, but I wanted more to find out what it was that Josie did or didn't know. I sat down on the back steps.

If I could learn and tell Josie, maybe she could go back to school and Thee would not have to sit on the sweetgum stump by himself. I listened for sounds from the kitchen.

"Does she know?" Mama asked.

"She know, but she still cain understan," Donie said.

"I was afraid of that." Mama rattled the stove lids. "Whose is it, for Heaven's sake? That's the first thing we have to know, and then we'll see what we can do about it."

"We cain do nothin." Donie sounded scared. "It—it Mister Billy Bob's."

"Billy Bob Jackson?" Mama was quiet for a minute. "Donie, are you sure?"

"As sho as I am that weah settin in this house. Ain nobody else been messen aroun her, Miss Venie. You know that."

"Well, I didn't know he had been," Mama said. *"When?"*

"He come to the house one day." Donie still sounded scared. "One day when he know I ovah washin fo Miss Una. An he hol her an do it."

"But didn't she tell you afterward, when you came home?" Pots and pans rattled as Mama took them down to cook supper.

"No'm. He say ef she tell he come back an kill 'er. And she bleve it, she so scahed. Then he come back agin nex week an some mo later, an——"

"Well God in Heaven!" Mama said. "She's still just a child, just a *baby* herself! And don't call that thing Mister! Will Jackson should have drowned him when he was born. Does Lewis know?"

"Yes'm he know. An it's th' onliest time I evah see Lewis cry. He take it bad. But what he kin do?" Donie started crying. "Mister Billy Bob Lewis's boss down in th' tie woods, an we all got to eat. An goin hongry f'm speakin out t' Mister Billy Bob ain

119

go' do nothing but bring on th' night riders. Lewis, he know he cain do nothin."

"Ohhh, forget about the night riders. You know you're not afraid of them, and right now you have something real to worry about. Here, drink this coffee. It's this morning's coffee warmed over, but it's hot and strong." I heard a spoon clink against a cup.

"Didn't Josie know what he was doing? Didn't you ever tell her anything?" Mama asked.

"No'm, I ain tell 'er nothin. I ain nevah tell 'er to keep the doe lock, Miss Venie. I ain had th' mine fo tellin Josie bout men lak Mister Billy Bob. An seem lak she ain been ready fo me to tell yit, Miss Venie."

"When is it supposed to be?" Mama's voice sounded worried. "How far along is she?"

"Doctor John say it be bout th' end o' December. Maybe Christmas week, he say. He say, Donie, what you think when she miss 'er monthly, an I say I ain think nothin since she ain but thirteen."

"Let's see," Mama said. "About four months from now. Does Trudy know? Does she have any suggestions we can use?"

"Yes'm, Trudy know. She say give Josie a whole bottle o' tur-pemtime an teach er to run faster nex time."

Nobody said anything for a while after that, until Donie spoke again.

"I jes cain bring myself to do that, Miss Venie. It's like Brother Amos say, it's too much like real killin."

"It is real killing," Mama said. "It's murder. No, we won't do that. Drink your coffee before it gets cold, and we'll find a way somehow to handle all this. This coffee tastes pretty good, doesn't it? We'll face it, Donie. It's not the worst thing that ever happened. It just seems like it right now—"

So it was something that old Billy Bob Jackson had done to Josie that had made her quit school.

I went out to the washbench and sat down between Thee and Josie.

"You're getting fatter every day," I said to Josie.

"I know it," she said. "But I ain feel good."

We got some pears from the box in the smokehouse and sat there and ate them and talked for a while, and then we picked up some from the ground and took them down to Peccavi. We stood there and scratched him through the side of his pen.

"Does your teacher know that you can read some words?" I asked Thee. In the summer I had taught him a lot of words, and James had taught him a few numbers. "Do you get to read a lot?"

"I tol her I k'n awready read, the first day." Thee looked skinnier than ever, standing there beside Josie. "She didn't bleve me, at firs."

"Mine doesn't know." I handed my pear core in to old Peck and he ate it and waddled over to another corner and lay down. "I don't think she believes anything I say."

Peccavi was as fat as Josie. It was funny how much we all loved him; all he ever did was grunt and eat and roll in the mud over in the low corner of his pen. He didn't look anything at all like the pretty baby pig they'd given to us in the spring, but he was our pet and we loved him.

"Are old Peck's brothers and sisters as big as he is?" I asked.

"Huh. Ain none of em left." Thee scratched around on the ground and found some acorns and threw them in to Peck. "We done kilt all of em except the two Daddy swapped to Mister Byrd fo groceries. An th' ol mammy died. Jes died."

"You killed them? What for?"

"We et em." Josie grinned and rolled her eyes. "An now we got ham an sausage an souse meat, and we give Brother Amos some, too."

"You're always giving Brother Amos something. Why do you give him everything you get?"

"He our pastor," Thee said. "Everbody at Mount Carmel Church give to Brother Amos."

"Well, anyhow, we'd better go back up toward the house. I sure hope old Peck doesn't have any hams or sausages on him. You might eat him up."

We all laughed and went back to the house. In the back yard we drew some squares on the ground and found some glass and played hopscotch for a while, but it wasn't much fun. Josie was too slow. She couldn't hop very good any more. She was tired before Donie came out the back door and called to them.

I sat on the back steps and ate another pear, and thought about things.

"Hello, out there!"

Daddy stood at the back door and called out to me. "How's everything at school and abroad?"

I clasped my hands and raised them and made the OK sign to Daddy, and he smiled and made the OK sign back at me. After that he left the door to go to the kitchen to see Mama. I wasn't really being untruthful; I just wasn't ready to talk about anything.

I guess Daddy was worried about something too, because in a few minutes he exploded.

I couldn't understand much of what he was saying, because Mama kept saying Jim Jim Jim, but I heard this much. He was damned if he'd ever sit through another one of old Will Jackson's long-assed prayers again and Mama said Jim! again and Daddy said "That's right! I won't, not if it harelips all of Arkansas. A tree is known by its fruit, isn't it? He raised him! He made him the blob of sadistic idiocy that he is!"

I didn't like Will Jackson's prayers, either. Besides looking like the North Wind and standing up when he prayed, he always said the same things. About the widows and orphans and how bad we needed rain. At the end he always reminded God to take care of us as we tabernickle here in these low grounds of sin and sorrow. That was how we'd come to name the little house at the schoolbus stop.

"The right word is taber*nacle*," Daddy had said. "And it means a temporary shelter."

But after that the little shelter at the crossroads where we waited for the schoolbus was always a tabernickle. We loved to call it that, and nobody in the world could have made us change the way we said it.

I went in to set the table for supper.

"Mama!" I called out that night from the washtub behind the stove. "Mama, do you think I could have some ducks?"

"Some what? I can't hear you!" In the living room Mama turned the radio down and came into the kitchen and stuck her head around the stove. "What do you want?"

"Some ducks. May I have some ducks?"

"Some *ducks?*" Mama frowned. "Well, I hadn't really thought about getting you any. Why in the world would you want *ducks?* What brought that about?"

I scrubbed the bottom of one foot.

"Mosquito said you had some ducks when you were a little girl."

"Some *ducks?*" Mama said again. "I never owned a duck in my life. Not that there's anything wrong with ducks, of course, but I never owned one. What in the world made her say that? You must have misunderstood."

I lifted the other foot. "She was talking to some other teachers today, and she said that you were a sweet little girl and that you drove your ducks to a bad market. I may be stupid, but I'm not deaf." I held both legs over the edge of the washtub and slid down until only my nose was above the water. Then I sat up and looked around for Mama.

Mama was still standing by the stove, but she wasn't saying anything and her fingers were making little pleats in her skirt.

"Silly," she said then. "That doesn't mean that I really had a bunch of ducks. That's just something people say when— Well, that's just her opinion." She reached for the towel she'd hung on the back of a chair. "You hurry and get out of that tub. You're dripping all over the floor."

I stepped out of the tub and dried off. Mama started back toward the living room. As I reached for my gown, I thought of something else.

"Mama!" I called again. "Mama, does Josie have worms?"

Mama came back to the kitchen door. "Good Heavens, how would I know? What's the matter with you tonight?"

"Oh, nothing."

I stood there for a moment holding my gown and remembering the time that Aunt Neevy had said that old Peanut had worms and we had given him a bottle of turpentine and it had made him worse.

Josie was too fat to run around the house in circles the way old Peanut did.

You can see how, by Friday, I had forgotten all about Recitation Day. I hadn't remembered a thing about it until, on Friday after lunch, Mosquito started calling on people. And I knew I had to think of something. I had to come up with something quick, or I'd be dead.

I was lucky. Mine was the last name Mosquito called that day, and by that time I'd remembered something to tell. It was a book I'd found in Mama's trunk one rainy day.

I stood beside my desk and looked around the room.

"It's this book that I read this summer, that I'm going to tell." I hitched up my bloomer leg and looked at Mosquito. She sighed, and her look at me said I-know-you-didn't-read-a-real-book, but she nodded for me to go ahead.

"The name of the book was *Bad Girl*. And it's about this boy and girl who—"

"Thorpe!" Mosquito's voice crackled through the air and my other bloomer leg fell. I told Mama they were miles too big when she was making them.

"You may be seated, please." Mosquito looked like I'd scared her. "That's enough."

"But that's not all, at all. I only just started. They didn't have any money, this boy and girl, and she had this ba—"

Mosquito shoved me down into my seat so hard that the cracked place in it pinched me.

I stood back up and let both legs drag. "There was this doctor in the book who wanted to—"

Mosquito stood over me, and her fingers dug into my shoulders. Her face was red as she dragged me out into the hall and stood me against the wall.

"You stand here until I dismiss the rest of the class and have time to talk to you! Don't come back inside this room until you can think and talk like a decent little girl! Until you can say I'm sorry."

The door to the classroom closed behind her, and I stood against the wall, disgraced and outcast.

When the bell rang, the kids all filed past without looking at me. I knew, then, what was wrong and what I had to do. It wasn't my fault, but I would do it.

I turned the knob gently to open the door, and stuck my head inside.

Mosquito looked up from her desk. "Well?"

"I'm sorry," I said. "I'm sorry I let both legs drag when I was up telling the story, but they really are too big, you know. I tried to tell Mama, when she was making them."

I fled down the hall and out the door to the bus that Leo had kept loaded and waiting.

124

"You knew."

Martin sat on his steps scraping the mud from his good shoes. He walked a lot and his shoes were always getting muddy. James opened his pocket knife to help Martin scrape mud. I went inside the house and came back with a wet rag to wash the shoes. We all three sat on Martin's steps and cleaned his shoes. It was a beautiful Saturday morning, with the pinoak and sweetgum and hickory trees around us all red and yellow. The sky was clear and blue.

"You know that little girls don't read the kind of books mothers hide in trunks. When you found it in Venie's trunk, you knew better. It was your fault, you know, and had nothing at all to do with your, ah, clothes. But what impelled you—" Martin looked down at me and shook his head. Then he said "Ah" and put his shoe down and let his hand rest on my head for a second. He said "Ah, Thorpe" again, and got up and went inside his house.

In a few minutes he came back out and handed me a book. "Here, try this one. Maybe we're taking you too fast." He smiled at James, who nodded. "And the next time you want to give a book report in school, maybe you'd better ask your father—or me—for advice, if you're tempted to use the ones you find in Venie's trunk. Okay?"

"She's stupid," James said. "It was a damn fool thing to do."

"Oh, not that bad," Martin smiled at James again. "And I'll bet that calling her stupid is a privilege you don't grant to anyone else."

"I'm sorry." Which was something James never said to anybody but Martin.

On the way home, James said that in the sixth grade they could show things on Recitation Day and tell about them. "Why don't you be safe and take something from home to show next week?" he asked. "Just to be safe and not get caught with your pants down."

"That's crude. Daddy said never be crude to your little sister."

But I liked his idea. I already knew exactly what I'd take. It was in my cigar box of treasures under my bed, and I would have bet there wasn't another kid in the first grade who had one.

On Friday morning while Mama poured the oatmeal and Daddy polished our shoes and shook his head over the holes, I stood around feeling in my pockets to be sure I had it. It felt dry and scratchy, and how could I help but please Mosquito this time?

"Mama, why can't I take one of Eloise's pictures to Leo? He is so nice. . . ." I watched her look into the sugar bowl to see if it needed filling.

"Because. Get your hands out of your pockets before you tear them off." She cut the cinnamon bread she'd made yesterday into thick slices. "Eat your breakfast and forget about Eloise and Leo. It's none of your business to be—"

"Watch it," Daddy said, setting my shoes over by James' to dry. "Unless you want her *really* asking questions."

I stirred my oatmeal and wondered how I could forget about Eloise and Leo. You don't just forget about your friends. But I did sort of forget about them, because it was time to go and I was going to do the right thing this Recitation Day and please everybody. With what I had taken from under my bed and put into my pocket, before breakfast.

"This is a owl foot. From a real owl." I took it from my pocket and pulled the tendon thing sticking out of it. The toes curled and uncurled. The girls all screamed and the boys looked jealous. "My best friend gave it to me, and he has the other one."

"Oh, how nice!" I could feel Mosquito relaxing. "Can you tell us something about it?"

"Yes, ma'am. His uncle shot it and cut off the feet. My best friend's uncle."

"Tell us about the little friend who gave it to you. What's his name? Where does he live? Does he go to school?"

"Yes, ma'am. But not here at this school. He lives down in the woods and his name's Theotus and he goes to Washington Carver."

I stood out in the hall in disgrace again, and I wondered about it while the other kids marched past me. Could it have been the damned bloomers again? I sighed and wished for the thousandth time for nice fat legs like Dawn Starr's.

Junie Thompson bumped me with her dinner bucket as she went by. "Nigger-lover," she hissed, and I knew what was wrong. I was not supposed to be friends with Thee. Mosquito had thrown me a stick and I'd run the wrong way, exactly like old Peanut. That was what Mama and James and everybody else had been trying to tell me. You couldn't be friends with nigras. Not if you wanted to be friends with white kids.

Maybe they wouldn't let me go to school here any more, with James. Maybe they'd take me out of school and let me grow up ignorant. I leaned against the wall and hoped that they would.

Mosquito stood in the door tapping her yellow nickel pencil against her big white teeth. When the other kids had all gone she looked down at me.

"Go on home." She sounded tired. "Just go on home. I don't know what to do. Get your sweater and go to your bus."

Back in the room we each gathered up our things and I followed her down the hall and watched her disappear into Mr. Whitehall's office.

James was standing outside the bus waiting for me. He'd already heard.

"Get on the bus," he whispered fiercely. "Fool!"

"We-elll," Daddy said the next morning. "This thing has reached a kind of situation, I believe, between you and Miss Keeter. And you can read, if given the opportunity, so maybe it's time to prove it."

I had followed Daddy from the living room onto the front porch, and we sat there and watched the clouds making pictures over us and talked about Recitation Day.

"Dammit," Daddy said. "Why didn't you tell them something from your Shakespeare book?"

"Because she'd never have believed that. She doesn't think I can read it, see? Most of the time she just kind of skips over me, and so she hasn't found out whether I can read at *all*."

"I expect she will eventually."

Daddy got up and went in the house, and when he came back out he had on his good clothes. He started down the steps.

"Are you going somewhere?" Mama stood in the door with a dishtowel in her hand. At the gate, Daddy stopped and looked back at us.

"I'm going to Wellco. I'll be home by noon."

"To Wellco? At this time of day? What for? Why?"

Daddy opened the car door and shouted over the top of the car to Mama. "I'm going to find Mr. Bond and talk to him about a little school business!"

"School business? You don't have any school business now!"

"Oh yes, I still have an interest in it," Daddy said. He got in the car and looked back at us and drove off.

Mama and I watched him turn at the mailbox. We went back into the house wondering about Daddy's school business. In his room, James heard us, and called out that maybe Daddy was going to be a principal somewhere again. I said I hoped not because I didn't want to leave the breezeway house and James said Stupid and Mama said for both of us to hush and go out and rake the leaves off the front yard.

Nobody had told Mama about the owl foot, and so I couldn't tell her why, on Monday morning, I didn't want to go to school. She felt my forehead and looked at my throat, and said I'd better go on to school.

Sure enough, when the bell rang for recess that Monday morning, Mosquito told me to get back into my seat and stay in the room.

Mosquito sat at her desk and ignored me. She kept looking down at her little brown register, and back at my desk. I wanted somebody there with me so bad I couldn't breathe deep. I would have settled for Billy Bob Jackson's face in the door right then, just to see somebody I knew. Then the door opened and Mosquito looked up and smiled so sweet it was like a bow and said, "Hello, Mister Bond!"

The fat man with white hair who stood in the door didn't smile back at her. He only grunted and came on across the room to me, and I felt better already, because I knew somehow that he didn't like her much either. He stood beside my desk and looked down at me for a minute, before he put his hand on the top of my head.

"Don't be frightened, Thorpe," he said. "You are Thorpe, aren't you?"

If Mama could have looked in my throat then, she wouldn't have made me go to school, because she would have seen this big hard lump that had come from somewhere and couldn't be swallowed back. I gazed up at the man with white hair and nodded.

"I'm Mister Bond," he said. "And I'm only going to talk to you, so don't be frightened." He looked around at Mosquito, and then back down at me. "Would you like to come down the hall to Mr. Whitehall's office with me?"

Of course I wouldn't *like* to. I'd like to go home. Or go hide in my ditch. I stood up and hitched at my bloomer legs and we went out the door. Because I knew who Mr. Bond was, of course. He was the County School Superintendent. I had seen him coming and going from the schoolhouse last year when Daddy was there. He was over all of the schools in the county. We went down the hall to Mr. Whitehall's office.

They were going to send me away to another county, because I wasn't fit to be in this one. They were going to make me sign a paper saying that I couldn't really read *Tales from Shakespeare* and that I would never again stand up before the whole room and say my best friend went to Washington Carver School. They were going to——

"This is Miss Simpson, our health nurse, Thorpe." Mr. Bond sat down in Mr. Whitehall's chair, and Mr. Whitehall, who had been looking out the window, looked around for a place to sit and couldn't find one, because Miss Simpson was in the other chair.

I knew who Miss Simpson was, too. I had seen her coming and going from the schoolhouse last year, and she had given James a typhoid shot that had made him sick. She had made the whole room sick.

"Thorpe, you sit here." Miss Simpson stood up. She had on a stiff white uniform like Trudy wore and she smelled like face powder and iodine. Her hair was gray and crinkly and her face was kind.

And the tests. The tests weren't anything at all except the kind of games that Daddy played with me nearly every night.

Out in the hall, later, as I waited for them to decide what to do with me, I could hear them talking.

"She really should be in the fourth, or maybe even the fifth," Miss Simpson said.

Nobody said anything, and I could almost hear Miss Simpson's pencil tapping her teeth, like Mosquito did when she was thinking.

"Oh, I don't know about that," Mr. Bond said. "Let's don't go overboard. This thing will set a precedent, you know. I'd say third, or maybe second."

"Second," Miss Simpson said, "will present no challenge at all to that child, I tell you. And you'll end up with the same situation."

And they'd told me not to be frightened! The way their voices sounded, you'd think they were all in there deciding on what to get me for my birthday, instead of whether to send me off to the third—or the fifth county!

Miss Simpson came to the door and called me. All that I could think of as I went back into the office was that I hoped that Mama would come with me. But I doubted that she would. She wouldn't even go anywhere else with Daddy to live.

"How would you like to be in the third grade, Thorpe?" Miss Simpson smiled and tapped her pencil against her teeth and looked down at me. "Why are you shaking? Oh, child, did we frighten you?" She put her arm around me. "Wouldn't you like to be in the third grade?"

I had to swallow three times before I could answer her.

"You—you mean in Miss Wooley's room? In the same grade as Dawn Starr?"

"Well, I don't know who Dawn Starr is," Miss Simpson said. "But if she's in the third grade, yes. In Miss Wooley's room."

I felt a little bad about Mosquito disliking me so much that she had asked for the whole second grade to be put between us, but mostly I was so relieved that it wasn't something worse that I was glad.

As I went back to Mosquito's room for my books and papers I was already aching for Tuesday to come, so we could have recess and I could be called. Because in the third grade, you were big enough to play Red Rover.

> Red Rover, Red Rover,
> Let Thorpe come over! . . .

It was a good dream.

9

Miss Wooley was soft and pretty like Mama. She smelled like flowers and like the spices Mama used in pies. She laughed a lot and played games with us, and she always had a clean, flowered handkerchief to wipe our eyes. If, in our games, she tore her stocking or got mud on her dress, she'd laugh and say don't worry about it. She had long red hair that hung down on her shoulders and curled up on the ends.

I guess Mosquito had told her to be careful about Recitation Day, because she came around that first week with a poem for me to learn for Friday. I learned it and said it on Friday and after that we didn't have any mix-ups. I learned a lot of poems that winter.

At recess the kids let me hang onto the end of the Red Rover line, and I hung onto the end of the line every time they let me. Hoping and praying, with my fingers crossed and sometimes my legs, because if I ran inside to the bathroom they might call let Thorpe come over! while I was gone.

At the tabernickle, though, nothing had changed. Thee still sat on his stump every morning, and we still rode past his schoolhouse twice a day. The schoolhouse sat there, gray and ugly, and there wasn't anything you could do about it except look the other way. It was like a stone bruise on your foot from jumping off the porch. You lived with it and you hopped around on it and tried to forget that it hurt. But there was a difference. You knew that a stone bruise would go away and the ugly, ragged schoolhouse would never go away. It sat there, like the wart on Aunt Neevy's chin that was another of the things God had wanted that way, and you learned not to look at it.

With the new happiness I had found with Miss Wooley, the days and the weeks began to pass more quickly. More of the red and yellow leaves fell from the trees and we didn't have as much time to play in the evenings before dark and one morning there was ice in the water bucket on the back porch.

Daddy came out into the yard to get a fresh bucket of water, and he called to us—to Thee and Josie and me—to come and see the wild geese flying over. We left the hopscotch game we had drawn in the sunny spot behind the smokehouse and went to watch the wild geese with Daddy.

"They're stragglers," Daddy said. "Hurrying to catch the rest of their flock before winter gets here." He picked up his bucket of water and started to the house. Then he turned back to us. "You might find some persimmons fallen to the ground down along the trail to Martin's house," he said. "You might pick up a bucketful for Peccavi to eat."

We did. Daddy went with us, and we spent the whole morning picking up persimmons, chinquapins and hickory nuts. We kept the nuts, but old Peck got all the persimmons, because they weren't ready for us to eat yet. They were still sharp-tasting and too hard, and they puckered your mouth.

"You know," Mama said while we were eating lunch, "I'd like to get out and walk through the woods while they're still pretty. I think we'll just walk over and visit Sister Mearl this afternoon, Thorpe and I. It's no wonder she doesn't get out and go very much, if everybody else in the community has been as lax as I have about visiting her. She's going to get the idea that she's not welcome."

"Now I don't know where she'd get an idea like that," Daddy said. "But I'll tell you what. If you'll go, James and I will do the dishes. Won't we, James?"

James didn't look too happy, but he didn't argue. Not with Daddy. After lunch Mama brushed my hair and we started for Sister Mearl's house. We went through the woods and cut across

Uncle Elmer's cotton field and ended up at Sister Mearl's back gate.

I wanted to go in through the back gate so we could look at her bottles and sandbags again, but Mama said you were supposed to use the front entrance when you went calling.

Brother Mearl's car was gone and nobody was in the yard, but inside the house somebody was singing. We could hear Sister Mearl singing before we opened the front gate. We went up the walk and knocked on the door.

> *"Walk down to the altar*
> *And buy your ticket*
> *And get on the Glo-ree train!*
> *Walk down to the altar*
> *And buy your ticket——"*

Mama knocked again.

"Come in!" Sister Mearl called out to us. "It's not locked!" She kept singing.

> *"Better hurry, sister,*
> *Throw away that paint*
> *And get on the Glo-ree train!"*

Mama stood on the porch a minute, looking around. She opened the door and I followed her into Sister Mearl's front room.

Sister Mearl was sitting in a rocking chair by the window. She was rocking back and forth as she sang, and when she rocked backward her feet came up from the floor. Her yellow hair was hanging down around her shoulders and she was wearing those blue cotton men's pants that Aunt Neevy had told Mama about last week. On the table beside her chair was a medicine bottle with a little pink stuff left in the bottom. When she saw us Sister Mearl stood up and waved the empty glass she was holding. Then she felt behind her for her chair and sat down again real fast.

"Sister Torrance!" She put the glass on the table with the bottle. "Come in! No—" she wiped her hand over her face. "Have a chair, thass it. Have a chair. There's lots of 'em in here. Have one."

Mama kind of sank down into a big wine-colored chair. She kept looking at Sister Mearl and didn't say a word. I went over to

133

stand beside Sister Mearl's chair. After a minute or two of nobody saying anything, I eased my hand over to the bottle and picked it up to read the words on it.

"Put that back, Thorpe!" Mama's voice was sharp. "You know better than to meddle!"

"Well, hi there Thorpe!" Sister Mearl ran her fingers through her tangled hair and lifted it up and tried to put it in a knot. It fell back down. "Excuse me, Sister Torrance, I'm not dressed for comp'ny. Cause I never have any, thass why. 'Cep' li'l Thorpe, here. An' she probly won't be aroun' any more, since she started to school. You are in the firs' grade now, aren't you, honey?"

"No ma'am," I said. "I'm in the third grade." I couldn't read the name of the medicine in the bottle, but underneath the name it said *For That Rundown Feeling*.

Sister Mearl looked at me. She picked up her glass and peered through it at me. "If you say you're a third-grader, you are. But I din' know I'd been married to him that long!" She sighed. "Time sure passes, don' it, Sister Torrance. You know wha' we need? Some good hot coffee."

"Oh no." Mama took her white handkerchief from her pocket but she didn't use it. She twisted it and looked down at it. "Don't bother. We can't stay. We just ran by for a minute."

"No bother." Sister Mearl got up and started into the kitchen and bumped into the door facing. She stepped back and looked at it. "Who put that thing right there in the door? Now you jus' sit still, Sister Torrance, an' we'll have that coffee in no time."

Mama nodded and looked worried. I went across the room and looked at Sister Mearl's rifle hanging over the fireplace. In the kitchen we could hear drawers and doors slamming and pots and dishes rattling.

I liked Sister Mearl. Maybe like James said, sometimes at church she looked like Brother Mearl had jammed her hat down over her head and dragged her to the car and maybe she did nod when old Will's prayers were too long, but I liked her. When I grew up I might be a sharpshooter in a carnival instead of a working girl like Eloise. I thought of the time Eloise had taken us to the carnival in Wellco, and I went over and sat down on the scratchy wine-colored couch and thought about Sister Mearl. I could see the bright lights and the Ferris wheel and hear the men calling to us from their tents. I could almost see Sister Mearl in her bright green shirt and her tight men's pants, holding her rifle and offering to outshoot any man in town.

"I can't fin' the perco-latel." Sister Mearl stood in the door. She rubbed her hand across her face. "I know iss in there somewhere. But after I take my tonic I can't remember where I put things."

Mama went to the kitchen door and put her hand on Sister Mearl's arm. "You just forget about that old coffee and come over here and sit down. Let's visit. We don't need coffee."

They sat down on the couch and looked at each other.

Sister Mearl spoke first. "You're a good woman, Sister Torrance. It's this tonic. You know that, don't you?" She rubbed her head again. "I never had a headache in my life till I got converted."

"Well," Mama said. "I expect a lot of people take wine tonic. My mother used to take it. You just took a little too much."

Sister Mearl moved back into her rocking chair. "Ever'thing's too much. It's this bein' converted, thass what it is. You know, Sister Torrance, I'm havin' an awful hard time keepin' my seat on that Glory train!" She started rocking again. "Sometimes I wanna jump off. Offa the Glory train. An' I go out in the back yard an' I shoot the necks offa all the bottles I can fin'." She looked at the tonic bottle. "I bet this stuff rots your guts the same as any ol' white lightnin."

"Maybe you ought to take something else for your headaches. Why don't you go and lie down and get over this one, so you can come home with us for dinner tomorrow?"

Sister Mearl rocked for a while without answering Mama. "Brother Mearl's the only man I ever knew offered to marry me. You know that?"

"Well," Mama said. "Well."

"Been lotsa men offered me lotsa things. Ever since I lef that ol' catfish-eatin' swamp when I was sixteen. You know how I lef that swamp, Sister Torrance? I lef with a real, honest-to-Pete gamblin' man! Jus like in the song." She started singing again.

> "Oh, mother, dear mo-ther, you know I love you well,
> But th' love I have for this gam-blin man
> Is more than tongue can tell."

135

Mama stood up. "We'd better run along, so you can go and lie down. Would you like me to find your percolator and make some coffee before we go?"

"No coffee. But jus tell me one thing before you go, Sister Torrance. You're a good woman. Can I sit by you on th' Glory train, a person like me? Do you think I can stay on that bloomin' train?"

"Of course you can." Mama picked up her purse. "And I'm going to expect you for dinner tomorrow."

We stood there for a minute trying to say goodbye, but Sister Mearl was rocking again, faster and faster. She rocked and her feet went higher and higher as her chair went back, and then she reached up into the air and closed her hand around something that wasn't there and pulled down.

"Whooooo-eeeeee. . . ." She sounded like a train whistle at night.

> *"Walk down to the altar*
> *And buy your ticket*
> *And get on the Glory train. . . ."*

We eased out the door and down the walk.

When we'd reached Uncle Elmer's fence again, Mama stopped.

"We'll turn here," she said. "And go by Neevy's house for that cup of coffee. And we won't say a word about Sister Mearl's Glory Train. Not a word, remember. We'll just say that we were out gathering nuts and decided to stop by."

"But where are our nuts?" I followed along the fence behind Mama.

"We didn't find any," she said.

The evenings got shorter every day. We noticed the short evenings especially on Wednesdays, because by the time we left Miss Mildred's house and walked down the railroad track, the sun was down before we started through the tie yard toward home.

One Wednesday when I went to Miss Mildred's, Callie was sitting in the porch swing, and so I knew that Miss Una was there visiting. I liked the days that Miss Una visited, because I always had coffee with them, and sometimes we had cake or cookies. It was much nicer than when Brother Mearl was there, because then all we ever had was prayer.

"Hi, Callie," I said as I went up onto the porch.

Callie looked at me and didn't answer, but I hadn't expected her to. I was glad she didn't, because I was afraid of Callie. Something about her bothered me. Maybe it was her eyes, and the way she looked at you without showing a thing she was feeling inside. Or maybe it was her big tan hands and the way they closed onto Miss Una's shoulder and turned her around. I stepped out of my shoes and left them outside the door and went into the house.

When I came into the front room Miss Una jumped and sloshed her coffee onto the arm of her chair. Miss Una looked more than ever like a little bird that day. It was hard to believe that she was Miss Mildred's baby sister. She looked a lot older.

"It's all right, honey," Miss Mildred said from the couch. "It's Thorpe come to take her piano lesson." She went over to Miss Una's chair and wiped the faded green velvet with her napkin before she rang the little bell that called Trudy.

Trudy had seen me from the kitchen window, and she came into the living room with a cup of coffee for me. It was really warm milk with a little coffee and a lot of sugar in it, but it was warm and sweet and it made you feel good to sit and drink it with them. We sat around the little low round table that held the blackened silver tray Trudy always brought in, and nobody said much.

Outside, the porch swing creaked with Callie, and in the kitchen Trudy rattled pots and pans, and we rocked and sipped. Through the window came the sound of James and Miss Mildred's boys playing cat-a-bat, but it was like sounds you hear in a dream. Just pieces of words and yells muffled by the wind.

Every time Miss Una set her cup back down on the little table, some of the coffee spilled over into her saucer. Her head bobbed up and down as her face quivered and trembled, and her hands fluttered back and forth like she was talking without making any sound. Sometimes when Miss Una visited, she would sit there the whole time without saying a word, just nodding and shaking and trying to smile. I had about decided that we were in for one of those days without a word from Miss Una when she spoke.

"My boys never get to play, to play like that."

She was talking about James and Winfred and Wilbur playing outside. She fluttered one little hand toward the drapes that were closed over the windows. "They always had to work," she said. "Because Will, Will, he thought that was what counted. Earn more, more money, and buy, buy more land, more land, and cut more timber and wait. Wait for the oil, oil leases to sell——"

Miss Mildred went over and patted her sister on her round little shoulders.

"It's all right now, honey," she said. "Everything's all right now. They're grown now, your boys, and they can do what they want."

Miss Una nodded. "That's what, that's what hurts. All that land and timber and oil, oil money, that they worked like nigras and got whipped like dogs, like dogs for, and—and there's Thad, stayin' in the Army and John Tom, John Tom don't even write."

"Miss Una," I said. "I have a new teacher in school."

Miss Una didn't answer. Miss Mildred and I talked about school for a while, before I tried again. I got up and went to the piano.

"Miss Una, would you like me to play 'Rock of Ages' for you now?"

Miss Una still didn't act like she'd heard me. "And Billy, Billy Bob," she said. "He, he got knocked around by all, by all of them. And I had to take up for him, didn't I? He's my, he's my baby. He's all I've got left . . ."

"Would you like me to play 'Jesus Lover of My Soul'?" I still stood at the piano.

"Someday," Miss Una said, and she looked toward the door. "Someday I'm going to run, to run away. You know that, don't you?" She looked around toward Miss Mildred. "You do believe me, don't you?"

Miss Mildred didn't answer. She stood there over Miss Una's chair and kept patting her shoulders.

"I will. I'll go, I'll go, someday, where Will Jackson can't ever, can't ever find me. Because I'll keep tryin'." She looked toward the sound of the porch swing creaking and nodded. "Old black Callie, she'll turn, she'll turn her back, and when she looks around, I'll be, I'll be gone. And then he can have, old black, old black Callie in his, in his parlor! That's the only room she don't—"

Miss Mildred put her hand over Miss Una's mouth, gently, and nodded to me. I sat down at the piano, and I played "Rock of Ages" and "Jesus Lover of My Soul" all the way through two times. Because they were the only church songs that I could play yet. But that didn't matter that day, because they were Miss Una's favorites, and that was why I had learned them.

Miss Una leaned back in the rocking chair and closed her eyes. Her hands fluttered a little bit, but nothing else about her moved. She listened until I had played through the songs two more times. Then she picked up her purse from the floor beside her chair, opened it and fumbled around inside. She smiled and nodded and brought out this red bandanna handkerchief tied in a bundle.

"Here," she said. "This is, this is for you." She held a quarter toward me.

"Oh, no," I said. "You don't have to pay me."

"Take it." She reached over to the piano bench and laid the quarter on it. "I'm not paying you. I'm, I'm giving it to you. And it's good money. Nobody got, nobody got cheated or whipped to, to earn it. It's my egg, my egg money, and I can do, I can do what I want to with it."

"You should take it to the bank," Miss Mildred said, and shook her head. "You must have forty or fifty dollars there."

"Seventy-five, a hundred." Miss Una looked down into her purse. "And there's some more, some more handkerchiefs-full in here. And it don't, it don't belong to any bank. It belongs to me, to *me!*" She looked around at us, scared. "You won't, you won't tell will you?"

We had been through this money talk before. Sometimes it was two hundred dollars she said was in her bandanna—sometimes one hundred. And sometimes it was only seventy-five.

"Callie!" Miss Mildred had stepped to the front door. "Miss Una's ready to go home now."

Callie came in and went to the closet for Miss Una's shawl, and Miss Una started shaking again, but nobody asked why or said anything about it. Callie put the knitted shawl around Miss Una's shoulders and turned her toward the door.

"Your new shawl turned out real pretty," Miss Mildred said. She tucked it up around Miss Una's face. "I'm glad you got it finished. The wind's cold out."

Miss Una tried to smile. "Well, of course I got, I got it finished. I still have my hands, you know." She held her little bird-claw hands out and looked at them. "It's my soul, my soul that's gone . . . gone, gone . . ." Her voice trailed off.

At the door she pulled loose from Callie's big hand and turned back to us.

"He, he had to fight back, you know," she said. "And I had to take up for him. Didn't I? He's my, he's my baby, and some-body was always knockin' him around . . ."

Callie pulled her out the door and down the walk. Miss Mildred stood and watched them. When they reached the end of the walk, she smiled down at me.

"Shall we begin?" she asked. "Maybe we'd better have a short lesson today. The evenings are getting shorter, aren't they, and Venie might start worrying if you're not home by dark."

Miss Mildred was right. The evenings were a lot shorter, and the rain that fell almost every day was cold and sad. Not like the warm happy rains we'd had when school first started. Down at the tie yard there was frost on the rails of the railroad track, and once when Soggum Thompson dared me I put my tongue on a frosty rail and it stuck and made my tongue sore. James called me a fool again and said he ought to scob my noggin hard, but my tongue got well before Soggum's jaw did.

Mama's flowers and the other things out in the garden all hud-dled away from the cold and turned brown and died. When there wasn't anything left in the garden, we had to start eating from the jars of stuff that Mama and Donie had canned in the summer. There just wasn't much money for food. Old Will Jackson hadn't closed the mill down but he only had it running two days a week.

The frosty mornings were cold. We wore both coats and sweat-ers to school instead of just sweaters. Mama worried about the cold lunches we had to eat at school, and twice a week she baked bread to make sandwiches for us because we didn't have enough money to keep bought bread and she knew that nobody took biscuits to school.

Every morning Thee was sitting on his sweetgum stump with red clay caked on his bare feet. Donie had told Mama that there wasn't enough work at the tie yard for Mister Billy Bob to need Lewis any more, and so they didn't have any money either. Not even for shoes for Thee. Every morning I looked at Thee's feet and hoped that Trudy would bring him some shoes that day. Lewis worked around for the farmers and nearly every evening he passed our house with a bucket of syrup or a big greasy bag of meat or something, but he never brought home any shoes.

"Don't worry about them," Mama said one evening. "I expect they're eating better than we are!"

"It's not their eating that bothers me." I sliced the apple she had handed across the table to me. "It's Thee's feet that bother me. They look so bare and cold and muddy. Mama, could we buy him some shoes?"

"Don't be silly. We can't even buy shoes for you and James!" Mama handed me another apple to slice and looked cross.

It was the evening before Thanksgiving, and we were in the kitchen making pies. Mama waved her knife toward the sound of Daddy's hammer in the living room.

"Don't you hear that? Don't you know what he's doing right now?"

Daddy had been out all day looking for a better job. He had come home looking cold, and sad and hungry. Now he had had supper. He was in the living room singing as he resoled mine and James' shoes.

> *"Down under the we-eping willow,*
> *Down where the sweet violets bloom,*
> *There lies a fai-air young maiden,*
> *A-sleeping i-in her tomb."*

It was a sad song, but it made me feel happy to hear Daddy singing it. Mama used to sing with him. She never did any more.

"But don't we have some kind of old shoes, Mama? Just some of James' old shoes that Daddy could fix for him?"

"We wear our old shoes, Thorpe. For as long as they hold together." Mama put her knife on the table and sat there looking across at me. "Thorpe, Theotus doesn't feel the cold like you do, because he's never known anything else. He doesn't really mind it." She reached for an apple from the blue bowl and started peeling again. "I don't guess Theotus has ever had very many pairs of shoes that were bought brand-new just for him. And if people haven't ever known anything better, they don't feel miserable with what they have. You only miss something you had and lost."

Mama sat there holding the half-peeled apple and looking down at the table but not really seeing it, and I knew that she was thinking of the yellow house in Strawne with the shiny green stove and a real bathroom and an iceman. Right then I wanted Daddy to go to Will Jackson and promise to take the awful White Supremacy no matter how bitter it was, to make everything all right so that we could get Mama back into the yellow house before the baby came.

I left half an apple on the table, unsliced, and went around the table to her. I put my hand on her shoulder, but all I could think of to say was I love you and I wanted to say a lot more than that. I stood there beside Mama's chair, and we were both quiet.

"Where's the milk bucket?"

Daddy had put his hammer aside and had come into the kitchen. Since that awful night of shouting out at the well just before school started, he had been doing all of the milking. He wouldn't even let Mama touch the bucket. Not even to pour the milk out and strain it.

"In the pantry, where you put it. Where it always is." Mama didn't look up. She was still in the yellow house in Strawne.

Daddy took the milk bucket and left the kitchen and James came down through the hall and went out the back door. It made me kind of sad about James. He was growing up a little bit; he was getting pretty good about filling the water tank on the side of the cookstove without being told.

"Go back to your apple-slicing, Thorpe," Mama said. "You're getting behind." She started peeling again.

James came into the kitchen with a bucket of water, and I sneaked him a slice of apple that I had dipped into the sugar bowl and he started back out chewing it. At the door, he stopped and we grinned at each other. From the barn we could hear Daddy.

"Back that leg, dammit!" he shouted. "Stand still, dammit! Get away from there, dammit!"

"I wonder," James said. "If she ever remembers that her real name is Brownie? I bet she's forgotten."

IO

I knew when I woke up on Thanksgiving morning that it was going to be a good day. It *felt* like a good day. My bed felt soft and warm, and the sunshine coming through the windows into the cold corners of my room was extra bright. Something about the whole room was different, and better, but I didn't know what it was until I went into the kitchen.

Eloise was sitting at the kitchen table drinking coffee and watching Mama stir something on the stove.

"Didn't you know that I slept with you last night, Goosie?" Eloise kissed me, laughed, and lit a cigarette. I knew then what it was about my room and my bed. The bed had been still warm from Eloise, and her smell had still been in it and in the whole room—the smell of face powder and chewing gum and flowers and cigarettes. I always kept the same sheets on the bed for as long as Mama would let me after Eloise visited us.

She was Mama's baby sister and I wanted to be just like her when I grew up. Like Eloise, with her red hair and her red finger-nails and her thick, black eyelashes that fluttered up and down over the love and the laughter in her green eyes. That morning, she had on a shiny blue silk robe with feathers around the neck and down the front, and her shoes were red and gold with turned-up toes. She always had beautiful clothes.

143

I took my hotcakes from the back of the stove and sat there looking at Eloise's shoes. They were like a queen's shoes, and someday I meant to have some just like them. Eloise blew out a puff of smoke, sipped her coffee, and laughed at something Mama had said. I held my fork halfway to my mouth and looked down at her tiny feet in the red-and-gold shoes, and as I looked they began to blur. They turned into two brown feet with pink bottoms, each smearing mud onto the other one. Trying to rub away the cold.

"Wake up and eat your hotcakes," Mama said, but she didn't sound cross. Mama was always happy when Eloise came.

I wondered if Eloise could buy Thee a pair of shoes. I sighed and ate my hotcakes. It would make Mama cross if I asked Eloise to, and anyhow Trudy would buy them. Surely Trudy would.

Mama and Eloise drank some more coffee and talked and laughed and then we went into my room to clean it up. But instead they sat on the bed and talked and giggled some more. I went over to the dresser and put a lot of Eloise's stuff on my face and eyes, and we heard a car drive up out front.

"Oh my God." Mama jumped up and yanked the sheets up on one side of my bed. "Grab the other side, Eloise, and let's get this bed made up before Neevy comes in here and swears I never clean house. Get that stuff off your face, Thorpe! She'll swear you're immoral. I'm sorry, Eloise, I didn't mean that you are but let's get this bed smoothed up before Neevy comes in."

"Well holy cow, it's your bed, isn't it?" Eloise yanked the sheets straight and they smoothed the spread.

"Yes, but it's half her house, you know. And I swear she comes in looking for signs of neglect." Mama scrubbed at my mouth. "You know, you're lucky, Eloise. You got the little dab of money and you don't have to share this old house with Neevy. Stand still, Thorpe!"

"Oh, well, just tell her that you learned your memory verse and tithed last Sunday, and she'll forgive you," Eloise said. "Is she still committin' emotional adultrey with the preacher?" She stuffed her pajamas under the pillow.

"Eloise!" Mama frowned, then she laughed. "Anyhow, the word would be mental, or spiritual. Maybe intellectual."

"That's right." Eloise rubbed her little finger over the fresh

144

lipstick she'd just put on. "Neevy couldn't be emotional, even in adultrey, could she? And I bet anything intellectual puts a helluva strain on her—"

"Eloise!" Mama said again and hit her on the seat. Eloise wrinkled her nose and blew a puff of smoke out toward Aunt Neevy's voice in the hall, and they went out the door laughing to meet Aunt Neevy and Uncle Elmer and Dawn Starr.

Mama had on her blue silk dress, and Eloise had on a yellow silk dress with green flowers and a flounce at the bottom. They looked a lot alike except that Mama was fatter than Eloise. Mama looked like a picture of Eloise that had blurred a little. Because of James and me and the baby, I guess. But Mama and Eloise both could have crawled into the purple-flowered tent that Aunt Neevy had on. Aunt Neevy's dress didn't touch her anywhere.

Aunt Neevy looked clean, her face and her dress and all, but you couldn't help thinking about all that stuff with bones and wires and hooks and eyes that she wore underneath. She smelled clean, too, but not like flowers and powder. It was more like the gritty-gray Lava soap Daddy used on his hands when he came home from work at the mill.

Dawn Starr had all these fat Shirley Temple curls bouncing around her fat face and her dress had ruffles all over it. She had on new black patent-leather shoes with red cuffs around the tops, and Aunt Neevy was holding her coat. Dawn Starr's coat was bright blue and brand-new, because she had given her plaid one to me last spring.

There isn't too much to say about Uncle Elmer. There never was. Most of the time he wore striped overalls, and I can see him perched on a ladder painting the sign that said THORPE'S CHAPEL BAPTIST, but most of the time nobody really saw Uncle Elmer. Aunt Neevy was always telling him to stand up straight or not to mumble and after that you couldn't see anybody but her. She always nodded to him at mealtimes and after he said the blessing he kind of faded away.

On that Thanksgiving Day, Uncle Elmer didn't have on his striped overalls. He had on his gray suit and gray shirt and gray tie that he wore to church. Also he had on high-top black shoes that were knobby on the toes.

I was looking at everybody's shoes that Thanksgiving Day.

Aunt Neevy believed in folks eating dinner at dinnertime. She was always saying so, and she had started setting the table as soon as she got her coat off. After Aunt Neevy came Mama, and Eloise bustled around the kitchen, hurrying dinner.

"Venie!" Aunt Neevy held one of Mama's blue-flowered plates up closer to her face and looked at it. "You've cracked one of these good plates!"

"I always break dishes when I'm pregnant." Mama reached back into the oven for the little turkey she had bought at Mr. Byrd's. The smallest one he had. "Some folks crave dill pickles, but when I'm pregnant, I always—"

"Venie!" Aunt Neevy looked toward my bedroom door. Because Dawn Starr had disappeared through it. "Use another word, please!" She looked at the turkey Mama was moving onto a platter. "My, is that a turkey or a *chicken?* I should have brought a ham, I guess. We have some good ones in the smokehouse this year."

"Yes, you should have." Eloise took Mama's Sunday silverware from the chest. "Why didn't you bring us a good old sugar-cured hickory-smoked ham?"

"Well," Aunt Neevy looked down at the plate again. "I just never thought about Venie's turkey being this little. . . . I guess it's all right to break all your dishes when you're that way if you can afford to. Why do you use your good dishes every day, Venie? Don't you have any old ones?"

"No." Mama laughed. "I've already broken all of them. No, really, Neevy, I just like to use the pretty ones, and I don't *mean* to break them."

"Well, good G— good heavens," Eloise butted in. "What's all this beef about a cracked plate? They're Venie's dishes. If she wants to use them for chamber pots and throw them over the fence, I don't see what—"

"I wish you wouldn't talk like a toughie, Eloise." Aunt Neevy said. "Especially around the children." She fanned in front of her face and Eloise wrinkled her nose again and put her cigarette out.

When she finally had us all seated around the table, Aunt Neevy nodded to Uncle Elmer. He said the blessing and faded

146

away, and everybody started passing food and talking about different things.

"Isn't it awful, Jim," Eloise looked up from her plate at Daddy, "what that devil Mussolini's doing to those poor Ethiopians?"

"It is, Eloise." Daddy passed the bread to James. "It's—"

"Oh, them?" Aunt Neevy looked up from her turkey. "Just a bunch of Catholics and heathens. All them Eyetalians are Catholics, you know. Pope-worshipers. So as long as they're just killin heathens, an' it's not in our country, I say let all of 'em alone. Here in our country we—"

"Here in our country," Daddy said, "we do it more gently. We go to church and sing songs about love while they die from ignorance and malnutrition. Now and then we hang one, or burn one, but mostly we sing while they starve."

Aunt Neevy's mouth got tight. "If you're talkin' about our nigras, why I don't know of many that ever starved to death. Not if they're willin' to work. You look too hard for evil, Jim. The soul of the wicked desireth evil; his neighbor findeth no favor in his eyes. That's from Proverbs, chapter—"

"We know," Daddy said. "And have you read this one? Eat not the bread of him that hath an evil eye. The morsel which thou hast eaten shalt thou vomit up and lose thy sweet words."

"Jim!" Mama held her napkin up to her mouth. Her eyes were big and round and they were beginning to fill with tears. "Jim!"

"I'm sorry, Venie." Daddy looked around the table. "I apologize to everybody." He picked up a piece of turkey on his fork and looked at it. "What I said is in the same book of the same Bible that Geneva quoted. I'm sorry, however, and I shouldn't have said it."

There was a little silence at the table. They all sat there and stirred the food around on their plates until Uncle Elmer spoke. It was the first time he'd spoken since he'd said the blessing. He looked around at everybody with a worried look on his face and cleared his throat.

"Now if you got to worry about somebody, why don't all of us worry about us farmers? You think we git a fair deal? I tell you, if Huey P. Long hadna got shot, things would be different."

"This dressing isn't as good as I usually make," Mama said. "Not enough sage, maybe." Her voice was a little trembly.

147

"I think it's good." Eloise passed her plate over to Mama. "May I have some more?"

Everybody started talking again and there weren't any more arguments. Uncle Elmer leaned back in his chair and burped and Aunt Neevy frowned at him and Dawn Starr giggled. Dawn Starr hadn't eaten anything except three pieces of pie, because that was all we had on the table that she liked. She kept fidgeting around in her chair until Aunt Neevy finally let her leave the table and she went into my bedroom. Eloise started talking about New Orleans, and that was what they talked about for the rest of the dinner.

"You'll never guess," Eloise said, "who got off the bus out here at the crossroads with me." She was telling about her trip from New Orleans the night before.

"Who?" Mama asked. "Somebody we know?"

Eloise laughed. "It was old Lewis Johnson. Wasn't that his name, Venie, the one who married old Alma's daughter? Yes, I remember— Well, he got off the bus right behind me when I got off, and there we were, at midnight. I didn't know what to do. I mean, at midnight, on a country road, and suppose some of the people around here had seen me walking down the road with him?"

"Excuse me." Daddy stood up and left the table. A few minutes later, he came back with the coffee pot. Eloise was still talking.

"I mean, you never know what's in their minds," she said. "And I was afraid to tell him I didn't want to walk along with him, because it might have made him mad enough to try something, and—Jim, are you all right?"

Daddy had choked on his coffee. He took a drink of water and said "Excuse me" again and his face was red from choking.

"But I guess old black Lewis was feeling as puzzled as I was about what to do," Eloise said. "Because we stood there a minute and the bus went out of sight over the hill and Lewis spoke first. He said, 'Miss Eloise, I'm going to walk on ahead of you, but not too far. I'll stay in sight,' he said, 'and don't you be scared.' So I stood still and he walked on ahead."

"I wonder what Lewis was doing riding the bus home from Wellco," Mama said. "That was where he got on, wasn't it?"

"I guess he got on the bus at Wellco, because we didn't stop

148

anywhere else to pick up passengers. Venie, this pie is good. Your pies always are." Eloise reached for another piece of pie.

"My goodness," Mama said. "Busfare from Wellco costs a dollar. What in the world was Lewis doing in Wellco?"

"I don't know, but there he was. And I think he'd been drinking, because I could smell it. And he was singing most of the way home. But you know, that might have been so I could tell how far ahead of me he was, because it was as dark as he—as dark as pitch."

Daddy stood up and filled two coffee cups and picked them up and handed one to Uncle Elmer.

"Come on, Elmer," he said. "Let's go into the living room and drink this and listen to the news broadcast."

Aunt Neevy stood up, too, and picked up what was left of the fruitcake that Eloise had brought. She reached for a plate with half a pie left on it.

"Sit down, Neevy," Mama said. "What are you doing? Just let these things alone and let's visit. Donie's coming in to clean up for me."

"I know it." Aunt Neevy went into the kitchen with the pie and the cake and came back and picked up the turkey. "That's why I'm taking these things from the table. I'll go ahead and hide these and—"

"Well, don't!" Mama pushed her chair back and went into the kitchen and brought back all the stuff Aunt Neevy had taken out. "I don't take anything from the table before Donie eats. You know that."

"It's your food." Aunt Neevy sat back down at the table and her mouth was tight. "But I think it's like Elmer said in the blessing. The Lord has blessed our struggles with His grace, and as far as I'm concerned, they can struggle a little harder if they want pie and cake. And turkey." She looked around the dining room, at the wallpaper that was spotted and yellow, and at the boards Daddy had nailed over the hole in the corner. "Of course, I don't guess it matters as much if you're married to a man like—I mean if it was up to Elmer we wouldn't have anything either."

Eloise lit a cigarette and looked around for an ashtray. "If you're trying to say something about Venie and Jim, I think Venie's got the best man God ever put a gut in. And if you've got a beef against him, why don't you cut out all that Lord talk

149

and come out with what it is?" Eloise's eyes were narrow, and she made an *O* with her mouth and blew the smoke right toward Aunt Neevy's face.

Aunt Neevy fanned again. "Well, all I said, was that I'm not going to leave out the best I have for them to eat so they can cavort around all night riding buses and drinking whiskey and—"

"Oh, both of you calm down. Eloise, behave." Mama got up again and went to the back door. Donie came through and went into the kitchen, and Mama stood and looked at Aunt Neevy. "Her dinner's all she gets for washing those great mounds of dishes, and if we can't afford a piece of cake for her once in a while, let's wash them ourselves."

Of course they didn't, and of course that wasn't all that Donie got. She took home a big box of stuff with a whole pie in it, and I saw Eloise give her fifty cents and Aunt Neevy glared at all of them. But that was later.

"Donie," Aunt Neevy finally had to ask it. "What was Lewis doing in Wellco last night?" She winked at Mama and Eloise.

They had come back into the kitchen to drink more coffee and to talk, because Uncle Elmer and Daddy were asleep in chairs in the living room. Dawn Starr was in my room prowling for something to break, but I had spread a jigsaw puzzle on the floor in the kitchen so I could stay in there.

"He was—" Donie turned and said it to Mama. "He went wi' Trudy. Trudy done got herself mah'd las night. They go to Wellco cause Trudy have to slip off f'm Miss Mildred, an they want us to go stan up fo em, but Josie ain feelin good, so I don go." Donie smiled, showing all her big white strong teeth. Donie could crack hickory nuts with her teeth without even trying, but I hadn't seen all her beautiful strong teeth in a smile like that for a long time.

"They have this pahty aftuh the weddin, and Lewis, he still feelin real good when he come home." She smiled again. "Musta been some pahty!"

"For goodness sake, who'd Trudy marry?" Mama asked.

"She mah'y a Ferguson boy. He a cuzin to Callie on the Darsey side, and he come down f'm Chicago on a visit. I think he visit Trudy mostly, though. He wuk in a fac'try up there, an he come down once befo in this big shiny blue cah, an when he come back this time Trudy leave wif 'em."

150

"A visit!" Aunt Neevy sniffed into her cup. "He better get back up there and stay, before he *gets* visited! They got no business down here among you folks after they go up there around all them smart-alecks and agitators." She moved Eloise's ashtray across the table. "Trudy should have stayed where she was, if you ask me. She might find herself in a real mess, with one of them Northen nig—"

"Why in the world did Trudy have to slip off from Mildred Hagan?"

Eloise lit another cigarette and looked around for her ashtray. I found it and handed it to her. "Why should Mildred Hagan give a hoot in hell who Trudy marries, or when?"

Donie grinned and shook her head. "Miss Mildred know she can't git another gal who cook lak Trudy fo two dollahs a week. Trudy tole me a long time ago that Miss Mildred say ef she leave her kitchen she have her thowed in jail fo—fo—fo what happen at night in Trudy's house."

"For illegal cohabitation, probably!" Aunt Neevy looked as happy as she had that time she'd found a dead fly in somebody's pie at a church dinner.

"Yes'm, thas it." Donie hung up the dishtowel and looked around the kitchen to see if everything was clean. "Where Trudy made her mistake, she move into that little house Miss Mildred had built fo her. She oughta stayed in the flats, where Miss Mildred cain't see who comin an goin. Trudy, she too man-minded anyhow, an she lak pretty things you cain't buy fo two dollahs a week, an——"

"My God, you mean she knew Trudy was like that and she built her a house where she could keep check on her? And worked her for two dollars a week? Why, that mealy-mouthed, skinny-footed old—old Sunday School teacher!" Eloise lit another cigarette and laid it beside the one she already had burning and Aunt Neevy put them both out. Eloise tried to laugh but it didn't quite come out. "Yikes, she *is* your Sunday School teacher, isn't she, Thorpe?"

"She's also my piano teacher," I said. "For free, now, because we used up the cabinets that Daddy built for her a long time ago, but she still wants me to learn to play the piano. She does have ugly skinny feet, but she's kind of nice to me." I'd been wondering if maybe I should put Miss Mildred's name inside my magic circle and call her one of my friends.

"Well," Eloise said. "Well, maybe." She bent over the puzzle I had spread. "Look, Thorpe, isn't that a piece of blue sky? Try it here." Eloise and I worked on the puzzle then, and nobody said anything else about Miss Mildred and Trudy.

Donie took her coat from its hook by the door.

"I guess I go now, Miss Venie. You ain have much to do fo the rest of the day."

That was when Mama gathered up the pie and stuff for her and Eloise gave her the fifty cents.

After Donie left we went back into the living room and Eloise woke up Daddy and Uncle Elmer. She took Daddy's mandolin down and put it in his lap, and we sat and listened while Daddy sang. James came in from the front yard to listen, and everybody was in the living room except Dawn Starr. She was in my room undressing my dolls and screwing their heads around backward. Daddy sang "Pretty Mohee" and "You're as Welcome as the Flowers in May" and then Aunt Neevy asked him to sing "Allan Bane."

He did, and we all sang with him:

> They're taking me to the gallows, dear mother
> They're going to ha-ang me high.
> They're going to gather around me there,
> And watch me till I die. . . .

Uncle Elmer was sound asleep again before we got to the part where the prop would fall from beneath the man's feet and leave him in the air.

"Have you taken any more owl feet to school, Thorpe?"

Aunt Neevy was gathering up their things to go home, and the tight look around her mouth that had almost gone away while we were singing had come back, and kept her little smile too tight to reach to her eyes.

"Owl feet?" Mama stood in the hall door and looked down to where I sat on a pillow by Daddy's feet. "She took owl feet to school? For goodness sake, when? What?"

"Oh, I thought you knew." Aunt Neevy laid her purse and Uncle Elmer's hat back on the table and looked around, but

Eloise had her feet stretched across into the chair Aunt Neevy had been sitting in, and she didn't move them.

"Well," Aunt Neevy stood in the door and looked happy. "Dawn Starr says everybody in school was laughing at her. I thought you heard about it when they took her out of Ruth Keeter's first grade room and put her in the other one. I mean, didn't that start all of it?"

Uncle Elmer had settled back down in his chair and was snoring again.

"She took this old owl foot or wing or something," Aunt Neevy said. "She took it to school and told everybody her best friend gave it to her. Well, it turned out this best friend was Donie's Theotus! And to Ruth Keeter that was a personal insult. Because everybody knows how she hates *nigras,* and always has!"

Mama went over and shook Uncle Elmer. "Elmer, wake up. Neevy's ready to go." She stopped beside Daddy's chair, but I didn't look up at her. I kept my eyes on Mama's feet. Daddy put his hand on top of my head and it lay there until Neevy moved away.

"Well, good heavens, Neevy, we could have said that, when we were— Remember how we used to climb that pecan tree out back with Donie and Lewis and any other colored children that were around! And how we caught Grandpa Thorpe's barn on fire that time, going down there to hide from Eloise and Trudy and smoke his Bull Durham?"

"All of that was before we started to school." Aunt Neevy's mouth was stiff again.

"Not the smoking, Neevy! You were a great big—"

"Anyhow," Aunt Neevy picked up her purse again. "We knew better than to go around saying they were our best friends. Because they knew their place, and they stayed in it! And what I heard was that Ruth Keeter went to Mr. Whitehall and asked that your child be taken out of her room. After that they found room for her in the third grade!"

"You heard wrong." Daddy moved his hand from my head and stood up. "I went to Mr. Bond and asked that Thorpe be tested. And the tests proved that she was equipped to do third-grade work." His voice was quiet and even. "Do you have any more wrong impressions you'd like to have corrected today?"

"Well! Well, I never thought!" Aunt Neevy's face was red.

"I'm sure glad you came over today." Mama jammed Uncle Elmer's hat down on his head. He jumped and woke up, and Mama herded him out into the hall with Aunt Neevy. Eloise got up and kissed them all goodbye and when she kissed Dawn Starr she took one of my doll dresses out of Dawn Starr's coat pocket.

"We ought to do this more often," Mama said. "Dawn Starr, you come over and spend the night with Thorpe sometime soon. She loves to have you."

"Like a fish in a pickle dish," I said to the floor in the living room and Daddy put his hand under my chin and raised my head.

"It's all right, baby," he said. "Don't worry about it. Get your coat and we'll all take Eloise to the tabernacle to wait for her bus."

I went into my room to get my coat. Eloise came in and sat down at the dresser. "That Neevy!" she said. "I could shake Venie for letting her— Hells' bells, look at me! I'll have to put on a whole new face before I go catch the bus."

I watched her put on her new face. "Eloise—" I watched her draw a curved half-moon eyebrow with the little pencil. "Eloise, did you know that Leo knows you? Leo's our bus driver. And our mailman. And I didn't know that you knew him! He wants me to bring him a picture of you, and Mama won't let me do it."

The little pencil dropped from her hand and rolled under my bed. Eloise looked funny with one eyebrow and her face white like that.

"Leo," she said. "Leo."

"Leo Tolliver." I was on my knees looking under the bed for the eyebrow pencil. "Every time Leo brings us a letter from you, he asks me the next day what did you have to say and did you send any pictures."

Eloise had gotten down on her hands and knees with me, but instead of looking under the bed, she put her forehead down against the floor. I crawled under the bed and got the little pencil and gave it to her. She put it in her purse and sat back down at the dresser.

"Heavens, it's turning cold outside!" Mama came in and picked up a comb from the dresser and stood behind Eloise. "I guess we'll get some snow out of this by morning. Eloise, are you all right? Are you sick?"

154

"That bitch. That fat ugly bitch. I hate her, I hate her!" Eloise sat there looking in the mirror. "I wonder if she still thinks I'm too good for a Tolliver? I wonder if she'd still tell a bunch of lies to keep me from marrying one? Or does she know that not even a Tolliver would have me now?"

"You hush that, Eloise." Mama looked tired, and scared. "You hush that now. It's all over, and hating anybody about anything doesn't do any good. Neevy did what she thought was best for you. And she did give up a lot, after Mama died, staying home and taking care of Papa and of us."

"She didn't give up anything for anybody, and you know it." Eloise was still looking in the mirror. "She sat around and waited for old lady King to die so she could marry one of the biggest farms in the country. And when old lady King took so long dying she got scared to death that we'd be married before she would and she—"

"Well, anyhow, it's all over now," Mama said. "It doesn't do any good to talk."

"And you made it. You married before she did. And I could have. We could have a little boy in school by now. Like James. And I could buy him books and crayons and he'd be losing his front teeth. . . . Or would he have already lost them? Because all I know about kids is from watching Thorpe and James."

"Don't, Eloise." Mama knelt down on the floor and put her face against Eloise's. "Don't keep hurting yourself." Mama got to her feet and leaned against the dresser. "I'm tired," she said.

Eloise sat up straight and reached her hand up to Mama's cheek. "I'm all right now," she said. "It's your life she's still ruining. And Jim's." She started combing her hair. "God, I look a fright!"

"You only have on one eyebrow." I picked up her purse from the bed and handed it to her.

Mama turned like she hadn't noticed me sitting there on the bed. "You! You go in the living room, Missy, and you sit down and don't move or speak until you're spoken to!"

All I did was crawl under the bed and get an eyebrow pencil! As I went out the door, I heard Eloise say, "That's not fair, Venie. Thorpe didn't have anything to do with any—"

I sat down in the living room and waited for Eloise to put her other eyebrow on and wondered what Mama thought I had done.

The sun had quit shining right after dinner, and while we were sitting in the car at the tabernickle waiting for Eloise's bus, it started raining and the rain turned to sleet. Most of the leaves were gone from the trees along the road and the clouds hung right down over the bare trees. The sound of sleet hitting the car was the end of the day that had started with sunshine that morning. I rubbed my face against the fur of Eloise's coat sleeve, and it felt dark and rich and warm. Eloise's hand closed over mine and placed something in my palm.

"Give it to him," she whispered, and I knew who she meant. I put the little picture in my pocket without looking at it.

"I never did get a chance to ask how the new job's coming along." Daddy tried to roll a cigarette and spilled most of the tobacco out of it into Mama's lap. He threw it out the car window and turned toward Eloise, who was sitting in the back seat between James and me.

"It's not." Eloise handed her cigarette package up to Daddy. "Keep it. I have a carton in my suitcase. I quit, Jim. The job, not smoking. Oh, sure, I'm a sucker for a sob story, but this gal came around looking for work and she had a sick husband and so—"

"Gaw!" James rubbed her coat sleeve. "You're *lucky*. You never work. You're always between jobs when you come to see us, and you always bring us presents and wear fur coats and silk and stuff."

"James!" Mama turned and frowned at him and pulled her coat collar up around her neck. It was cold in the car, and getting colder.

"It's all right, Venie." Eloise laughed and hugged James. "The fur coat was a gift, James, and it's true I don't miss many meals. I laugh for my supper, I guess. You'd be surprised at the people who like a good laugh." She rolled the car window down and threw out her cigarette. "Is that my bus, Jim? Oh, keep the cigarettes, for goodness sake!"

Daddy made Eloise take her cigarettes back and we all got out of the car and kissed her. Thanksgiving Day was ending. Nobody said much on the way home. Daddy had a toothache and Mama sat looking down in her lap like she was thinking about a lot of things. I didn't mind that. What I dreaded was when she got ready to start talking about them. I slipped the picture

156

out of my pocket and looked at it. Eloise was standing in front of a gate and there were a lot of flowers around and she didn't have on her fur coat, so it must have been made last summer. Eloise was beautiful. No wonder Leo wanted her picture.

I heard Mama and Daddy fussing again after I went to bed.

"Next she'll be telling everybody old Trudy is her aunt!" Mama was crying and she didn't need to. I wasn't that stupid. Trudy was my best—Trudy was Thee's aunt. Eloise was mine— and Aunt Neevy, of course.

"I never was so humiliated!"

"And Geneva was tickled as hell to get to humiliate you!" Daddy shouted. "Do you realize there was your perfect chance to prove something that I suspect Thorpe needs badly to have proved? You could have said that if any friendship, black skin or otherwise, would move that fat moron of hers up two grades in school, she'd better cultivate it! She'll never make it otherwise. How do you think Thorpe—"

"Oh, Jim," Mama said. "I still say it's mostly your fault and we're just lucky she didn't say Trudy was her aunt."

"Well, Eloise *is* her aunt! Do you and Geneva mind her telling that? Does the difference lie in the fur coats and swank apartments or in the discretion used? Because Eloise and Trudy are sisters under the sk—"

"Go ahead and evade! Attack my family!" Mama was screaming. "If you're trying to hit back at the world by suggesting that Eloise is a— You've lost your mind. I don't see any similarity!"

"And I don't see much damned difference!" Daddy was still shouting. "When you come out of that filthy hole you Thorpes dug a hundred years ago and look at things honestly, Venie, you're going to grow up into a good woman. I hope. Or else lose your mind, like the rest of this damned sick . . ."

"Oh, God." Mama was talking real quiet now. "Now it's not just me and my family and old Will Jackson. Now it's the whole country."

Daddy said, "Oh hell."

"And that's another thing!" I wondered if James could hear them. "What do you think people think about a schoolteacher helling and damning with every other word he says? If anybody had told me you would talk . . ." Her voice was muffled then, like in a pillow.

There wasn't any sound through the wall for a moment, and then Daddy said, "I'm sorry, Venie. Are we quarreling about Eloise, or what? I don't care about Eloise. She's fighting her own battle, and all I feel for her is love and pity. I guess I yell about other people, Venie, because I'm such a sorry damned excuse for a man myself." His shoe hit the floor like he'd been sitting there holding it. "Sometimes I think the best thing I could do would be to butt my brains out against a brick wall." His other shoe fell to the floor.

Mama didn't say anything for so long I thought she'd gone to sleep. Then she said, "I know, Jim, and I'm sorry too. I guess I should have gone on with you when you found that place in St. Louis. But Jim, I can't. I *have* to raise my family like I was raised, among the people I love. It's all I know!"

Daddy didn't answer.

A few minutes later, Mama said, "I know about Eloise, Jim, but I can't bear to talk about it. She's my baby sister and—well, as long as we don't take anything except Christmas gifts from her, it's not like we're condoning it. I mean, I wouldn't accept money from her at all."

I did. I accepted money from Eloise. There was a quarter in the plaid coat pocket that Eloise had given me.

I heard Daddy say, "Oh, forget about Eloise," but a long time after Mama and Daddy were quiet, I lay awake wondering what was wrong with the quarter and what to do about it. Finally I hopped out of bed and raised the window and threw the quarter out into the grape arbor.

The red coat still hung in Mr. Byrd's window, soft and warm and bright. Sometimes, when we went to buy groceries, I didn't go inside the store with Mama; I stood outside and watched the coat. I had looked at it from one side, from the other side, from up on High Pockets' shoulder one day when he came along the sidewalk, and from squatting on the sidewalk looking up at it, and then I'd started watching it. Guarding it. Because as long as it hung in the window it was mine. Even though Mama had said that she didn't see how we could afford it and that she wished I'd hush about it.

One day while I was standing watch, Mr. Byrd stepped up into the window and took the coat from the rack, folded it over his arm and stepped back down into his store. Somebody had bought it. I didn't go inside the store to see who had bought it, because I didn't want to know. I sat down on the pavement and waited for Mama to come back out.

I had been wishing for the coat in every way I knew. On black crows flying alone in the sky, on loads of hay, on one-eyed cars —and it was gone.

"Well," I said to Mama on the way home that day. "I guess I won't wish for the red coat for Christmas any more."

"Why?" Mama turned to the back seat.

"Because it's gone. Somebody bought it today."

"Oh," Mama said. "I expect Mr. Byrd has more than one red coat. We'll see. And if you act real nice and keep wishing, you might get it."

"No. It's gone now. I wanted that one, not another one just like it." I kicked the back of the car seat. "I'll just wish for Thee a pair of shoes for Christmas." I looked out the car window and saw something in the sky overhead to wish on. . . . "See one buzzard, don't see two, make a wish and it'll come true. I wish that Thee had some shoes to wear to school on Monday morning. . . ."

He did. On Monday morning, Thee was sitting on his stump across from the tabernickle, and he had on shoes. But not shoes like I'd meant to wish for. He had on this big old pair of shoes with holes in the sides, and they were tied onto his feet over about three pairs of socks.

His feet might have been warmer and dryer, but they looked worse. And of course old Soggum Thompson had to try to make something out of it as soon as he saw the shoes.

"Hay, Thee!" Soggum grabbed Thee's ruff of hair that morning and lifted Thee's head until it looked like his neck would break. "Where'd you git them shoes?"

All of the Thompsons sniggered, and Soggum kept on.

"Them's pinpoint shoes, boy! Oooo-weeeee!" He pranced around the stump, still holding Thee's ruff of hair. "Ain't we dressed up today!" Then he started singing.

"Coon, coon, coon, Oh I wisht my color would fade . . ."

Thee twisted his head out of reach and started scratching on the ground with a stick, but Soggum kept on.

"Look up at me, boy, an' answer me. I said where'd you git them ol' pinpoint shoes? Huh?"

"Mama fount em. By th' road." Thee kept scratching the ground with his stick, still looking down.

"Found em? Aw, naw, who'd thow *them* shoes away?" Soggum looked around and laughed, real happy, and all the other Thompsons laughed again too.

"Say, now, Thee," Soggum said. "Is your feet shaped that way? Huh? Is you got pinpoint feet? Yo mammy had to look hard to find shoes to fit yo pinpoint feet. . . . Is that right? Coon, coon, coon, oh I wisht my color would fade—"

James had put his books and his lunch inside the tabernickle and had gone over to stand behind Soggum. He reached up and got Soggum's hair and twisted Soggum's head around like Thee's had been twisted.

"Let me tell you something, you slow-witted morfydite. If he's got pinpoint feet, that's fine. But when he gets a pinpoint head like you, we'll start worrying about him. Now get back across that road!"

Soggum was already crying when he got back to his side of the road, and he picked up a big rock, but he didn't throw it. The bus was coming, and I was glad, because Mr. Whitehall had already told James and Soggum that the next time they traded licks he meant to get a few licks of his own on both of them.

I stepped onto the bus, wondering about James' new word. James was always coming up with a new word he'd heard at the tie yard or somewhere, and most of the words he shared with me. But when I asked him, that evening, what a morfydite was, he said he didn't know for sure and that I didn't need to know. I said I'd ask Daddy or Martin, and he said that if I did he'd never tell me anything else or even speak to me any more.

It wasn't in the dictionary.

II

It was the week before Christmas that we had the surprise. Since the weather had turned colder, Donie had been coming by herself to wash for us on Saturday mornings, but when she came that Saturday Thee and Josie were both with her. Josie was carrying a big box. She brought the box into the kitchen and put it on a chair. "Heah he is," she said and stood by the chair and looked up at the ceiling and around the kitchen.

Inside the box, on a pillow, was a real baby.

It looked like a doll. Mama dried her hands on the dishtowel and came over to the box, and James came in from the front room, and we stood around the box on the chair and looked at the baby. Its face was the color of Mama's three-o'clock coffee after she put the cream in, and its hair lay in little black curls all over its head. It had on a blue silk dress the color of Mama's church dress that Aunt Neevy had given her, and it was wrapped in a little white quilt made from flour sacks.

"Why, Donie!" I was so glad for Donie I grabbed her legs and hugged them. "I didn't even know you were that way!"

Mama looked at the baby, and looked at Donie, and they both laughed. After a while it sounded more like they were crying, but then Donie wiped her eyes and got her breath.

Mama sat down in a chair and kept looking in the box and sort of rocked back and forth and I still couldn't tell whether she was laughing or crying.

"Oh, Miss Venie, don' feel bad." Donie's big brown twisted hand patted Mama's shoulder, and then she took her apron and wiped Mama's eyes. "Miss Thorpe, she gon take it fine. She lak you, Miss Venie, she got a heart big as the moon an a mine almos' so. She ain say why with the ones she love, Miss Thorpe ain't. She jes say *is.*"

"It's not Donie's baby, stupid." James had come into the kitchen and he stood over the box and looked down at the baby. "It's Josie's."

"Josie's!" I looked at Josie and she nodded. She looked like she didn't much believe it was hers either.

"He mine, awright," she said. "He borned las week, after I done got sick an—"

"Josie!" I looked in the box again. There he was. "Well, am I stupid! I should have known why you were getting so fat, but . . ." I looked at Mama. "I didn't know kids like us could get that way."

"Dummox, you can't." James scobbed my noggin. "It takes two. Josie couldn't either, except she got ra—"

"James! Hush and get away from that baby, both of you, before you wake it up." Mama moved the box back to a bench in the corner behind the stove and told James to fill the woodbox and not call his little sister things like dummox.

Donie told Josie they'd better get out to the wash place and Mama said leave the baby in where it was warm. She hadn't said anything to me, so I went back to the box again. Thee was leaning over it grinning and saying "Goochy" and stuff like that and laying his finger against its nose and on top of its head real easy.

"Is it a boy or a girl?" I asked.

"He a boy," Thee said. "He name Junior."

Mama went into her room and started sewing and I started out to the wash place with Thee. On the way out we met James coming in with a load of stovewood.

"The baby's a boy," I told James. "Named Junior."

James stopped with his armful of wood and looked at us. "Junior what?" he asked. *"What* Junior?"

I stood on the bottom step and looked up at James on the top one. "What do you mean, what Junior?"

162

"Well, gaw, stupid. You can't be named just Junior. You've got to be something, Junior. Henry, or John. Or James. Go ask them what his real name is. It's not Junior!" James went into the kitchen and dumped his load of wood into the box.

Josie was poking clothes down in the boiling pot.

"He ain nothin Junior," she said when I asked her. "He jes Junior. I name him myself."

James still didn't believe it, so we took the argument into Mama's room. She straightened up from the little nightgown she was cutting and glared at us.

"Get out of here," Mama said. "And find something else to do besides argue about what nigras name their kids. I guess you can name them Junior if you want to. You can name them Peter Rabbit if you want to. Now stop that arguing and go do something else, or I'll find something else for you to do!"

We went, but we were still arguing. James kept mouthing around about it. "Junior!" he said. "It's still not a name! *Nothing, Junior*. Well, I'm not calling him *Nothing*. I'm gonna call him Peter Rabbit."

Peter Rabbit was a good baby. He lay in his box in the kitchen and when Josie had the clothes boiling good she played with us while Donie washed another load. James played with us for a while before he went on down to the tie yard and we had to run fast to keep warm and I could hear Thee:

> *"Honey in the bee-ball, bee-ball, bee-ball,*
> *I cain't see y'all, see y'all, see y'all,*
> *All ain hid, holler ha-aay yo. . . ."*

Mama came to the back door and said the baby was crying in the kitchen and Donie told Josie to quit running and go feed it. Josie brought it back out and sat down on the washbench looking up into the bare limbs of the peach trees until Donie told her that was enough and to change its pants. Donie had to help her change it and she took it back into the kitchen and Mama called me to come and eat dinner.

On the back porch I met Josie coming back out and I asked her if it hurt when the baby chewed on her, but she said, "Naw, he cain't chew. He borned wifout no toofs."

That was the day the mill closed down.

Daddy handed Mama the money before he sat down to eat.

"That's it," he said, and kept looking down at the yellow checks in the oilcloth. "He closed her down today."

"One week. One week until Christmas!"

Mama's face was white, and her hand that wasn't holding onto the table went to her stomach and kind of cradled the baby, like it was suddenly too heavy. That was the day, too, that Mama started holding her stomach.

"Oh, hell," Daddy said. "I'd forgotten about Christmas." He rubbed his jaw. Daddy's jaw had been swollen since Thanksgiving Day with the toothache that had started that day. "Venie, can we make it? Maybe I'll find something . . . somewhere. . . ." He rubbed his jaw again.

Mama shut her eyes and it was like you could see and feel her reaching deep down inside for the right words. Then, still holding onto the table and her stomach, she nodded.

"We'll make it, Jim. I—I've been sticking a little back every week, for Christmas. And we still have credit at Walter Byrd's. Don't we?"

She watched Daddy rub his jaw and waited for his answer.

Mama had ten nickles and five dimes in a pint jar in the pantry. That was what she had stuck back. But I knew, that day, watching both of them, that she meant for Daddy to think it was more than that. I kept quiet.

"We should have," Daddy said. "If, after six years of paying up regularly, he can't trust us now—"

Mama bent and looked at Daddy's jaw. "Jim, how much does Dr. Johnson charge to pull a tooth?"

"I don't know. Seventy-five cents, I guess. A dollar maybe. This is a hell of a time to talk about that."

"This *is* the time to talk about it, while we still have the dollar." Mama handed him a bill from the little pile he'd given her. "You take this and go to Strawne this afternoon, and you let Dr. John Johnson pull that tooth. You know it's not going to get any better, and it might get worse!"

Daddy reached down into his pocket and pulled out a quarter and sat there rubbing it before he laid it on the table.

"I found this in the grape arbor the other day," he said. "They say you can drink a quarter's worth of old Jelly Thompson's moonshine and you don't feel a thing. For hours. And the old ball of obscenity might be just sadistic enough to pull it for me. I might go over—"

"Don't talk like a fool." Mama stuck the dollar bill into his shirt pocket. "Let's eat, so you can get off to town and get Dr. John onto that tooth."

"Will we go get the Christmas tree first?" I asked, and Daddy smiled and said he thought we had time for that.

Going after the Christmas tree was one of the best parts of Christmas. I ran to call James, and I forgot to ask about sadistic and obscenity.

After lunch Mama bundled us up in mittens and scarves and she even tied a red-and-green wool scarf over Daddy's head and down around his sore jaw. Daddy fussed and twisted his head around, but it must have felt pretty good, because he didn't take it off after we got out of sight like James had thought he would.

The hickory and black gum and oak trees were all stripped by the wind and the cold, and the sky that you could see up through the bare branches was gray and low-hanging, like it might open and let the snow and the sleet start falling before we were back home. Once in a while a rabbit ran across the trail, and a big gray fox squirrel in a tree over our heads dropped a hickory nut right onto Daddy's head. Daddy looked up and laughed and rubbed his head. We stood under the tree with Daddy and watched the squirrel scamper up to the top limb, fussing and chattering and waving his fluffy gray tail like a big round gray feather.

The best trees were down around the old Pig White place, where the pines and cedars grew taller, and where James and I had already found and marked the tree we wanted. We went along Uncle Elmer's fence and down through the undergrowth to old Pig's place.

"Here's a good one." Daddy stopped and took the axe from his shoulder and leaned it against Uncle Elmer's fence. He walked around the little pine tree and looked at it. It was just a little taller than his head, and the branches tapered almost to a point at the top. "How about this one?"

James looked at the pine tree. "It's lopsided. Here's a better one over the fence. See?" He pointed over Uncle Elmer's fence to a perfect holly, with leaves that looked like they'd been waxed and berries as big as the buttons on his coat. "How about this one?"

Daddy looked at the holly tree and at James.

"You know better than that. Elmer sells those trees. He planted them for that reason! See, that one's already marked to sell." He turned back to the pine.

"But, gaw, what's one little old tree!" James hung over the fence and he could almost touch the berries when he stretched his arm. "Nobody's sure it would sell, even if he cuts it and hauls it off to Wellco or somewhere. It might just lay there in the truck and die. Can't we—"

Daddy went over to the fence and stood beside James and put his arm across James' shoulder. "There's not any right time or reason for stealing, son. But I guess if there were a worse time, Christmas would be it."

He left James at the fence and picked up his axe again. "Come on, son. There's possibly a holly tree just that pretty down in the woods somewhere. On the right side of the fence. So if the pine won't do—"

The wind was cold and damp-smelling. I looked at the red-and-green scarf that Daddy had not untied from around his jaw, and I knew what we had to do. "I think this tree is just perfect," I said. "And anyhow, pine always smells better than holly."

It had been a good try, but it hadn't worked. And I knew that we mustn't ever let Daddy know that the holly tree just over the fence had been marked by us and not by Uncle Elmer. Daddy cut the pine tree, and we dragged it home. We stopped once and cut some limbs of holly for Mama to put in vases. While Daddy was cutting the holly, James climbed up into a big tall bare tree just off the trail and cut some mistletoe and dropped it down to us, and we were almost to the back gate with our loads of stuff when it started snowing.

After Daddy left to go and have his tooth pulled, I went into the living room and curled up in the big red chair to look at the Christmas tree. Daddy had nailed it onto a platform of boards, and Mama had spread cotton over the boards. It looked beautiful. It *was* a little lopsided, but that wasn't Daddy's fault. And the lopside was against the window, so you really didn't notice it.

We didn't have lights, because in the old breezeway house there wasn't any electricity, but when we'd finished with the tree you didn't miss the lights. Most of the shiny decorations on it—except for the sweetgum balls that James and I had covered with the tinfoil we'd been saving all year—were older than I was, and we'd talked about each one as we'd hung it on the tree. Mama even had some glass angels and birds that she and Daddy had used on their first Christmas tree together. Angels and birds so shiny and light that they just floated in the tree and you didn't dare touch them. There it stood, so beautiful it made your stomach hurt.

It was better, even, than holding Grandma Thorpe's gold watch and looking at it, because you had to be sick to get to hold the gold watch. Mama came in and lay down on the couch with a magazine, and James stuck his head in the door and said he was going down to the tie yard.

"Don't you stay out in that snow all evening," Mama said, and James looked in at the Christmas tree again and left.

It was warm and quiet in the big red chair, with the glowing red sides of the big wood heater making lights on the shiny tree decorations. One silver ball looked bigger than the rest. . . . It got bigger . . . and bigger . . . until it looked like the magic balls used by fortune tellers. . . . I lay back with my legs across the arm of the red chair and on the couch Mama snored a little bit—

I floated down the hall at school, taller than before because my feet weren't touching the floor. The teachers all stood in the doors of their rooms and bowed as I went past, and Mosquito said Bow to me, too. I used to be her teacher. . . . Out the door like a red flame I burst, and on the school ground everybody shouted I choose Thorpe. I want Thorpe. Let Thorpe come over! And as we chose the lines to play Red Rover old Billy Bob Jackson drove his car right up onto the schoolground and splashed mud on my new red coat and Thee was there and he said Old ball Obscenity and kicked Billy Bob's tires with his new shoes and all of the tires went flat. Boy, I'm gonna have to take you in— Billy Bob got out of his car with a star as big as a saucer pinned to his chest and I tried to call for Daddy but all that came out was I cain't see y'all, see y'all, see y'all and Mama shook my shoulder and said why did you get the new coat all muddy why why why——

"Why don't you get up and take your bath and get ready for bed?" Mama had lit the lamps and turned on the radio. Somewhere somebody was singing about hearing the bells on Christmas Day. "I wonder what's keeping Jim? He should have been home hours ago." Mama pulled the drapes apart and looked out the window.

I went into the kitchen, and a few minutes later I could hear Mama and James laughing at Amos 'n Andy—or maybe it was Lum and Abner—and I hurried and jumped into my gown to join them.

Mama dipped all of us a bowl of corn-meal mush from the pot she had bubbling on the living-room heater. We ate it with sugar and butter and with a lot of laughter about things we heard on the radio. When we were through, Mama gathered up the bowls and started to the kitchen with them, and in the door she stopped.

"I wonder where on earth Jim is," she said again. And then we heard the car outside. Mama picked up the lamp from the library table and we all went to the front door.

When Daddy got out of the car he was singing. "Throw out the lifeline, throw out the lifeline. . . ." He sang all the way through the gate and up to the steps, brushing the snow from in front of his face with one hand, and waving it in time with his singing. On the steps he stopped and looked up at us standing there in the door.

Mama held the lamp toward him, closer to the screen, and the wind blew the flame. Daddy held onto a pillar and looked at us and blinked. He looked happy.

"Open the door to me," he said. "My love, my dove. For my head is filled with dew and my locks with the drops of the night." He turned loose of the pillar and almost fell off the porch backward.

"Jim!" Mama shoved the lamp into James' hands and darted out the door to Daddy. She held him up, from the back, and pushed him into the living room. "Jim, what in the world?"

Daddy was holding a paper sack in one hand and trying to push his shirttail back in with the other. His shirt was bloody. He stood there, holding his paper sack, and looking around the room at all of us and at the Christmas tree. He smiled happily. "Ho ho ho!" he said.

Then he rubbed his hand over his face. " 'Sawfully hot in here," he said. He smelled like the fruit cake that Aunt Neevy had in her safe for Christmas. He looked around the room again until he'd found me and turned and bowed to me. And started singing again.

168

"Santa Claus, you dear old man—" he sang. "Lean your ear this way. Don't you tell a single— By golly, you know something, Thorpe? You can't lean your ear. Jus' can't be done. You have to lean your whole da— your whole head. So."

He handed me the paper sack and bowed again and folded on down to the floor. And there he lay, looking surprised and happy.

"Jim, you're drun—" Mama put her hand up to her mouth.

"No," Daddy said from the floor. "My head is filled with dew." He looked up at Mama standing there over him. "How beautiful are thy feet with shoes, O prince's daughter! And thy belly is like an heap of wheat set about with lilies. . . ."

He went to sleep, with his mouth half open and a happy, surprised look still on his face.

Mama stood there over him for a little while before she left the room and went to the kitchen. She came back a few minutes later with the coffee pot, and put it on the heater.

James and I looked inside the sack, and in it was a pair of brown high-topped shoes. They were boys' shoes, but they were too little for James, and I knew, before Daddy woke up and told us, who they were for and how he had gotten them.

"James," Mama said, "get over here and hold his head up and help me pour this coffee down him."

They poured three cups down him before they quit, and then Mama washed his face with a cold cloth, and Daddy rolled around and looked up at us again. They took him in to his bed, and after a while I went in to see about him. I put my hand against his jaw, and he opened his eyes.

"Does the hole hurt," I asked, "where the tooth came out?"

Daddy put his hand over mine and held it there against his jaw. "Not a bit," he said. "Nothing to it. Old Jelly's a damned good dentist. He just missed his calling."

"Let's all go to bed now," Mama said. "And I charge you, that ye stir not up nor awake my love, till he please."

And, like she'd been on that day that Josie first brought her baby up, you couldn't tell whether she was laughing or crying.

That was why, the next morning, Brother Mearl came by to say he'd missed us at church, he found us still sitting at the breakfast table.

Everybody was through eating but Daddy. He hadn't had anything except three cups of coffee and a big glass of tomato juice that Mama had made last summer, and he was holding his head instead of his jaw.

"It's Brother Mearl," James whispered when he looked out the front door and saw the car.

"Good Heavens!" Mama stood up and pushed her plate back. "Go in the living room, quick, and talk to him while I take my apron off and find my shoes!"

Daddy moaned and started into the bedroom.

"Oh, no!" Mama took his arm and guided him into the living room with us. "You don't get out that easy. You sit right there, and you talk to him too, until I can get in here."

Brother Mearl wasn't all that easy to talk to. Not for James and me. He was always calling you things like flowers in the garden of the Lord, and wanting you to say verses from the Bible for him and saying Amen while you were still talking.

"Wake up!" James leaned across the couch and punched me with his elbow. "He asked if you knew your memory verse for today."

"Oh. Oh, yes sir. I was glad when they said unto me let us go unto the house of the Lord!"

"Amen," Brother Mearl said. From where he sat in Daddy's big red chair he leaned forward toward Daddy, who was on the couch beside James. "We missed your little family today, Brother Torrance."

Daddy turned his glass of tomato juice around and stared into it and didn't say anything.

"They follow in your footsteps, Brother Torrance. You must never forget that. Ah, hello, Sister Torrance. We missed you folks today, Praise the Lord."

"Well," Mama said. "Well, we— We—"

"During our prayers, I worried to the Lord about you. Is there trouble, I asked Him. And the Lord put his hands on that old steering wheel, Sister Torrance, and He turned that car off the highway, so I would come by and see."

"Nobody's sick, Brother Mearl," Mama said. "It's Jim. He had a— He had a tooth pulled yesterday. He had a tooth pulled, Brother Mearl, and he just didn't feel like—"

"Ah, yes," Brother Mearl said. "I saw Brother Torrance after he had his tooth pulled. He and High Pockets came by to sing for

170

the second Sister Mearl and myself when they were out, ah, caroling. They—"

"Caroling!" Mama looked at Daddy. "Caroling!"

Daddy slid down lower on the end of the couch, and his face was as red as the tomato juice in the bottom of his glass.

"Yes," Brother Mearl said. "They came by twice. And when they came the second time, Doctor John was, ah, caroling with them. I went back in my house then, Sister Torrance, and I got down on my knees, and I talked to the Lord about them. But I had interference, Sister Torrance. I had interference. Because the old Devil hisself was right there in the back seat of that car yesterday, cheering them on."

The room was so quiet you could hear the fire crackling in the big heater. In her chair by the window Mama rocked, and on the end of the couch Daddy looked down at his tomato juice.

Brother Mearl stood up and smiled around at all of us. "I wonder if we could get down on our knees today, Brother Torrance, and rout that old Devil. Let's get him by the horns, Brother Torrance, and throw him out the door!"

Daddy stood up from the couch and left the room with his hand over his mouth.

"Oh!" Mama looked from the door back to Brother Mearl. "Jim's not feeling very—"

We heard Daddy's axe out at the woodpile.

There was another little silence, and Brother Mearl heaved himself to his feet and knelt down on the floor beside the Christmas tree. "Let's rout that old Devil, Sister Torrance," he said, and I wished that I could go cut wood with Daddy. James closed his eyes and Mama put her hand over hers, and Brother Mearl started praying.

"Before You, in Your wrath, pluck a rose from this man's garden, oh Lord, we come to You in humbleness and in sorrow. That he not wait until he hears the clods of dirt falling, yea, falling over one of his loved ones, before he repents! This is our prayer. . . ."

Daddy's tomato juice was on the table beside the sack with the shoes for Thee, and out back his axe went *crack!* as it hit a slab of wood.

"Yes," Mama said after Brother Mearl had left. "Yes, you may go and take the shoes to Theotus." She poured water from the teakettle into the dishpan. "But remember, you're to take them straight to him and come straight back home. Just because you're out of school for Christmas holidays doesn't mean that you're going to start running all over the woods with them again. You give Theotus those shoes, and you come straight home!"

Outside the back gate, we stopped by the woodpile to talk to Daddy.

"Daddy, do you think that one of us could be plucked today?" I had to ask him. "Do you think we might be plucked and leave you to hear the clods falling over us?"

Daddy lowered his axe and looked us over.

"You look pretty healthy to me," he said. "Stick out your tongue."

I stuck my tongue out. James opened his mouth, but then he grinned and shook his head.

Daddy looked at my tongue and felt my forehead. "I believe you're in fine shape. Aside from a falling tree or a speeding truck —neither of which should cause us too much concern today—I don't believe we need to worry." He looked us over again and then he raised his axe and went back to chopping wood.

So Thee had shoes, and I could go back to wishing for the red coat. Mr. Byrd had already sold the coat to somebody else, but I could not quit wishing.

I tried hard, that week before Christmas, to be good. Mama had said that if I acted real nice, I might get it. And so no matter how stupid James said I was to keep hoping, I couldn't quit.

The night before Christmas Eve I even went over and spent the night with Dawn Starr. I wanted the coat that much, and I was doing everything I could to please Mama.

It was a sorry night, exactly like every other night I'd ever spent with Dawn Starr. Uncle Elmer pulled off his shoes and turned on the radio and put his paper over his face to go to sleep. Aunt Neevy read her Bible and started into the kitchen to fix their Crazy Water Crystals. As she was going down the hall, the telephone rang, and we could hear her answering it.

"Hello," she said. "Yes, yes . . . who? . . . No, there's nobody by that name here. No, I don't know him. Never heard of him. . . . No. . . . no. You must have the wrong— Yes, of course.

You're welcome." She hung the telephone up and went on into the kitchen.

"Who was that?" Uncle Elmer pushed his paper aside and walked to the door in his socks that still had holes and peered down the hall toward the kitchen.

"Just a wrong number," Aunt Neevy called back. "Wanted somebody, somebody that— Well, whoever they wanted don't live here. Never did."

"Sounds to me like they need some new operators in Wellco," Uncle Elmer said. "They ort to give us our exchange back in Strawne. That's twice this week you've took calls for somebody you never heard of."

"You kids better go to bed," Aunt Neevy called from the kitchen, "so you can get up early and get ready to go to town tomorrow."

The snow from the week before had almost all melted and gone, but Strawne was spotted with dirty gray patches of it. It was cold and cloudy, and the wet ground had frozen over, leaving a little crust on top that fooled you. If you stepped off the sidewalk onto that crust over the ground, you sank in mud up to your ankles.

We went into the Cheerful Corner because Dawn Starr kept whining about being hungry, and Uncle Elmer bought us some hot chocolate. It was warm and cozy in the Cheerful Corner, with the big Christmas tree against one wall and the radio playing "Silent Night" real loud. From behind the wall we could hear the nigras in their side of the café, laughing and singing.

"You kids quit lookin around an' drink that chocolate." Uncle Elmer pushed his cup back and stood up and reached in his pocket for four nickels. "Make it snappy. We ort to be on the road right now."

They were going to Wellco for Christmas, to visit Uncle Elmer's aunts.

It was sleeting when we came out of the Cheerful Corner. Cold, sharp little icicles that stung your face and melted and ran down inside your coat collar.

"Br-r-r!" Aunt Neevy shivered and turned her cottony-looking fur collar up around her face. "We better go on to the car. The roads'll be slick by evenin', an' we need to be in Wellco before then." Uncle Elmer left us to go by the bank, and we started back to the car.

173

Over in the park, some people were huddled together in their toboggan caps and scarves, singing Christmas carols, and Dawn Starr wanted to stop and listen.

"Hmp!" Aunt Neevy wrapped her collar tighter and frowned over toward the park. "We can hear better music than that at home on the radio. They're all probably half-drunk, anyhow, to stand out in the cold like that. An' if you think I'm going to stop an' listen to a bunch of half—"

But she did stop. She stood still on the sidewalk, and held her arm in front of us to keep us from hurrying on.

We had almost bumped into Nathaniel. Nathaniel, who worked at the tie yard and who was wearing the same red toboggan cap in town that he'd been wearing to the tie yard since it had turned cold. He was standing on the sidewalk with a little bunch of other nigra boys, and they were all looking toward the park. They were listening to the Christmas songs. As we stopped behind Aunt Neevy's arm, all of the boys except Nathaniel stepped from the pavement onto the frozen crust. Nathaniel stood there, on the edge of the pavement humming with the carol singers, and waiting for us to go past them. That wasn't any problem, really. I could have stepped behind Aunt Neevy and Dawn Starr, and there would have been plenty of room, but she wouldn't have it that way.

"You!" She barked out at Nathaniel. "Boy! You step off this sidewalk. Right now!"

"Yes?" Nathaniel raised his old stocking cap up from over one ear and turned his face away from the park, toward us. "Were you speaking to me?"

Aunt Neevy's face was red like it was going to burst, and she sputtered a little bit before she could say anything again. "You—you know I'm talking to you, boy! Don't you ever say yes to me like that again! Now you get off of this sidewalk, and you get off fast. And when you speak to a white lady, you say yes ma'am!"

She stood, holding her hand across in front of us, and glaring at Nathaniel, and he moved first. But not very fast.

Nathaniel pulled his cap back down over his ear, and his face was like the face of a brown statue. You couldn't tell a thing about what he was thinking, as he lifted one foot and put it back down, off the pavement and onto the frozen ground. Cra-a-ack went the ice around Nathaniel's foot as it sank down into the mud. He lifted his other foot, and slid a little bit on the first one, and then he put his second foot down, and what he said wasn't very loud, but it sounded like a firecracker in the cold air.

"Yes *ma'am!*" He turned his back to us and watched the carol singers.

We started on to the car, and Aunt Neevy stopped once more and looked back toward Nathaniel.

"Nothing irks me any more than a smart nigra," she said. "A thing like that's enough to ruin anybody's Christmas. I wish I knew who that one was, but I don't guess there'd be any way of finding out. They all look just alike."

"I don't know who he was," Dawn Starr said. "I don't know any nigra boys. Do I, Mama?"

I wondered what Aunt Neevy would do to Nathaniel if I told her his name.

"Me, neither," I said as we got in the car to wait for Uncle Elmer. "They all look just alike to me, too." I wondered when I was going to be plucked from the garden for lying. We sat in the car until Uncle Elmer came, and we could still hear the people singing in the park:

> ". . . *and wild and sweet, the words repeat,*
> *Of Peace on Earth, Good Will to Men.*"

The red coat was under the tree on Christmas morning. And so was *Tales from Dickens*. Daddy had gotten the book for me, to go with the book he'd given me last Christmas. I didn't know which to look at first. I put the red coat on over my gown and sat down and opened the book.

"I thought you were getting her a doll!"

I had put the empty coat box in Mama's lap, and she let it fall to the floor as she stood up and looked across at the book in my lap. "You *promised* you'd get the doll, if I went ahead and got the coat!"

"I bought the book in Wellco last fall, Venie," Daddy said. He picked the box up from the floor and sat there smoothing the ribbon on it. "I meant to get the doll later, but after the mill closed down, I—"

"Oh, what's a doll?" I opened to a picture of the Olde Curiosity Shoppe and started reading. "I have a whole shelf full of dolls."

"Yes, but this one I had picked out had red hair." Mama looked

175

like she was going to cry. "And a pink silk dress. You don't have a doll with real hair, and I wanted—"

"Look!" James was putting his new boots on. "Laced boots, just like Daddy's! Man!"

We all looked at James' boots and he put them both on and opened his present from Daddy, which was *Moby Dick*. Pretty soon everybody was happy again and we opened the box from Eloise. Leo had left the box at the mailbox more than a week ago, but it had this big sticker on it, with holly leaves and red flowers, and it said DO NOT OPEN UNTIL DECEMBER 25.

Just under the lid on the box, there was a lot of candy and nuts and firecrackers. Under that, in a flowered tin box, was a fruitcake bigger than the one Aunt Neevy had in her safe. And then a whole box of chocolates for Mama, and something in a gold box for Daddy. On the gold box it said KENTUCKY'S FINEST.

I hoped that when we got to our presents, mine would be pink silk, but it wasn't. It was a red sweater, and a skirt and a pair of mittens. For James there was a blue sweater and a pair of pants and some gloves.

"I wish you'd look!" Mama looked down at her present that she'd opened and held in her lap. "Five yards of *real* linen, and I wish you'd listen to what the note says. 'To make you a spring suit after the new baby comes. . . .'" She sat there, rubbing the white linen and looking down at it, and Daddy started to open his box.

"Kentucky's finest what?" James asked, and then he looked at it and said, "Oh."

Daddy laughed and put the sparkly glass bottle on the bookcase and pulled Mama to her feet.

"Let's go have an eggnog," he said. "*One,* I promise, and then we'll save the rest of it in case somebody needs to have a tooth pulled. By golly, a man might drink that and pull his own!"

"I'm not sure," Daddy was saying as they went into the kitchen, "that Eloise should have sent that through the mail. Isn't it illegal?"

"Oh, well," Mama said, "at Christmastime . . ."

The whirr of Mama's eggbeater was louder than the rest of Daddy's words. James and I sat under the Christmas tree and read our new books until Mama called us to breakfast.

Lewis knocked on the back door while we were eating. I slid from my chair and went to the door, and he stood there stamping the snow from his feet and smiling and when I opened the screen door he poked this package in at me.

"Fo Miss Venie," he said. The box he handed in to me for Mama was wrapped in colored funny papers, and it had a red bow and a twig of mistletoe tied on it.

"Mama!" I called her to the door and handed the package to her.

"Why, thank you, Lewis." Mama held the package and watched Lewis go down the steps. Then she called out to him. "Wait a minute, Lewis, and let me— Let me send Donie something too."

"Aw, hit ain much, Miss Venie." Lewis came back up onto the porch and stamped his feet again. "Hit a set o them yellow glass f'm Mister Byrd's store. Miss Mildred gived Trudy a bunch of em an Trudy gived Donie two sets." He looked through the screen at Mama holding the box. "She ain nevah taken em outen the box, Miss Venie. They clean."

"Wait a minute." Mama set the Christmas present from Donie on the hall table, and when she came back to the door she handed Lewis two packages of candy and some English walnuts and a big box of firecrackers. "Merry Christmas!"

Lewis went out the back gate whistling, and Mama and I sat back down to breakfast. "Well, now I have two sets of yellow glasses!" She buttered a biscuit and handed it to Daddy. "That's what was in the box Neevy left under our tree yesterday, too. A box of yellow glasses."

"Aunt Neevy has great slews of them, Mama." I reached for the jelly Mama had made from the mayhaws we'd picked last spring. "You ought to see the great slews of those yellow glasses Aunt Neevy has. She gave them to everybody she knew. You, and Sister Mearl, and Uncle Elmer's aunts—"

"Well." Mama looked at the box of glasses from Donie, wrapped in colored funnies and with the crooked red bow and mistletoe. "They're nice glasses. Now let's eat, so you can take a box down to Martin."

Mama had sent a note to Martin, inviting him to eat Christmas dinner with us, but Martin was sick with a cold, and so last night Mama had agreed that we could take a box of stuff down to him.

The box for Martin was heavy when we finally left with it, because besides the footwipers and blotters and handkerchiefs that we'd made for him and the scarf that Mama had knitted, we had

177

put in some of the candy and nuts and a piece of fruitcake from Eloise.

The snow crunched under our feet and twice little flocks of birds flew up into the trees.

"I thought the birds all went south in the winter," I said.

"No, stupid." James brushed the snow from a stump and set the heavy box on the stump. "Let's rest a minute. What did she put in that box, Daddy's iron shoelast? No, stupid, they don't *all* go south. Some birds stay in Arkansas for the winter. That's why Martin has those feeders around his house." He lifted the box and we went on through the snow.

We could hear the birds around Martin's feeders before we went around the curve in the trail. The smoke from his chimney was going straight up and floating out over the icy, sparkling trees, and icicles from his roof hung almost to the ground. Martin's house looked like a Christmas card.

"Knock on the door," James said. "Hurry. This thing's heavy."

I knocked.

"Come in, come in!" Martin called from inside. "Lift up the latch and come in!"

Martin was sitting in front of his fireplace, a blanket across his legs. Open, on the blanket over his lap, was a big Bible, and on the round table by his chair were the pictures of the woman and the little girl.

Martin put the big Bible on the table and stood up and his blanket slid down to the floor. James picked it up and put it back on the chair, and Martin went over to his shelves and took down the gifts he had for us. There was a book for Daddy and a book each for James and me. For Mama he had a little basket of perfect red apples, and you could tell that Martin had rubbed and polished every one of those apples.

"Would you like some chocolate?" Martin watched us warming our backsides at his fireplace. "I have a pot in the kitchen, with some marshmallows to drop in and some cinnamon sticks to stir it."

"Don't care if we do," James said.

I was cold and it sounded so good that I couldn't say anything. I swallowed and nodded.

James went into the kitchen with Martin and brought two more chairs in and set them at the little round table and when Martin

178

brought the chocolate in I found the fruitcake that Mama had sent in the box and put it on the table.

"Now isn't this cozy!" Martin said. "This is exactly the way Christmas ought to be. Warm fires and good friends and a hot cup to drink and a bite of a cake from faraway places." I had told Martin about Eloise sending the fruitcake when I was looking in the box for it.

"Drink your chocolate before it gets cold." James tapped me on the shoulder, but I wasn't really listening to him. "Don't be nosing into other people's things."

"She's all right," Martin said. "Don't bother her. Let her drink it when she gets ready for it."

I was looking at the Bible that Martin had left open on the table.

Mama had been right. Martin had a wife one time. It was on the page he had opened in the Bible. It said that he had been UNITED IN MATRIMONY with Mary Margaret Stegall on May 12, 1910, and around their names were angels holding streamers of pink and blue flowers. I looked at it for a long time, and then I turned the page.

The next two pages told about BIRTHS and DEATHS. That was the awful part.

Only one name was under BIRTHS. Frances Louise Ahrens had been born on June 20, 1912, and her name was on the facing page, too. Frances Louise had died on December 21, 1918, and Mary Margaret Stegall Ahrens had died on December 23, 1918. So I knew for sure who the pictures were on Martin's round table, and I knew what had made the lines on his face. And there wasn't one thing that I could do for him.

I stirred my chocolate and licked the cinnamon stick and put it in my pocket and looked around the room. On Martin's shelves were some more presents that he intended to give to people. There were some things for Donie's family, and for a lot of other people that I didn't know. There were even some things for the Thompson kids.

It was a kind of an odd Christmas Day, without any company at all—Eloise couldn't get off work and Aunt Neevy had gone to Wellco—but it was a good one. When we got home from Martin's, Daddy had put on his white shirt and tie. Mama had on her blue silk dress and a hen was baking in the oven. Everything was perfect. Mama's dress was getting tight around the middle, but when she put her apron on and pinned Grandma Thorpe's gold watch to her front, you couldn't tell that her dress was tight at all. You didn't even notice it.

After dinner James and Daddy put their laced-up boots on and went out to track rabbits through the snow, and Mama and I went into the kitchen to crack pecans for fudge.

I took out a perfect, unbroken half of pecan and put it in the little blue bowl. "Mama, may I go down, after a while, and show my new coat to Thee and Josie?"

She put the nutcracker down and frowned at me. "Go down to show— Of course not. On Christmas Day? Christmas is for family and friends, Thorpe."

"But you sent Donie a present and she gave you one. Why can't I—"

"Donie is my *washwoman,* Thorpe! Donie is a nigra, and they are her *nigra* children. Can't you understand the difference?"

I watched Mama measure sugar and cocoa into a pan. She poured a cup of milk into it, and took it to the stove and stood there stirring.

"Shouldn't people get to choose their own friends, Mama?"

"Well, maybe when they're old enough." She stirred the fudge and held her stomach. "There's no such thing as being friends with a nigra, Thorpe. A thing like that makes everybody concerned unhappy. And that's what you're doing! James gets into fights and Geneva breaks her neck getting over here to tell me about them, and the other children in school laugh at both— Don't crack that nut with your teeth! Use the nutcracker." She left the candy boiling, and sat down at the table.

"And it would hurt Thee and Josie most of all, don't you see, because when they grow up they'll be smart-aleck nigras, and Thee could get into bad trouble, even get killed, when he gets grown, if he doesn't know his place. So—"

"But what about the song we sing in Sunday School?"

"What song?"

"You know, the song about red and yellow and black and white and He loves all of them?"

Mama sighed. "Well, of course He loves them. So do we. Have you ever seen me hurt any— Oh, God in Heaven, what do you say? I think that's enough nuts. Listen, Thorpe, would you want to *marry* one of them? Or to see James marry one?"

I didn't want to marry anybody, and I didn't much think that James did.

"I wouldn't even have anything for the babies to eat." I looked down at my front and thought about Josie's baby chewing on her. "How could I marry?"

Mama just looked at me, and it was exactly the way she used to look at old Peanut, that old dog we had who couldn't learn to do tricks. She came over and took the bowl of nuts from my hand and poured them in the fudge.

She stood with her back to me, stirring again. "Thorpe, we got you the red coat because we love you. Now do you love us enough to do something for us? Something that would make us all very happy? Will you *try* to make some friends your own age at school, and give up this idea that you can ever be *friends* with our *nigra washwoman's* children?"

She poured the candy into the platter she had buttered, and sat down at the table and held her stomach. "Oh, God, I hate to drive a bargain with a Christmas present, but what else can I do?"

She looked so sad and miserable that I couldn't stand it. I went over and sat down on the floor at her feet and put my head in her lap. How beautiful were her feet with shoes.

"I love you, Mama," I said. "And I don't know how to make friends, but I'll try. I wish we lived in the yellow house in Strawne again, and you could have an iceman and—"

"Well, we don't." Mama put her hand on my head and rubbed my hair back from my face. "And so let's try to get along in this house. Let's all do what we can to make each other happy. Don't sit on that floor too long. You'll catch cold."

Daddy and James came home pretty soon after that. It had gotten too dark to track rabbits, and they came in cold and hungry. We took the fudge into the living room and listened to the radio and Daddy read aloud to us from my Dickens book. But when everybody went into the kitchen for cold chicken and fruitcake, I went to bed.

I lay there in bed for a long time, thinking about the whole day and about what Mama had said while we were making candy. Then I knew what I had to do. I got out of bed and took the red coat from my closet and put it back into its box.

Because I loved her so much that I could not bear to see her unhappy, and if that was what it took to make Mama happy, I would quit being friends with Thee and Josie. But I would *not* swap them for a red coat. I did not want the coat-box under my bed, either, so I looked around the room for a place for it. I stuck it in the corner with some clothes and toys and books on top of it. I crawled back into bed, and when Daddy came in to kiss me good night I pretended to be asleep.

Daddy leaned over and pushed my bangs back from my face, and his hand stayed on my cheek for a moment. He stood there over my bed, and I think he was looking down at me, but I did not open my eyes.

Mama found the red coat, later, in its box in the corner, and hung it back in my closet again, but I didn't wear it. I wore the plaid one of Dawn Starr's, and the red coat hung there, soft and bright and warm.

And who wanted to wear it?

Eloise came to see us before school started again after the holidays. She didn't come on the bus; she drove up in front of the gate one morning, in a big shiny black car, and she had a friend with her. We heard the car out front, and we ran out the gate to meet them.

"Gaw," James rubbed his hand over the hood of the car just before Eloise jumped out and grabbed him and hugged him. "A new car and a new fur coat and everything!" He pulled back from Eloise and looked at the car again. "You must really have a good job this time!"

Eloise laughed and turned James loose and hugged me.

"Silly goose, is the car all you're interested in? It's only borrowed, James. It belongs to my—to a friend. I just borrowed it for the day."

She hugged Mama, who had put on a sweater and come out the gate. "Venie, this is Sue Beth. Sue Beth, I want you to meet the sweetest, nicest big sister God ever put a gut—God ever made."

Everybody was laughing and talking at the same time.

"And you must be a *mar*velous person, all the *won*derful things Eloise is always telling us about you," Sue Beth was saying to Mama. Sue Beth was pretty, too, but not as pretty as Eloise. Sue Beth had real silver-white hair fluffed out around her face, and she had long black eyelashes and bright red lips like Eloise, but she was not as pretty. They both had on black silk dresses with a lot of glittery stuff around the bottom, and they had on spiky black high heels with glittery bows on them.

"And this must be little Thorpe." Sue Beth was still talking. "And James! What a big handsome boy!"

"Br-r-r!" Mama said. "It's cold out here. Let's go into the house where it's warm. James, get their suitcases."

"Oh, we didn't bring any suitcases." Sue Beth was *still* talking. "Only these little old make-up kits." She handed the two little brown cases to James, and we went in the gate behind Mama and Eloise, who were talking, too.

"Is that *your* car?" James asked Sue Beth. "Why was Eloise driving it?"

"No, honey." Sue Beth took her lipstick out of her purse and drew it around her mouth. "It's not my car. It belongs to Eloise's *gent*leman friend, and it's just one of his little old cars. Oooh, what a *gent*leman friend she has, that lucky old thing."

Her gentleman friend? Did that mean her boy friend? Her sweetheart? If Eloise had a sweetheart, then maybe I shouldn't give her the picture that had been in my pocket since before Christmas. . . . But I had promised Leo that I'd give it to her when she came. . . . I spent most of the day wondering what to do about Leo's picture.

"Where's Jim?" Eloise asked after they'd been there for an hour or two. "Is he at work? Has the mill started up again?"

"No, he's gone to Wellco." Mama stood at the pantry door and looked into it at the empty shelves. "He's gone in to Wellco to see about a job with the railroad. I'm going to open some chili and beans for dinner. I'll bet you're both starved, driving since midnight. Do you eat chili, Sue Beth?"

"I *love* it," Sue Beth said. Her coffee cup had a great thick rim of lipstick on it. "I could eat *chili* three times a day!"

Eloise set her cup down and went over and stood behind Mama and looked over Mama's shoulder into the pantry. She put her arm around Mama.

"I know what let's do!" She turned and spoke to the rest of us in the kitchen, and she had a funny look on her face, like she was about to cry. "Let's all get in the car and go somewhere and have hamburgers! Don't fix any chili, Venie! You need a day off, too!"

Mama argued a little bit, and said she didn't look presentable to go out to eat, but that's what we did. Mama sat in the front seat between Eloise and Sue Beth and when we passed Aunt Neevy's house on the highway Eloise thumbed her nose and didn't slow down. Mama laughed and talked and was happier than she had been since Eloise had come home for Thanksgiving.

We sat in the Cheerful Corner and ate hamburgers and hot dogs and nobody said make it snappy. James spilled his soda pop but nobody scolded and the music box kept playing. All the time Eloise kept watching everybody who came into the Cheerful Corner, like she was looking for somebody.

"Let's drive around a little while," she said after we left the café. "You're not in a hurry to go home, are you Venie?"

We drove around the block that had the Post Office, the bank, the park, and Mr. Byrd's store. That was about all of town there was. When we passed Mr. Byrd's store, Eloise slowed the car, and then she picked up speed again and eased on down the street to where the houses started. Most of the houses were neat and white in Strawne, with Christmas decorations still up around their fronts and wreaths on the doors. Eloise and Mama talked about who lived where in the houses along the muddy streets, and who was doing what to make a living. Finally we had seen all of the houses, except the flats, across the railroad track, and I guess Eloise didn't want to see them.

She turned up the highway toward home, but when we passed the tabernickle at the crossroads, Eloise kept on driving.

She drove clear to Wellco, and Mama laughed and said how foolish it was to burn up all that gas. Eloise kept saying that oh well Christmas came but once a year, and Sue Beth, who had gotten in the back seat when we left the café, kept saying what a *marvelous* time she was having.

In Wellco, Eloise stopped in front of a Piggly-Wiggly store, and turned and spoke to James in the back seat.

"Let's go in here, James, and get some Cracker Jacks and things, to munch on." She looked at me. "You, too, Thorpe. Come on."

Inside the store, I guess Eloise must have bought some of everything they had. She bought sacks and boxes of stuff, and a man helped her and James carry them out to the car.

"Sue Beth, you'll have to get back up front," she said, as they started loading the stuff in the car. "It's going to take the whole back seat for this stuff."

"I hope that's not *all* Cracker Jacks," Sue Beth said as she got in the front seat by Mama and drew another ring around her mouth with her bright red lipstick. "Are we goin' *camp*in' or somethin'?"

"We might," Eloise said and backed the car out and we started home.

When we got home she made James and Sue Beth help her unload every bit of that stuff and put it on the shelves in our pantry and Mama went out on the back porch and cried.

"Eloise," she said, and held Eloise's arm as she started into the pantry with two big cans of peaches. "I don't know what Jim will say. He might not like it."

"Oh, phooey." Eloise pulled her arm loose and set the peaches on the shelf. "Don't tell him. Just let him think you're one hell of a good manager, to stretch a dollar this far!"

Mama sat and watched them, and they barely had the last can put away when Daddy came in. And Mama got cross again.

Daddy was in the living room drinking coffee with Eloise and Sue Beth after he came home, and Mama was in the kitchen, and I guess she was worried because he hadn't found a job. She called him and he went into the kitchen. She asked him if he'd forgotten that the cow had to be milked and she said something about old fools ogling young girls. Daddy said that was too ridiculous to argue about and I didn't hear anything else they said. I followed Eloise into my room to give her the picture that Leo wanted her to have.

I put the picture down on the dresser in front of her, and Eloise sat and looked at it and then she picked it up and put it in her purse and she never did put on any fresh make-up. Sue Beth came in and put on powder and lipstick and eyebrows and fluffed her white hair.

"Are we ready?" she asked, and Eloise nodded. Eloise looked more like she'd taken her face off than like she'd put a fresh one on, but they put on their fur coats and Eloise kissed all of us and Sue Beth said what a *mar*velous time she'd had all day, and they left.

We stood at the gate and watched the long shiny new car easing

185

down toward our mailbox, and then we went in the house feeling sad.

"Gaw," James said. "Eloise is sure lucky."

It was that same night that I was sick three times before morning. Mama said it must have been the hot dogs, but it wasn't. Before daylight I started itching all over, and by breakfast time I broke out solid, with chickenpox.

When school started again on Monday, I was sick. Mama fixed me a bed in the front room by the heater, and Daddy got some ointment from Doctor John to rub on the bumps, and I lay in bed and held Grandma Thorpe's gold watch and broke out in sores. All over.

"Don't you dare drop that watch," Mama said. "I shouldn't let you kids hold it when you're sick. It's almost a hundred years old, you know. I remember my grandma used to wear it, pinned to the front of her best black dress."

Mama said these things about the watch every time she let us hold it. Which was only when we were sick. Of course it wasn't Grandma Thorpe's watch any more, really. It was Mama's. Like the big black bed and chest that were Aunt Neevy's, and the silver that had been Eloise's until she sold it and Mama and Aunt Neevy cried. It was Mama's watch, and she had said that some day it would be mine.

Mama moved and straightened the ointment and things on the table by my bed. Then she opened the heavy old red drapes. "Let's have a little sunshine in here." She sneezed. "Good Heavens! If we do have to have Dr. John out here with you, he'll say lady there's nothing wrong with the child except too much dust from those awful old drapes!"

We both laughed, and it was worth being sick. Holding the watch and laughing with Mama, I felt cared-for and happy.

"I remember," Mama said, "when I used to try to swing on those old drapes, and Mama would have a fit. And one time Donie hid behind them, before I started to school, and—"

I went to sleep holding the watch and listening to Mama's voice. When I woke up a few minutes later because my throat itched, she was still dusting and cleaning and talking.

"—and Neevy needn't gripe, about us living in her half of the house rent-free. If we weren't in it, it would be empty. Or have nigras living in it, like has happened to so many of the old houses around. Houses that I used to visit in and play in, and now nigras are living in them. And a house is gone, if they ever move into it—"

"Or Thompson?" I said sleepily. "Thompsons can ruin a house, too. Mama, aren't you glad that Junie Thompson's not my best friend?"

Mama had left the living room and gone to the back door to let Donie in. I heard Donie talking as she gathered up the washing and went back outside, and a few minutes later I heard Thee out back, coughing. And I could not go outside because I was sick, and Thee could not come in because he was a nigra and he could not be my friend. Ever.

Mama went to the back door, later, and called to Thee to come in the kitchen out of the cold, and he came in, but that was where he stayed. In the kitchen, and I did not see him.

It was hard to tell what was good and what was bad, when you had to choose somebody to hurt. I didn't laugh and talk any more with Mama that day.

12

The chickenpox bumps made blisters, and the blisters made sores. Before they all went away I had missed more than two weeks of school.

When I went back, Miss Wooley hugged me and said that she had missed me and that she had a whole new list of poems for me to learn. "Let's give a cheer for Thorpe's return!" she said to the class, and they all yelled Hooray! and one boy passed two marbles up the aisle to me in a sack. A few minutes later, Dawn Starr dropped a note on my desk that said I could be in her Red Rover line at recess. So it seemed like, to make friends, that all you had to do was to be absent and let them miss you.

"I thought you got a new coat for Christmas," Dawn Starr said as we went out the door at recess.

"I did but I don't wear it to school." Nor anywhere else, either, if I can help it.

"Want some hard candy?" Junie Thompson pulled a piece of candy out of her coat pocket and gave it to me and I said Thank you but I didn't eat it. It had dog hair or something on it, and I didn't feel *that* friendly. . . . Nobody called me, in Red Rover, but at least they weren't arguing over who had to take me onto the tail end of their line. It was a pretty good day.

Thee wasn't at the tabernickle all week. He was home, sick

with the cough he'd had that day in our kitchen. I missed seeing him at the tabernickle every morning, but after school and on Saturdays we wouldn't have had time to play, anyhow, because of this deal that James and I had made with the Candy Man.

The Candy Man came around every two weeks, and if you wanted to, you could sell candy for him and earn stuff. One day when he came around, James and I took ten boxes of candy to sell for him and earn a doll with a pink silk dress. To make Mama feel better.

So, on Friday, I said a sad poem about a boy who stood and let a whole ship burn up under him, and after school James and I went out to sell candy. We went again every time Mama would let us until the whole month of January was gone and it was Groundhog Day but we hadn't sold much candy.

About the only people who bought any of the candy were the railroad men at Miss Mildred's. They bought a box, if they were there, every time I went for a piano lesson. I guess Stella wasn't as good a cook as Trudy had been. Stella had moved into Trudy's little house and had taken Trudy's place in Miss Mildred's kitchen, but she was fat and she didn't look as clean as Trudy. Once when Miss Una was there Miss Mildred had to ring the little bell three times before we could have coffee, because Stella was in the kitchen talking to Callie and didn't hear the bell.

Miss Una wasn't talking much that day. We drank our coffee after Stella finally brought the tray in, and Miss Una sat there and looked at me.

I was telling them about Eloise having a friend who had this big new car that she drove, and about the groceries she had bought in Wellco for us, and right in the middle of it, Miss Una spoke.

"Will, he always wanted a, a little girl," she said. "If he's got a, a tender spot, it's for little girls. The Lord knows he wasn't ever tender with, with his boys."

"Oh, now don't talk that way, Una honey," Miss Mildred said. "Will's a good man. He brought those boys up in the church, didn't he? He works hard, and he tithes, and——"

"But after I saw how he was set, how he was set on treatin' the boys"—Miss Una was still talking like she hadn't heard Miss Mildred—"why, I never wanted a little girl. I'm real glad, glad we didn't have one. The, the boys would have noticed the difference, you know. And it would have been hard, hard on them."

She didn't say anything else after that, and pretty soon Callie took her home. I didn't play "Rock of Ages" for her that day.

It took all of February and most of March for us to sell that candy. We walked for miles, to every house we could find, but nobody had any money except the railroad men and sometimes the men at the tie yards. Every time Billy Bob Jackson bought a candy bar at the tie yard Nathaniel paid for it.

There were places in the woods down back of Donie's house that had never felt the sun in the summer. The big trees spread and locked together and the little trees grew up underneath, and walking through those places was like walking on a wet sponge. In the winter months, when the woods were still and quiet and the cold gray moss hung down and brushed you in the face and the briars caught and held you, it was dark and lonely and ghosty. Sometimes we ran through those places. Ran until our sides ached and our chests hurt. Then we had to sit down and rest when we'd reached the clearing on the other side. Sometimes we tiptoed, slow and easy, and James kept looking over his shoulder and we talked about every ghost story we'd ever heard.

"The Pig White place isn't really ghosted, is it?" I looked through the big dark trees toward the old tumbling-down shack that nobody had lived in for years.

"Of course not." James walked faster.

"Josie says it is. She says that when the moon is full blood comes out on the tree where the night riders tied her Uncle Bobo to whip him. And that you can hear screams and hear the clop of the horses and see the light—"

"You know that's not true! Shut up!" James looked back toward the old house and grabbed my hand. "Let's run a while and get warm," he said. "It's—it's just eerie around here, that's all."

Away from the shadows and the eerie places, I stooped and looked under the pinestraw, where Lewis had shown us to look for the first violets, and there they were, with little heart-shaped leaves and tiny buds, coming right on up through the straw. As the days got warmer, in March, we began to see the craw-dads out by the creeks, piling dirt, and I remembered how, last year, Donie had given us an old lard bucket to fry craw-dad tails in. James always pinched off the tails for us, and threw the craw-dads back into the creek, because he said it was all right if you threw them back in so they could grow new tails.

But we wouldn't—we couldn't—do those things together any more, James and Thee and Josie and I, because if you loved your mother you didn't have nigras for friends after you started to school. Sometimes my stomach hurt because I was so unhappy, but that was the way it was. And I wasn't alone in my unhappiness. Everybody at our house was kind of worried and sad.

It was because of the money, for the rest of them. We didn't have any.

One morning James asked Mama for a nickel to buy paper, and she said she didn't have one.

"But I *have* to have it," James said. "Miss Taunton said for me not to come to school another day, without paper."

Mama was in the pantry, opening a sack of cornmeal and when James said that, she gave a big jerk on the string at the top of the sack and it broke and cornmeal spilled all over the floor.

"Well, I'll be God-dern!" Mama sat down in the cornmeal and started crying. She hadn't talked that way, ever, and she didn't like for anybody else to. It scared us.

We left Mama sitting in the cornmeal and ran all the way to the tabernickle that morning, and James went to school without paper again. The next day Miss Una gave me a quarter again for playing her songs, and we had money for paper to write on at school.

Sometimes Daddy went through the woods with us, and we picked the poke salad that grew along the fences, but it wasn't for fun. It was so we could have it for supper. Once, after we'd picked a big basket of poke salad, Daddy broke off a branch of dogwood to take home to Mama, and James found a bush of wild honeysuckle already starting to bloom, but none of it smelled like it had last year when we'd picked it with Thee and Josie.

Daddy had planted a garden, and every day Mama walked up and down the rows to see if anything was ready to pick and eat. We ate a lot of cornmeal mush, even after Dammit had quit giving us milk to put on it, and of course, without any milk, we didn't have any butter for it. One Saturday when she came up to wash, Donie told Mama how to make dawg bread, and after that Mama made dawg bread to go with our poke salad.

"You jes poe boilin water ovah y' meal. Wif a spoonful o' salt,"

Donie said. "An a onion, ef you got one, chipped up in it. An nen you bake it, an eat it while it's hot."

"Why, that's just like hush puppies," Mama said. "Except that you bake it instead of frying it. And I guess you make it thinner?"

"Yes'm." Donie picked up the bundle of clothes and swung it over her shoulder. "Hush puppies is thicker dough, so you k'n make it into patties. But dawg bread's good, when you ain got the grease to deep-fry nothin." She took a jar of the soap that Mama and Aunt Neevy had made, and started to the back door.

"Donie." Mama reached for the jar of soap and took it from Donie's hand and set it back in the kitchen. "Donie, you mustn't wash for me today. Nor any other day, until I—I send for you. I don't have the money to pay you, nor any milk and butter to give you, and, and— Well, Jim can help me with the washing, and James, until . . ."

"Why, Miss Venie!" Donie swung the clothes bundle to her other shoulder and stepped back to the kitchen to pick up the soap again. "Me quit comin to help you when you that way? Miss Venie, you know they ain no nevah-min about the money when you helpin a fren! Now you git on back in that bedroom an make them baby cloes, an don you talk that way no moe!"

Mama went into her bedroom and made a baby dress from flour sacks she'd bleached white, but she didn't make any lace on it. And that afternoon, we went to Strawne, to Mr. Byrd's store, and didn't buy anything at all. Not anything at all.

"I guess there's maybe enough gasoline in the tank to get us to town and back." Daddy sat under the steering wheel and looked worried. "Dammit, I hate to ask Ben Joe Hudson to keep letting us have more credit, when—"

"Well, he'd just better not *stop* letting us have credit!" Mama settled down in the front seat beside Daddy, and James and I got in back. "After all, he is still my cousin, and blood's thicker than water, and—"

"But not thicker than gasoline. Gasoline he could be getting cash for." Daddy turned the car around and we were off, with them already arguing. Mama said that cousins just don't do each other that way and Daddy said that when she was ready to live off her relatives she might ought to go and live *with* them and that was the way it went all the way to town.

In town, we went straight to Mr. Byrd's store, and we all went in together. Mama had her grocery list in her hand, and the store was empty, except for us.

Mr. Byrd didn't come up front to meet us, smiling and rubbing his hands together and showing Mama all of his good deals like he'd always done. He was sitting at a big desk in the back of the store, and he kept sitting there, looking down at this big gray book that was open on his desk, and writing in it. We stood around and looked at things for a while, and Mama and Daddy looked at each other, and then Daddy went back to where Mr. Byrd was sitting. James and I started to go back with him, but Mama told us to stay up front with her.

We couldn't hear what they were saying, but we could see Mr. Byrd shaking his head and spreading his hands like he might be saying What can I do, and we could see the back of Daddy's neck turning red.

After a few minutes Daddy came back up front again.

"Let's go," he said, without slowing his steps up through the store, and we all started out.

"Oh, no," Mama said. "Jim, what—" and she put her hand to her stomach and followed him. James looked at me and said Come on and we went out the door behind them. Just as we were all outside the door, Mr. Byrd ran out onto the sidewalk after us.

"Aw, doggone, Jim," he said. "I'm sorry. I—"

"That's all right." Daddy looked down at Mr. Byrd's face, which was redder than Daddy's had been when we'd started out. "Forget it."

"Jim," Mr. Byrd looked down at a crack in the sidewalk and tried to rake a cigarette butt out of it with the toe of his shoe. "Jim, I want you to know that I'd help you, if it was up to me, but it's not. Ever since Mr. Jackson bought my mortgage from the bank, he's been the one to say yes or no. And he checked the books last week and he said—"

"Forget it." Daddy turned his back and started toward the car.

"Aw, Jim, if it was up to me, I'd let—"

"I said *forget it!*" Daddy turned and looked at Mr. Byrd again and his face was like a piece of the sidewalk that Mr. Byrd kept raking his toe over, and he was standing tall as a mountain.

Mr. Byrd scooted back inside his store, and after he was out of sight Daddy went all slumped, like all the air was gone out of him, and he walked so fast that he was at the car before the rest of us were halfway down the block.

Mama didn't slump. She walked straight and tall, all the way to the car. She was holding her stomach, but her face was quiet and proud, and her eyes looked straight ahead. She didn't look back at Mr. Byrd's store or down at the sidewalk, and the hand that wasn't holding her stomach went up to Grandma Thorpe's watch and rubbed over the red stones and the little pearls.

I walked beside her, carefully, matching my steps to hers and looking down at the sidewalk. It wasn't any time to step on a crack—and break your mother's back.

"Hi, Miss Thorpe, Mister James!"

Across the street, at the back door to the Cheerful Corner, Thee waved his hand and his teeth shone, white, in the big smile he always had when he saw us. He was standing beside Lewis, who was laughing at something one of the other nigras had said.

On the other side of Mama, James flipped his hand at Thee. "Hi!" James called out to him. I looked past Mama's hand, holding her stomach, and up to her face, so beautiful and so white it frightened you, and then I looked back down at the sidewalk and kept quiet.

I could not stand it. I slowed my steps, and when Mama was ahead of me I turned to wave at Thee. But it was too late. He and Lewis were going into the back door of the Cheerful Corner, and I had not spoken to him. It was done, and it could not be undone.

I crawled into the back seat of the car beside James.

"Well, shoot, we didn't buy anything!"

Nobody had said a word on the way home, until James leaned over the seat and shook Mama's shoulder. "I thought we went to buy some groceries!"

"Well," Daddy said, "we didn't. We don't really need anything. The poke salad's still good."

"Ugh!" James held his nose and made a gagging sound. "Let's go back and buy some meat! We've had so much poke salad now that I bet if we stood still by a fence we'd all take root!"

"And the garden should start producing next week." Daddy was still talking. He looked across at Mama. "I'll go back and talk to the railroad company again. Maybe I'll get on with them. That's one pie that Will Jackson can't help cut. And we ought to get that veterans' bonus by summer. I noticed in the paper that some places in Wellco are offering free help to veterans who need it in filling out the application. Maybe they mean business this time. Maybe we'll get it by summer."

"Have you filled out an application?" Mama was still holding her hand over Grandma Thorpe's watch and staring straight ahead down the highway.

"The last time I was in Wellco looking for work. My bonus should be around six or seven hundred dollars."

"Oh, sure." Mama didn't turn her head from looking down the highway. "Maybe we'll all fly to the moon. Maybe manna will fall from Heaven for us. Maybe a lot of things." She looked down at the watch. "Jim, we could probably get something for—I mean, maybe we ought to drive on to Wellco and try to sell this."

Daddy jumped around at her and we almost went off the road.

"Now who sounds crazy? Do you really think I'd let you sell that watch, Venie? Oh, Venie—" Daddy's voice was soft then, and he drove slow. In the back seat we couldn't hear much of what he was saying, but that was because he wasn't talking to us. He was talking to Mama, about borders of gold with studs of silver, that he had meant to bring to her to match the watch. And then his voice was louder, and we could hear him.

"Don't, Venie," he was saying. "Don't, please. Let me decide what dreams we'll sell, and for what price. And I promise we won't go hungry much longer."

"I know!" James' face looked like he'd just caught on to some kind of riddle that was being asked. "We could butcher old Dam—old Brownie!" He rubbed his stomach. "Oh, boy, what a beautiful steak she'd make! We could eat—"

"Butcher? You mean *kill* her, to *eat*?" I started crying. "Who could eat a murdered animal?"

In the front seat Mama started crying too.

"Oh, relax," Daddy said. "Both of you. Brownie's safe. She's not costing us anything, now that she can find grass to eat, and in a few weeks when she has her calf, we'll all have milk and butter again. She's perfectly safe."

"What—what about Peck?" I was remembering Thee's and Josie's hams and sausages and souse meat. "You're not thinking about—about eating him, too, are you?" James was evil. "I hate

195

you!" I screamed at him and bawled louder. Mama sniffed and blew her nose.

"I'm not thinking about killing anything." Daddy slowed at the tabernickle to turn. "But if some of this idiocy doesn't stop, I might go berserk and start it before we get home." He handed Mama his handkerchief. "James for God's sake, take your handkerchief to Thorpe, before we all have to swim the rest of the way home."

James mopped my face and held his handkerchief while I blew, and Daddy stopped at the mailbox.

"Roll your window down and reach in, James," he said. "And see if Leo left us anything today."

James reached in and pulled out the letter. He turned it over and looked at it. "Mr. James Torrance," he read. "Gaw, who do I know in Orchard Springs?" He started to open it, but we were home then, and Daddy took it from James' hand.

"I believe it's mine," he said, and his face looked like you'd lit a candle inside it.

"Well, I'll be damned. I'll be eternally damned."

Daddy sat in his big red chair and reread the letter he'd opened outside the front gate. James and I had followed him into the house, and we watched, still waiting for Daddy to tell us who it was from.

"You possibly will." Mama stuck her head out the bedroom door. "But we'd still like to know who on earth is writing to you from Orchard Springs. Where *is* Orchard Springs? What's that letter—"

"That sister of yours!" Daddy held the letter out to Mama, and then he pulled it back and looked at it again. "Here, I'll read it to you." He pushed his glasses back up onto his nose, and read.

"Mr. James Torrance, and so forth. . . . It's from a school board in Orchard Springs, Venie. Orchard Springs is right up on the Missouri line, and I sent them one of those letters I mailed out last fall. . . . Dear Mr. Torrance, it says, we received your letter of application and so forth, and so forth, and, having an unexpected vacancy beginning the following week, we tried to secure you for the position. However, upon calling the telephone number furnished in your letter of application, we were told that

196

the person answering the telephone knew of no such person as Mr. James Torrance, and, after receiving the same answer to a second telephone call and having to fill the position before the end of the Christmas holidays, we gave the position to another applicant."

"Oh, Jim!" Mama stood in the door and held her stomach. "Neevy didn't do *that* to you! How could— Oh, Jim, I'm sorry!"

"Sorry's hardly the word." Daddy looked back down at the letter. "However— Listen to the rest of it, Venie. However, with another vacancy to be filled by the first of April with a contract extending into next school term, we are now offering you an administrative position with—"

"Well, that's nice." Mama sat down on the couch. "But you know it's impossible. You'll just have to write and tell them it is."

"Impossible? Why?" Some of the light went out of Daddy's face and he looked puzzled.

"Because where would we get the money to move clear across the state? How will you pay rent and buy groc—"

Daddy looked across at Mama, hard, and she turned red. And then she kept on. "Suppose the baby comes before you even get a check? Jim, I won't go! I'm not going running off pregnant, dragging a bunch of hungry kids and—"

"I'll ask for an advance," Daddy said. "I'll go to town this evening and call them from John's office. And if I can't get an advance, I'll go to the bank Monday and borrow enough to move us. I'll mortgage everything we have. The old car and all the furniture ought to carry a hundred dollars! I'll work it out. You'll see!"

"And you'll see . . ." Mama stood up. "You'll see that I won't go with you, Jim. I won't. If you go, you'll go by yourself."

"Then, dammit, I'll go by myself!" Daddy stood up, too, facing Mama. "I'll go by myself, and I'll send you money to eat on, and you can stay here until you moss over!"

Mama ran out of the room and slammed her bedroom door and Daddy slammed out and got into the car and drove off. James and I looked at each other and neither of us said a word.

Daddy wasn't gone an hour, and when he came back nobody asked him about the advance. Mama was still lying down in her room, and James and I didn't want to know yet.

We guessed on Monday morning, that he didn't get it, because on Monday morning we didn't have to ride the schoolbus. We rode to town with Daddy, because he wanted to be there when the bank opened. And all day long, I felt like those people in one of Daddy's books who were chained to horses and pulled in half down the middle.

"When are we leaving?" James asked at supper that night, after we'd all been sitting there for hours pushing our food around and not wanting it. Mama glared at James and I started feeling pulled again. We all watched Daddy and waited for his answer.

"We aren't." Daddy's face was tired and gray, and there wasn't any light in it at all. "Money's scarce and tight, son, and they aren't making any new loans at the bank. At least that's what the man said, after keeping me waiting, hoping, supplicant at the throne of Will Jackson's mercy for half a day. I should have known." He sipped his water and turned the glass round and round. "I should have remembered that Will Jackson is not only the biggest investor in Strawne Savings and Loan; he's also on the Board of Directors."

Mama looked like invisible horses were pulling her apart, too. She reached across the table and her hand almost touched the back of Daddy's neck, and then she moved her hand back, and it lay beside the other one in her lap.

"Jim," she said. "Don't. Don't feel bad about it. These things usually work out for the best. I bet you that by next year you'll be back at Strawne High School, doing the best job of—"

"Of boot-licking in the country," Daddy said. "And of taking oaths that gag me to think of them. If that's what you see in our future, you watch it for me, too. Because I don't see it. Not yet. I'll leave walking!"

I sat on the porch with Daddy, after supper, and we watched the sunset above the trees change from gold to red to red-and-gray-streaked and finally to all gray like the rest of the sky, and we watched it without talking. Then I had to ask him.

"Daddy, are you going to leave us? Walking?"

Daddy stirred in his rocking chair and reached his hand out to my shoulder, where I sat on the floor at his feet.

"Thorpe, baby. Is all this talk frightening you? No, baby, I'm not going to leave you. Not any of you. When I leave, you'll all go with me, I promise. I won't hurt you *that* way."

It was good enough for me. I went in the house and went to bed.

13

13

"Complications?"

Daddy took a sip of his coffee and made a face like he had a bad taste, and looked at me and then at Mama.

James had left a few minutes earlier, to catch the school bus, but I woke up with a sore throat that morning, and I was still sitting at the table in my bathrobe, coloring the pictures in this old magazine that Eloise had brought to Mama. Daddy was making the face because of his coffee, not at Mama and me. Because of the way Mama made coffee those days. She didn't pour out the grounds and wash the pot; she just pushed it to the back of the stove and boiled it again next day.

"Well, complications or not," Mama poured hot water from the kettle into the dishpan. "I can't send her out in this damp weather with a sore throat. Why don't you just tell her the truth? She's old enough."

"No." Daddy put his cup over into the dishpan. "We'll do it this way, if we're going to do it. I'm not going to betray every confidence the child has, in one fell swoop. If it didn't mean her survival as well as ours, I wouldn't do it at all. Thorpe," he bent over me. "Gather up your things, honey, and I'll fix you a place on the couch, nice and comfortable."

I took my magazine and my crayons and followed Daddy into

200

the living room, and he wrapped me in a blanket on the couch and closed the drapes tighter to keep the sun from my eyes. I heard Daddy go out the back door. I left the crayons on the table and pulled the blanket over my head and listened to Mama's sounds from the kitchen. I was almost asleep when I heard old Peck squeal.

I sat up on the couch, and when Peck squealed again, like he was either being hurt or scared to death, I went to the window and looked out.

Lewis was coming from the barn. He had Peck's back feet in one big hand, and he was sort of dragging him. Lewis never stole things . . . did he? Maybe Daddy had told him to take old Peck down to the river bottom and turn him loose. I tied the belt of my robe and grabbed for my house shoes.

I could only find one shoe. The other one was way back under the couch but I couldn't take time to rake it out. I ran down the hall in one shoe, burst through the back door, missed the top step and rolled down the rest of them. I landed right beside Daddy, who was squatting over old Peck with a big shiny knife. They'd tied old Peck's back feet and Lewis was holding his head with one hand and his feet with the other.

"Oh Lordy," Lewis said when I rolled to a stop beside them. "Oh Lordy."

"Daddy! You promised, you *promised!* What are you *doing?*"

Daddy dropped the knife and helped me up and his eyes looked like they belonged to one of the animals we were always letting out of Billy Bob Jackson's traps.

"Baby, Thorpe," he said, trying to twist his face out of my hands. "We *have* to do this. We *have to.*"

"We have to what, Daddy?"

"We have to—oh God. We have to—to give old Peck a bath!"

"But the knife!" I screamed, "the knife!"

"Why, it's to clean and trim his toenails," Daddy answered me. "You ought to know. A nail file sure wouldn't do it."

Daddy squatted down beside Lewis again and Lewis held Peck and they cleaned and trimmed his nails. Old Peck squealed like they were killing him and I stood inside the back door and watched. Daddy's face looked like Uncle Elmer's did when Aunt Neevy caught him smoking inside the house, and I couldn't see

Lewis' face but his shoulders were shaking like he was coming down with something.

Mama watched them through the kitchen window for a while, and when I looked across the hall, her shoulders were shaking, too. Then she went back to the pantry and got out stuff and started making an eggless milkless sugarless cake with some of the sorghum syrup Donie had sent us. She was singing. For the first time in weeks.

"What have I to dread, what have I to fear, leaning on the everlasting arms. . . ."

Lewis dipped out some of the water they had boiling in the wash pot and set it on the bench to cool, and when they'd finished trimming his nails, they gave Peck a bath, with lye soap. They scrubbed him with Mama's broom, and he squealed, and neither one of them said a word the whole time.

Lewis spoke first, when they'd finished and stood back to look at Peck, lying there on the ground still snorting and squealing. Lewis' voice sounded kind of strangled, and his shoulders were still shaking.

"Seem a shame," he said, "puttin him back in that dirty old hawg-pen. Seem like we mought oughta hang 'im up to dry out some whilst we go clean it."

Daddy shuddered. "God, no," he said. "Don't hang him. I might still—"

"Here. You might as well go *whole hog*. Use some of this." Mama had come out the door with the bottle of lilac cologne Eloise left her New Year's Day, and they used it! Mama and Lewis both kept shaking, and their faces looked like they both needed to cough.

"Hell," Daddy said. "Let's take him back to that rarefied atmosphere he deserves, before we decide to go polish the rails around it."

They took Peck back to his pen, and when they came back to the yard, Daddy picked up the big shiny knife and put it on the back porch.

"Lewis," he said, "you figure what I owe you for this little fiasco, and I'll pay you someway, someday—"

"Aw, that's awright, Mr. Jim," Lewis kicked a burning slab back under the washpot. "Hit was the wrong time of year fo' fresh poke,—an I wouldn' rightly know how to figger it, anyhow. I ain nevah helped give no hawg a bath befo."

He went out the gate and off down the trail toward his house, and he must have thought of something funny right after he closed the gate, because he started laughing before he was out of sight, and we heard him whooping and yelling a long time after he went into the trees.

Mama pulled Daddy's head down and kissed him on the cheek. "You know," she said, "Eloise is right. You're the best man God ever put a gut in!"

Daddy smiled down at her, and some of the tired look was gone from his face.

"What else could I do?" He spanked Mama on the seat as she started back into the house. "And you and Lewis didn't make my role in it any easier. And what you just said about me—I want you to remember that, while we're eating that manna that's going to fall from Heaven for us."

In a way, Mama had been right about the manna. It didn't fall from Heaven for us, but that was the night that old Will Jackson brought us out a big box of relief groceries.

My sore throat was almost gone by evening, and I was able to play outside with James. But we didn't play much, because James looked funny when I told him about old Peck's bath. He fed Peccavi without being told, and brought in stovewood. Then he started bringing in water to fill the reservoir on the stove. We were out at the well, getting a bucket of water, when old Will's pickup truck drove up and stopped at the front gate.

In the kitchen Mama was singing again. Everybody felt good, that night, for some reason, until old Will came. "Lean-ning," Mama sang. "Lean-ning, safe and secure from all alarms. . . ." And then Mr. Jackson knocked on the door and a few minutes later Daddy exploded.

"Did you actually by Heaven do that?" he shouted. "Did you actually go to the Red Cross office and sign my name on the *relief* rolls?"

James dropped the water bucket back into the well. It hit with a bump and a splash, and the rope rolled out all the way to the knot in the end. We left our bucket from the back porch sitting there, empty, and scrambled onto the back porch to hear them.

"Aw, I didn't make a special trip," old Will was saying. "I had to go to Wellco, anyhow, and I thought if you was to of been there, you'd of signed for all them free groceries, and so I tuk that voucher right down to Walter Byrd's store an I filled it fer you."

"I don't accept charity, Will," Daddy said. "I haven't asked for it, and I shan't. Now suppose you just take the box home with you."

"Aw, this ain't charity, Jim. This here's help f'm the gummit. I know plenty of folks gittin' it, don't need it half ez bad as you do. Now—"

"*Now*," Daddy was shouting again. "You get out of my house! And you take that damned relief box with you!"

James opened the screen door quietly, and we eased into the kitchen.

Daddy was standing at the kitchen table, with his book flung across the checked oilcloth, and Mama was standing beside him holding the dishtowel under her stomach. "Get out, Will," Daddy said in a quiet voice, and his fists were clenched on the oilcloth until the knuckles were white. "Get out, now."

"Well, sure, Jim."

Old Will edged toward the back door, with his little pig eyes in his North Wind face going from Daddy's fists up to Daddy's face and back. But he didn't pick up the big box of groceries he'd set in the corner of our kitchen. "I'll get out, sure, Jim. But seein as how it's not your house to begin with, it's Venie's and Neevy's, why you got no call to be so high and mighty about a favor I tried to—"

Daddy's face was white as he started across the kitchen. Mama's dishtowel fell to the floor, and she grabbed and hung onto Daddy's arm. Old Will went down the hall and out the front door.

Outside, on the front porch, he stopped and looked back in through the screen door. "I'm goin', Jim. But I'm gonna leave that box. You'll hafta bring it back, an' you go' have some mighty hurt little tykes when you do. An' I still say there ain't no call for temper an' hard words."

He pressed his face to the screen wire and watched James and me as we lifted the stuff from the box and looked at it. The box said KELLOGG'S CORNFLAKES, but it looked like it had some of

204

everything in Mr. Byrd's store in it. Stuff that we hadn't bought since we'd moved into the breezeway house. Canned peaches and raisins and prunes and applesauce. And rice and sugar and corn-meal and a big slab of drysalt bacon and—

"If you feel reasonable enough to come outside an talk, Jim," old Will was saying through the screen door, "why, the main rea-son I come by was to tell ya that Jason Whitehall ain't comin back to principal for us next year. He's movin t' Wellco. They ain't no reason why you can't have that job next year, an' we talked about that very thing at the board meetin' the other night. Are you innarested, Jim?"

Daddy sat down at the table and looked across it at Mama. She sat down in her chair and reached for the dishtowel she'd dropped and folded it and pleated it and looked back at him. Daddy looked at James and me, still counting cans and stuff in the relief box, and then he stood up and pushed his chair back under the table and went outside to the front porch. To old Will, waiting there.

"Put that stuff back in the box," Mama said. "And go do your homework. And if you don't have any homework, turn the radio on and listen to it."

We went into the living room where the radio was already on and a man with a fast, clipped-off voice was giving the news. ". . . and the Haile Selassie frock, introduced in Bermuda last month," he was saying, "has been an immediate success. Cool white, with a slit, flowing skirt, the dress is being seen . . ."

James turned the knob, and Joe Penner's voice came out. "Quank! Wanna buy a duck?"

"Turn it down a little," I whispered. "So we can hear Daddy and old Will."

"Nope." James shook his head, and the radio stayed loud, but I moved over to sit by the window, with James, and we could still hear them.

Old Will coughed, and I heard the porch swing creak. So I thought that must be where he was sitting. If old Will was in the porch swing, then Daddy must be sitting on the top step. Or maybe not sitting. Just leaning against a pillar. I chose the pillar for Daddy, and I could almost see them out there.

"The main thing is, Jim," old Will was saying. "Right now, people don't trust you with their younguns. Or with the things their tax money bought. You done a crazy thing, an' now you got to prove y'self again."

"By riding with a pack of fools?" Daddy asked. "By aligning myself with that scum of creation, that riffraff?"

"Hold on there, now, Jim." The porch swing creaked again. "I ride with 'em sometimes, an' they ain't a banker nor a preacher in the county'll tell you I'm riffraff, nor scum. Billy Bob ain't riffraff, an'——"

There was a lot of laughter on the radio about something Joe Penner had said, and we couldn't hear them for a minute. Then old Will's voice came through the window again.

"Jim, we don't hurt nobody. We hafta keep 'em in their place, an' we may hafta whup a boy once in a while, but—"

Daddy said, "Boy, hell!" but old Will kept talking.

"The's one boy in yo' neck o' the woods needs it. I found out he went down to Dr. John's office last fall with some tale about his gal's woodscolt bein' Billy Bob's. Now I ain't sayin' Billy Bob don't like his poontang well as any young hot-blood, but he don't leave no woodscolts. He knows better. I remember when I liked a good piece of poon—"

"I'm not interested, Will. I don't want to hear it," Daddy said.

"An' this ol' looney back there that's goin' around preachin' to 'em, he ain't even a preacher! They ain't got no souls worth worryin' about, an' things like that makes trouble in a community. He—"

"What did you want to say about the next school term, Will?"

"I wanta say this first, Jim." Will cleared his throat and we heard him spit. I hoped it went off the porch. "I ain't got where I am by takin' up for other people, black or white. They's people works f'r me an' owes me money now that wouldn't spit on me when I used to walk up them red clay roads totin' biscuit an' lard in an' ol' bucket. I ain't got the education you got, cause I got wore out with sittin' on the back benches in them one-room schoolhouses so the other kids wouldn't catch itch an' lice f'm me, and I quit school after the third year, and I worked like a nigger an'—"

"I know, Will," Daddy said in a tired voice. "And I hope you get everything you have coming to you. You've earned it."

"Jim, I seen my mammy die when she'uz thirty, wore out, like that pretty little lady you've got in there's gonna be. Papa dug a

206

hole in th' red clay with a pick-ax, cause it wuz froze solid. An' after he buried her he took us younguns an' left out an' headed here to homestead. An' I made up my mind that some day I was gonna own half the county, I went after it an' I got it, th' hard way."

Daddy didn't say anything.

"When I went back to put a stone on my mammy's grave," Will said, "I couldn't even find it."

Daddy still didn't answer. Finally Will spoke again.

"Doggit, Jim, you know what I mean! This here's the United States where a man can be anything he wants to be. All you got to do is go after it in the right way. But you ain't going the right way, goin' against everybody in the country an' defyin God's plan for—"

"I guess not, Will," Daddy said. "But you have your ways and I have mine. And using brute force against a group of already—"

"Aw, look at it this way, Jim. They're like younguns. An' younguns need chastisin'. You admit that? Whom the Lord loveth, He chastiseth. An' sometimes He does it through His agents."

"It's not for me, Will." Daddy sounded tired. "Let's just forget the whole thing. I can't be one of the Lord's agents; I don't even have a horse to ride with you."

"You know I got plenty o' horses, Jim." Will coughed and the porch swing creaked. "I ain't pressin' you, but you better give it some thought. Ain't a man in the country agrees with what you done, an' ridin' with us is what you need to do to show you can get along with people." We heard old Will get up out of the swing and his steps sounded on the porch.

"I'll run along, Jim, but while you're thinkin' about it, you might think about how Venie and them little tykes looked at them groceries."

Old Will left then, and the front door opened and closed, as Daddy came back into the hall. We listened as he walked through the hall, and we heard the back door open and close. Daddy had gone through the hall and out into the back yard.

"You kids start getting ready for bed." Joe Penner was over and Mama had come into the living room to listen to her programs.

I started down the hall to the kitchen, but then I remembered.

There was something I had to ask Daddy. About poontang. I went out the back door and stood at the edge of the little porch and looked around the yard for him.

The night was still and quiet, with only the crickets chirping over by the fence, and once a whippoorwill called. I shivered. Josie had said that if a whippoorwill came into your yard and called, someone would die. The lopsided moon shone down through the pink-and-white blossoms that were already on the fruit trees, and there, in the moonlight on the ground, over by the smokehouse, I saw Daddy's feet. He was sitting on the washbench, and leaning back against the wall of the smokehouse, as still as the night.

I went down the steps. I stood beside the washbench in the dark that the moonlight could not reach. Beside Daddy. "Daddy, I love you" I said, and I put my hand up to his face and when I took it away it was wet.

We went back into the house then, and Daddy never did take the box of relief groceries back to Mr. Jackson.

14

"I cannot go to Canton in the rain, rain, rain—"

I sang, as I skipped out the gate to go down to the mailbox to
wait for Leo. It was a Saturday afternoon in spring, the first
Saturday in April, and everybody had something to do except me.
So I would wait and talk to Leo for a while. I could smell the
yellow jasmine and wild honeysuckle down in the woods, and
there was an ocean of blue daisies to wade through on my way
to the mailbox.

Daddy had gone to Wellco to talk to the railroad people again
—Ben Joe was still letting us have gasoline—and James had wandered off from the tie yard to look at some trees with Billy Bob
and Nathaniel. Mama was sewing baby clothes, and waiting about
thirty minutes to answer everything I said to her. So I'd come
down to wait at the mailbox and talk to Leo.

I went over to the twisted old peach tree by the barn and
pulled some green peaches to throw them in to Peccavi. After
that I wandered around through the ocean of daisies and picked
a great handful of the tiny blue flowers to take back to Mama,
but Leo still hadn't come. I sat down on the ground beside the
mailbox and waited some more.

I wondered if Mama would care if I walked down to Rocky

Bottom. Just to watch the craw-dads piling dirt, and see if the fish were jumping. It was time for her nap, and she'd be cross if I woke her up to ask her.

It was a warm day even under the trees along the trail. All kinds of flowers had pushed up through last year's rotted leaves, and the Spanish moss that Mama's Grandma Thorpe had brought with her from Louisiana looked old and sick against the new pale-green leaves. The earth is the Lord's and the fullness thereof —that was the memory verse we'd learned for Miss Mildred last Sunday, and on that Saturday afternoon in April I was sure glad the Lord was sharing His earth with me. I skipped a little bit, and stopped to caw back at a crow on a treelimb above me.

Thee and Josie were both out in their yard when I went by Donie's house.

Josie was sitting on an old chair with a cowhide bottom with the cowhair still on it, watching the chickens scratch and letting Peter Rabbit eat. That was the only place where Josie was still fat; the rest of her was just skin stretched over bones. Peter Rabbit was fat. He had on the little white apron Mama had made for him and trimmed with blue cross-stich, and he looked like a cream-colored dumpling.

Thee was standing over the washpot with an old butcher knife, cutting some bacon into strips to cook over the coals that were still under Donie's washpot. Over on the washbench were some forked sticks he'd already cut to hold the bacon while it cooked.

Donie came out the door with a basket of wet clothes and started toward the clothesline that ran from the house to a tree. "Don you catch on faar, now," she said to Thee. "An don be slicin on yo han none, either. Well, hi, Miss Thorpe."

I had been standing behind this big tree at the edge of the yard, watching them. When Donie spoke, they looked around and saw me and I went on into the yard. Mama wouldn't care if I just stopped and spoke. They didn't have to be my best friends if I just spoke to them.

"Hi, Josie. Hi, Thee. Is that real bacon?"

I hadn't smelled bacon cooking since I'd spent the night with Dawn Starr. Aunt Neevy had a whole smokehouse out back full of bacon and hams. Sometimes it got so old that she would find these little white worms in it. When she did, she just brushed them off on a paper and said Waste not want not and kept on slicing. I told Mama about the waste not and she said that much as she'd been craving a good thick slice of home-cured bacon, she was glad Neevy thought she hadn't made enough effort to deserve it and that Neevy hadn't been brought up that way.

"Daddy he brought in a whole side uv bacon las night," Thee said. "Fo plowin. Wait, I put you on a strip, too." The bacon grease dripped onto the coals around the washpot and sizzled and sputtered. The smoky smell of it filled the whole yard.

I started across the yard to join Thee at the washplace. Then I remembered. I had just stopped to speak to them, not to visit. "Oh, I can't. I have to go now. I'm just walking down to Rocky Bottom, to watch the craw-dads."

"By yo'self?" Thee asked. I nodded. "Wait, we might kin go with you." Thee propped the sticks of bacon over the black-iron washpot so that the bacon hung just over the heat from the coals, and ran around the corner of the house. I could hear him talking to Donie there, and her answering.

I went over and rubbed my hand over Peter Rabbit's head. He burped and rolled his head lazily around and smiled up at me. His black-silk hair curled around my finger.

"Mama say leave the bacon ovah th' coals an put Junior in his box an fix im a sugar-tit an we kin go!" Thee was back, looking happy. He took Peter Rabbit from Josie while she went inside to fix the sugar-tit. Thee walked around the yard with Peter Rabbit, and I followed him.

"Aw, now, you fat rascal," Thee kept talking to the baby. "You quit jumpin. I go drop you. Quit now, you fat rascal!" Peter Rabbit had punched Thee in the eye with his fist. We laughed and Thee juggled him up and down until Josie came back out with some sugar and butter tied up in a clean white cloth. Thee put Peter Rabbit in this big wooden box with a ragged old quilt in it, and we were off down the trail. Just like we used to do.

"I go be in a Tom Thumb weddin," Thee said after we'd walked a little piece. "For th' end o' school."

"What's a Tom Thumb wedding?"

We were practicing for an operetta for the end of school, but I wasn't too excited about it, because all I was going to do was be a firefly and wiggle a little flashlight tied on back. We didn't even get to keep the flashlights.

"It a play. Like somebody gits married. An I git to be th' preacher, like Brother Amos an Mister Martin. An I haf to wear a tie an a white suit." He kicked a clod of dirt from the trail, and his bright, happy smile faded a little. "Ef Mama kin git me one."

Josie hadn't said a word. She just walked along with us and looked down the trail and up into the trees and smiled and smiled. She was happy, too.

When we got to Rocky Bottom, the Thompson kids were already there. Old Soggum was swinging out on the grapevine and dropping down into the water. Lester was holding Junie's head under and trying to drown her. Little Thompsons were playing around the edges of the water, and they all looked blue with cold. While we were watching, the littlest one stood there in the water and went outdoors.

"Hay, watch it there!" Soggum had crawled back up onto the bank and seen us. He stood there blue and shivering, with his skinny arms stretched between us and the creek like he was guarding something. "Where's J-James?" His teeth were chattering.

"Down at the tie yard, I guess."

"Well, go home. You can't get in the creek while we're in the water."

"We didn't aim to," I said. "It's not summertime yet. And anyhow, if we did aim to, we wouldn't, now, after what *he* did." I pointed to John-bo, the littlest one.

"Yeah?" Soggum stared at us. "What'd he do?"

"He went outdoors in the creek," I said. Thee and Josie hadn't said a word.

"That's a lie," old Soggum said. "You ain't goin' in cause you're scared to. Whyncha go back to school an' tell some more crazy things aboutcha black nigger frens?" The other Thompsons all laughed and Soggum grabbed the vine and swung out and dropped down into the Mouth of Hell. Lester had turned Junie loose and she ran up onto the bank.

"Yeah, nigger-lover!" she yelled, and ran back and got behind Lester.

"Oh, you're not so smart," I said to Junie. "And quit slinging

212

your damned old drippy hair toward us. The only time it ever gets washed is when you go in swimming. And you eat candy with dog hair on it. I wouldn't play Red Rover with you if you got down on your knees and begged me!"

Junie stared at me. "You're crazy." She stood there in the water behind Lester, shivering.

"You call me crazy?" This was fun. "You stand there freezing to death and call me—"

"Yeah, you're crazy," old Soggum said from the Mouth of Hell. "Yeah, crazy an' scared too. You're scared to jump in this water while we're here. Scared to when we ain't here, too."

"She ain't scared, neither." Thee stepped in front of Josie and me. "Ain't none of us scared. We jes ain't s'posed to."

"*You* ain't s'posed to git in th' water with white folks. That's wha*chu* ain't s'posed to do. You're scareder than she is."

"I ain't neither." Thee stepped closer to the edge of the water.

"Okay, black boy, if you ain't scared of what I'll do to ya, come on! Come on, grab that vine an' swing out an' drop right down here by me! We'll see how brave ya are!"

Thee looked up at the grapevine that hung from the big tree, and took a step toward it.

"No, Thee, don you do it!" Josie was shaking. It was the first thing she had said since I'd walked up in front of their house. She held Thee's arm in both hands and pulled him back to where we were standing.

"Aw, you scared he'll drownd?" Old Soggum yelled up at us. "He won't drownd! Hay, Thee, how come they call you a nigger? You too yeller to be a nigger! You mus be a Chink!"

Thee pulled his arm from Josie's hands and ran to the grapevine. He looked back at us once, and then he grabbed the vine with both hands and swung out over the water. Before he even dropped, the Thompsons were all scrambling for the banks.

"Don't!" I screamed at them. "Stay there! Stay in the water! He can't even swim—"

"He cain swim, he cain swim—" Josie put her hands over her eyes.

"We ain't stayin in th' water with no nigg—" the rest of Soggum's words were lost in Thee's splash and Josie's screams.

Thee fell tumbling and he hit the water hard and it closed

over his head as he went down down down. And then there were only the ripples of the water and some bubbles. The ripples kept hitting the banks on all sides.

We waited, and he did not come back up. Nobody said a word. There was only the sound of the little waves and ripples still hitting the banks and a bird in the tree overhead singing. Josie's hands were still over her eyes, but she wasn't screaming. She was listening.

We stood there, and the water got still and quiet, and we looked around at each other.

Then we ran.

The Thompsons scattered into the trees and Josie turned into her yard and I kept running. I slowed at our gate, and past our house down at the mailbox I saw Leo stopping his mail truck. I ran toward Leo, and he waited.

"I left you a letter from Eloise." Leo said, but who cared then?

"It's Thee, it's Thee." I sobbed after Leo had held me and made me breathe again. "Thee's in the Mouth of Hell and he didn't come back up."

In the mail truck we bounced over the ruts and the weeds and down into the trees and around them, and when Leo jumped from the truck at Rocky Bottom, Donie was running down into the water. Leo kicked his shoes off and followed her.

"Thee, baby, Thee. . . . Theotus, baby? . . . Come on, baby, come on—" Donie was calling, like Thee might hear her from under the water and come up. "Theotus, Thee, come on—"

"Can you swim?" Leo asked Donie as he stopped and looked out over the creek. Donie looked at Leo like she wasn't really seeing him or anything else and shook her head.

"You get back up on the bank and sit down," Leo said. His voice was gentle. "Go on, now, get back up here and sit down and I'll find him."

Donie sat down. Right there in the water she sat down and waited. "Thee, baby," she kept calling, and on the bank Josie held Peter Rabbit like a sack of meal on her hip and looked up into the trees.

Mama and James came through the trees and stood on the

214

bank beside me. Old Jelly Thompson waddled up with Soggum, and all the Thompsons came out of the trees and stood around watching.

Soggum could not have yelled Chink at Thee when Leo brought him up from the water. Thee was all gray and water came from his mouth and nose when Leo bent over him and did things. Leo straightened up and looked at Donie and shook his head.

"He was caught on an old tree limb," Leo said. "We'll take him in to the hospital at Wellco if you want to, but—"

"She wants to." Mama pushed me closer to James and went over to where Donie was squatted on the ground over Thee and still talking to him. "Mr. Thompson," she looked at old Jelly. "Will you go and find Lewis and send him home? I believe he's over working for Elmer today." She put her arms around Donie, wet dress and all, and helped Donie to stand up. "And, James, you and Thorpe go by Josie's house with her, and when Lewis gets there you go straight home. And *stay* there. I'm going with Donie."

"Yes'm," old Jelly said, and Leo lifted Thee and they all got into the mail truck. Mama took Thee's head in her lap and they left.

Soggum watched them leave and then he picked up a clod of dirt and threw it into the water. "Wonder what he's go' do about people's mail?"

"I magine he's fixin to lose a dern good job." Old Jelly took a step or two back toward the trail and then he turned and bumped into Soggum, who was right behind him. "Ain't no use to take that nigger to a hospital, he's dead. You didn't push that nigger in, did you?"

"Me?" Soggum backed up a step or two and looked at his daddy. "I didn' have nothin to do with it! He jis jumped in."

I tugged at James' arm.

"Quick, what's the worst, the very *worst* word you know?"

James' freckles all stood out like bumps on his face and for a minute I didn't think he'd heard me. "I d'no," he said. "Bastid, I guess, or sonbitch. . . . Why?"

Soggum was walking off through the jasmine and honeysuckle along the trail with old Jelly. I ran, and when I reached them I stood in front of Soggum and looked up into his ugly face.

"You bastid," I said. "You stinking ugly sonbitch bastid, you! You sob!"

Old Jelly turned and looked back and down at me.

"You need a whuppin'," he said. "A hard whuppin'."

Overhead in the tree the bird was still singing, and in my hand, bruised and dead, were the blue daisies that I had picked a long time ago to take to Mama.

"His bacon's still cooking," I said, and nobody answered me.

We sat on the washbench, James and me, and Josie sat in her cowhide chair and fed Peter Rabbit, and we waited for Lewis to come, and nobody was talking. "It's still cooking," I said again, and the bacon grease sizzled as it dropped onto the coals that had turned to gray ashes and the smell of it was more than you could stand, but nobody moved it and nobody said anything else.

Lewis came into the yard and took Peter Rabbit from Josie's lap, and we knew that he knew. Lewis sat down on the end of the washbench and leaned back against the wall of his house and with his eyes closed he bumped Peter Rabbit up and down on his knee.

"Lordy," he kept saying. Just that. "Oh, Lordy, Lordy."

James stood up.

"See ya, Lewis," he said. I followed James out of the yard and Josie moved over to the washbench with Lewis, and we went home.

I went around the house and sat on the back steps. I wondered what it was like to be dead. Just, in one minute, not to be living any more. . . . How? What was it like?

"Well, I don't know, stupid!" James had come out to sit by me and I had tried to ask him. "It's not like anything, I guess. You're just *dead* and they put you in this pine box in the ground and put the dirt on top of you and—" He didn't finish. We sat there in the sunshine.

"How do you get out of the box to go to Heaven?"

James thought for a moment. "Well, stupid, you don't get out of the box. Your *soul* does!"

"Will they put Thee in a box and his soul have to get out of it?"

James shook his head. "From what Brother Mearl says, I don't know for sure. But the way it figures out, they—nigras—don't have souls."

"Don't have souls? You mean they can't go to Heaven?"

"Well, stupid!" James looked miserable, and glared at me. "Why don't you hush? How do I know? You don't think horses and cows and—and things go to the same Heaven we do, do you? And God put them here, I guess, to be servants, like horses, and so . . ."

"That's not right." I moved away from James and stood up. "I'll ask Martin. Here he comes now."

Martin didn't stop. He went past our house, and instead of turning off the trail to go home, he went on down toward Donie's house. We went to the fence and watched him until he was out of sight.

"Wonder why he's going down there?" I hung on the fence. "Nobody's home but Josie and Lewis."

"Well, fool," James said. "He knows that, I guess. I guess he's going down to sit with them."

"Sit with them? Out on the washbench? Why?"

"No, not on the washbench. You just sit with people when somebody dies. Can't you ever be quiet?" James stood away from the fence and looked back at me and his face was all screwed up. "Just shut up them damfool questions! If I'da been along, it wouldn't've happened!" He went toward the back door, all humped over and digging his fists into his eyes.

"Well, if they're people," I jumped back from the fence and shouted after him, "why don't they go to Heaven? Why don't they have souls? Why can't we all just be people together?"

James banged the back door and after a while I went into the house, too. I had something to do.

I took the red coat from its hanger in my closet and threw it to the floor. I stomped it, and that was not enough.

I ran into Mama's room and scratched through her sewing box until I found the scissors, and then I slashed and cut until all I had left of the coat was a bunch of red ribbons. I dragged the ribbons outside and stuck them under the wash pot and went back inside after matches.

The smell of the red coat burning was thick and sour, and it came in the back door and filled the breezeway hall.

Mama and Donie came home from Wellco in the car with Daddy, but Thee was not with them. Donie sat in the car while Mama came in the house and put on her blue silk dress. She put her flowered smock on over it, because the dress wouldn't button any more, and then she pinned Grandma Thorpe's watch onto her smock and they left again. . . .

James found some cereal in the relief box and poured it into bowls for us, but neither of us ate anything. We sat in the living room. It got dark and James lit a lamp and I went in my room and sat on the floor in the corner. The lights of the car flashed into the darkness of my bedroom when Mama and Daddy drove up out front again, and I did not move.

"Where's Thorpe?" They had come in the front door and were in the living room talking to James.

"In bed, I guess," he said.

"Oh, well, we won't waken her," Mama said, and went into her room and started sewing. *Sewing.* I did not go in to tell her that I was still awake nor to see what was so important about baby clothes that she had to sew on them on *that* night. I did not want to talk to her.

It wasn't like any other Sunday morning we'd ever had.

When I woke up, Mama was in her room sewing again, and except for the sewing machine the house was quiet. In the kitchen, James was sitting looking out the window, and when he saw me he pointed to the oatmeal Mama had cooked and left on the back of the stove. Oatmeal from the relief box.

I dipped up a spoonful of the oatmeal and dropped it back into the pot and went to stand beside James at the window.

"You should eat something. Both of you." Mama had quit sewing and come into the kitchen. "Well, that job's finished. I think I'll just make an eggless chocolate cake." She went to the relief box in the corner and bent over it. Then she thought of something else, and she went to the door and called Daddy in from the yard and they talked for a minute. Daddy followed Mama into the bedroom and came out with a bundle and got in the car and left, and Mama went back to her cakemaking.

I wondered where Daddy was going, but I was too tired to ask. I went out in the yard with James and we walked around under the peach trees and James pinched off one of the tight little rose-buds on the fence and broke it open.

"See," he said. "They don't really have fairies in them. I told you they didn't." But I didn't answer. I didn't care.

When Daddy came home the cake was on a plate on the kitchen table and Mama had on her flowered smock again.

"Everything's ready," Daddy said. "Are you ready to go down there for a few minutes?"

Mama nodded. "James, get a can of those peaches from that box. No, Jim, I'll carry the cake. It won't bear any juggling around. Come on, Thorpe."

. . . Come on, Thee baby. Theotus, come on. . . .

We went along the trail, and Daddy stopped once and looked down among the leaves beside it. "Some late violets," he said, and he stooped and picked them and handed them to me. "Take them for the— Give them to Donie," he said.

Donie's house was full of people, and they were all nigras except Martin and us. Martin was there, and Brother Amos from Mount Carmel, and Nathaniel and Callie, and a lot more that I didn't know.

Thee wasn't in a pine box. He was lying in a gray box with silk around and under him and a silk pillow under his head, and he had on a white suit and a blue bow tie. Maybe it was the suit that Donie had meant for him to wear in the Tom Thumb Wedding. . . . He looked asleep, like he'd wake up and grin, if you touched him and I didn't know that my hand was reaching for his until Mama took my hand and held it. "Don't touch him," she said.

The gray box was on a bench in front of the fireplace. If Thee could have opened his eyes he could have read the colored funnies on the ceiling over him. But he was asleep in the gray box, and the peacock spread on his bed was smooth and stiff and clean. The cracked mirror over the fireplace mantel had been turned around and you couldn't see yourself in it.

Fat Stella from Miss Mildred's was there. She and Callie and some more women were sitting in cowhide chairs around the gray box, and they were singing, sad and low, and kind of moaning. Once in a while one of them would quit singing and say Lord, Lord, and they would all sway back and forth and moan together and then they would sing again. Mama pulled me into the kitchen, and I gave Donie the violets that Daddy had picked. She put them in a glass of water and took them into the front room and set them on the gray box that Thee was in.

In the corner of the kitchen, Lewis was sitting in his old rocking chair with one arm, rocking Peter Rabbit and talking to him. Josie sat on the floor beside the chair and looked up at the ceiling.

"—an he ain hongry an cole no moe," Lewis was saying. "He ain worrit, an he ain weary."

"An I take 'im back, hongry an cole an all!" Donie leaned her face against the wall and moaned. "I want my baby back. I wan' im *now*."

The kitchen was quiet. Donie started crying and Mama patted her on the back. Lewis quit rocking and sat still and looked at Donie.

"You hush, woman. You hush that, now. You don' know what you sayin, wishin 'im back. He waitin fo us to come home now, not us fo him."

"Hello, Thorpe," Martin said and reached for my hand. "Let's go back in here for a minute." We went into the front room and Martin took some of the violets from the glass and put them in Thee's hand and stood there and looked down at them. "He's God's child now," he said, and I think that he was talking to himself. "He's God's alone, and what we have here is not even a good imitation of what he found waiting for him. . . ."

We went back into the kitchen, and Martin left me with Mama and he went over to stand at the wall again with Brother Amos.

"Mister Martin," Lewis said from his rocking chair. "Would you—could you say a few words at the— Ah cain't say it. Would you speak ovah Theotus? You was his fren, an he loved you."

"Certainly I can," Martin said, "if you want me to. And if Brother Amos doesn't object."

"I be proud to have you stan by me," Brother Amos said. He took off his thick glasses and wiped them and put them back onto his long sad face, and then he straightened his long skinny body away from the wall. "I go in here an lead a prayer, now." He went into the front room, and Nathaniel stood against another wall and watched us all.

"Theotus be proud, too, ef he knowed it." Donie had quit crying. "To have you speakin ovah him, Mister Martin." Then she walked around the kitchen tall and straight, nodding to people.

"Is Trudy coming for the funeral?" Mama asked Lewis.

"No'om, she ain have time to git here by tomorrow," Lewis said. "Mister Martin call 'er, on the phone in town, an she say she ain have time, but she mought come later. I sho wisht she was here."

Mama looked tired and whispered for me to pull up my bloomers and we left pretty soon after that. Daddy had gone over to talk to Nathaniel, and when we went out the door Naye came out behind us. And outside, around the yard, I noticed something that I hadn't noticed before we went in. Tied onto the crepe myrtle and cape jasmine bushes were a lot of blue and green glass bottles and jars, and when the wind moved them they clashed and tinkled like little glass bells.

"Who put those there?" I pulled Mama over to look at the bottles and little jars. "Who put the bottles in the bushes? What for?"

"They're to—" Mama pulled me back, and she didn't say anything for a minute as we stood and looked at them. "I think each person who comes brings one," she said. "Kind of like bringing flowers. They put them on the grave, I believe."

"I know what they're for." James stood behind us and listened to the tinkle with us. "They're to keep evil spirits away from the house, like turning the mirrors around so evil spirits can't call Thee into the mirrors and—"

"Well, hush," Mama said. "Quit staring. Let's go."

"Mister Jim, do you believe in God?"

Daddy and Nathaniel were waiting for us at the edge of the trees, and Naye was asking Daddy that question as we came up to them. I listened, to Daddy's answer.

"Do you mean God-with-a-long-white-beard, Naye?" Daddy asked. "Or do you mean God the Creator, the Supreme Being?"

"I don't know what I mean, Mister Jim. I don't know." Naye's mouth was a straight line, and his eyes didn't make you think of any kind of music. "I guess what I mean is this. There, in that house. A dead little black boy and a half-white baby. No father for the baby and no obituary for the son! Because they don't print obituaries for dead pickaninnies, do they? Don't you think that's a kind of unfair division of sorrow, Mister Jim, to wish it all off on that one family?"

"Well, yes," Daddy said. "But—"

"And what does Lewis do about it? He sits there and moans Lordy Lordy and rocks his daughter's half-white bas— baby. Look at those bottles back there!" Naye waved his hand toward the bottles tinkling in the wind. "You know what I ought to do, Mister Jim? I ought to go back there and smash every one of those bottles before they can take them to put around over that grave! Smash the ignorance and superstition! Pull Uncle Tom to his feet and go with him after the man who fathered that baby! That's what I ought—"

"Whoa, there," Daddy said. "Back up, Naye. Nobody ever cured ignorance and superstition by smashing things. You know that."

Ahead of them, Mama jerked my hand and said, "He's a fine one to talk about smashing things not being the answer! Come on, Thorpe. Hurry. You're walking too slow."

I pulled my hand loose from Mama's and when she walked on ahead I hung back to walk with James.

"You think I have time to back up, Mister Jim?" Behind us Naye and Daddy were still talking. "You want me to end up sitting around moaning Lordy Lordy? Or tied to a tree somewhere? I have to hurry, Mister Jim. I have to do something or bust wide open!"

"Then the first thing to do," Daddy said, "is to get an education."

"You think it's that pat, Mister Jim, really? Just get an education? And what comes after that?"

"After that it's up to you. If you can't gain a little wisdom with the education, you can come back here—or go anywhere else—and be the best-educated man ever tied to a tree. You have a brain, Naye. Use it. Take one step at a time, and keep in mind that they're giant steps . . ."

"Listen!" James held me back and pointed to a clump of bushes just off the trail. Something in the bushes was making a squeaking, frightened sound. James eased over and looked and then he called to Daddy. To come and help him free the rabbit that was caught in one of Billy Bob Jackson's traps.

They set the rabbit free and stood there looking at the trap

222

and talking. I ran the rest of the way home and when I caught up with Mama at the gate I darted past her into the house.

What was an Eggless Chocolate Cake? She'd been making them for months.

On Monday morning it was drizzling rain. Daddy took us to the tabernickle in the car and stayed there with us until the bus came, so that we didn't have to crowd under the tabernickle with the Thompson kids.

The skies hung low and gray, and the drizzle turned to cold heavy rain that fell all day. The warm sunny world we'd had last Saturday was as far away as it had been in November, and Monday was a bad day.

I kept thinking about what was happening over at Mount Carmel Cemetery, and I wondered if the cold rain would soak through the ground and would the gray box leak onto Thee? I stared around the room at the other kids and I tried to see them in the gray box with their faces wet and the gray silk cold and damp and spotted and streaked. . . .

"Thorpe."

Miss Wooley had come back to my desk and was standing beside it. "Thorpe, I've asked you three times to read the next page, honey." Her voice came through the fog around me as soft and beautiful as her face, and I tried to think what she was saying.

"Ma'am?"

"Thorpe, I've asked you three times to read. Never mind. Go ahead, Dawn Starr. Take your hand down and read the next page." She squatted beside my desk. "Thorpe, honey, you haven't paid attention all day. You haven't done any of your work, or read any of your . . ."

Thee would never read again. . . . My best friend is dead and they are putting him into this hole they dug in the ground and I cannot tell you because it is wrong for him to be my friend and when I saw him on the street I did not speak and now he is dead. . . . A bee flew in through the door that was opened to the hall and lit on my desk. Thee would never, any more, call out Honey in the bee-ball and he would never read even the colored funnies on his walls that we had read together.

And Mama had found the little burned pieces of the red coat and she had cried and said Why Thorpe Why but who knew why?

223

And so I got through two more days, and it was Wednesday again.

"Thorpe, please tell me what's the matter with you this week."

I sat at my desk after the rest of the kids had gone, waiting for James to beckon at the door that he was ready to walk to Miss Mildred's with me, and Miss Wooley knelt on the floor and put her arms around me. "Are you sick, Thorpe? Is something at home bothering you?"

"No ma'am."

"Is it because you're going to have a new baby at your house? Is that worrying you?" She had seen Mama at church and in town and she knew about the baby.

"No ma'am."

Miss Wooley sighed. "Thorpe, what is Jim— What is your father doing now? I mean, where is he working?"

"He's not working. Old—Mr. Jackson closed the mill down. May I go now?" James was standing outside the door, waiting for me to go to Miss Mildred's.

Miss Wooley stood up and her hand stayed on my shoulder for a moment and it felt soft and kind. When she moved her hand, I wanted to reach out for it and hold it against my cheek. She started back up the aisle to her desk.

"Miss Wooley," I said. "Daddy would work now if he could. He would like to be teaching again, you know, but Mr. Jackson says they don't want him to teach here any more until he takes some Awful White Supremacy." I stood up and picked up the books I was taking home. "Miss Wooley, is Mr. Jackson your boss, too? Did you have to take some Awful White Supremacy?"

Miss Wooley sat down in her chair and looked across her desk at me, puzzled. "Awful white supremacy?" she said. "What—" Then she said, "You don't mean *Oath* of white . . ."

She looked scared. "Yes, you do mean oath," she said. "They're doing that to him, just because of those old books!" She stood up again and came around her desk and then she did something real odd. She sat down in Dawn Starr's desk on the front row and held my face between her hands and looked at me for a long time.

"You are not a liar," she said. "You didn't make that up."

"No ma'am."

Miss Wooley was quiet for a while, and I stood there, waiting, until she spoke again.

"You'd better run along to your music lesson. And what you said about White Supremacy, Thorpe, you mustn't repeat that to anybody else. Not *anybody*. Because, somewhere, you've heard words not meant for a child. Or for a woman. Words best forgotten. Do you understand?"

"Yes ma'am."

Miss Wooley went back to her desk and picked up her grade book, but instead of writing in it, she watched me start out the door.

"It's a sorry world, Thorpe. Maybe you can make it better."

"Yes ma'am." But it was the only world we had for now, and if James was right, the only world that Thee would ever have. I went on to Miss Mildred's house and tried to play the piano.

At home everything was different. The house was quiet all week, with nobody laughing, nobody singing, nobody cross and yelling. At night I went from one room to another and looked at the quiet people in the quiet house, and it was like each of us had a worry that we had to think about alone. I thought about the night I'd teased Mama about being a butterfly in a glass jar and, that week, I saw us all in glass jars. You could see the other people moving around and hear them talking and all, but you couldn't really join them and they couldn't join you.

"Do you think," I asked James one evening, "that maybe a whippoorwill flew into Donie's yard or something? I mean, Josie said one time that if a whippoorwill flew into your yard and called, somebody would die."

"Oh, fool!" James glared across the kitchen at me. "How do I know why it happened? It just did! Why don't you go on to bed?"

The week had passed, and it was Friday evening. I was standing on the back porch, watching Daddy sharpen his last razor blade in a glass of water.

It had been his last razor blade for a long time. What he did was, he put it in this glass of water, and with his finger he rubbed it around and around inside the glass, and when he took it out it was as sharp as a new one. I swung around the porch column, watching him.

"Didn't Dawn Starr come home with you from school?" Daddy dried his razor blade carefully on the towel and looked up at me before he started putting it in his razor.

"Yes. She did, but Daddy, do I have to go in the house and talk to her? I didn't *ask* her. She just came up to me and said Guess what, I'm going home with you. Do I have to—"

"We-ell . . ." Daddy poured hot water into the washbasin from the teakettle he'd brought from the kitchen. "Somebody asked her. Evidently. So, yes, I'd say maybe you'd better go along with it." He started soaping his face.

"Go along with what?"

"With the conspiracy. It's called distracting—" He laid the little brush back in the cup and reached for his razor again. "Never mind. Your mother means well, Thorpe. She thinks it's for your own good."

"Thorpe!" Mama called from the kitchen. "Come in here and help Dawn Starr set the table!"

I pretended not to hear Mama calling. I had to be on the porch with Daddy, and not in there with Mama and Dawn Starr with the walls closing in around us. Because, with Mama, my throat ached and hurt and got tighter and I could not say anything at all.

Daddy was through shaving, and a little trickle of blood was running from his cheek down onto his neck, and another trickle was starting on the other side. He took the blade from his razor and looked at it and turned it and frowned and shook his head.

"That damned thing should have been thrown away six months ago," he muttered, and threw it over into the pink-and-white four o'clocks that grew up around the porch.

"Daddy, why are you always cross before you go to Masons?" I held onto the column with one hand and swung out into space from the edge of the porch. "Don't you like to go to Masons? You should, because a Mason is a fine and honorable thing to be."

Daddy was standing there wiping his face and looking down into the four o'clocks. "That's all we need around here," he said. "Blood poison in a cut foot." He went down the steps and into the flowers and found the old razor blade that had made his face bleed and picked it up. "I agree with you about the Masonic

Lodge," he said as he came back up the steps. "Is that an original statement, or did you hear it somewhere?"

"Martin said it. Last week I asked Martin if he was a Mason, and he said he wasn't an active one. Are you an active Mason?"

"You asked him if he *were* a Mason." Daddy rinsed his face in cold water and dried it. "And yes, I suppose you could say I'm an active one. In the Masonic Lodge, yes. In what takes place afterward, when the riffraff gathers, no." With the towel still across his shoulder, he started refilling the teakettle.

"You forgot to hang the towel back on the hook, Daddy. What's riffraff?"

"It's—"

"Thorpe!" Mama came out the back door. "Thorpe, I have called you three times to come in and set the table. Now go in there and help Dawn Starr."

I went into the house, and Mama stayed out, talking to Daddy.

"Jim, I don't want to be cross with her, but she hasn't answered a thing I've said all week. And the only time she gets out from under your shadow is to go to school! What's the matter with her? How long is it supposed to last?"

"Young Lycidas is dead, Venie." Daddy's voice was soft, and his words came out slow. "You know what's the matter with her."

"Young who?" Mama said. "Lycidas?"

"Oh, forget it, Venie," Daddy said. "You don't know who young Lycidas is, and I can't conform to—so we are none of us perfect and I don't feel like explaining anything. I don't know any answers, any more than you do."

"Are you both crazy?"

Mama didn't sound cross. She sounded lonely. So lonely that for just a second—and then it went away again—I knew something terrible. Something as big as the world. I knew that every single person in the world could be lonely at the same time, and nobody, *nobody* able to do anything at all about it. It was the glass jars. . . .

I pushed Dawn Starr out of my way and reached for the plates.

"What'd you push me for? I'm going to tell Aunt Venie."

"Go ahead." I shifted the stack of plates to my left hand and pressed my right hand against the top of the stove. "Go ahead, tell her."

I held my hand there, against the stove, but either the stove was not hot enough to burn or else I could not feel it. It was not on purpose that I put the cracked plate at Mama's place, but when I noticed, I did not move it.

"This rice came from the relief box," I told Dawn Starr after Mama had put a big fluffy spoonful of it onto Dawn Starr's plate and covered it with gravy. "Everything we eat comes out of the relief box, because we don't have any money. The meal and the flour and the sugar and—"

"Thorpe!" Mama's face was red. "Eat your supper!"

"Of course the peas came from the garden," I said. "But we *don't* have any money. Sometimes there isn't even a nickel in this house, for tablet paper. And the other night Daddy said that if Mama didn't hush about it he was going to do something drastic. I guess like hitting her."

"Thorpe." James reached over and shook my shoulder and I threw my fork across the table at him and it missed him and hit the floor and everybody was quiet.

"Thorpe," James said in a sad voice, and Daddy pushed his his chair back and left the table without saying Excuse me or anything.

"Go to your room, Thorpe," Mama whispered, and her face wasn't red any more. It was white. "Go to your room, and don't come out until I say you may."

She couldn't cook very good anyhow. Who wanted any of her old supper?

I went into my room and reached for *Tales from Dickens*. But instead of reading it, I lay across my bed and looked at my hand that I had stuck to the stove. I was still feeling things, because, inside, I was feeling bad about Daddy. Daddy was big and kind and gentle and wise, and he'd never hurt anybody. And I had hurt him. I had been rude and unmannerly and I had hurt Daddy so bad that he had left the table without eating. . . .

Outside the front gate, I could hear James and Dawn Starr and the Thompson kids playing. When Mama came in and said that I could, I would go outside and play with them. Even playing with old Soggum Thompson would be better than lying across the bed wanting to throw up and not being able to do even that. But I would not call Mama and ask her if I could go out. She had to care enough to come in and forgive me and ask me if I *want*ed to.

The room got darker, and in the darkness was the smell of honeysuckle and the sound of Dawn Starr squealing and giggling. I closed my eyes and tried not to hear or smell or think, and so I went to sleep.

When I woke up moonlight was coming into my room through the window, and Mama had not cared enough to come in and say anything at all to me. I went over to the window and looked out. The moon was a big round ball hanging just over the trees, with little stringy white clouds floating around and across it.

"The moon was a ghostly galleon, tossed upon cloudy seas," I said, remembering the poem that Miss Wooley had me learn once for Recitation Day. "A ghostly galleon—"

"Hey, it's dark in here!" Dawn Starr came into the room and fell across my bed, giggling and shivering. Aunt Neevy wouldn't let anybody even *sit* on her beds, but old Dawn Starr always rolled all over mine. "Ugh," she said. "You missed the fun! You oughta hear what we've been doing! We've been telling ghost stories, and boy, do they know some good ones. Is the Pig White place really ghosted?"

James had laughed at Thee and Josie and me when we'd talked about it, and said that I knew damned well there wasn't any such thing as ghosts. But James was afraid of Pig's old place, too, when we had to walk by it. I looked at the side of my room that the moonlight didn't reach, where the doll from the candy man was still in her box on the shelf.

"Well, of course it's—it's ghosted," I said. "When the moon is full like tonight, blood runs from the trees. And ghostly riders gallop around the yard and screams come from the tree where they tied Pig's husband to whip him." I tried to see Dawn Starr's face, in the moonlight. "He died there, you know, and they say you can see him there tied to the tree, and hear him moaning, and"—I got carried away—"and a maiden leans from the window, tying a dark red love knot into her long black hair!"

There was only one window in Pig's old house, with no glass and a ragged shutter hanging by one hinge, and the kind of ghost maidens that might lean from that window wouldn't have long black hair unless they'd used Trudy's straightening iron on it, but you could count on old Dawn Starr not to think about that.

"Ugh," she whispered. "Could we go down there sometime and see it? Do you think James would go with us?"

"We don't need James," I said. This was too good to quit. "We can go down there tonight. I'll go with you, if you'll go with me to take a book back to Martin. I've been down there lots of times." I hadn't seen Martin all week, and maybe if I could talk to him for a while, Martin could make everything all right again.

"That crazy old man? That old coot?" Dawn Starr had stood up, but she sat back down on the bed. "What do you want to borrow books from him for? Mama says he's—"

"Martin is my friend." I found my shoes under the bed and sat down to put them on. "He is my friend, and I need to take his book home. He might need it."

We argued for a while. Then we unhooked the screen and crawled out through the window.

James and the Thompson boys were still out by the front gate, telling ghost stories, but they didn't see us climb over the fence. And they didn't see us ease around the corner and onto the trail that went through the trees to Martin's house.

15

The woods were quiet. An owl hooted once, but nothing answered him, and we walked closer together. A whippoorwill called, and a mockingbird tried to mock him and didn't quite make it.

"If a whippoorwill comes near your yard," I said, "point your finger at it. Because if one comes in your yard and sings, it means someone is going to die. Unless you point your finger and scare the death away."

"I know it," Dawn Starr whispered and held my arm tighter.

"Or if a bird taps on your window somebody's going to die," I whispered. "Or if you sweep your trash out after dark, you sweep out one of your family."

"Where'd you learn all those things?" Dawn Starr held my arm and shivered.

"From—from a friend of mine."

We were quiet then, slipping along through the trees and thinking how easy any of those things could happen to you. . . .

Dawn Starr tripped over this old tree root and went sprawling. She got up rubbing her knee and crying.

"Let's go back home," she moaned. "I don't want to see any old ghosts tonight. Let's go home, Thorpe!"

"Oh, come on!" I held her arm, and she was shivering like she'd already seen a ghost. "If you can't walk faster, I'm going

231

on to Martin's house by myself, and you can just forget about going to the Pig White place."

"I don't care," she whimpered. "I don't want to see any old ghosts. I want to go home."

"Go home, then," I said. "But if you do, I'm going to tell Mama that I looked out the window and saw you kissing old Soggum Thompson under the grape arbor. I'll tell Aunt Neevy, too."

I hadn't seen any such thing, but I knew Dawn Starr and I knew Soggum, and it must have been a pretty good guess. She held onto my dress and followed me as I walked on ahead to Martin's house.

The big moon came through the trees and made eerie shadows on the ground and the night was still and quiet. No more owls hooted, and no more whippoorwills called. It was a night waiting for something to happen.

We knew, when we went around the curve in the trail, that what we saw in front of Martin's house was one more part of that night. A big torch thing, shaped like a cross was stuck down in the earth of one of Martin's flower beds, and burning. On *fire*. There it was, jammed down among the mashed and trampled lilies and buttercups. Jammed down into the ground and burning with a bright light.

Nothing moved anywhere about Martin's yard, except the flame on the torch thing. The flame crackled and jumped, high and then low, and the smoke drifted up and away and you could smell burning pitch and pine tar, like the smell when they burned scrap lumber around the sawmill.

"What is it?" Dawn Starr asked. She had come from behind me when we walked into Martin's yard, and we walked around the cross and we looked at it and little grains of soot fell from the black smoke onto our faces.

"I don't know." We were not whispering, for the first time since we'd crawled out the window. "Maybe Martin put it out to scare off burglars. Let's go in and ask him."

I knocked on Martin's door. Nobody came to let us in.

I called, and we stood there waiting, but nobody answered.

Martin wasn't home. I pushed the door open, because Martin had said once that we could do that to leave books or to get more books, and we went inside to leave Martin's book that I had brought back.

232

Martin's rocking chair was turned over and his house looked like James' room looked after James left for school every morning. I put the book on a table and set Martin's rocking chair straight, and we left.

"Let's go on to the Pig White place," I said as we started up the trail. "We may as well, while we're this close."

"No. No! I want to go home." Dawn Starr grabbed my arm again and started crying. "I don't want to see any ghosts tonight. I was joking you. I don't want to go down there! I want to go home!"

"I keep my bargains." I kept walking. "And, anyhow, tomorrow you'll be telling everybody it was me that got scared. So come on!" I turned and looked back and waited for her. "I'm not going to walk home with you right now, so come on."

We crept through the woods, with Dawn Starr whimpering and shivering and dragging at my arm. James had said that I knew damned well there wasn't any such thing as ghosts, and I had believed him, but James might not be right. This was a good night to prove to myself that James had told me the truth—and a good night for ghosts, if he hadn't.

And that was how we almost walked right up onto the whole bunch of them under this old walnut tree in Pig's yard. The bunch of ghosts.

We stopped, quick, behind a big huckleberry bush, and squatted there, to keep from being seen. I'd meant to scare Dawn Starr, but not that much.

Her teeth were clicking, and her hand on my arm was shaking.

"Let's go home," she moaned, but I didn't answer her. I was too busy watching the ghosts.

For something that damned well wasn't, the ghosts were sure busy in Pig's old ragged, weed-covered yard that night. We'd never have as good a chance as this to watch real ghosts again. There were a lot more of them than the bunch we'd almost walked into. They were moving around all over the yard, and some of them were on ghost horses. There was another one of the big cross-shaped torches burning in Pig's yard, and the light from it and the light of the moon made everything as bright as day. The ghosts were all in white robes, and so were their horses.

Dawn Starr's whisper was too loud. "I didn't know horses

had ghosts! I didn't know horses came back when they died! I'm going home!" She straightened her legs to stand up.

"Sh-h-h—" I put my hand on top of her head and pushed her back down and tried to hold her, but she pulled away from me.

"Go on, then," I hissed at her. "But I'm staying. I want to watch them."

Dawn Starr scuttled off up the trail on her hands and knees, crying and shaking. When an owl hooted above her she stood up and ran without looking back.

I watched her fade into the shadows and bushes along the trail. When I looked toward Pig's yard again, the little huddle of ghosts had moved away from the big walnut tree. Under the tree, tied to it, was a ghost without a robe. He wasn't even wearing a shirt. I could not see his face, because it was against the tree, but he looked exactly like a real man.

Maybe ghosts did, underneath all the white stuff. Maybe they looked like real people. Anyway, after this night, James couldn't tell me what was damned well what again, about *anything*.

The ghosts all came together again, in the middle of the yard, and had a ghostly conference.

Except for one. One ghost was still on his horse, and as I watched, he eased around the edge of the yard toward the walnut tree until he was right over the big huckleberry bush. The one I was crouched beneath.

Somewhere in the trees an owl hooted again. One of the horses jumped and one of the ghosts laughed. I had not been afraid until I heard the laugh. It was a laugh I'd heard before. It was the same laugh that we'd all heard at the tabernickle when Billy Bob Jackson splashed mud on us. And down at the tie yard, when he bought chocolate and didn't pay for it. I listened to their voices, then, and they were real men's voices. It was then that I began to be afraid.

If these were real men, then the night was ugly and real and terrible, and something ugly and real and terrible was about to happen. It was in the wind that rustled the leaves over us, the ugliness and the terror, and in the soft, frightened whinnies and restless feet of the horses. It passed among the little groups of men standing around old Pig's yard, and leaped and flickered from the burning cross.

I wanted to run after Dawn Starr and yell at her to wait for me, but I could not move. So I watched the ghosts that had turned to men, and I knew some of them.

The tall one. He was so tall that his robe only came to his knees, and he kind of stooped to listen to the others talking. That one was High Pockets. It had to be. Nobody else in the county was that tall. There, in another bunch, was Ben Joe Hudson, with his stomach holding his robe up and out in front . . . and the shiny black shoes and black Sunday pants under the robe beside Ben Joe belonged to Doctor John.

Then the biggest group began to separate. One of them stepped to the center of the yard while the rest eased back. The one who had stepped out had something in his hand, and it dangled to the ground as he turned toward the man who was tied to the walnut tree. He held it dangling while he took the bottle that somebody passed up to him. He pushed his hood up over his mouth and drank from the bottle and handed it back and then he held his arm out and the whip still dangled as he bent and straightened his arm and worked his wrist around and around and his hand up and down. The whip flashed across the yard and hit with a thud and when he pulled it back a streak of blood oozed from the back of the man who was tied to the tree.

The fire of the cross flickered and burned brighter and the only sound was another thud.

I crouched closer to the ground and shut my eyes so tight it made my face hurt, and pressed both hands over my eyes.

It was not real. It could not be. It was a dream, and the kind of dream that leaves you with the memory of fear for days afterward. . . . I was not in the woods at night, watching blood ooze from the back of a real live man while another real man swung a whip—I was in the ditch at school, and the *thud* was the sound of somebody's jump rope hitting the ground. . . .

. . . One, two, buckle my *thud*. . . . Three, four, shut the *thud*. . . . Five, six, pickup *thud*. . . .

The man on the horse standing right over my huckleberry bush groaned and said God, and I looked up. Up and across at his boots in the stirrups over my bush. They were lace-up boots, like Daddy's, and they had been resoled, like Daddy's. With red tacks.

It was Daddy on the horse, watching them whip the man who was tied to the tree and could not help himself. The sickness that had been in my stomach all week since Thee had died jumped up into my mouth and my throat and I leaned over and was sick on the ground.

I did not want to look again, but I could not help it. I had to look toward the man under the walnut tree. His back was a blur of red stripes, and his blood had spattered onto the ground and spotted the weeds and grass around him. His face was still against the tree, but as I watched, he turned it. He looked at the man with the whip, and then his head fell to one side and hung down onto his shoulder. It was Martin.

It was Martin, who had walked in muddy shoes to help people and who gave us books to read and polished the apples he gave to Mama for Christmas and who had a little girl one time and Daddy was watching as Martin's blood spattered onto the ground.

The light from the cross was bright in my eyes as I ran to him. I ran to Martin, and as the whip came at us I put my back against Martin's back and my arms went up, in front of my face.

I screamed once, but it was for Martin, because at first I did not feel the whip. I saw the blood on my arms as I lowered them, and then I felt it warm in my eyes and could not see anything at all. But I did not feel the searing streak of fire that ran across my chest and cut into my arms. Not until after Daddy had joined us under the tree and had picked me up.

Daddy held me for a minute against him, and then he knelt on the ground and held me on his knee. With one arm still around me, he tore at his hood and when it was off he used it to wipe the blood from my face and eyes. And I could not tell whether, kneeling there, he was cursing or praying.

"Where'd that kid come from?"

"I d'no, but ain't that the dawggonedst thing—"

The whispers from the robes sounded ashamed and frightened. For a time there was only the sound of the muffled whispers and the crackle of the burning cross and the wind in the trees, and then somebody spoke aloud.

"She's Jim Torrance's young'un, that's who she is."

"Whut's she doin' in th woods at night?"

Billy Bob said something then that I did not hear, and he tried to laugh. But his laugh died off into a whimper when Will's voice came out of the robes.

"Shut up, you fool! That's a little girl you done hit!"

Daddy had wiped the blood from my face and eyes, and from the circle of his arms as he still knelt there, I could see them. They were moving about again, moving into little groups and huddles like they had been at first, and whispering together. Billy Bob was left standing alone in the center of the yard, still holding the whip that dangled to the ground.

"*I* done hit 'er!" Billy Bob whirled completely around, looking from one group to another. "*I* done hit 'er! Lissen, ol' man, les don't be layin all th' blame on me, cause I ain't takin' it!" He reached down inside his robe for another bottle and lifted his hood again. He stood there in the center and there was not even a whisper as he drained the bottle and threw it against a tree and wiped his mouth on the back of his hand.

"I mighta used this thing." He held the whip out in front and shook it at the men. "But I never braided it! An' I never rode by myself. None o' th' rest of you had th' guts to use it, that's all! An' if I'da had me that nigger to whup, I wouldna used it on a white man. *Maybe.*"

He waited, but nobody answered. "Well, I'm still gonna find me that nigger before daylight, an I'm gonna whup 'im! Anybody gits in my way, well, they better not, that's all! That kid wouldna got in th' way, she wouldna got hit! Anybody comin' with me?"

Will's big muddy feet were heavy under his robe as he stepped out from the crowd around High Pockets, and the crunch was loud as his big hard fist hit Billy Bob's jaw bone. He nodded his hood toward High Pockets.

"Take 'im home," he said.

High Pockets walked out and looked down at Billy Bob and his voice was as nice and mild as it was when you met him at Ben Joe's station, as he prodded Billy Bob with his foot. "You better take care of 'im, Will. You raised 'im." He stood there, looking down at Billy Bob.

Billy Bob's arms and legs twitched, and then he rolled over and raised himself to his hands and knees. Everybody watched as he finally stood up, and nobody helped him. He stood there, rocking back and forth a little bit.

"Aw, why don' *you* jus go on home, ol' man, to Callie?" His words sounded thick and awful. "Ain' nobody taking me home, til I find an' whip me a nigger."

Daddy swung me up against his shoulder and stood up.

"Why don't all of you just go home?" He wasn't shouting. He didn't need to. "Unless you want to pull off your hoods and step out here and try to repair some of the damage this night has done."

Nobody said a word. There was only the crackle and the wind and the sound of their robes brushing together.

"Then by God, if He still listens to any of us," Daddy said, "ride off! The party's over!" He kicked the whip that Billy Bob had dropped when Will had knocked him to the ground. "And take that thing with you!"

Billy Bob was the first one to his horse. He grabbed for the whip and tucked it up onto his saddle and when he got on his horse he almost fell off on the other side. He steadied himself, and then he turned and glared across the yard at Daddy.

"I'd still like to know who tol that nigger we was comin'!" He rode off into the trees by himself.

One man walked out and pulled his hood off and dropped it to the ground and stooped over Martin.

"I'm with you, Jim," Doctor John said. "I think you need me, and I've lost sleep to ride with that bunch for twenty years, afraid they'd do some actual damage sometime and I'd be needed." He started untying the rope around Martin's ankles. "Now let's get these folks down to my office. That's our problem, right now."

The rest of the men sat on their horses, mumbling and whispering through their hoods, but nobody lifted a hood, and nobody offered to help with Martin. They sidled to the edges of the yard, and, in twos and in threes, they began leaving. Daddy whacked the rump of the big brown horse he'd been riding, so it would follow them, as he rode by us behind the big brown horse, High Pockets stopped and looked down at us. I turned my head. High Pockets would never again swing me up onto his shoulder, because I would not let him.

The *clop-clop* of their horses and the rustle of the undergrowth around them faded into the night, and they were gone.

Doctor John moved the rope from around Martin's shoulders and lifted him onto a horse and held the reins as they followed behind Daddy and me. On the horse Martin moaned softly, and at the edge of the trees we met Mama and James starting out with a lantern. To look for me.

Brother Mearl was with them, and his car was parked in front of our gate.

Brother Mearl took us to Strawne in his car, and the shot that Doctor John gave me stung my arm and made me sleepy. Back in the car again, I went to sleep, warm and safe in Mama's lap, and I did not know it when they took us home and put me in my bed and Martin in James'.

I lost the next day from my life. Because I did not wake up until Sunday morning.

I tried to turn over, onto my side, but I couldn't. The bandages were across my chest, around my arms and shoulders, and they pulled when I turned. I looked around. The sunshine came through the window and my room was the same as it had always been, except for James. James was asleep with his mouth open in the big red chair. Somebody had moved Daddy's big red chair into my room, and James slept like he had been there all night.

In the kitchen, with their voices coming through the quiet house into the open door of my room, Mama and Daddy were talking. And instead of waking James to help me turn over, I lay and listened to them.

"Jim, did she really shoot him *there?*" Mama was saying. "Oh, I wish you'd waited until Thorpe was well to tell me, so I could laugh!" The oven door creaked open and closed again, and the smell of something baking drifted across the hall and into my room. "It's not really funny," Mama said. "But good Heavens! She could have killed him!"

"No danger of her killing him unless she'd meant to," Daddy said. "She shot what she aimed at, I'm sure. And from what High Pockets says, her target must have been right there in plain sight."

"Good Heavens!" Mama said again. "What do you suppose will happen now? Can she be prosecuted?"

"Of course not," Daddy answered her. "It was self-defense, pure and simple. Nobody'll be prosecuted; everybody concerned is trying to keep the whole thing quiet. Quite a few things happened to make that Friday night memorable in this community, but you won't find anybody wanting it publicized."

"Is that why nobody's called the sheriff from Wellco to look for Una?"

"Exactly. Can't you see what a field day the Wellco *Herald* would have with the whole stinking fiasco? Una's run away before, you know, and they've always found her. And the story about Billy Bob's being shot, I believe, is that he accidentally shot himself while cleaning his gun." Daddy waited a minute, and when he spoke again his voice sounded tickled. "Damnation, Venie! Think how he'd have to be holding a gun, to shoot off his—"

"Jim! You quit making jokes with Thorpe lying in there!" Mama rattled pots and pans. "Wonder why Billy Bob tried a thing like that?"

"I'm as worried about Thorpe as you are, Venie. But John said we could expect some shock for a few days, and I guess this is it. I don't think Billy Bob planned an attempted rape on Bertha Mearl, but why does a drunk fool do anything? You have to remember that he was feeling cheated because he couldn't find Lewis, and old Will had just knocked him sprawling, and when he passed Bertha Mearl's house and saw her sitting out on the porch in her nightgown, singing, he translated it as an invitation. Or, if not, a chance to even up a lot of scores. He didn't think it would take much force, at any rate, to get on that Glory Train with her, and so he reined up his horse and went in. And got a bear by the tail."

They were both quiet for a while, and then Daddy said, "By golly, Venie, do you know what position this puts me in? I have to go to church every Sunday now!"

"You what?"

"Remember when I said that if that hunk of lard ever did or caused to be done anything that would benefit anybody, I'd go and listen to him every Sunday? By golly, he brought her here, didn't he? So she could shoot . . ."

"Jim!" Mama said. "You quit talking like that! I wonder who warned Lewis? Did you?"

"I didn't, but I wish I could say I did. I would have, if I'd known what they had in mind. Venie, I think I'll go in and wake Thorpe."

"No," Mama said. "I've been wanting to wake her all morning, but Doctor John looked in on her when he'd finished with Martin. He said that it was good sleep and to let her alone until

240

she wakes. That was right after High Pockets came by looking for Una, and you were out talking to him."

My back hurt, and I tried to turn onto my side again. And in the red chair James wiggled and woke and rubbed his eyes.

"Gaw, are you awake?" He yawned and came and stood and looked down at me, grinning so big his ears wiggled. "Gaw, I'll go get Mama!"

"No, wait." I held his hand so he could not leave yet. "James, who got shot? Who shot somebody? What are they talking about in the kitchen?"

"Sister Mearl shot Billy Bob," James said. "Right in the—" He turned red. "Well, anyway, he's not old Bullet*head* now!"

"Will he live?" I asked, and from the kitchen, I heard the answer.

"And John had an ambulance sent from Wellco, and that's where he is now. In the hospital. He's too damned mean to die. But he won't ever be Bull of the Woods any more. I hope poor little Una is all right somewhere. I guess if Thorpe's all right when she wakes up, I'll go help look for Una. Who brought the big ham?"

"Neevy brought it," Mama said. "I never saw so much food. Everybody in the country brought something, like we'd had a— a death in the family." She rattled the oven door again. "The ham's about done, too. Jim, see who's at the door."

Daddy's footsteps went out of the kitchen and down the hall.

"You can call them now, if you want to," I said to James. "I'm aw'fly tired . . ."

"Anybody home?" Eloise's voice came through the hall. "You people all still in bed around here? Hi, Jim, where's the rest of your crew?"

Mama's little ragged felt houseshoes went running down the hall, and James went out the door to join them, and they were all talking at once. "We weren't expecting you until tomorrow," I heard Mama say. "You must have left as soon as Jim called you. And, Jim, don't let me forget that we owe Neevy for that call. She'll—"

"Don't worry about that," Eloise said. "Neevy won't let you forget, so how's if I pay her, and you can owe me? And with

Thorpe sick, you didn't think I'd come until tomorrow? Thanks. Thanks loads."

"But I was thinking about your job." Mama's voice sounded like it always did when Eloise came—like she had somebody on her side now. "How did you find somebody to replace you so soon?"

"Oh, heck with the job," Eloise said. "Where's Thorpe? How is she? Let's go in and see about her. Is she asleep? Is she sick?"

"She's awake," James said, and they came into the room and stood around my bed.

"Look, baby, pink silk!" Eloise put this package on my bed, and then she took it and unwrapped it, and the pink silk step-ins slid from my hand onto the pink bedspread, and I was too tired to look at them. I closed my eyes and wished that they would all go away and let me talk to James.

"Oh my God!" Eloise looked at Daddy. "You said on the phone that the doctor said she was okay. Look at her!"

"It's shock, Eloise." Daddy's voice was low. "John said that *physically* she would be all right, but that the shock reaction might last for days. Only *days,* if we're lucky." He took my hand and held it, and then he rubbed his hand across my forehead. "Thorpe? I wonder if John ought to see her again?"

"What in the name of God was she doing in the woods around that place at night?" Eloise looked across my bed at Mama. "Didn't you even know where she was, Venie?"

My eyes were open again and I watched them and listened, but it did not really matter what any of them said.

"I thought she was in her room asleep." Mama sat down on the bed and picked up the pink silk step-ins and looked at them and smoothed them across her lap. "I had sent her to her room, and I thought she was still in there. Don't look like that, Eloise, you have to discipline them! I went in to see about her, I *did,* and she was sound asleep. And then when I heard Dawn Starr come in and heard them whispering I thought they were both in bed."

Mama's voice went on explaining, and I went back to sleep.

"Just let her alone. If she shows any response to James, then I say let him take over as much as possible."

When I woke again, Doctor John was in the room. "These

242

things just take a little time," he said. "And sometimes the body heals more quickly than the mind. Now I'll just look in on Martin again, and I'll be off. And Thorpe's going to be fine."

The days and the nights passed, and if James slept, it was in the big red chair beside my bed, because he was always in it. Because Martin was in James' bed, and the only time James left my bedside was when Mama and Eloise came in to give me baths. Leo sent a sack of oranges to me, for juice, and I drank some of the juice to please James, because he looked so sad and tired.

"Mister James-e-o! Wake up!"

James was asleep again in the big chair, and Eloise stood over him, shaking his shoulder. "It's beautiful outside this morning," she said when James finally opened his eyes and stretched his arms and legs. "The sun's shining, and the birds are singing, and Mister James-e-o is going outside and get some of that fresh air and sunshine. Go on, scoot!"

She pulled him up, and James yawned and stretched again and went out the door and Eloise sat down in the chair and leaned back. She looked around the room. "My gosh," she said, "are those oranges or basketballs in that bowl by your bed? Toss me one, and I'll see."

I looked at the oranges and at Eloise. I was too tired to play games. But Eloise sat and waited, her hands out in front cupped to catch the orange, and I raised myself to one elbow and reached for an orange.

"See?" Eloise said. "The bandages are most all gone now, and it doesn't hurt you to move, does it? Come on, throw me one, right in here."

I had to use both hands to throw the orange, and to do that, I had to sit up in bed. I threw it, and sat there on the bed and watched Eloise stoop, laughing, to pick it up from the floor.

"They're oranges, all right," she said. "A basketball would have bounced up into my lap, wouldn't it? Now I'm going to peel this one, and we'll each eat half. Where in the world did you get such big monster oranges?"

"Leo sent them to me. I guess he got them in Wellco."

Eloise kept peeling, and the thick black fringe of her lashes hid her eyes as she looked down at the orange. "How is old Leo these days?"

"He's okay." I lay back against the pillows. "He comes to church sometimes, now, with Miss Wooley."

"With Miss Wooley?" Eloise's hands on the orange were perfectly still. "Who's Miss Wooley? . . . Oh, she's your teacher, isn't she? Sit up and talk to me, goosie! I can't talk to you with you lying there looking like something the cat dragged in an' wouldn't eat! Tell me about Miss Wooley. Is she nice? Does Leo like her?" Eloise came over to my bed and put the half-peeled orange on the table and bent and fluffed and pounded my pillows. "Now," she said, "sit up and lean against these, so we can see each other while we talk. Tell me about Leo and Miss Wooley. Does he like her?"

"I don't know." It felt good to sit up, after the dizziness went away. "I don't know if he likes her, but I think she likes him. She always turns pink and looks happy when he comes in to talk to her after school."

"Comes in where? In the schoolroom?"

I nodded. "Sometimes we have to sit on the bus and wait, while Leo's in talking to Miss Wooley."

"Doesn't anybody fuss about having to wait for him to visit before he takes you home?" Eloise pulled off two sections of the orange and handed one across to me and popped the other into her mouth.

"We don't mind. They're both nice. James says they like each other. Eloise, if I have to sit up and talk, may I talk to James? Eloise, do you have something in your eye?"

Eloise had reached for her purse and pulled out a handkerchief with white lace all around it to wipe in the corner of her eye.

"I sure-God do. Half the juice in that orange, I think." She groped in her purse for another handkerchief, and when she pulled it out a key fell out on the floor. Eloise picked up the key and held it out and looked at it. "And you, goosie, you've got to hurry up and get well before I lose the key to my apartment. Or before old Sue Beth moves her butt into it."

She laughed and wrinkled her nose and stuck out her tongue to show what she thought of old Sue Beth moving into her apartment while she was gone, and I was laughing with her, as she went out the door to call James.

He came in the door talking and shaking his head. "Gaw, some people just don't know when they're well off! Imagine everybody gettin all excited because you're talkin to 'em!" He stood at the bed and looked down at me and grinned, and then he sat down in the big chair.

"James, don't lean back and go to sleep! If you do, I will, too. James, how long have I been sick?"

"Oh—two or three—maybe four—days. But you're not sick." He grabbed for one of my pillows and tucked it under his head. "You're just tired, from running around through the woods tending to other people's business." He yawned.

"James," I said. "I had this dream. A dream so bad that I don't want to talk about it, but it's all I can think about. . . . I dreamed that Thee died. He drowned, in the Mouth of Hell, and water came out of his mouth and nose and he was dead. And I didn't cry or anything, but it went on for days and days, this dream, and some men with ghost clothes on tied Martin to a tree and whipped him. And when I ran out to help him, the whip hit me." I held my arms over my face to show James how it had happened in the dream—and the bandage that was still on my chest pulled and stung a little.

James sat up straight and watched me looking down at the bandages under my gown.

"Still want to talk about your dream, stupid?" he asked. His voice was soft, and his hand, when he came over and tousled my hair, was gentle.

I nodded.

James stood there looking down at me for a minute, with his lower lip between his teeth and his eyes worried, and then he went over to my dresser.

He came back to the bed with a cigar box and stood there looking at the box and at me. "Here!" he said then, and shoved the box into my hands. "It wasn't a dream. You know that. Open the box."

The top of the cigar box had THEE printed on it in crooked letters. Printed with a black crayola, and I remembered printing it. It was the box I'd given to Thee once, to keep his treasures in. Like my cigar box under the bed, with the owl foot and things in it.

Under Thee's name on the lid, somebody had printed TO MISS THROP, and so I opened it. Inside was a bird nest and a cracked blue marble and some rocks that we'd found once at Rocky

Bottom. And the other owl foot. And a note. TO MISS THROP.
I unfolded the note, and James read it over my shoulder with
me.

Dere miss Throp, we have gone before the riders git us.
Thee wud hav wanted you to hav thes things becaws he luved
you. you was his fren   Donie

I didn't have to ask James anything about what the note meant.
I knew. . . . *Shut up, you fool, that's a little girl you done hit.*
. . . I'D STILL LIKE TO KNOW WHO TOL THAT NIGGER
WE WAS COMIN'. . . . Theotus, come on. Come on, Thee
baby. . . .
"Where did they go?" I asked James. "They aren't really gone,
are they, not for good? They're coming back."
"I doubt it." James sat down on the bed beside me and took
the box from my lap. "They're gone, Thorpe. And nobody knows
where. Somebody told Lewis the night riders were coming after
him, and they just disappeared."
He pulled a flower from the glass of roses that Eloise had
put on the table by my bed, and sat there pulling off the petals
and watching them float down to the floor. "Mama sent me down,
the next day, after Donie, and they were gone." He looked up
from the rose petals and tried to smile. "Maybe they went to
Trudy's. Maybe she came after them, and took them back with
her."
Or maybe they had to slip through the woods at night, running
and hiding, and Josie carrying Peter Rabbit like a sack of meal on
her hip.
"I don't believe it," I said. "I bet you they're back by now. Have
you been down to see?"
James dropped the rose stem in the wastebasket and went
back to his chair and kind of fell into it and leaned his head
back. "They're gone, all right," he said tiredly. "And the best
thing you can do is to get well. And quit lying there not talking
to people." He tucked the pillow under his head and yawned,
and I wondered if he had slept any at all since I had been sick.
"James," I said. "In my dream, I burned the red coat."
James did not answer. His eyes were closed and he yawned
again and his mouth stayed open. He was asleep again.
I lay there thinking about all of it until James started snoring,

246

and then I pushed the blanket and the spread back and eased my feet down to the floor. I stood up, and the room whirled and spun around. I caught at the little table, and the glass of roses turned over. The water poured straight down into my rabbit houseshoes and they spun around, too, and then they sat still in the little puddle of water. I eased out of the room barefoot without trying to catch the rabbit houseshoes.

Because I wanted to go back. Back to a long time ago, when being sick meant lying in bed and smelling like Vicks salve and holding Grandma Thorpe's gold watch and making jokes with Mama.

I went out the door, and into Mama's room.

The old blue velvet box that always held the watch wasn't on Mama's dresser. Nor in any of the drawers. I went to her trunk in the corner and dumped things from the trunk onto the floor, and, pawing through the things with my good hand—the one the whip didn't hit—I found the box.

The watch was not in the box.

I opened it wide, and turned it upside down and shook it, and two pieces of paper fell from the box and floated down to the floor like James' rose petals had. I picked the papers up, and then I sat down on the floor to look at them. Mama's name was on both pieces: Mrs. Jim Torrance.

PAID . . . the first paper said . . . TO *Mrs. Jim Torrance* THE SUM OF *thirty dollars* . . . FOR . . . *one watch and chain* . . . TO BE REDEEMED IN . . . *sixty* . . . DAYS. . . .

The other paper said RECEIVED OF . . . *Mrs. Jim Torrance* . . . *thirty dollars* . . . FOR . . . *one casket, gray, silk-lined* . . . *Paid in Full.* . . .

In Mama's trunk underneath the place where the watch box had been there was a pattern for a boy's suit, size six. And some pieces of white cloth. The white pure linen that Eloise had sent to Mama in the Christmas box. Mama had sat in her room sewing at night and I had thought that she did not care that Thee was dead.

There was also, tied around a pattern for a baby's dress, a scrap of the blue silk that she had taken from the skirt of the dress Aunt Neevy gave her. A scrap left when Mama made the dress that Peter Rabbit wore for best.

16

Under the trees along the trail my bare feet sank into the spongy cushion of last year's leaves, and a bush caught at my gown and tore the lace around the hem.

I had tumbled the things back into Mama's trunk and on my way through the hall I had peeped in at Martin, who was asleep, and then I had slipped through the door and out the gate. I ran, the two pieces of paper in my good hand and my breath coming in little gasps, to Donie's house.

Because of course it was not true. They had left, but they were back. They would be there, with Josie watching chickens scratch in the dirt while Lewis filed a saw and Donie's biscuits rose on the back of the stove in the kitchen.

The house sat under the trees exactly like it always had, and the chickens were clucking and scratching in the yard. But Josie wasn't watching them, and the rack where Lewis filed saws was empty.

"Thee!"

I stood in the yard and called. "Thee! Josie! Donie! . . . Thee?"

Thee, baby, come on. Come on, Theotus——

The front door was shut, and nobody came to open it. Nobody

looked out the window, nor around the corner of the house, and the chickens kept on scratching.

I stumbled up onto the rickety steps and leaned against the door and pounded on it. It opened, and I fell into the front room and the wind from the open door rattled some empty coat-hangers on a rod in the corner. The brass bed in the corner was stripped and bare. The peacock spread was gone and cotton stuck through the holes in the blue-striped ticking.

In the kitchen, the feed-sack curtains were still up at the windows with the red and green flowers that Donie had sewn over the writing on them. But there was no fire in the stove and no biscuits set to rise on the back of it. Josie's little bed in the corner was bare, and the box that Peter Rabbit played in was empty. I stuck my head into the little leanto room that was just big enough for Donie's bed, but it was empty except for a little stack of colored funny papers in the corner and a ragged quilt on the foot of the bed.

I pulled one of the cowhide-bottomed stools from under the kitchen table and sat down. I sat so still that a big rat came out from the woodbox in the corner and looked at me before he ran across the floor.

Somebody—or something—was in the house. It wasn't the rat. I could tell. Somebody—or something—was stiller than I was, watching and listening. I opened the kitchen door and looked out, and I went to the little windows. Nothing was out there except the chickens in the yard and the birds in the trees.

I went across to the pantry that Lewis had built behind the stove for Donie to keep her groceries in, and listened. I pulled on the door. It was stuck. I jerked it, quick and hard, and it came open.

Miss Una almost fell out on me.

"*Miss Una!*" I sat down on the cowhide stool and looked at her sitting there on the floor where she'd tumbled when the pantry door opened. "Miss Una, are you looking for them too? Because they're gone. They're really gone, and I doubt if they'll be back."

Miss Una nibbled on a piece of hard cornbread that she must have found in Donie's pantry and looked sideways at me without turning her head.

She said, after she'd chewed for a while, "I'm not looking for them. I'm not looking for, for anybody. But I bet you, I bet you somebody's looking for me!" She nibbled again, and chewed and giggled. "If they're not, they will be, when they find out I told those nigras to leave the country. I, I told them, you know." She stood up and shoved her cornbread down into her sweater pocket. "Are you, are you looking for me?"

"Me?" I shook my head. "I'm not looking for anybody. Not now."

We watched each other, and Miss Una kept chewing. "Did you really tell them?" I asked her.

She nodded. "I sure did. I had gone down to the barn, to visit, to visit Nathaniel, and I heard the men talking. And I knew the nigras had to be, to be warned." She giggled again. "I gave the nigras my egg, my egg money, you know. And I told them to go straight to Wellco and send that, that Trudy a telegram. I even told them how to send one!"

"Why didn't you go and tell Martin? Didn't you know they were going after him, too?

Miss Una nodded again. "I knew. But I didn't figure they'd do anything to a, a white man. It was the nigra I was worried about. I went, I went by Brother Mearl's house first, to see if he could go stop, stop the whole shebang. Brother Mearl told me to go home, and he'd go, he'd go after them. But I ran, I ran through the woods an' I beat them to old Pig White's place, and I watched, I watched through the trees. What they did."

"You *saw* it? Miss Una, you saw them whipping Martin?"

She pulled the other cowhide stool from under the table and sat down on it. Her little bird-claw hand eased over and patted the back of my hand that was on the table, and she wasn't giggling. She looked sad. "I'm not, I'm not as brave as you are, child. I'm just a wore-out, wore-out, crazy old woman, and they'd've sent me back to old Callie and—" Then she looked pleased. "I wonder what old, what old Callie thought, when she turned off her radio and came in to, to check on me. . . ." She sat there smiling and looking pleased, thinking about Callie.

"Miss Una, they might call the sheriff out from Wellco to look for you. Why don't you come to our house to live?"

Miss Una pulled her cornbread from her pocket and looked at it. "I had me a apple in my pocket," she said. "But I ate it. Did you ever eat a raw, a raw egg? They're not, not bad." She bit off a corner of the bread. "Jim Torrance's had enough, enough trouble from the Jacksons, without me, without me addin' to it. I'll just stay here," she nodded. "Till they find me."

"You could go live with Miss Mildred. I bet *she* loves you."

"Pee," Miss Una said. "I mean *fiddle,* child. She'd shoot me back to, back to Will an' Callie so fast. . . . No, I'll just, I'll just stay here. They've done looked here, while I, I hid in a tree outside. Course if they come back with, with dawgs, I might not—"

"I'll stay with you." I stood up. "I mean, I'll go home and get a dress and some—some oranges and stuff, and I'll come back."

Daddy had sat and watched them whip Martin, and so my days on earth, according to Brother Mearl, would not be long. Because I could not honor my father and my mother. But for what days I had left, I would stay in Donie's house with Miss Una.

"Daddy watched them whip Martin, you know," I said. "He went out with them to whip people, and he sat on his horse and watched. Until I ran out."

Miss Una looked up from the top of Donie's table to my face, and her fingers caught and held the hem of my nightgown.

"Wait a minute, child. We need to get somethin' straight, straight here. You don't think that Jim Torrance, Jim Torrance rode out with them knowin' somebody was goin' to get hurt, do you? Is that what you're thinkin'?" Her head bobbed up and down and the little hand that held my gown was shaking. "Oh no, child, no! They didn't set out to whip, whip nobody that night. Not till after they started passin' the bottle, I reckon."

"But Daddy still watched them whip Martin."

"Be quiet. Be quiet an' lissen. I heard, I heard them down at the barn. No rough stuff, they said, till after, after Torrance has rode with us for a while. They aimed to just ride around an' talk big an' scare people. That's what they said, but I was still worried about that nigra. Anyhow, I tell you, I tell you this. I was there, an' I saw it all. An' *Jim Torrance was off his horse an' aimin' to stop them before you ran out from behind that huckleberry bush!"*

Miss Una turned loose my gown and sat there nodding. Her lips moved but no words came out. Then she stood up and put her arms around me.

"I told you I'm a crazy, crazy ol' fool," she said. "I guess

251

you got hit with somethin' bigger, bigger than a whip, didn't you Thorpe honey? How can I tell you, child, how long grown-ups watch things sometimes before they decide to act? I know what Jim Torrance stood to gain by settin' on that horse, that horse, for just a while longer. But he didn't set there, did he? He made his decision, an' he jumped off. Before he saw you."

"But I thought Daddy was—was good!"

"Honey, he *is* good. But he's just a man, just a man. An' you got to learn that what he does will be right sometimes, and wrong sometimes. An' Venie too. But they're both, both good people. An' they mighty apt to have to make some more decisions that won't be easy. Decisions that hurt, whichever way it goes. That's what we pay, pay for bein' grown-up."

She pulled me to my feet.

"I guess if you're ready, I'll, I'll walk home with you."

Outside, I wanted to run. To run home. But I stayed with Miss Una, and held her hand and pulled her along the trail.

"You know," Miss Una's other hand went up and stroked the shawl that was around her shoulders over her sweater. "I could, I could stay with Mildred, couldn't I? I could sew. I could sew for the, for the railroad men. . . ." She held my hand tighter. "But it's *my* house! My own house, that Papa gave me when he, when he gave Mildred the town propity. An' I might, I might go back to it an' take the broom to all of 'em! Ever' last one!"

We laughed. When we reached the edge of the trees, we saw Mama, walking slow and holding her stomach. But walking toward us. I ran, then, toward Mama, and I buried my face in her apron. She wiped my face with it and then she reached into her apron pocket for the clean handkerchief she always carried there.

"For the love of God," Mama said. "For the love of God!" She smelled like Ivory soap and powder and vanilla.

252

epilogue

It was a week later.

The places on Martin's back were healing into scars. His hands only shook sometimes when he tried to eat or drink, and he had wanted to go home. So Martin had gone back to his little house in the woods, to weed his flowers and feed his animals and, later, walk in his muddy shoes to help people.

Eloise had gone to Strawne and called, and Sue Beth had come after her, in the big shiny black car. Eloise had gone out the front gate to meet her, and after she'd thrown her suitcases in, she'd made Sue Beth move from under the steering wheel and let her in the driver's seat.

"Move over," she'd said. "And fork over." She'd held out her hand. Sue Beth's little red bow-shaped mouth had pouted for a minute before she'd handed over the car keys. "Oh, well, I'd hoped you'd stay longer," Sue Beth had said, and fluffed her white hair. "But it was fun while it lasted."

Eloise had started the motor. "And if I find," she said, "even so much as a cigarette butt in that apartment with your lipstick on it— Here, hold your foot on the brake!" And she had jumped out of the car and kissed all of us again and they had left.

"Well, you aren't going with him, are you?" Aunt Neevy asked.

She had come to visit Mama while Uncle Elmer went to Wellco, and Leo had just brought Daddy another letter.

"Of course I'm going." Mama waddled over to the couch, like a duck, and sat down. She was so fat with the baby she couldn't walk right.

"You sit there and rest," Daddy said, and put a pillow behind her back. "I'll pour the coffee and serve it. How's that?"

"But, Venie, a *Thorpe* dragging around like . . ." Aunt Neevy frowned.

"Neevy, I'm not a Thorpe," Mama said. "I'm a Torrance. And I don't think that Jim should have to dwell any longer in the corner of a housetop."

"I don't know what you mean," Aunt Neevy said stiffly, and took the cup of coffee that Daddy brought her.

"Well, Jim does," Mama said. "Thank you, Jim. Yes, I'm going with him, Neevy, just as soon as the baby's born. And if we end up gypsies, I'll put a rose between my teeth and dance while Jim plays the mandolin."

Something fell to the floor and broke with a crash, and from the circle of Mama's arm around me on the couch, I heard the sound of tinkling glass.

Aunt Neevy had dropped her coffee cup. It lay on the dark wood floor beside the faded rug and the coffee made a wet ragged circle around it. "Oh my," Aunt Neevy said. "One of your best cups. How did I do that? Well, maybe you can glue it back together. Sure made a lot of noise, didn't it, for one little old cup!"

And to Aunt Neevy it might have been the sound of a cup breaking. But I knew better. It was the sound of a glass jar shattering and of the invisible pieces falling.

A rustling, whispering sound filled the quiet room. The quiet in which Mama and Daddy looked at each other and nobody answered Aunt Neevy about the broken cup. And that sound could have been the wind blowing through the open window and moving the dusty, faded red drapes. But it wasn't. It was the rustling and whispering of invisible wings. Unfolding, lifting, drying . . . getting ready to fly out into the world.